"I CAN'T POSSIBLY BE CONDUCTING SUCH AN IMPROPER CONVERSATION!"

"A very proper attitude for a governess, Miss Smith, but quite unnecessary at the moment. I prefer your frankness." Deverell cocked a quizzical brow at her. "Nor can I believe that you haven't attracted a gentleman's attention before, even under more conventional circumstances."

Phoebe sank back to the sofa as if her legs had turned to water. "Well, yes..." But these attentions were certainly unlike the attentions she had attracted before—*they* had caused her to lose two previous posts.

"I don't understand *why*," she almost wailed.

"Because I find you...intriguing," he said softly.

Julia Byrne lives in Australia with her husband, daughter and two overgrown cats. She started her career as a secretary, taught ballroom dancing after several successful years as a competitor, and presently works part-time in the history department of a Melbourne university. She enjoys reading, tapestry and playing mah-jongg.

SCANDAL AND MISS SMITH
JULIA BYRNE

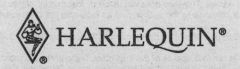

HARLEQUIN®

TORONTO • NEW YORK • LONDON
AMSTERDAM • PARIS • SYDNEY • HAMBURG
STOCKHOLM • ATHENS • TOKYO • MILAN • MADRID
PRAGUE • WARSAW • BUDAPEST • AUCKLAND

If you purchased this book without a cover you should be aware
that this book is stolen property. It was reported as "unsold and
destroyed" to the publisher, and neither the author nor the
publisher has received any payment for this "stripped book."

For my father, in loving memory
You were always there for me
The best of fathers
The best of friends

ISBN 0-373-51117-5

SCANDAL AND MISS SMITH

Copyright © 1997 by Julia Byrne.

All rights reserved. Except for use in any review, the reproduction or
utilization of this work in whole or in part in any form by any electronic,
mechanical or other means, now known or hereafter invented, including
xerography, photocopying and recording, or in any information storage
or retrieval system, is forbidden without the written permission of the
publisher, Harlequin Enterprises Limited, 225 Duncan Mill Road,
Don Mills, Ontario, Canada M3B 3K9.

All characters in this book have no existence outside the imagination of the
author and have no relation whatsoever to anyone bearing the same
name or names. They are not even distantly inspired by any individual
known or unknown to the author, and all incidents are pure invention.

This edition published by arrangement with Harlequin Books S.A.

® and TM are trademarks of the publisher. Trademarks indicated with
® are registered in the United States Patent and Trademark Office, the
Canadian Trade Marks Office and in other countries.

Visit us at www.eHarlequin.com

Printed in U.S.A.

Chapter One

"Thanks to your lordship's unwarranted and selfish reluctance to assume the sacred charge laid upon you three years ago, I have been forced to take matters into my own hands. Not without considerable inconvenience, I might add."

There was no reply.

Phoebe would have been surprised if an answer had been forthcoming, since she'd addressed her strictures to the portrait of a long-dead Deverell that was hanging over the mantelpiece in the library into which she had been ushered ten minutes ago.

She knew the gentleman immortalised by Lely was a Deverell. He possessed the same raven-black hair, lean, aristocratic countenance and ice-cold sapphire eyes that characterised every generation of Deverells. Phoebe studied the portrait with a jaundiced eye and decided she had become rather tired of that particular combination of colouring and feature. The occasional blonde or redhead would have broken the monotony somewhat. It might at least have infused some badly needed warmth into the family bloodlines.

Unfortunately, Deverells bred true, no matter what new blood was introduced into the family. In fact, they had probably looked exactly like the gentleman in the portrait when they had crouched over fires and worn mammoth skins. Doubtless the mammoths had been rendered easy prey by the same piercing, basilisk stare that arrowed down at her from the painted canvas.

Phoebe had had a great deal of experience with that stare.

And with Deverells in general. Which was why she was busily
rehearsing the opening lines of a speech destined to be delivered to her employer, the Honourable Sebastian Alexander
Deverell, newly created—for services to the Crown that were
of an unspecified and mysterious nature—Baron of that name.

The reason for the creation of a barony to grace the younger
son of an old, distinguished family whose present head was an
Earl was only the latest mystery surrounding Deverell. Despite
the rumours abounding in the *ton,* Phoebe knew next to nothing
about the man. According to family lore, he had sailed off to
India at a young age and had remained there for several years,
after which he had travelled throughout the East, engaging in
whatever shadowy activities had resulted in his new title.

At any other time, Phoebe might have found such highly
rewarded patriotism reassuring. Even comforting. Quite conducive to a measure of peace of mind, in fact. But comfort,
peace of mind and other such necessities for a well-ordered
existence had vanished from her life the day Deverell's aunt
had hired her to take up the position of governess to his orphaned nieces and nephew.

Two years of living on the edge of disaster had ensued; the
minions who were supposed to answer her queries and lend
assistance when required failing dismally to do either. Nor had
the trenchant letters she had been sending post-haste to
Deverell since his return to England three months ago elicited
a more satisfactory response.

The only alternative, as far as Phoebe could see, was a verbal
assault.

Her attack on the gentleman in the portrait was not the first
such speech she'd rehearsed. She had begun the practice a
week ago, when she'd reached the conclusion that she either
handed over control of the younger members of the family to
their uncle and guardian, or presented herself at the gates of
Bedlam in a state of babbling witlessness.

The opening lines of her speech had rapidly become less
civil as her meeting with Deverell loomed closer, with the result that, after a journey to London fraught with adventures of
nightmarish proportions, Phoebe was feeling extremely *uncivil.*

Not to say desperate.

She quelled that last thought immediately. Dramatic emotions such as desperation were no help at all when dealing with Deverells. One had to remain calm and in control of oneself.

Phoebe lifted a hand to her head to assure herself that she still appeared calm and in control of herself, even though her stomach persisted in performing such acrobatic feats as somersaults.

Her old-fashioned bonnet seemed to have remained in place. Its nondescript fawn hue did not show her light brown hair, brown eyes and fair complexion to advantage. That knowledge, borne in on her when she'd inspected her appearance prior to leaving Grillon's Hotel for Deverell's town house, had caused a pang in her secretly fashionable heart. She had sternly suppressed it. Governesses were expected to look plain and unremarkable. They were supposed to fade into the background.

In this case, she reflected, casting a glance at her surroundings, such a task would not be difficult. Her severe chocolate-brown pelisse not only matched the bookshelves lining most of the wall space, but also blended in rather well with the commodious sofa and armchairs grouped in a cosy arrangement about the fireplace. If she sat on one, she would probably disappear altogether.

A rueful smile curved her lips as she ran one gloved hand over the back of a nearby chair. Clearly, one of the rumours about Deverell was true. He appeared to have made a fortune in India. The rich brown leather beneath her fingers was the finest Cordovan, heavy drapes of dark gold velvet, tied back with brown and gold silk tassels, framed the long windows, and the floor was covered by an exquisite Oriental rug into which her half-boots sank to a positively decadent degree.

The rug wasn't the only object of beauty in the room. Jade statues and antique urns loomed from pedestals or from behind glass-fronted cabinets; a heavy globe on a gold inlay and ebony stand graced the corner near Deverell's solid mahogany desk; and on the desk itself, illuminated by a shaft of sunlight, a graceful Psyche held aloft a branched candelabra.

Phoebe found herself staring at the sculpted figure with fascinated interest. Its creator had not believed in covering the female form in anything but the flimsiest of draperies, but what struck her was its setting. The flowing lines of the statue were so fragilely feminine, a waterfall in pure white marble, frozen forever in time, that it should have looked out of place in such a darkly masculine room. The fact that the statue looked perfectly at home on the desk raised some equally interesting questions about its owner.

She frowned and returned her gaze to the painted visage above her. The saturnine features reminded her that she was not here to be distracted by statues.

"On the contrary," she informed the portrait sternly, "I am here to condemn your lordship's utterly incomprehensible behaviour in the strongest possible terms."

"How very unfortunate," drawled a deep male voice from the doorway behind her. "The third Earl was notoriously profligate, but condemnation a hundred and fifty years after the event seems a trifle unfair. Even for him."

Phoebe spun around with a startled gasp. And went completely still.

The gentleman standing in the doorway, one hand resting on the door knob, black brows raised in faintly mocking enquiry, was unmistakably a Deverell. The height, the careless arrogance in his stance, the midnight-dark hair were all as she had expected.

What startled her wits into temporary paralysis were his eyes. Instead of the hard sapphire orbs she had anticipated, she was transfixed by a glittering aquamarine gaze that was as changeable and mysterious as the sea; blue one moment, green the next, shot through with shards of gold.

She had never seen eyes like them.

"Miss...Smith, I believe," he murmured, coming into the room and pushing the door closed behind him.

The latch slid home with a decisive little click that succeeded in snapping Phoebe out of her trance. She opened her mouth.

"And this," he continued, eyeing her attire, "is, I presume, Lord Pendleton's idea of a disguise." One black brow went up. "Dear me. I must have sounded more than normally disapproving if he thought my tastes ran to buttoned-up Puritans."

Phoebe felt her mouth drop open further. She blinked. "I beg your pardon, my lord?"

"Ah, but the voice is very good." A lazy smile curved Deverell's mouth as he came closer. He began to walk around her, circling her slowly while he made a comprehensive sweep of her person from her bonnet to the tips of her brown suede half-boots. "Melodious and refined, with just a hint of provocative huskiness. Pen is to be congratulated."

"What...? Pen...*who?*"

Phoebe shook her head in an attempt to recover her senses. It was not easy. Trying to keep track of Deverell while he circled around her was making her positively dizzy. So was the sudden breathlessness she was experiencing at his close proximity. She couldn't understand it. She was used to Deverells staring down at her. They did it all the time. But this particular example of the species was rather taller than the rest.

And larger.

He finally came to a halt directly in front of her, but Phoebe's relief that he'd stopped moving was short-lived. Up close, he towered over her. And, she noted with some annoyance, she couldn't even see past him to the door. Far from rejoicing in the slim willowy build of the rest of his family, Deverell looked as if he'd spent his years abroad engaging in hard physical labour.

His shoulders were intimidatingly broad and the excellent tailoring of his coat of dark blue superfine did nothing to disguise the formidable proportions of the body beneath. Tightly fitting buckskins adhered faithfully to the long, powerful muscles of his thighs, and his topboots appeared to be on the extremely large side.

His size was not the only difference, Phoebe saw, as her bemused gaze travelled upwards to rest on the strong planes and angles of his face. Polite society would have deemed him handsome, but, allied to that powerful build, on him the chiselled Deverell features took on an edge that sent visions of medieval knights and crusading warriors flitting through her mind.

There was nothing romantic about the visions. The warrior studying her with a coolly assessing intelligence gleaming in his blue-green gaze was straight off the battlefield. There was no obvious gore, but the classical nose looked as if it had been broken at one time, and a small scar curved around the angle of his jaw. Two deep grooves were carved on either side of his mouth, and while its thin, almost cruel, top lip was familiar,

the lower one was disturbingly sensual and strangely compel-
ling.

Phoebe gazed up at it and felt a very odd tremour somewhere
deep inside her. A medieval warrior. As fierce in love as in
battle.

"Miss Smith? Are you all right?"

"Uhh…" Phoebe wrenched her gaze upward and encountered a sardonic gleam that had her straightening her spine with
an almost audible snap. "Oh. Yes. Of course I am, my lord.
Um…you were saying?" She could have sunk through the
floor.

"Lord Pendleton," he repeated dryly. "He is to be congratulated. When he told me about the latest establishment ca-
tering to a gentleman's every whim, I confess it held no appeal
for me. But I do believe, my dear Miss Smith, that you could
change my mind."

"I could?" Phoebe searched vainly for the rapidly unrav-
elling thread of the conversation.

"My fantasies don't run to the peculiar or overly exotic,"
he explained when she frowned. "On the other hand, there was
no need to get yourself up as a governess. I hate to disillusion
you, but, as a disguise, it is really quite hopelessly inadequate."

"Disguise? But…"

"And couldn't you have come up with a more diverting…
er…*nom de boudoir,* than 'Smith'?"

Shock hit her heart like a small velvet fist. Her breath caught.
Her knees wobbled. She forgot about medieval warriors and
the strange statements issuing from Deverell's lips. She even
forgot her speech. One thought, and one thought alone, reverberated inside her head.

He didn't believe Smith was her name!

But he couldn't know… She had used Smith for several
years. He couldn't possibly know…

"Smith *is* my real name, sir," she managed at last, hoping
the warmth staining her cheeks was not too visible beneath her
bonnet. It seemed to be but a faint hope. The critical assessment
lingering in his eyes sharpened abruptly to a knife-edged interest that set her babbling. "And I do not have the least idea
of what you are talking about. Clearly I have come to the
wrong house. Although, when I asked for Lord Deverell, your

butler did not so much as blink. However, if you would kindly direct me…"

"Oh, you're in the right house," he murmured. "So there's no need to continue the charade." He took a step closer, his gaze narrowing further when Phoebe promptly retreated. "But surely you're not going to run away. Did Pendleton send you here only to have you vanish after you'd proven his point? How very disappointing. I can provide several inducements for you to stay, you know."

"Stay? Point?" Phoebe took a deep breath and decided she was dealing with a lunatic. "Sir, this has gone on long enough. If you are indeed Lord Deverell, which I doubt, you obviously belong in Bedlam. Of course, it is quite possible that I made my way there this morning and am experiencing some sort of delusion. In which case you are another inmate, which does not surprise me in the least. However, you do not appear to be overly irrational, so perhaps you would be kind enough to fetch someone in authority so the mistake may be rectified."

The intent look vanished from Deverell's face. He laughed softly. A low growl of amusement that sent a series of nerve-tingling ripples down Phoebe's spine. She couldn't have said why, but that deep purr sounded distinctly dangerous.

"I can assure you, Miss Smith, that you're not presently in the madhouse. A Deverell's house is often unconventional, but madness hasn't overtaken the family. At least, not yet. Now perhaps if we start—"

But the word family had a galvanizing effect on Phoebe's senses. Drawing herself up to her full height, she launched into a diatribe that bore no resemblance whatsoever to any of her rehearsed lectures.

"Well, madness may not have overtaken the family, sir, but it is about to overtake *me* if I do not receive a more satisfactory reply to my petitions than mealy-mouthed put-offs from your man of business, and injunctions to use my own judgement from your secretary." Her voice rose. "Not to mention the total absence of any reply from *you!*"

"Uhh—"

She levelled a finger at him before he could elaborate. "You, my lord, are about to take charge of your nephew and nieces whether you want to or not. *I* have had enough!'' She shook her finger vigorously. "Enough, I say! Do you hear me?"

"I hear you," Deverell said mildly, eyeing the finger waving back and forth in front of his chest with great interest. Phoebe flushed and lowered her hand. He brought his gaze back to her indignant countenance, made another thorough survey of her costume and a smile of unholy amusement crept into his eyes. "Ah-ha. You're *that* Miss Smith."

Heat almost lifted her bonnet off her head. "Furthermore, my lord, while you may consider the behaviour of your family to be unconventional, others may find it scandalous, shameless and downright shocking. And at whose door will the blame be laid when scandal erupts, as will surely happen if nothing is done?" Infuriated anew at this rhetorical question, she abandoned finger-shaking and began to pace. "At the governess's door, that's whose! Well, I will not have it, my lord."

She turned at the window, skirts flying. "I have my future to think of. My living to earn. I will not tolerate the situation a moment longer!" She fetched up abruptly in front of him and returned his look of amusement with a ferocious glare. "Do you understand me, sir?"

"Well, I didn't at first, but I think I'm beginning to see a glimmer of light."

"I can't tell you how reassuring I find that information. Perhaps, now, you will refrain from circling me, weighing me up and looking me over as though…as though I was a horse for sale at Tattersall's!"

"I shall refrain immediately, Miss Smith. Believe me, even in those hideous clothes, the last thing you resemble is a horse." He grinned.

The sudden change wrought to his stern features momentarily halted Phoebe in her tracks. She could, however, see nothing remotely contrite in the expression. "I do not resemble anything other than what I am. Really! I cannot imagine what you must have been think—"

She broke off, staring at Deverell as a dreadful suspicion filled her mind. A muscle quivered near his mouth once and was ruthlessly stilled.

"Oh, my goodness!" Her eyes flew wide. Her reticule fell from suddenly nerveless fingers. "Lord Pendleton…

establishment…gentlemen's whims. You thought… *Oh, my goodness!*''

This time her knees did buckle. Fortunately for her dignity, Deverell seized her arm before she actually hit the floor and steered her over to the sofa. Phoebe sank onto it without a murmur, her stunned gaze fixed on his face as he sat beside her.

''You thought…? You really thought…?''

He raised a brow encouragingly.

With a heroic effort, Phoebe plastered a hideously bright smile onto her face. ''Goodness me, my lord, no doubt you thought I had met Lord Pendleton at some function or another, although I must tell you that I've never been to London before and—''

''No, don't spoil it,'' he murmured, smiling back at her. ''You've no idea how refreshing it is to meet a female of practical sensibilities who neither feigns ignorance nor goes off into exaggerated hysterics at the mention of a gentleman's… ah…conveniences.''

''Conveniences!'' Her smile vanished. ''But I *am* ignorant. That is, I am not precisely acquainted with— Ohh!'' She blushed wildly when he burst out laughing. ''Oh, you are quite shameless, my lord. How dare you discompose me like this! I can only suppose you *are* mad if you mistook your nieces' governess for a…a…''

''Barque of frailty?''

She glared at him.

''Bird of Paradise?''

Phoebe arose in her wrath. Before she could annihilate her tormentor, he rose also and took her hand in a strong clasp. Her breath promptly deserted her. She stared at the long fingers wrapped around her own and wondered wildly if she was embroiled in some demented sort of nightmare.

''Miss Smith, I do most sincerely apologise for not immediately remembering who you are. Please allow me to explain. You see, my friend Lord Pendleton decided to enliven what he refers to as my 'deadly boring existence' by challenging me to fault the…er…gentility of some females of his acquaintance. I was expecting the first one this morning and—''

"The *first* one? Good heavens! How many—? I mean…oh, no!" It was a wail of despair.

His aquamarine eyes gleamed with silent laughter. "Aha. I was right. A female of practical sensibilities. How could it be otherwise when you've been out in the world earning your living?" Then, as her face turned stormy, "But before you apostrophize me as being quite beyond the pale, Miss Smith, please recall that parading Incognitas through the house was Pendleton's idea, not mine."

Phoebe was having trouble recalling her own name, let alone any ideas. Never had she been assaulted by so many emotions at one and the same time. Shock, outrage and dazed disbelief jostled about in her brain until she could scarcely think. Not to mention the uneasy feeling engendered by Deverell's remark about earning her living. Just what sort of a living did he think she'd been earning?

Several pithy words on the subject rose to her mind. Unfortunately, before she could utter them, she made the mistake of looking up. Wicked humour still gleamed in Deverell's eyes—and, to her horror, Phoebe was seized by a wild and irresistible urge to laugh back. She choked instead.

"This *is* a nightmare," she finally gasped, snatching her hand from Deverell's as if he were the devil incarnate. Her fingers felt all warm and tingly. The circumstance only added to her agitation. "I can't possibly be standing here conducting such an improper conversation with you, my lord!"

"A very proper attitude for a governess, Miss Smith, but quite unnecessary at the moment. As I said a minute ago, I prefer your frankness." He cocked a quizzical brow at her. "Nor can I believe that you haven't attracted a gentleman's attentions before, even under more conventional circumstances."

Phoebe sank back to the sofa as if her legs turned to water. "Well, yes, but…"

These were attentions? They were certainly unlike the attentions she had indeed attracted before—*they* had caused her to lose two previous posts, but—

"I don't understand *why*," she almost wailed.

"Then you don't spend a great deal of time studying a mirror," he said softly. "I find you…intriguing."

Her eyes widened before her gaze went to the large gilt-framed mirror hanging on the opposite wall. The drab reflection staring back at her made her wonder again about his sanity. *"Me?"*

He smiled.

Annoyed at the startled squeak that had emerged from her throat, Phoebe scowled back at him. "Sir, your existence must indeed be boring if you find anything to intrigue you in your wards' governess. Nor did I come here to discuss— What *are* you doing?"

The demand was uttered in an even higher squeak as Deverell resumed his seat and, without so much as a by-your-leave, captured her chin with one large hand. He turned her face towards him, his grip gentle but quite inescapable.

"I see you're now determined to throw the governess at me at every turn," he murmured, his slow survey of her features causing her heart to leap into her throat. It stayed there, fluttering.

"Why is that, I wonder? Do you hide behind her, Miss Smith? Is that why you disguise yourself in colours that dim your own?"

"C-colours? I'm as colourless as this costume, sir."

He raised a brow.

"I…I mean…everything's brown." She gestured helplessly. "Bonnet, hair, dress, pelisse. Even my shoes. Brown, brown, brown."

"You forgot your eyes," he said, gazing straight into them.

Phoebe swallowed. "They're brown, too," she whispered. "Plain, ordinary brown." And she couldn't tear them away from his. He's casting a spell on me, she thought. Some exotic, eastern spell that made her wonder if she was drowning. Drowning in a deep blue-green sea. She could scarcely hear him over the rushing in her ears, but his words stroked over her nerves like warm silk over bare flesh.

"Plain? Ordinary? With those long lashes? Oh, no, Miss Smith. There's fire within." His mouth curved lazily. "Amber flames that could singe a man if he wasn't very careful. And when you remember propriety the fire darkens and goes still, waiting behind a haze of smoke, hiding secrets."

"S-secrets? No, I... That is...we should both remember propriety right now, sir."

He ignored this feeble attempt to distract him. "And while you may try to imitate a brown wren by your costume, your hair is every shade of fawn and sunlight and honey ever imagined."

"Oh, my good— I mean...how very poetic, my lord, but—"

"As to the rest, your complexion is flawless, your mouth a perfect bow that defies the governess no matter what words she utters, and—" he turned her head to the side "—although that little chin is nothing less than determined, your profile is really quite exquisite. No, Miss Smith, to the discerning observer you are anything but plain and ordinary."

She was now also anything but calm and in control. Deverell's low, caressing tone made her feel flushed all over. She had never had such things said to her. She should not be listening to them now. But protest was the last thing on her mind. On the contrary. She wanted to hear more.

It was shocking! It was scandalous! It was horrifyingly delicious.

"My lord..."

"Relax, Miss Smith," he said, his tone suddenly so curt that she started. He removed his hand. "I didn't mean to alarm you."

Phoebe took a steadying breath and realised she hadn't been breathing for what felt like several minutes. "I am not alarmed," she informed him, sounding distinctly rattled.

"No? I suppose that's why you just lost every vestige of colour in your cheeks." He got to his feet with a rather abrupt movement and crossed the room to a small table on which reposed a crystal decanter and several glasses. "Stay there. I'll pour you a restorative. And perhaps, in future, you might be more cautious about calling on a bachelor without escort of maid or footman."

"Maid! Foot—"

The terse words stunned her into silence for as much as ten seconds. Then enlightenment dawned. She stared at Deverell's back and didn't know whether to succumb to outrage or relief. Had he said all those shockingly exciting things to her merely to teach her a lesson? Who did the man think he was? *Her* guardian?

She eyed him for a moment longer in fulminating silence and then decided it was safer to let the matter drop. Something told her a protest on the grounds that she was a mature woman of four-and-twenty, and a mere governess besides, would go unheeded. And lesson or not, Deverell's description of her had left her decidedly unsettled. She had never met anyone like him before in her life.

Not even another Deverell.

Frowning, she watched him pick up the decanter and a glass and realised she was holding her breath again. The delicate vessels looked in imminent danger of shattering in the grip of those big hands. But the only sound that disturbed the stillness was the polite plink of liquid against crystal. Everything remained intact.

In fact, the only things in danger of shattering, Phoebe discovered, were her nerves. It was not a reassuring thought. Her frown deepened. Why had this particular Deverell so easily overset her composure when the others had not succeeded in doing so?

It was not the outward differences in him. The superficial contrasts of eye-colour and a more powerful physique might engage the interest momentarily, but surely not fluster one. They didn't explain the fluttery sensations still lingering inside her, or the fact that she'd forgotten every precept of proper behaviour and modest demeanour that had been drummed into her head since childhood. Good heavens, she had even forgotten her speech. Calmness and control had been things of the past. It had been Deverell who—

Phoebe stopped right there, eyes widening as the flickering candle flame of puzzlement in her brain roared into a sudden blazing inferno. Stunned, she raised a hand to her face, her fingertips brushing the place where Deverell had held her captive for those few heart-stopping seconds. She could almost feel his touch there still, the steely strength in his fingers, the careful restraint of his hold.

He was a man in complete command of both his physical power and whatever emotions lay hidden behind the glittering colours of his eyes. The emotions were there, almost palpably intense, but controlled by a force of will she'd never before encountered.

The notion was enthralling. Utterly, insidiously, enthralling.

Control and restraint were, as Phoebe knew only too well, completely foreign concepts to Deverells. Although they were all dissimilar in personality, they shared one trait; no matter what mood they were indulging in at any given time, they could be counted on to indulge it to the hilt. A Deverell who understood control, therefore, was something of a rarity.

She had just reached that interesting point in her ruminations when the object of her study turned and met her gaze. It was like taking a hit from one of the prize-fighters Gerald was always talking about. All the breath seemed to leave her lungs. She watched Deverell start towards her and was shaken by a most unaccountable desire to leap to her feet and flee.

Why hadn't she seen the powerful restraint in him before? It was in the way he moved, with a lithe, predatory grace that was riveting. It was in the firm line of his mouth, and the piercing assessment in his eyes. She was reminded once again of a medieval warrior—one who was deliberating the chances of storming a citadel.

Phoebe shivered, then gave herself a mental shake. Fanciful nonsense, she scolded herself, as he bent to scoop up her abandoned reticule on his way across the room. He hadn't really looked at her as if he intended to discover every one of her secrets. Those unusual eyes appeared so light and piercing only because his face was tanned; a legacy of his years in India, no doubt.

Her head jerked up as she realised Deverell had closed the distance between them and was standing beside the sofa. He was watching her from beneath half-lowered lashes and, as her eyes met his, she wondered abruptly if he'd ever been like the others, and if so, what price he had paid to acquire that cool veneer.

A very high one, she decided, and shivered again. She knew then the real difference that set him apart from his family. This man had looked danger in the face—and survived.

And to think she had come here to lecture him.

Phoebe blinked. What on earth was she about? She *had* come here to lecture Deverell. She'd been lecturing Deverells for two years. True, they seldom paid any attention to her homilies, but she'd never let one intimidate her before.

Feeling as if she was seizing her wits with both hands, she took the glass he was offering her, placed it firmly on the small fluted table beside the sofa and rose to her feet.

"I am not in need of a restorative, sir," she stated in her sternest governessy tones. "And it is past time we returned to the purpose of my visit. I can understand you delegating the care of your wards to others while you were out of the country, but that circumstance no longer applies."

Deverell's brows shot up. He glanced down at her discarded brandy, aimed a narrow-eyed look at her face that rivalled the portrait above them for sheer intimidation, then tossed her reticule onto the sofa.

"Perhaps you should sit down again. Miss Smith. Something tells me this is not going to be a short visit."

"Did you expect it to be?" Phoebe resumed her seat, waiting with primly folded hands while Deverell seated himself opposite her. The dangerous stare had gone, she was thankful to see. Now he just looked annoyed. For some reason she found the expression unexpectedly reviving.

"Since your mind seems fixed on my wards, yes," he said, leaning back and crossing one booted foot over his knee. He rested his elbows on the arms of the chair and sent her a faintly menacing smile over the tops of his steepled fingers. "However, let us get business out of the way first, by all means. Don't think I'm not happy to make your acquaintance, Miss Smith, but if you wanted to complain about the brats' behaviour, wouldn't a letter have been less trouble than a journey from Sussex?"

"Less trouble for you," Phoebe retorted, feeling better by the minute. "And I did write you a letter. Several letters! In fact I have sent you eight letters in the past three months!"

Deverell frowned. "Ah, yes. I recall. I had to pay for them."

"Well, if you'd extended me the courtesy of a reply to the first one," she pointed out, "you would not have been put to the expense of receiving the other seven!"

"You mean I wouldn't have been put to that expense if you'd accepted my secretary's initial reply," he shot back. "Mr Charlton attends to all the correspondence from Kerslake Park.

I'm sure he wouldn't have been so remiss in his duties as to ignore your reports.''

She ground her teeth. "Oh, yes, he replied, my lord. No doubt as instructed by you, with more useless injunctions to use my own judgement. If I'd used my own judgement, sir, I would have abandoned your charges months ago. The only reason I didn't is because I expected you to visit Kerslake Park shortly after you returned to England.''

"Good God, did you? Why?''

"Why?" She stared at him in astonishment. "They're your brother's orphaned children, sir. Surely the smallest degree of family feeling—''

"Miss Smith, I have no family feeling. You'd best know that now, before you get carried away on this tide of sentiment. As for my late, unlamented brother, I imagine he took even less interest in his offspring than I do.''

"But—'' Quite nonplussed, Phoebe found all her well-rehearsed arguments deserting her. She had been prepared for reluctance on Deverell's part, but his outright indifference to his nephew and nieces managed to deflate her wrath before she'd fairly got started.

The thought of her probable future if she remained in her present post, however, had her rallying. Reminding herself that she needed Deverell's co-operation, she tried a sympathetic smile.

"Well, I know that family relationships are not always felicitous, sir, but—''

"Yes, I imagine you've encountered several examples of infelicitous family relationships in the course of your career, Miss Smith. The sorry details of which were no doubt recounted to you by the males in the situation.''

Her mouth fell open. A second later she blushed hotly. "That has nothing to do with the case,'' she stated, resisting the urge to wriggle under his unnervingly penetrating gaze. "I was referring to my own family, sir. I, too, was orphaned at a young age and had to—'' She stopped dead.

"Please go on, Miss Smith. You had to—?''

The enquiry was delivered smoothly, but Phoebe found herself gripping her hands together.

"Your aunt, Lady Grismead, was given all the relevant information about my background when she hired me," she finally replied after a taut little silence. She felt another blush burn her cheeks and silently cursed both Deverell and the strange effect he was having on her. "The point I wished to make, sir, was that my relatives were always punctilious in their duty, and, if I am independent now, it is because I wish to be, not because of any neglect on their part."

His brows snapped together. "You can hardly claim my brother's children are neglected, Miss Smith."

Phoebe swallowed. It was quite impossible, of course, but the temperature in the room seemed to have fallen by several degrees.

"I am not claiming any such thing, sir, but there is more to caring for children than providing them with servants to see to their physical needs. Besides, Gerald and the girls are hardly children anymore and—"

"There are also others apart from the servants living at Kerslake Park," he interrupted curtly. "If I recall, my Uncle Thurston can't be dislodged short of a volcanic eruption, and isn't there some sort of cousin to chaperon the girls? Clara…"

"Miss Pomfret," supplied Phoebe. "Yes, she's there, but I have to tell you, my lord, that Mr Thurston Deverell left before I took up the position of governess. He is presently residing in Harrogate."

"Harrogate?" To Phoebe's relief, the ice in his eyes was replaced by genuine, if irritated, surprise. "What the devil's he doing there?"

"According to Miss Pomfret, he said Harrogate was the most distant watering-place from Sussex he could find, and that nothing would induce him to set foot in Kerslake Park again while his nephew's whelps were in residence."

"Good God!"

"Precisely, my lord." She smiled with grim satisfaction at finally eliciting a proper response. "Since you care nothing for your family, you are obviously unaware that Gerald is turned eighteen. In fact, he will be going up to Oxford at the start of the Hilary Term, but how long he remains there is quite another matter. The boy is uncontrollable.

"As for Theodosia and Cressida, they will be presented next Season and will no longer require a governess. However, I have no intention of remaining in charge for so much as another day, sir, let alone several months, so—''

''So you came up to London to tender your resignation, Miss Smith. Is that it?'' He crossed his legs and leant forward to fix her with a smile of relentless determination. His voice lowered to a note that made the smile seem positively benign. ''That is most unfortunate. You see, I have no intention of accepting it.''

''In-deed?''

Her minatory tone had surprise and then narrow-eyed speculation replacing his smile. Phoebe was rather pleased to see the rapid changes of expression cross his face. For one dizzying minute she might actually get the upper hand with a Deverell.

With that delirious thought in mind, she delivered her *coup de grâce.*

''I'm afraid you will have no choice, sir, when Grillon's Hotel sends to ask what you intend doing with your unchaperoned wards.''

Chapter Two

His wards were in London?

Sebastian stared at the small, triumphant figure opposite him and decided that Miss Phoebe Smith was in need of a sharp set-down. Unfortunately, she did not appear to be the type of female to stay down once she'd been set there. She hadn't even looked overly alarmed when he'd been waxing lyrical about her disturbingly lovely face. More than a little stunned perhaps, but not overly alarmed. He'd had to put that word on it to put some distance between them.

Keeping his hands busy hadn't been a bad idea either.

Sebastian frowned. He wasn't accustomed to needing an excuse to draw back from a woman. An experienced hunter, he knew the advantages of retreat, but it had always been an orderly manoeuvre, carefully planned and executed.

It had never been necessary to employ the strategem because he'd been a breath away from thrusting his fingers into the silky fawn and gold mass coiled primly at the nape of her neck, and finding out if freeing her hair from its tight confinement would have a similar effect on the passionate little creature held in check by the governess.

To make matters worse, he was finding the governess just as appealing. She was so delightfully disapproving.

The thought was unexpectedly pleasant.

Sebastian's frown vanished. The challenge of melting that disapproval into sweet feminine surrender would, he mused, prove far more interesting than exposing Pendleton's high-flying ladybirds for the rapacious harpies they were. It might even ease the restlessness that had been plaguing him lately. A restlessness not even his sculpting could alleviate.

He would need to move slowly, of course. The delectably disapproving Miss Smith was not a complete innocent, even if she did look as if she was scarcely out of the schoolroom herself. She'd known precisely what he'd been talking about when he'd mistaken her for a Cyprian, and she'd been within an Ames' ace of sharing the humour of the situation with him. But she had obviously survived an unpleasant experience or two, hence her attempt to render herself as unattractive as possible.

It would be his pleasure to change her mind. Not to mention her wardrobe.

Unfortunately, before he could implement the various schemes for Miss Phoebe Smith's re-education that were flitting through his brain, he had to put an end to her foolhardy intention of giving him her notice and disappearing from his life after leaving his brother's brats on his hands.

That thought was not so pleasant. And, he reflected, eyeing her grimly, the cause of it did not even seem to realise the danger she was courting in threatening him. Certain matters would need to be made clear right from the start.

Such as who was in charge.

Sebastian rose and walked over to the fireplace to prop one broad shoulder against the mantel. He folded his arms across his chest and fixed his visitor with a disapproving frown. It wasn't a difficult task. He was experiencing a quite irrational surge of frustration at the thought of the three objects in his path.

"Do you mean to tell me you went to the unnecessary expense of bringing my wards to London with you?" he demanded. "That action was rather improvident, Miss Smith. If my memory serves me correctly, Kerslake's estate is almost under the hatches."

His quarry looked annoyingly pleased with herself. "Oh, there was very little expense involved, my lord. We came on the stage."

Sebastian narrowed his eyes at her. The glare that had been

known to cause grown men to quail seemed to have little effect. "You travelled on the common stage? Unescorted?"

"Well, of course." Phoebe bristled. She had never heard that the British population in India still lived in the dark ages, but perhaps she'd missed something.

"Really, my lord, you have some very antiquated notions of what is proper, do you not? I am not a green girl, and though it may be the custom in India for ladies to be chaperoned at all times, there is nothing improper in my calling on you on a matter of business, nor in travelling up to London by stage. And, as I keep on telling you, your wards are no longer children. Gerald is perfectly capable—"

"Yes?" he prompted when she fell silent.

Something in the silky anticipation in his tone stirred her temper.

"I was going to say, my lord, that Gerald is now of an age where he would be considered an adequate escort. That is, if he had any notions of responsible conduct. But I'm sorry to say that notions of responsibility and proper conduct have never entered his head. That journey, sir, is an experience I do not intend to repeat. In fact, it is a matter for astonishment to me that we're all alive to tell the tale."

"That bad, was it?" he said with a mocking smile that made Phoebe grind her teeth. "Let it be a lesson to you, Miss Smith. I suppose Gerald wanted to tool the horses. Driving a yellow bounder is the ambition of every would-be young whip."

"No. Gerald did not want to tool the horses," she retorted through clenched teeth. "He was perfectly happy with the guard's yard of tin, until the other passengers wrested it from him before we were all rendered quite deaf! It was Theodosia who drove for several miles, my lord. At the gallop! On a particularly winding stretch of road!"

His expression turned ironic. "Well, you appear to be in one piece so I assume she didn't land the coach in a ditch. Be grateful."

"Grateful!" Phoebe bounced to her feet in indignation. "For heaven's sake, sir, how can you dismiss Theodosia's reckless behaviour with such unbecoming levity and yet take me to task for not bringing a maid—?"

She swallowed the rest on a startled gasp as Deverell unfolded his arms, straightened and began to stalk towards her.

Phoebe sat down hurriedly. The action didn't halt his progress in the least. He leaned over her, propped one large hand on the back of the sofa and his other on the arm, caging her between them, and pinned her to her seat with a distinctly menacing stare.

"There is one difference in the consequences of those actions, Miss Smith, that I shall take great pleasure in demonstrating to you at a later date. As it is, unless several other members of Polite Society have taken to posting about the country in stagecoaches, I hardly think the knowledge that Theodosia drove one will be bruited abroad. I suggest you put the episode behind you."

"I would be happy to do so," she managed, refusing to be cowed, "but that is not all."

It was all she was capable of for the moment, however. Phoebe stared up into the dangerous glitter in her captor's eyes and tried to remind herself that she was used to the Deverell glare. The reminder did nothing to calm her suddenly tumultuous pulse.

Heat and terror and excitement swirled around her in a strange kaleidoscope of blues, greens and golds. She felt like a moth, drawn helplessly towards the flames, but before she could decide what to do about such a perilous situation, Deverell's brows met in a dark scowl and he jerked upright as if she'd struck him.

Startled, Phoebe jumped a good three inches off the sofa. She was immediately furious with herself. Her only consolation was that her host didn't seem any happier. Still scowling, he turned, strode back to his chair and sat down. When his eyes met hers she could have sworn she heard the clash of steel.

The reverberations seemed to echo in the silence for several seconds. Determined not to lose the contest, Phoebe continued to glare at him until, slowly, gradually, she became aware of a new element in his frowning gaze.

Surprise. Puzzlement. As if *she'd* managed to startle *him.*

Then, as her gaze wavered, as she felt uncertainty shake her resolve, the intent frown vanished and his mouth started to curve.

"I believe you were about to continue the tale of your perilous journey, Miss Smith."

The gentle reminder was all she needed to reanimate her wrath. The spate of words jammed in her throat spilled forth in a rush.

"Other members of Polite Society might not notice a young lady driving a stagecoach, my lord, but some of them—gentlemen to be precise—do attend prize fights. I expect your response to the knowledge that Theodosia prevailed upon Gerald to interrupt our journey so she could also attend one, to elicit a more satisfactory response than a metaphorical pat on the head!"

He seemed to consider the matter. "I doubt it," he finally pronounced judiciously. "For one thing, I hardly think Theodosia was entirely truthful if she told you she attended a mill. She may have given you the slip with that intention, but females are not admitted to such events."

"That circumstance, sir, had been anticipated. She dressed in some of Gerald's clothes."

He smiled soothingly. "Well, in that case, you have nothing to worry about."

"What?" For a moment Phoebe could only stare at him. "That might have been true had nothing untoward occurred," she finally gasped. "But, although I don't like to be put into the position of having to tell tales, in this instance Gerald led his sister into danger. Apparently someone in the crowd took offence at a remark she made and an altercation started, in the course of which her cap fell off. She was unmasked immediately. According to Gerald, it was only Theo's punishing left that enabled them to escape."

He raised a brow in surprised approval. "Sounds as if she gave a good account of herself."

Phoebe could hardly believe her ears. "Is that all you have to say?" she all but shrieked.

"Calm yourself, Miss Smith."

"Calm myself?" Your niece takes part in a common brawl and I'm supposed to calm myself? Theodosia may be utterly ruined! What if someone noticed the fracas and recognised her? The Deverell features are not exactly unremarkable, you know."

"Yes, there's no need to glare at me as if I'm responsible for the Deverell features. I assure you, they've been a source of considerable irritation to me, also. But to put your mind at rest, I doubt if anyone of influence was present at an obscure mill held in a small country town. Be assured, however, that I will instruct Gerald that, if he wishes to reach a respectable old age, he won't take his sisters to any mills on your way back to Kerslake."

"I do not intend to return to Kerslake," Phoebe declared in a voice that shook with the effort of holding onto her temper. "So the enormous effort of instructing Gerald will not be necessary."

"Sarcasm does not become you, Miss Smith."

"Perhaps you'd prefer to hear the details of Cressida's elopement instead," she suggested, not moderating her sarcastic tone one whit.

"Not particularly. But I can see you're going to enlighten me anyway."

"I certainly am," she declared in a tone as menacing as anything a Deverell could produce. "Let us see how much amusement you derive from the information that Cressy ran off last week with a man from a company of play actors."

He looked thoughtful. "Not a great deal, I should think. Especially if you expect me to go after the runaways." His eyes gleamed. "You see, I'd be obliged to disappoint you, Miss Smith, and I have the distinct impression you don't take disappointment silently."

"Disappoint— You mean…your own niece…" She swallowed the other disjointed utterances trying to escape her lips and made a grab for her rapidly disintegrating wits. "Then how fortunate that I don't have to suffer a blow of such magnitude," she said with spurious sweetness. "No doubt you'll be overwhelmingly relieved to learn, my lord, that Cressida was returned within twenty minutes of her departure."

He burst out laughing. "Twenty *minutes?*"

Phoebe glared at him. "Apparently she spent that time describing their future life to her suitor. The knowledge that Cressy intended to join him on the stage was enough to cause him to turn his gig around, restore her to her family and flee."

"Hmm. I can see how that circumstance would overset you.

You probably thought you were getting rid of one of the brats.''

"Getting rid of…" She stopped, dragged in a badly needed breath and tried again. "Have you no proper feeling, sir?"

"I believe I've already answered that question, Miss Smith."

"But you must have some family sentiment," she cried, waving a hand wildly towards the portrait she'd been addressing earlier. "You've got one of them on your library wall."

He glanced briefly at the painting. "Ah, yes. Another black sheep, but as you discovered for yourself, he doesn't talk back. Believe me, that's the only reason he's been permitted to take up residence here."

"Good heavens!" Brain whirling, Phoebe sagged limply back against the sofa. "This is beyond belief."

He grinned. "Why don't you take a sip of brandy? It might help."

The suggestion brought her upright again. "I do not need any brandy, sir. What I need is for you to pay attention to me."

"Oh, I'm paying attention, Miss Smith, I'm paying attention. You've no idea how much I'm learning."

She glared at him suspiciously for a moment, then decided to ignore that obscure comment. She was probably better off not knowing what he meant anyway.

"Fortunately, no harm was done on that occasion," she said. "However, the same cannot be said for some of Gerald's latest pranks."

"Gerald? I thought we'd disposed of him."

"I am referring to the events that occurred last Saturday evening, my lord. Gerald and his friends tied flags to all the toll-gates and signposts in the vicinity of Kerslake Park so that everyone for miles around saw them when they went to church the next morning." The memory had her shuddering. "It was the outside of enough. Every proper feeling was offended. In fact, poor Miss Pomfret swooned away as soon as she saw the first one."

"Well, my opinion of Cousin Clara's good sense was never high," he said dryly. "But what caused such an excess of sensibility? Were they French flags? Navy flags denoting an outbreak of yellow fever, perhaps?"

She set her teeth. "Where would Gerald get hold of French

flags, sir? Or flags used by the Navy, come to that. They were—''

There was an uncomfortable pause. Phoebe knew she was blushing, but now that she was launched on the tale, there was really nothing to be done except continue. With extreme caution.

''It was not the flags themselves,'' she finally muttered, ''but what they were made of.''

Deverell regarded the rosy hue washing over her face with fascinated interest. ''Dear me. You positively alarm me, Miss Smith. I must insist that you put me out of my suspense immediately. What were the flags made of?''

''Well...'' Phoebe began to feel rather desperate. ''They were lacy.''

''Lacy?''

She nodded.

He waited. He was probably capable of waiting until the proverbial crack of doom, she thought despairingly. Or until she became frozen where she sat. Her spine felt so stiff she wondered it didn't snap in two. She took a deep breath and was careful to address his cravat. ''They were ladies' unmentionables, sir.''

''Ladies'...unmentionables?''

Her gaze whipped back to his. ''Drawers,'' she snapped, goaded.

''Ah.'' His grin held pure male wickedness. ''In that case, Miss Smith, the real question is, how did Gerald get hold of so many...uh...items of intimate apparel?''

''I don't care how he got hold of them, sir. Nor did I ask. Gerald is not, strictly speaking, in my care. Not that anybody bothered about that little fact when the local magistrate became involved,'' she added bitterly.

''The magistrate became involved in the unmentionables?''

Phoebe scowled quite ferociously. ''Sir, you will oblige me by not mentioning the unmentionables again. Fortunately, the father of one of the boys made sure they were removed. The entire episode, however regrettable, on the whole, regarded as a prank. Perpetrated by boys with nothing better to do with their time.''

''Quite harmless, in fact.''

Phoebe had a quick vision of the usual serene village church-yard enlivened by carriages and gigs full of shrieking, moaning and swooning females, and had to bite her lip.

"Some people might consider it so," she agreed carefully, unwilling to perjure herself any more than was necessary. When his lips twitched, she rallied herself and frowned reprovingly. "What is not so harmless, my lord, is the consequence of Gerald joining a gang of dissatisfied tenants in poaching from their landlord, and then marching on the man's house when several were caught and arrested."

"Good God!" The amusement in his eyes was replaced by sheer masculine disgust. "Don't tell me Gerald was caught. What a clunch."

"A clunch?" All desire to laugh vanished from Phoebe's mind. "A *clunch? Does nothing* make an impression on you, sir? We are now talking about a criminal action! Do you wish to see your nephew shipped off to the Antipodes in leg-irons?"

He shrugged. "It didn't do me any harm."

She gaped at him, utterly speechless. Seconds passed. Phoebe's gaze fell on the glass of brandy set before her. Without a thought, she snatched it up and gulped down a healthy dose in the manner of one in dire need of revivification. She nearly choked as liquid fire hit the back of her throat, but at least the shock restored her voice.

"You were shipped off to the colonies in leg-irons?" she squeaked.

He studied her rather enigmatically for a moment, then rose and walked over to the mantelpiece again. He thrust both hands into his pockets and leaned against the cool marble. "It wasn't quite as dramatic as that, Miss Smith. The leg-irons were a figure of speech, and some parts of India are quite civilised."

"Oh."

"And in justice to my father, I must tell you that in those days I was what is commonly referred to as a hell-born babe."

"Oh, my goodness."

He smiled faintly. "I'm surprised you haven't heard the tale."

"No." She shook her head, still dazed. "Only that you'd gone to India several years ago."

"Fifteen to be precise." Something she couldn't decipher flickered briefly in his eyes. "A long time."

There was not a lot to be said about that. But as Phoebe looked at the faintly bitter set to Deverell's mouth, she felt impatience seep out of her to be replaced with an odd sense of empathy. Fifteen years. He must have been very young, she thought. Not much older than Gerald perhaps.

"Well," she began on a calmer note, "I must say that sending a boy to the far ends of the earth seems somewhat drastic. No doubt you found it quite upsetting at the time, my lord, whatever you may say now, which is all the more reason for you to ensure that a similar fate doesn't befall Gerald. I'm told he was not a robust child. Indeed, that was why he's been taught by the local vicar all these years. Miss Pomfret wished to protect him from the rigours of school and—"

"Cousin Clara is an idiot," he interrupted, not mincing matters. "School would have given Gerald some discipline. It's plain to see he's been allowed to run wild at home. The girls, too."

Phoebe briefly considered pointing out that they were talking about Deverells and not more amenable mortals, then dismissed the notion. It would be difficult to win the argument when her opponent was a Deverell who had achieved self-control under what she strongly suspected had been extremely harsh conditions.

"Yes, well, that is what I've been telling you," she pointed out. "I regret having to admit defeat, my lord, but it is no use blinking at the facts. I cannot afford to be involved in a scandal—and so far it has only been by the merest stroke of good fortune that scandal has been avoided. Your wards need a stronger hand than mine. They need a man's guidance. They need a man's authority. They need—"

"Yes, yes." He held up a hand. "Please spare me the rest of the clarion call, Miss Smith. The plight of my orphaned wards leaves me singularly unmoved. As I told you before, I have no intention of accepting your resignation."

Phoebe's sympathy vanished as swiftly as her earlier desire to laugh. "Well, *I* do not intend to argue with you any further, my lord. Especially as nothing I say has any effect." She rose to her feet. "You may collect your wards from Grillon's or wait until the hotel sends a cry for help, as I assure you they will. Unless you intend to imprison me—''

"An interesting thought."

"I am leaving," she finished, pointedly ignoring this blatant provocation. "Perhaps you would be good enough to instruct Mr Charlton to forward the requisite recommendation to Mrs Arbuthnot's Employment Registry. Good day, sir.''

Snatching up her reticule, she started towards the door.

"One moment, Miss Smith.''

The command was so soft that for a moment Phoebe wasn't certain she'd heard it. She paused, glancing back over her shoulder.

Deverell stood before the fireplace, his powerful frame seeming to take up all the available space. His eyes were narrowed and glittering, and intent on hers.

"Did all your previous employers provide you with a character?'' he asked very gently.

Phoebe's lips parted on a shocked little intake of air. By what diabolical twist of logic had he thought to ask that home question? she wondered nervously. And how was she to answer it without tripping herself up with a lie?

"I have had only three previous employers, my lord. The first, an elderly lady to whom I was companion, died quite suddenly. Unfortunately, she was the last of her family, but the parish vicar was kind enough to write a letter of recommendation for me.''

"And the others?''

She was silent.

"I thought so," he murmured. "Tell me, Miss Smith, what are you chances for immediate employment when you have only one recommendation that is second-hand and several years old?''

A rather unpleasant hollow sensation made itself felt in the pit of Phoebe's stomach. Lifting her chin, she turned fully to face him. "Are you threatening me, my lord?''

"I was under the impression it was the other way around," he said drily. "No, Miss Smith, I'm not threatening you, but it occurs to me that we would both benefit from...re-negotiating the terms of your employment.''

The hollow sensation increased. Phoebe stood as if glued to

the floor, conscious of a strange tightness in her throat. Ridiculous, she thought. Utterly ridiculous, to feel a pang of disappointment so sharp it suspended her voice and caused a hot prickling behind her eyelids. This had happened before. Why would Deverell be any different to the other males of her acquaintance?

"You mean *you* would benefit from blackmailing me," she managed at last.

He shook his head. "When you know me better, Miss Smith, you'll discover that I never waste time with blackmail or threats. I'm merely pointing out the possible consequences of your abandoning your responsibilities without proper notice. Although," he added when she opened her mouth to protest, "I understand why you did it."

She shut her mouth again.

"Come." Deverell held out a hand and smiled at her—a slow smile that seemed to tempt and beguile even as it pulled her already taut nerves tighter. "Won't you sit down again, Miss Smith? The solution seems perfectly logical to me. I have no experience in looking after youths or girls. You need a stronger hand to back you up. Why don't we pool our resources?"

"Pool our resources?" Taken completely by surprise, Phoebe could only stare at him. Her thoughts scurried in several directions at once. Had she misjudged him? It appeared she had, and yet there was a disturbing stillness in the way he watched her that reminded her forcibly of a hunter waiting for its quarry to make a false move.

But what would become of her if she obeyed the instincts urging caution and walked out of the house? She had already left two positions under a cloud, and had only obtained this present post because Lady Grimsmead had been so desperate to obtain a governess that she hadn't been fussy about a lack of recommendations.

On top of that, there was the unpleasant fact that she would forfeit half a year's pay if she left at once—no small sum when her future was so uncertain. And underlying everything, hovering in the back of her mind, was an insidious desire to stay. She didn't want to leave. Especially now.

Well, of course not, Phoebe assured herself, hurriedly consigning that last thought to oblivion. It was quite natural to want to stay. She had lived with her charges for two years. She was, despite everything, quite fond of them, even thinking of them sometimes as the younger brother and sisters she'd never had. Given that, she could at least listen to what Deverell had to say. If she didn't like it, then she could leave.

Bolstering herself with this practical advice, she took a small step forward. The next one was a little easier. But when she resumed her seat on the sofa, she perched right on the edge with her reticule held like a shield in front of her.

"I'm not going to bite you, Miss Smith," Deverell said, sitting down and crossing one leg over the other.

Feeling foolish, she blushed. "I will pay you the courtesy of listening to you, my lord. Although, I should warn you that even the prospect of applying for a position without the proper references is less daunting than whatever disaster your wards may inflict upon us at any moment."

"Then we shall have to ensure that disaster doesn't strike us. Fortunately, I don't anticipate any trouble knocking Gerald into shape." He returned her startled gaze with a bland smile.

"Er...no. I mean, I trust you're speaking metaphorically, my lord. Gerald indulges in his pranks from boredom, I think, not from any serious defect of character."

He didn't appear convinced. "I daresay. Is boredom Theodosia's and Cressida's excuse also?"

"Very likely, sir. They were hoping Lady Grismead would present them this year, but she still has her own daughter to establish, so the event was put off." She frowned. "I'm afraid they didn't take the delay at all well. In fact, if their antics continue, they might ruin their chances before the Season even commences."

"I doubt it. They're twins, aren't they? Identical twins? Knowing Society's constant greed for anything out of the ordinary, they'll probably take London by storm, whatever their antics."

Phoebe was about to debate this cynical assessment of the situation when Deverell continued. "However, perhaps they might feel more inclined to accept a companion, Miss Smith, rather than a governess."

"A companion?"

"Yes. You could take them about London, do a little shopping. No doubt my aunt knows other young ladies who have left the schoolroom, but won't be presented until next spring. They must do something with their days."

"Yes," she said slowly, struck by the notion. "Quite a lot, I expect." She nodded, considering. "It might work. Theodosia and Cressida are only seventeen, after all, and if Lady Grismead could be prevailed upon to introduce them to other girls in the same situation…"

"There will be no difficulty about that, I assure you."

She regarded him doubtfully. "If you say so, my lord. But I must still warn you that Cressy and Theo are not overly given to obeying my instructions or listening to advice."

"They won't need to obey your instructions, Miss Smith," he stated gently. "They will obey mine, or find themselves banished to Kerslake and faced with the prospect of relying on their brother's generosity when they make their come-out next year."

"But Gerald has nothing to be generous with," she protested.

"Precisely. I, however, do."

"Oh, goodness." Phoebe gazed at him with a certain amount of appreciative awe. A second later, she couldn't suppress a wry smile. "More of your 'possible consequences,' sir?"

The swift, slashing grin that crossed his face sent a wholly unexpected and not altogether unpleasant shiver down her spine.

"I'm glad you approve, Miss Smith. Consider, also, that our plot has the added advantage of removing any burden of blame from your shoulders should disaster strike despite our efforts. Mine are broad enough to withstand the blow."

Phoebe's gaze fell to the shoulders in question. She was about to agree that they were certainly broad enough to withstand several blows, when the voice of caution intervened once more. She quickly rearranged her features into an expression of sober contemplation.

"Your proposition does seem to have some merit, my lord."

"I would, of course, make the exercise worth your while," he murmured.

Her spine stiffened immediately. "The remuneration paid me by the estate is more than adequate, my lord."

"Adequate by today's standards, perhaps. But what future awaits you when your days as a governess are over?"

Phoebe suppressed another shiver. This one was definitely unpleasant. Genteel circumstances was the usual lot of retired governesses unless they were fortunate enough to receive a pension from affectionate and grateful former pupils. Genteel circumstances was also a euphemism for grinding, relentless poverty.

She reminded herself that such a dismal prospect was still a long way off. "I suppose that depends on how provident one is during one's years of employment, sir."

"A courageous answer, Miss Smith. But it takes no account of illness or accident or any one of a number of circumstances. On the other hand, if you accept my offer, I would settle a sum of money on you sufficient to ensure your future financial security."

She frowned thoughtfully. "That sounds like a great deal of money, sir."

"I can afford it."

Yes, but could she?

It was tempting, Phoebe mused. A large sum of money would, if she wished, enable her to open her own academy for young ladies. It would banish the ever-present spectres of uncertain employment, unpleasant employers and grim old age.

It would also put her under a considerable obligation to a man who, in the space of one short hour, had caused her to experience more baffling emotions than she'd ever felt before in her life. And none of them had anything to do with safety or security.

Phoebe took a firmer hold on her reticule. She would think about that later. "I appreciate your generous offer, my lord, but I must decline."

His eyes narrowed. "You insist on leaving?"

"Oh, no. No, you misunderstood me. I would like to stay, but I must insist on receiving no more than the usual remuneration for a companion." She glanced away, unable to meet the sudden frowning intensity in his eyes. "You don't have to bribe me, sir. Despite everything I said earlier, I do care about your wards.''

''Yes,'' he murmured after a moment's silence. ''That was perfectly obvious from the start.''

Startled, her gaze flashed back to his.

''As for payment, Miss Smith, shall we see how our arrangement works out? Naturally your living expenses will be included. And,'' he continued smoothly, ''a more suitable wardrobe.''

Phoebe's jaw dropped. ''Wardrobe? Certainly not!''

''Why not?'' he countered at once. ''Recollect that maids and footmen and the like are provided with their working clothes. You can't expect to accompany my wards around town in your present attire. This is London. They'd probably refuse to be seen with you.''

''Well, that is just too bad!'' Affronted, she glared at him as if he was personally responsible for her drab costume. ''I can make up one or two gowns myself if you consider it necessary, but—''

He shook his head in gentle reproof. ''Not good enough, Miss Smith. You'll need morning dresses, carriage dresses, evening dresses—''

''Evening dresses?''

He ignored this startled interjection and began ticking off items on his fingers. ''Possibly a riding habit, a pelisse, gloves, bonnets—''

''But I already have—''

''Half-boots, slippers, reticules, a fur muff—winter is coming on, you know—a shawl for evenings at home, a warm dressing-robe, stockings—''

''For goodness' sake, sir!''

''And—'' a gleam of sheer devilment came into his eyes ''—last but not least, we mustn't forget unmentionables.''

''Ohh!'' Phoebe leapt to her feet.

He laughed and rose also, uncoiling from his chair with a lithe, unexpectedly swift movement that caused her to take a quick step back. Just for a moment, the sheer threat of his size rolled over her like a swamping wave. She'd never considered herself a delicate creature, Phoebe thought, shaken. It was a considerable shock to discover she could feel so small and vulnerable.

"Calm yourself, Miss Smith. I was only teasing you. Reprehensible, I know, but you were looking so outraged, the temptation was irresistible."

"Try harder to resist it!" she retorted, still grappling with hitherto unknown sensations. When he burst out laughing again, she ordered herself to stick to the point. "Sir, you must know it would be quite improper for you to provide me with such a wardrobe."

He grinned down at her. "What about a modified version?"

"A modified version?" she repeated weakly.

"Why don't we compromise, Miss Smith? I'll leave it to your discretion to decide on a suitable wardrobe, as long as I have final approval of your purchases."

"That isn't a compromise," she protested indignantly. "And—"

"You could regard it as a loan if you insist."

"A loan?"

"When your tenure as a companion is over, you could return the garments." He smiled blandly. "They could be donated to a worthy charity."

"Well, I..."

Oh, goodness, surely she wasn't going to accept. She was certain it wasn't the wise thing to do, but her mind was quite unequal to the task of summoning any further protests. She was positively exhausted. Arguing with Deverell was worse than facing a combined assault by his wards. And surely if the clothes were merely *loaned*...

If only he wouldn't watch her with those wickedly challenging eyes. If only the expression in the blue-green depths gave her some hint as to what sort of bargain she would be entering into. Despite having infuriated her earlier, he now seemed quite sincere. Even reasonable. The only trouble with that was, in her experience, Deverells were only reasonable when they wanted something.

But that "something" was merely to have her take his wards off his hands. Wasn't it?

Oh, dear, her imagination was running away with her. All she had to do was make it very clear to Deverell that she wasn't accepting anything from him that could be misconstrued. Well, not accepting anything *permanently*.

"You're looking quite torn, Miss Smith," he murmured, breaking into the myriad thoughts spinning around in her head. "Is it such a difficult decision? Perhaps you'd like a written guarantee that your...er...uniform will be forfeited at the end of our arrangement."

"What I'd like," she stated, desperately gathering her wits for a final rally, "is a guarantee that you won't—"

He tilted his head slightly and waited.

"That there will be no—"

He raised a brow in polite enquiry.

"That I won't have to—"

He put her out of her misery. "That you won't have to listen to the sorry details of infelicitous family relationships, Miss Smith?"

"Ohh. Yes." Phoebe's pent-up breath escaped her in a long sigh of relief. Why, Deverell or not, he could be perfectly gentlemanly. What on earth had she been worried about?

"No doubt it is immodest of me to mention such things," she confided in a relieved little rush, "but I only wished to make it perfectly clear that my acceptance of a temporary wardrobe does not mean I will be amenable to the distasteful advances that always seem to follow such sorry details."

A slow smile began in his eyes and crept to the corners of his mouth. "Miss Smith, you have my word of honour that if I am ever tempted to pester you with the sorry details of my family relationships, they will not be followed by advances of any kind."

"Thank you, sir." Phoebe rewarded him with the first real smile she'd felt like in weeks and held out her hand. "In that case, I accept your offer."

Something fierce flared in his eyes. Shaken once more, Phoebe almost withdrew both acceptance and hand. Before she could, Deverell's strong fingers closed around hers. For an instant she felt as if her entire body was captured, enveloped by heat and strength, then he gave her hand a brief, business-like shake and released her.

Phoebe ordered her heart back to its proper place. She'd been mistaken. She had *not* been captured. Deverell had *not* looked predatory, merely pleased. Her fingers were *not* tingling, merely warm. And the rest of her merely felt limp with relief that the interview was over.

"Good," he said briskly. "Now, the only question remaining, Miss Smith, is where you're going to reside."

Chapter Three

"Far be it from me to agree with anything Deverell might say, my dear Miss Smith, but in this particular instance I must admit he is right. It would be highly inappropriate for you to live in his house. Highly inappropriate."

Lady Grismead, her tall, commanding figure resplendent in sable-trimmed, violet silk, made the statement in her usual manner—as one pronouncing an immutable law. The fact that she was seated in the largest chair in the parlour at Grillon's Hotel reinforced the image of royalty deigning to address the peasants.

As did her ladyship's appearance, Phoebe reflected, nodding obediently. Despite gaining weight in her middle years, Lady Grismead was dressed in a fashionably high-waisted pelisse that, ruffled to within an inch of its life, emphasised an expanse of bosom that took imposing and majestic to new heights. A matching violet turban rested upon hair that was still rather defiantly black, and her Deverell eyes had lost nothing of their hard sapphire snap.

Phoebe had felt the effect of those eyes already. Having apparently received a note sadly lacking in details from Deverell yesterday afternoon, Lady Grismead had arrived at Grillon's at an hour far in advance of the usual time devoted to morning calls, for the express purpose of inspecting her young relatives.

They had not passed muster. As a result of a shopping trip when they'd been left to their own devices yesterday, Theo-

dosia and Cressida were garbed in scandalously low-cut, bright
gold muslin gowns that, thanks to a deficiency of undergar-
ments, clung to every curve. Their matching bonnets were
adorned with a wealth of multi-hued feathers that threatened to
seriously endanger the eyesight of anyone in the immediate
vicinity. Had they been inhabitants of the establishment pa-
tronised by Lord Pendleton, the clothes would have suited ad-
mirably.

Lady Grismead had taken one look and sent the twins upstairs to change.

Gerald had been likewise banished for permitting his sisters
to purchase gowns totally unsuited to their youth and station,
not to mention his straitened pocket. He was also instructed to
remove the Belcher handkerchief knotted carelessly about his
throat and to replace it with a cravat more suited to assisting
his sisters' companion in her forthcoming house-hunting expedition.

To Phoebe's utter astonishment, the trio had obeyed, meekly
filing up the stairs with no more protest than a few muttered
grumbles. She could only suppose they'd been momentarily
overwhelmed by an older, more intimidating version of themselves. When Lady Grismead took command, Phoebe expected
her victims felt much like a blade of grass facing a lawn-roller
in the hands of a determined gardener. One simply bowed to
the inevitable.

She had done so herself. As soon as her charges were out
of sight, it had taken her visitor less than five minutes to learn
the details omitted from Deverell's sorry excuse for a note.
Much to Phoebe's relief, no word of blame had crossed Lady
Grismead's rather thin lips. Obviously, the events which would
have horrified lesser families were water off a Deverell's back.

Her ladyship, however, was not ready to depart. She fixed
Phoebe with an interrogatory stare and continued declaiming
on the matter of where she should reside.

"Had Cousin Clara come with you, it would, of course, have
been a different matter."

Dragging her fascinated gaze from the lorgnette bouncing
about on Lady Grismead's ample bodice whenever she drew
breath to speak, Phoebe hastened to reply to the implied query.

"Miss Pomfret feared the journey would be too much for her health, ma'am."

Her ladyship raised a delicately arched eyebrow. "The truth, if you please, Miss Smith."

"Well...I'm afraid nothing would persuade Miss Pomfret to have anything to do with Gerald after the...er...unfortunate episode with the flags. In fact, even as we started off, she was laid out on the floor in the hall, drumming her heels and screaming, because he'd tried to persuade her to accompany us."

"Clara is a fool. Always was," stated her ladyship, unwittingly agreeing with Deverell for the second time in as many minutes. "More of a Pomfret than a Deverell from the day she came into the world. Of course, she's only a cousin in the third or fourth degree, so what can one expect?" Clearly this was the only allowable excuse for Miss Pomfret's behaviour. "However, that is neither here nor there.

"I am astonished, Miss Smith, positively astonished, that Deverell has permitted his wards to remain in London. Had you applied to me, I would have advised most strongly against your plan. You are not familiar with the metropolis, and as I am fully engaged in taking Pamela about—"

"I hope Miss Grismead is enjoying the Little Season," Phoebe interposed in a vain attempt to stem the tide.

"Whether or not Pamela enjoys herself is not the question, Miss Smith. This is her Last Chance." The words were emphasised with ominous foreboding. "She is five-and-twenty and not a single eligible gentleman has she encouraged in all these years."

"Miss Grismead has not formed an attachment to *any* of her suitors, ma'am?"

Her ladyship bent a severe frown upon her. "What has that to say to anything? You don't suppose I married Grismead because I had formed an attachment to him, do you?"

"Well..."

"Foolish sentiment," dismissed her ladyship. "I accepted Grismead's offer because he was in possession of a comfortable fortune and he never argued with me. You may have noticed, Miss Smith, that we Deverells like our own way."

"Er...yes, ma'am."

"Unfortunately, Pamela takes after me," continued Lady Grismead, sublimely unconscious of any irony in the statement. "And who must she now decide to marry but a poet. A poet, Miss Smith!"

"Oh, dear." Phoebe could readily understand her ladyship's concern. "Poets are usually impecunious."

"That is not the problem. The problem is he *wishes* to be impecunious. Something about suffering for his writing, or some such fustian. He has cast off his family! His exceedingly wealthy and well-connected family. Can you imagine that, Miss Smith?"

"Well, actually—"

"Of course you cannot. No sensible person could. I have told Pamela that her father has been instructed to accept the next respectable offer made for her hand, whether she likes it or not."

"What did she say to that, ma'am?"

"That she would rather starve in an attic with her Norvel than feast with anyone else. Did you ever hear such nonsense?"

"Well, as it happens—"

"You can see, Miss Smith, why I have no time to devote to Cressida and Theodosia. Whatever Deverell may try in the way of bribery and blackmail," she finished darkly.

Phoebe's eyes widened. "Deverell tried to bribe you, ma'am?"

"He had the temerity to remind me that Grismead's investments have suffered several losses over the years, and the possible consequences to Pamela's chances should such a fact be made known."

"Possible consequences? Oh, my goodness!"

Lady Grismead eyed her with grim approval. "I don't wonder at your shock, Miss Smith. And I know I may rely upon your discretion. After all, Kerslake's estate has suffered the same setbacks. It is too bad. Poor Grismead has had the entire responsibility for all our finances while Deverell was off making that disgusting fortune of his.

"And now he is rude enough to bribe me with the offer of a new wardrobe for Pamela to distract a possible husband from her die-away airs, as he put it. How heartless! Pamela is delicate. She always has been. But one cannot expect a man to understand anything.''

Phoebe's mind balked at the thought of anyone in possession of a Deverell parent being delicate. Fortunately, while she was racking her brains for a soothing answer the door opened to admit Gerald and his sisters, with the news that Mr Charlton was that moment stepping out of a hackney and requesting the driver to wait.

''You are inspecting houses with Mr Charlton?'' demanded Lady Grismead before Phoebe could respond. ''Upon my word, what does Deverell think he is about to send an inexperienced girl and his secretary to choose a suitable house?''

''I'm sure Mr Charlton will be very helpful, ma'am,'' Phoebe murmured, refraining from reminding her ladyship that she had not been considered inexperienced when she'd been hired. She turned to inspect her charges.

Both girls were now properly attired in cambric walking dresses of gentian blue that suited their ebony locks and sapphire eyes to perfection. Being possessed of the aristocratic Deverell features and height, they were striking rather than conventionally pretty, and as their uncle had remarked yesterday, identical in every respect, even to the way they dressed; the single outward difference being the jaunty epaulettes adorning Theodosia's slim shoulders. Only the most alert observer might note from this small distinction that the twins possessed very different personalities.

''Besides, what do we need with a fashionable house, Aunt Ottilia?'' demanded Theo with a distressing lack of respect. ''It's not as if we're going to be giving stupid dances and parties.''

''Yes. We don't really need a house at all,'' put in Cressida. ''I, for one, would be happy in lodgings as long as they're within easy reach of the theatres.''

''I'm sure we'll find something to suit everyone,'' Phoebe intervened hastily before Lady Grismead recovered from her shock at being so addressed and actually heard what was being said.

''Well! This is a come-about.'' Gerald stared at his sisters in the liveliest astonishment. ''You've been moaning to Phoebe for months about missing the Season, and now you say parties are stupid. Girls! Featherbrained ninnyhammers.''

Cressida sent him a pitying look. ''We wanted to come to London, Gerald. The Season was only an excuse.''

''Yes, anyone who wasn't a ninnyhammer would have seen—''

''That will do, Theo.'' Phoebe stood up in the hope that the gesture would lend her some authority. Interrupting Deverells engaged in combat was no easy task.

She had to admit, however, that the combatants made a riveting picture, Gerald's resemblance to his sisters, who were only a year younger, often causing strangers to mistake them for triplets. They usually caused a sensation wherever they went, although Phoebe had long ago discovered how very disconcerting it could be to see three mirror images every time she turned around. No wonder she'd been struck by Deverell's unusual aquamarine gaze.

She pushed the surprisingly vivid memory hastily out of her mind. She'd already told herself she'd been quite wrong about his eyes. The strain of the interview had no doubt affected her normally sensible judgement. His eyes were probably plain green. Or perhaps hazel. Yes, hazel was a nice, non-threatening colour.

Feeling exceptionally pleased with this conclusion, she returned her attention to the battle now being waged in acrimonious undertones.

''Cressida, stop arguing with your brother. Gerald, perhaps you would step outside and tell Mr Charlton we shall be with him directly. I expect Lord Deverell has asked him to draw up a list of suitable houses and—''

''How typical,'' stated Lady Grismead in the satisfied tones of one who could have predicted the outcome had anyone thought to consult her.

Phoebe forgot her squabbling charges and flushed guiltily at having ignored her ladyship for several minutes. ''I'm afraid I said much the same thing, ma'am, when Deverell suggested Mr Charlton's escort.''

''Did you, indeed, Miss Smith?'' A rather thoughtful look crossed her ladyship's face. ''And what was Deverell's reply?''

"He said I should be grateful for whatever assistance he chose to give."

"Hmm." Lady Grismead appeared to consider the statement for a minute, then come to a sudden decision. She glanced at Phoebe's brown pelisse, shuddered, but stood up as one determined to sacrifice good taste for the sake of duty. "*I* shall accompany you, Miss Smith."

"Oh, ma'am, I wouldn't have you put yourself out for the world. I'm sure between the five of us—"

"You don't expect the children to aid you in your endeavour, do you?" Ignoring the lightning-bright glares being aimed at her by three pairs of eyes, she gathered up her reticule and sable stole. "No doubt Mr Charlton is an excellent secretary, but what does a man know about choosing a house? Besides, my carriage will be more comfortable than a hackney. Come along, now. Standing about chatting will not solve the problem of where you are to live."

Having had the last word to say on the subject, her ladyship sailed out of the parlour in much the same manner as Boadicea going into battle. Only the spear and chariot were missing.

"You know what the problem is, don't you, Deverell?"

Lord Pendleton tossed aside the newspaper he'd been reading and lounged back in his chair at White's Club.

"You wish they'd hurry up and serve breakfast?"

"No, damn it!"

Sebastian looked up from the sheaf of papers he was perusing and frowned. "As a matter of fact I do know what the problem is, Pen, so you can save yourself the trouble of telling me."

It was clear Lord Pendleton intended to ignore this sage advice. He ran a hand through his already fashionably tousled brown locks and bent stern hazel eyes upon his friend.

"You're too accustomed to women falling all over themselves trying to please you. I dare say it has its advantages, but a man needs a little spice occasionally. Not to mention intelligent conversation."

"I hope you're not referring to the succession of lightskirts who called yesterday. I wager the only time they show any signs of intelligence is when they're assessing the value of a piece of jewellery. As for gentility—''

"And there's another thing," Pendleton interrupted. "Your tastes are too nice."

Sebastian snorted. "Good God, Pen! You're not so desperate for a ladybird that you consider the denizens of Madame Felice's establishment suitably entertaining, are you? Set up a widow as your mistress if you want gentility, intelligence and reasonably priced entertainment."

Pendleton cocked a brow. "Is that what you're planning to do? I would've thought a high-flying Society wife who knows the rules would suit you better. God knows, there's plenty of 'em."

Sebastian's eyes went cold. "I never conduct my liaisons with married women."

"Dare say you're wise," Pendleton agreed, making haste to retreat from a suddenly precarious position. "Not but what half of London isn't at it. Well, we'll have to think of something else. Not widows, though." He shook his head and added darkly, "Expectations. Before a man knows it, they want a ring on their finger."

Sebastian thought briefly of the pretty young widow with whom he'd enjoyed a discreet arrangement until a week ago. She, too, had had expectations but, fortunately, she'd had the wit to see that he wasn't going to meet them and, with his good wishes for success, had turned her attention to a rich, elderly banker whom she'd recently met.

Not so fortunate was the gap her departure had left in his life. Pen was right about one thing. He'd become too accustomed to the gentle, softly spoken women of the East, who were trained from girlhood in the arts of pleasing a man. The hard-eyed, grasping courtesans and bored ladies of the *ton* filled him with nothing but distaste.

Trying to impress that fact upon his well-meaning friend, however, was no easy task.

"Don't think I'm not grateful for your...er...altruistic interest in my *affaires*, Pen, but—"

"Well, I have to do something," Pendleton muttered. "If it hadn't been for the sound investment advice you've been giving me over the past couple of months, I wouldn't be in a fair way to recovering the family fortunes. Probably be waiting for breakfast in the Fleet. If they serve it there, which I doubt.''

Sebastian grinned. ''You'd have to send out for dinner, too.''

''Yes, it's all very well to laugh, Deverell, but I was getting pretty desperate, I can tell you. Seems to me the least I can do is return the favour.'' He intercepted a quizzical look and couldn't help but grin back.

''I'm not giving up, you know, just because we've eliminated wives, widows and ladybirds. There's still one other possibility. Wedburne told me only the other day about a little governess he's set up in a cosy house in St John's Wood. All perfectly discreet, and the poor girl is so grateful to be rescued from a life of teaching other people's brats, she's as happy as a cat with cream.''

Sebastian's grin vanished. ''You may oblige me, Pen, by contriving to forget about my current lack of a mistress. The situation is very temporary, I assure you.'' He proffered the papers in his hand with something of a snap. ''What's more important is this new shipping prospectus. Read it!''

Pendleton's instincts for self-preservation finally took the hint. He forgot about mistresses or the lack thereof and, rather in the manner of a rabbit diving down a rabbit-hole, buried his nose in the papers.

Just as well, Sebastian reflected. He did not want to discuss the possibilities of making a governess his mistress. It was a little too close to the intention he'd all but formed yesterday. An intention that, since then, was making him increasingly uncomfortable. And he wasn't precisely sure why.

He'd lain awake last night, his hands folded beneath his head as he'd stared at the shadowy ceiling, and had reminded himself that Miss Phoebe Smith was no innocent young girl. Not only had she known what he was talking about when he'd mistaken her for a Cyprian, the little minx had almost succumbed to curiosity on the subject of numbers before respectability had got the better of her.

She'd also been earning her own living for several years; had been clearly accustomed to dealing with the male of the species; and had seemed totally impervious to the threat of his displeasure. Instead, she'd been only too ready to lecture him on his shortcomings.

Obviously Miss Smith did not subscribe to the generally accepted view that governesses were seldom seen or heard outside the schoolroom.

But as soon as he'd convinced himself she was not without experience, he'd remembered the quick succession of emotions that had fled across her face when he'd momentarily intimidated her into silence. His satisfaction at the shock and startled feminine awareness in her eyes when he'd loomed over her had instantly coalesced into an almost uncontrollable urge to pull her into his arms and kiss her senseless.

The force of his desire had stunned him, but it hadn't been nearly as startling as the suspicion, when her defiance had shattered into an utterly unexpected vulnerability, that she hadn't been as experienced as he'd thought.

And the doubts, once insidiously planted in his brain, had proceeded to roll other pictures past his eyes. The starched-up costume that had gone far beyond subdued dressing. The ruthless restraint she'd used to bury the laughter in her eyes. The delicate colour that had tinted her cheeks when he'd commented on her name, and again when they'd touched on her past.

The contradictions had intrigued him. The image of her delicately etched profile had stirred the artist in him. And the memory of graceful movement and suppressed energy had aroused a damned inconvenient urge to discover the soft curves and slender limbs hinted at beneath the hideous clothes. To know how she would look, how she would feel in his arms, when freed of the restraints imposed by the governess.

All in all, he had not spent a restful night. Had the problem been caused by any of the other women he'd had under his protection over the years, he would have taken immediate steps to eradicate it. However, he'd doubted Grillon's Hotel would take kindly to admitting a short-tempered male into a lady's bedchamber at three o'clock in the morning.

No, the situation called for more subtlety than that.

And at that point, suddenly, inexplicably, plotting to free Phoebe of restraints and himself of frustrating nights had made him...

Yes, damn it...uncomfortable.

Sebastian frowned. He wasn't used to feeling protective

about a woman. Blast it, he wasn't even sure just what sort of protection she needed. That flicker of vulnerability might as easily have been surprise; she'd certainly recovered her sharp tongue fast enough. He could assume she was innocent and abandon the chase, only to find Miss Phoebe Smith enlivening the existence of some other gentleman who was presently lacking a mistress.

Especially as it seemed half the males in London were going about setting up governesses in cosy cottages.

What madness had made him agree to let his wards remain in town? He should have bundled the whole crowd back to Kerslake—forcibly if necessary—and found another widow. One who didn't come with complications. But no. He'd watched shock, defiance and doubt chase each other across an exquisite countenance and had proceeded to outsmart himself.

And now it was too late.

She was here. Or rather, out there.

Looking at houses.

With his secretary.

With a barely suppressed snarl that startled awake an elderly Viscount who'd been snoring comfortably nearby, Sebastian surged to his feet, scattering papers all over the floor.

"I'll see you later, Pen," he announced, as his friend glanced up, jaw dropping in surprise. "I've just remembered some urgent business that needs my immediate attention."

He was out of the room and striding towards the street before Pendleton could do more than gape after him.

Phoebe was feeling extremely frayed around the edges. She was also beginning to question the wisdom of coming to London. If yesterday and today were anything to go by, she would be laid low with nervous exhaustion before the week was out.

And she didn't even believe in nervous exhaustion.

At the moment, the only thing keeping her from emulating Miss Pomfret's farewell performance was the calm presence of Mr Charlton. For some reason, the three Deverells had taken an instant liking to their uncle's quiet, fair-haired young secretary, while he in turn seemed to be thoroughly fascinated by

Theodosia. He had scarcely taken his eyes off her all morning, but Phoebe was too distracted by Lady Grismead to worry about the possible ramifications of this new development.

After listening to her ladyship criticise every aspect of the house they were inspecting, as well as the previous four houses they'd visited, two of which in Phoebe's opinion had been perfectly suitable, she was more than ready to put an end to the entire business. But first, she had to locate her charges, who seemed to have vanished in three different directions.

"I say, Phoebe, Aunt Ottilia, this is the best place yet."

Gerald's voice, wafting down from above, caught her attention. She looked up to see him leaning perilously over the railing at the top of the staircase, the upper flight of which descended to curve sharply around a small half-landing before continuing down to the hall. From Gerald's appearance, Phoebe could only deduce he'd been exploring an attic so far removed from civilisation it had never seen a broom or duster.

"It has the oddest little rooms up here, and look at this capital bannister."

Before Phoebe could ask why they should look at a perfectly ordinary bannister that was clearly too broad for grace or beauty, a door leading off the half-landing was flung open with a crash. Cressida stepped forward to the balustrade overlooking the hall, hands clasped at her breast, gaze uplifted.

"'O, shut the door! / and when thou hast done so, / Come weep with me; / past hope...past cure...past help!'"

"Upon my word!" Lady Grismead stared upward as if she'd never seen her great-niece before. "What on earth is the child talking about?"

"Cressy has a decided liking for drama, ma'am," Phoebe began. "Especially Shakes—"

The rest of her explanation was destined to go unheard. With what she could only consider to be typical Deverell deliquency, Gerald chose that moment to launch himself on a life-threatening descent to the hall using the bannister he'd just been extolling. At the same time, his sister flung out her arm in a dramatic gesture worthy of Mrs Siddons.

Phoebe squeezed her eyes shut as the inevitable sounds of collision rent the air. She opened them in time to see Gerald skidding onwards while Cressida, describing several turns at high speed, reeled sideways into the cupboard from which she'd emerged. She landed on the floor in a dishevelled but extremely vocal heap.

"You horrid little toad!" she shrieked. "You did that deliberately." Picking herself up, she rushed forward to continue her tirade just as Theodosia, following Gerald's example, whizzed around the angle of the staircase.

Another outraged shriek ricocheted hideously around the hall as Cressida was sent flying again. The sound had scarcely died away when it was followed by the quiet closing of the front door and a firm footfall.

Phoebe, still standing frozen with the expectation of broken limbs or worse, had her back to the door, but everyone else suddenly assumed the appearance of stunned mutes. Even Lady Grismead was struck dumb. She stared past Phoebe, her eyes almost starting out of her head in astonishment.

"Good heavens!" she exclaimed at last. "Deverell!"

By the greatest exercise of self-control, Phoebe resisted the temptation to close her eyes again and pretend she hadn't seen her charges risking life and limb in front of their guardian.

She turned and smiled brightly. "Oh! Good afternoon, my lord."

Deverell's cool gaze swept over the scene in front of him. "Miss Smith," he acknowledged. "Good afternoon, Aunt. Edward, would you mind telling me why you appeared to be standing ready to catch my niece instead of preventing her from a hoydenish activity guaranteed to distress her companion?"

There was another dumbfounded silence while everyone digested this acid request. Then a rueful smile crept into Mr Charlton's grey eyes.

"I'm afraid I was not in a position to do anything but stand by, sir. Your niece was too quick for me."

Theodosia tossed her head. "I don't see why Gerald should have all the fun just because he's a boy. It wasn't in the least bit dangerous." Having obviously been aware of Edward Charlton's interest all morning, she turned to him with a brilliant smile. "Was it, Mr Charlton?"

Phoebe resigned herself to witnessing another victim fall prey to Deverell manipulation.

"I dare say you enjoyed yourself," Mr Charlton said quietly, surprising her. "But perhaps it wasn't quite as harmless a prank as you suppose, Lady Theodosia."

To Phoebe's further surprise, Theodosia seemed to accept this mild rebuke without a blink. She beamed at her new admirer. "Oh, how clever of you to guess who I am. No one can ever tell Cressy and I apart. How did you do it?"

"It wasn't difficult." He smiled back at her. "There really are several clues."

"I'm happy to hear you say so, Edward," Deverell put in with some asperity. "Since you'll be in charge of my wards for the rest of the day."

"What?" Phoebe looked up at him, startled. It wasn't a wise thing to do. She discovered she hadn't been wrong about his eyes, after all. There was nothing in the penetrating aquamarine gaze focused on her face that could be described as either nice or unthreatening.

"You and I have some shopping to do, Miss Smith," he informed her before she could recover the breath that had mysteriously disappeared from her lungs.

He turned to his aunt. "And you'll be wishing to go about your business, Aunt. In fact, I can't think why you're here in the first place."

"Well! Upon my word, Deverell! If this is the sort of ungrateful manner you expect will reinstate you in your family's affections, you sadly mistake the matter. As for your note yesterday—"

"If I ever had any such expectations, madam," Deverell bit out in a voice abruptly edged with the chill of an ice-tipped wind, "they were forgotten years ago."

Lady Grismead's already indignant colour rose. "That was your own doing, sir."

"Was it?" Deverell said cryptically. "You may be right, Aunt, but in any event, I don't intend to debate the matter with you. I've arranged for any bills you incur at Cecile's to be forwarded to me, if you wish to take Pamela there for some new gowns."

From the tight-lipped set of Lady Grismead's mouth, Phoebe fully expected her to toss Deverell's offer back in his face. Practicality, however, won over outrage. Her blue eyes flashing angrily, she turned on her heel and waited in imperious silence for Mr Charlton to open the front door.

"Thank you for your advice this morning, Lady Grismead," Phoebe ventured, hoping to smooth a few ruffled feathers.

Her ladyship paused at the top of the front steps and looked back. "I hope I know my duty, Miss Smith. You and the girls may call upon me in a day or two. I shall send my carriage for you when I have your direction. Good day."

"Well, really, my lord," Phoebe began as the door closed behind Lady Grismead's rigid back. "How could you—?"

"Does anyone care about *me*?" demanded Cressida from the landing above them, her throbbing tones completely drowning out the rest of Phoebe's lecture. "Does anyone care that *I* could have broken every bone in my body? Does anyone care that—?"

"Stop ranting and come down here!" ordered Deverell in a voice that made everyone jump visibly.

Cressida blinked at him, her mouth open in shock.

"Here!" thundered Deverell, pointing at the floor in front of him.

"For heaven's sake, my lord," Phoebe protested in an agitated undertone, "Cressy is not a recalcitrant puppy."

"You will kindly stay out of this, Miss Smith. You wanted a strong hand. You're getting one."

"Yes, but—"

He ignored her.

"Thank you," he said when Cressida, still stunned, obeyed.

Theodosia and Gerald moved at once to flank her in a show of unity that raised Deverell's eyebrows. All three stared at their uncle with varying degrees of resentment, rebellion and curiosity, but in Gerald's eyes Phoebe saw the dawning of the boy's half-reluctant, half-cautious respect for an older, more powerful male.

She swallowed her instinctive desire to intervene and waited.

"Now," Deverell began in the tone of one addressing troops, "you will accompany Mr Charlton and you will oblige him by not engaging in the type of activities that brought Miss Smith to the point of resigning her post."

Three pairs of astonished blue eyes turned towards Phoebe.

The trio then looked at each other, communed silently and shook their heads.

"You must be mistaken, sir," Gerald said, appointing himself spokesman. "Phoebe wouldn't leave. Why," he added ingenuously, "we've done far worse things since she came to Kerslake than we ever did when the other governesses were there."

"Yes, one left after only two days," Theodosia added helpfully.

Cressida, still brooding, contented herself with a baleful nod.

"Indeed? Am I to understand that only Miss Smith's strong sense of duty has withstood all your attempts to be rid of her?"

"Oh, no!" Gerald looked shocked. "We'd never want to get rid of Phoebe. We like her."

Touched, Phoebe smiled. "Thank you, Gerald."

Deverell slanted a brief, amused glance down at her. "Good. Then it shouldn't be too much of a hardship to comport yourselves in a manner she would approve." He let that sink in and turned to his secretary. "Give me the keys to this house, Edward, and then take my wards away. They can visit the Exeter Exchange or some such attraction."

"What's at the Exeter Exchange, Uncle Sebastian?"

Phoebe saw Deverell wince. "For God's sake, Gerald, don't call me Uncle Sebastian," he said with so much disgust in his voice that Gerald grinned. "Sebastian or Deverell will do. As for the Exeter Exchange, they house an exhibition of wild beasts there. You should feel perfectly at home."

"Wild beasts!" Cressida shrieked, as her brother chuckled at this sally. She clutched at her sister and lowered her voice dramatically. "Did you hear that, Theo? He's going to throw us to wild beasts! Our own uncle! Oh, wicked, wicked world that condones such a dastardly act."

"Try to contain your transport of delight," Deverell ordered sarcastically, eyeing his niece with disfavour. "Even I draw the line at inflicting you upon helpless wild animals."

Incensed at this cavalier reception of her performance, Cressida straightened and resumed scowling.

"I'm sure between the two of us, your brother and I will be able to protect you from an untimely end, Lady Cressida," Mr Charlton soothed, handing over a bunch of keys to Deverell.

He cast a laughing glance at his employer as he did so and moved forward to open the front door again.

"Oh, Mr Charlton!" Phoebe exclaimed, belatedly remembering the main business of the day. "The second house we looked at—"

"Leave it to me, Miss Smith," Edward Charlton called back as he was swept through the doorway on a small tidal wave of Deverells.

"Oh, dear." Phoebe gazed anxiously after the departing expedition. "I do hope they don't contrive to lose him."

"It's far more likely he'll wish to lose them," Deverell retorted. "Gerald and Theodosia seem comparatively rational, but what the devil is wrong with Cressida?"

"Well..." Phoebe turned back to him with a rueful smile "...I'm afraid she is much addicted to melodrama, sir. I think that's why her actor held so much appeal for her."

"Hmm. Her heart doesn't appear to be irrevocably broken."

"Oh, no." Phoebe laughed. "Mr Corby's unromantic behaviour in returning her to Kerslake and then driving away faster than when they'd departed quite tore the scales from her eyes. She discovered that, away from the stage, he was really a very ordinary young man.

"In fact," she added thoughtfully, "I'm not even sure he knew he was eloping until Cressy embarked on their excursion to the village carrying a large bandbox. Of course, I may be wrong. When Gerald dashed out of the house waving a duelling pistol, Mr Corby didn't wait around to explain."

She thought Deverell might appreciate the picture she'd evoked of Cressida's actor fleeing the scene of his short-lived betrothal, but although he did indeed glance down at her, his smile was rather perfunctory and his gaze returned almost immediately to the open front door.

The prospect of a quiet street in a genteel neighbourhood was pleasant enough, but, watching him, Phoebe had the strangest feeling Deverell was seeing something else entirely. Something far distant, she thought, in time and place.

Only when the silence was broken by the rattle of carriage wheels on the road outside, did she venture to speak, instinctively softening her voice. "What is it, my lord?"

He half-turned his head as if, for a moment, though hearing

her, he was still in that faraway time and place. "I beg your pardon, Miss Smith. It was nothing. Merely, I was remembering…"

Remembering a pair of tiny, doll-like Deverells gazing up at him with identical solemn blue eyes from their cradles, and a little boy scarcely out of leading-strings who had pestered to be taken up on his uncle's favourite hunter for a ride, and the unexpected pleasure it had given his younger self to grant the treat.

Sebastian shook the memory aside and looked down at the gently enquiring expression on Phoebe's face. She couldn't read his mind, of course, but in the luminous golden brown glow of her eyes he saw something that looked very like understanding.

He frowned, the deeply rooted wariness that had seen him return to England relatively unscathed raising its head like an animal scenting the air. "You were right yesterday, Miss Smith," he admitted curtly. "I hadn't considered the fact that Gerald and the girls are no longer children."

"A quite understandable misapprehension, my lord. They must have been little more than babies when you left."

There was a faint coolness in her tone as though she'd sensed his withdrawal and responded in kind. Sebastian found himself regretting the change even as he told himself Miss Phoebe Smith sensed far too much.

And yet, he'd almost told her of those long-forgotten memories, was conscious, still, that the impulse to let her draw closer, to allow her inside the invisible barrier of his defences, lingered. Even the legacy of rage and pain left over from a past that would forever remain unresolved, seemed, in her presence, to have faded to a faint echo.

"Yes," he said slowly, "the twins were still in the nursery. You know my sister-in-law died while they were quite young?"

Her wide gaze searched his for a moment. "Miss Pomfret told me."

He nodded. "Perhaps things might have been different for them had she lived. She was…gentle. Far too gentle to cope with my brother. Theirs was an arranged match and very—"

He broke off, suddenly realising where the conversation was

going. And then couldn't help laughing in rueful acknowledgement. "Infelicitous, Miss Smith. But don't worry. I won't bore you with the sorry details thereof."

His smile was returned with a brilliance that made him blink. "Your sentiments do you credit, my lord, but you mustn't think your wards have *suffered* from not remembering their mother. The situation seems to have had the effect of making them closer, perhaps, than other siblings."

Sebastian hadn't been thinking any such thing. The wildly conflicting sensations aroused by Phoebe's smile simply didn't allow room for extraneous thoughts. On the one hand, he wanted to disabuse her mind of the naïve assumption that he'd ever entertain such mawkish sentiments, while at the same time protect her from that knowledge. The warm approval in her eyes was surprisingly sweet. He could have basked in it for a very long time.

Unfortunately, her smile also aroused a shockingly fierce urge to sweep her up in his arms and carry her up the stairs where he could bask in private. His resistance wasn't helped when the loud striking of a clock in the adjoining drawing-room reminded him that they were completely alone in the house.

"Yes, well, I shall bow to your superior judgement in such matters, Miss Smith," he said, turning on his heel and striding purposefully towards the front door. There was still a rather imperative point to be established, damn it. *And* he'd made her a promise. "Shall we go?"

Phoebe blinked. Really! What had caused such a snappish reply? Just when she was feeling quite in charity with the man, he turned around and behaved in a manner that was totally incomprehensible. As if she hadn't put up with enough from Deverells today.

Elevating her small nose, she sailed past the door he was holding open for her. "As it happens, my lord, my judgement in such matters may indeed be relied upon. I have had a great deal of experience with Deverells, you see. Despite their various foibles and faults, they do care about each other."

"I shall have to take your word for that, too, Miss Smith," he retorted, locking the door behind them.

His true opinion was only too plain. Phoebe levelled her

brows at him. "It is surely obvious, sir. Look at Lady Grismead's kindness in accompanying me this morning."

For some reason, this remark elicited a savage scowl.

"Good God! You don't really believe she came along out of kindness, do you?" Taking her hand, he clamped it down on his arm and began striding down the street.

Almost whisked off her feet, Phoebe had perforce to follow. She didn't make the mistake of reading anything gallant into the gesture. If she snatched her hand away, she was quite certain Deverell would simply continue walking.

That realisation, however, did nothing to lessen the stunning impact of sheer male power in the steely muscles beneath her fingertips, or distract her from the tension emanating from her escort. It was so forceful, she wondered the air about them didn't crackle like one of the new electricity machines she'd read about.

And suddenly, without knowing precisely why, she felt an urgent need to have him believe her, to have him see his family as she did.

"Well, perhaps not kindness exactly," she temporised. "But certainly Lady Grismead wished to be helpful."

He sent her an impatient glance.

Phoebe frowned right back at him. "You seem to forget, sir, that she cared enough about Gerald and your nieces to take over the hiring of a governess when all Miss Pomfret's candidates left, one after the other."

"Yes, you have me there, Miss Smith. since my aunt had the good sense to engage you in the first place, I suppose I'll have to forgive her for dragging you all over London."

"I'm sorry if I appear sadly wilted," she retorted, incensed all over again. "But I could hardly refuse Lady Grismead's offer. And it wouldn't have hurt *you* to have shown a little gratitude. This isn't an easy time for her, you know. Your aunt is extremely concerned about Miss Grismead."

"Understandable," Deverell allowed with a sardonic curl to his lip. "My pea-brained cousin seems to spend her time either swooning, drooping or languishing."

"Well, it doesn't help to have you pointing out 'possible consequences,'" Phoebe scolded, warming to the subject. "How could you, sir? Poor Lady Grismead is probably living in fear of having it known that their circumstances are severely reduced.''

He shrugged. ''It's none of my concern if my aunt chooses to lose sleep over the matter. I'm quite sure you don't intend to spread the news abroad and nor do I.''

''I didn't for a moment think you had any such intention, my lord, despite what your note might have implied. But does Lady Grismead know that?''

Deverell stopped short in the middle of the footpath, the look he cast down at her almost making her gasp aloud. For one infinitesimal instant, bitterness, violent rage, and the shadows of years-old pain seethed like a sea-witch's cauldron in the blue-green depths of his eyes before vanishing beneath the frozen surface.

''She should,'' he bit out. And stepped away from her to hail an approaching hackney.

Phoebe stood motionless as the driver reined his horse in at the curb. She was scarcely conscious of breathing. Never had she seen such raging emotions in a man's eyes. Nor the icy implacability that had followed. The Deverell stare was a benevolent gaze by comparison.

A warrior, she remembered, with a small inward shiver. The trappings of civilisation were in place, even elegantly in place, she thought, eyeing the snowy folds of his cravat and the superb tailoring of the coat covering those broad shoulders, but underneath was a warrior. Hard, powerful, and dangerous.

Her mind whirled with questions as Deverell handed her into the hackney and seated himself opposite her. For a long time no one spoke. Phoebe's gaze remained riveted on the stern lines of Deverell's profile, illuminated by a pale September sun as he stared out of the window at the passing scene. His brows were drawn together in a frown, and she was startled by an impulse to reach out and touch him.

Was it because she'd caught a glimpse of invisible scars? she wondered. A warrior, yes, but alone. A law unto himself. She suspected he'd been alone for a very long time.

''How did you know we've been all over London?'' she finally asked softly.

Deverell shifted his gaze from the cab window to her face. ''I had a copy of Edward's list of houses,'' he said. ''And followed you.'' He was silent for a heartbeat and then a wry smile touched his mouth. ''When I learned my aunt was with you, I thought you might need rescuing, Miss Smith.''

''Oh...no, I...'' Feeling oddly shy, she glanced away. Then humour came to her rescue and she smiled back at him. ''Do I really look so wilted, sir?''

He shook his head, reached out and took her hand. ''I'm sorry,' he said very soberly. ''I shouldn't have snapped at you like that. I frightened you.''

''Not at all, my lord.'' Phoebe lifted her chin, but her heart was racing. His hand felt very warm and strong wrapped around her smaller one. She suddenly noticed how much room he was taking up in the hackney. He was so big, so close, she could feel the heat from his body. Perhaps that was the reason her pulse was jumping about beneath his fingers. ''As I pointed out earlier, I am quite accustomed to Deverells.''

He smiled faintly at that and released her. ''Some of us are less easy to control than others, Miss Smith,'' he murmured, and returned to his contemplation of the street.

With that enigmatic remark echoing in her ears, Phoebe did likewise.

The rest of the short drive passed in a not-uncompanionable silence. All was not serene, however, inside her head. No matter how diligently she ordered herself to take heed of Deverell's warning—if warning it had been—her brain refused to co-operate. It was too busy grappling with another problem.

Deverell's indifference to his family had not been feigned yesterday in order to amuse himself by teasing her—an explanation that had occurred to her once or twice since their meeting. Though his wealth put him in a position of some power, he was indeed estranged from them.

And she was very much afraid that she wanted to hear every sorry detail of the infelicitous circumstances surrounding the rift.

Chapter Four

Half an hour later, the dangers of listening to sorry details had given way to the dangers of temptation—in the form of the loveliest pelisse Phoebe had ever beheld.

Modish, high-waisted, with shoulder-puffs and a neat up-standing collar fashioned to frame her face like a small ruff, its soft ivory hue was beautifully set off by the delicate gold-scalloped trim on collar, puffs and hem and a row of tiny gold buttons marching down the front. A large sable muff and a jaunty ivory bonnet, sporting gold ribbons and a sable-tinted plume, completed an ensemble that was both elegant and feminine.

And totally impractical, Phoebe told herself firmly.

She took one last look at the transformation reflected in the mirror in Madame Cecile's fitting-room and shook her head in genuine regret.

"Oh, but, ma'mselle, the fit, it is perfect. And see how the trim brings out the gold in your hair."

Bustling about, twitching a fold into place here and stroking a sleeve there, Madame Cecile paused long enough to inspect the curls she had insisted on freeing from their usual tight knot at Phoebe's nape. "Such pretty hair, but ma'mselle must have been out in the sun without a bonnet or parasol." The plump little modiste clucked in disapproval.

"No, it's quite natural," Phoebe murmured, marvelling that

soft ringlets framing her face could make her eyes appear so dark and large. And oddly vulnerable.

She frowned. She wasn't entirely certain she approved of vulnerable. "The pelisse is very beautiful, madame, but—"

"Ah, you think the ivory too pale, perhaps? Not every lady can wear such a colour, but with ma'mselle's eyes and complexion—" Cecile broke off with an eloquent gesture. "But come," she insisted, beginning to prod Phoebe gently towards the outer room of the shop. "We will show milord Deverell. He will decide."

"What does he know about fashion?" Phoebe grumbled as she was propelled through the curtain separating the two rooms.

"Enough to know what pleases me, Miss Smith," Deverell replied, turning from his contemplation of the street beyond the window. Something dark flashed in his eyes before his gaze travelled over her from her bonnet to the tips of her tan suede half-boots.

Phoebe had time to be thankful the late hour meant they were the only customers in the shop before he very slowly reversed the procedure.

"And the vision of you in that pelisse definitely pleases me," he murmured in a soft growl that sent a series of tiny shivers rippling down her spine.

She stared back at him, wondering if her imagination was suddenly running riot or if the light aquamarine of his eyes really had darkened to a deep sea-green.

Impossible, she told herself hastily. It was only because he was watching her so intently. She wished he wouldn't. She wished he had waited outside. She wished he looked ludicrously out of place surrounded by gowns and fabrics and fashionable feminine knick-knacks.

It was as if an extremely large predator had somehow found his way into a chamber full of dainty treasures, she thought crossly. But instead of appearing in the least uncomfortable with his surroundings, Deverell conveyed the distinct impression that if the shop had been filled to overflowing with breakable objects, he would prowl among them without so much as brushing a single one.

The image of incredible masculine strength under such powerful control set off another ripple of sensation, this time from her throat to her knees.

"Is not ma'mselle a beauty, milord?" Cecile crooned, lovingly curling the sable plume so that it brushed Phoebe's cheek.

She started at the touch and sternly ordered her throat to unlock and her knees to cease trembling. From the gleam in Deverell's eyes she knew she was about to have the same argument that had ensued with every other article of apparel she'd been shown. She needed her wits about her.

"The pelisse is lovely, sir," she agreed. "For a young lady of fashion. Not for a companion."

"Miss Smith, my nieces will be young ladies of fashion once they're let loose in here with my purse. Their companion most definitely cannot look like a dowd in comparison."

"Mais oui," confirmed Cecile, nodding vigorously. She cast a mischievous glance at Deverell. "Milord is very right. He usually is, ma'mselle."

"Is he?" muttered Phoebe, noticing this little byplay. She hadn't been much surprised to find that Deverell was on terms of friendship with his secretary. But a modiste?

A second later the likeliest explanation occurred to her. She promptly blushed bright scarlet.

"The pelisse is really, how you say, not fussy, ma'mselle," Cecile began, hurrying to avert customer embarrassment. She fluttered her hands expressively. "Most suitable. There are no ruffles, no bows or frogging."

"It isn't that." Phoebe sighed. And seeing genuine puzzlement on the modiste's face, she launched into an explanation in French, hoping to make the situation clearer.

It only took her seconds to realise she'd made the situation much worse. Cecile was now looking positively blank.

Exasperated, she turned to Deverell, only to see him wheel hurriedly towards the window. He seemed to be fascinated by a high-perch phaeton drawn up on the opposite side of the street, but there was a suspicious hint of movement about his shoulders.

Phoebe narrowed her eyes at him. "The plume," she stated very clearly, "will have to go."

"Plume? Go?" Cecile appeared more puzzled than ever.

"Plumes are provocative. Companions are not. At least,

they're not supposed to be. My lord, will you kindly look at me when I'm addressing you.''

"My apologies, Miss Smith. I thought you were still arguing with Cecile.'' Deverell turned, his eyes brilliant with barely suppressed laughter. ''Am I to understand that you've decided to bow to the inevitable?''

Phoebe glared at him. ''That's what we blades of grass have to do.''

He raised an eyebrow. ''I beg your pardon?''

"Nothing, sir.''

He grinned wickedly. ''If you say so, Miss Smith. Cecile, remove the plume and send it along with the other packages. One of the girls may wish to have it.''

"*Oui*, m'sieur. What shall I do with ma'mselle's old pelisse?''

"Send that along, too,'' Phoebe instructed with another minatory frown at Deverell. ''This one is only being loaned.''

Shaking her head over the vagaries of customers, Cecile directed her minions to obey.

"And I still say this pelisse is highly impractical,'' Phoebe added when she and Deverell were once again seated in a hackney and bowling along towards Grillon's. ''Whoever heard of wearing a white pelisse in winter?''

Deverell lounged back in his corner of the cab and regarded her with lazily smiling eyes. Apparently, getting the better of her by purchasing several gowns for her use had put him in an indulgent mood.

"There's no need to create problems, Miss Smith. When the weather is inclement, you will naturally instruct your footman to send for your carriage.''

"Carriage? Footman? Oh, my goodness. Servants. I'll have to—''

"You will have to do nothing. Mr Charlton already has the matter well in hand.''

"Oh.'' She mulled that over for a minute. ''Mr Charlton seems to be an excellent young man,'' she observed at last.

"He also has political ambitions and has already attracted the notice of an influential sponsor, so you may cease worrying about his obvious attraction to Theodosia. In a few years, if he's still of a like mind and she's unattached, he'll be perfectly eligible.''

"Good heavens, sir. Do you ever miss anything?"

"Very little, Miss Smith."

"Yes, well..." She eyed him narrowly. "Not all of us are blessed with your powers of observation, my lord. Would you mind telling me what you found so hilarious about me trying to communicate with Madame Cecile in French? I am accounted quite proficient in the language, you know."

"You may well be, Miss Smith. Cecile, however, is not."

"Not? But she spoke with an accent."

Deverell threw back his head and laughed. The sound bounced around the hackney for a full minute before he managed to control himself.

"Well?" Phoebe demanded when his laughter faded to intermittent chuckles. When chuckles seemed to be the only answer forthcoming, she scowled even more ferociously. "I am, of course, delighted to afford you so much amusement, my lord, but I am still waiting for an answer."

"Miss Smith," he said, grinning. "You are a delight. Madame Cecile, I regret to inform you, started life as Sally Mutworthy. After advancing by way of the streets to...er...more salubrious places of employment, she became the mistress of a French émigré from whom she picked up an accent and the odd phrase or two."

"Oh. I see. And th—?"

She stopped, appalled. Good heavens! She had been about to succumb to a scandalous urge to enquire about the next step in Cecile's career. And if Deverell had had anything to do with said step. She must be going mad!

"No, Miss Smith," he said smoothly. "I've tossed some business Sally's way, but by the time I made her acquaintance she was already well-established in her new profession."

Phoebe felt herself blushing again. Now he was reading her mind. This was what came of challenging a Deverell. She should have known better.

"Oh. I mean...I am not surprised, my lord. She has excellent taste. One could purchase an entire wardrobe there. In fact, we seem to have done so. How am I ever going to find the time to wear all those clothes? We will have to—"

He leaned forward and laid his hand over hers, successfully putting an end to her babbling. Phoebe stared at him, transfixed, her fingers quivering once beneath his touch before she went very still.

Gently, slowly, he wrapped his fingers around hers until she could feel her own pulse fluttering madly against his palm. His eyes, glittering in the shadows of the hackney, gazed straight into hers for a long time. Then he raised her hand to his lips and held it there.

Phoebe jerked back immediately, her breath catching on a small startled gasp. He must have felt her resistance but he ignored her struggles, his gaze continuing to pin hers. Then he nodded once, lowered her hand and released it.

"You really are innocent, aren't you?" The words were spoken with absolute conviction.

Her lips parted. "Well, yes. I mean…that is to say…"

"No, not ignorant. Innocent, Miss Smith. There's a difference."

"If you say so, my lord." She could scarcely get the words out. Her heart was beating somewhere in her throat and she felt as breathless as if she'd run all the way from Kerslake to London. "But what has that to do with shopping…or anything?"

"Quite a lot, Miss Smith." He sat back in his corner of the hackney, his gaze going to the window, eyes narrowing as he stared out at the gathering shadows of late afternoon. "Quite. A. Lot."

Phoebe looked down at her tingling hand and tried to restore order to her wildly disordered senses. The task took an inordinate amount of time. Clearly, something had put a swift and comprehensive end to Deverell's mood of amused indulgence. She couldn't imagine what it was.

The only explanation that occurred to her was that he'd been testing her in some way. Perhaps he wanted to make sure his nieces' companion was a woman of high moral standards. Although after yesterday's confrontation, she was rather inclined to resent any need for confirmation of the fact.

But then, if he'd been testing her, why was he now looking so grim? No, she amended, studying him cautiously from beneath her lashes, not grim precisely. More brooding, as if someone has just presented him with a totally unexpected and not altogether welcome solution to a puzzle.

There was no need to puzzle over what she should do next, however. This time she had no intention of asking for enlightenment. It was definitely safer to remain silent. Very silent.

Several days later, Phoebe followed her charges through the gates of Hyde Park, and decided it was quite possible she would survive the move to London after all.

They were settled in a pleasant house in the fashionable area around Grosvenor Square; Theodosia and Cressida had already struck up a friendship with another pair of sisters whom they'd met while shopping with Lady Grismead; and apart from such minor domestic upsets as Cressida scaring the wits out of the housemaid with a rendition of Lady Macbeth's most bloodthirsty speech, and Gerald falling asleep on the back doorstep after an overly-convivial evening with a new acquaintance, life had been relatively peaceful.

True, she was experiencing some moments of concern over Gerald's suddenly busy social calendar, but, in an abrupt reversal of her original plan, Phoebe was determined not to apply to her employer for assistance unless it became absolutely necessary.

Her decision had not been influenced by his odd behaviour at their last meeting. Well, not entirely. After a period of calm reflection, she had come to the conclusion that Deverell had indeed been testing her. After all, she'd come to her post without proper letters of recommendation—which only went to prove that he was not so uncaring of his wards as he appeared.

Unfortunately, this happy exercise of logic had been overturned as the days passed. Not only had Deverell failed to call upon them at their new abode, he hadn't even sent to enquire as to how they were settling in. The omission had at first surprised, then disappointed her. Both reactions had given her a rather nasty jolt.

It was fortunate, she'd told herself sternly, that she'd been so summarily reminded of his indifference to his family. Otherwise, she might have been in danger of changing her mind about him. Or of thinking about him several times a day.

Phoebe frowned. She had finally succeeded in putting Deverell out of her mind, and she was not going to let him sneak
back in now.

"Phoebe, look! Several ladies are riding in the Park. It isn't
fair that Deverell has permitted Gerald to purchase a horse
while we have to walk."

So much for keeping Deverell out of her head.

"I don't think your style of neck-or-nothing would suit Hyde
Park, Theo," she said, studying the riders trotting sedately up
and down the Row a few yards to their right.

"I don't know why we have to walk here at all," Cressida
grumbled. "I wanted to visit the theatres."

"Mr Charlton kindly escorted us to the theatre the other
night," Phoebe reminded her.

"Yes, and it was all very exciting, but I want to *act*."

Phoebe suppressed a shudder.

"Gerald says he's going to buy a phaeton. Why can't I have
a phaeton, too?"

"I'm going to be the greatest dramatic actress the world has
ever—"

"Ladies can drive just as well as gentlemen, you know."

"I'm sure once Mr Kemble hears me, he'll—"

"There's Gerald now," Phoebe interrupted hastily. She
waved with enthusiasm. It wasn't easy fielding complaints and
unsuitable ambitions; Gerald had appeared in the nick of time.
"And see," she continued, "he's on foot, as we are. Who's
that with him?"

"I think it's Mr Filby," Theodosia said, momentarily di-
verted. She studied Gerald's friend with a critical eye as the
two young men approached. "Gerald says he's all the crack,
but if you ask me, he looks like he belongs in a Fair."

Cressida giggled. "What do you think will attack him first,
Theo? The points of his collar or that bunch of flowers he has
in his buttonhole?"

"Hush," commanded Phoebe, not feeling greatly inclined to
share her charges' mirth. Mr Filby had been the gentleman who
had deposited Gerald on the back doorstep at an ungodly hour
two nights ago. Adorning his rather plump person with every
extravagance of male fashion, which included a waistcoat of
palest rose embroidered with blue and purple unicorns frolick-

ing in an improbable forest of greenery, did not predispose her
to alter an already unfavourable opinion.

"Phoebe!" exclaimed Gerald. "We're devilish pleased to
see you. Some enterprising rogue is selling ices over there by
the hedge. Has a deuced clever box with ice beneath to keep
them frozen. Dare say it'll melt before long, but Reggie and I
thought we'd sample a few. Only trouble is, we can't hold more
than two at a time. Oh, forgot! You haven't met m'friend,
Filby. M'sisters and Miss Smith, Reggie."

This offhand introduction made Phoebe wince. Mr Filby apparently shared her view. After favouring each twin with a
polite nod precisely calculated for young ladies not yet out, he
bowed low over the hand she felt obliged to offer him.

"Reginald Filby at your service, ma'am. Very happy to
make your acquaintance. Told Gerald he should present me,
but didn't mean him to do it in such a shambling fashion. Feel
I should apologise."

Phoebe retrieved her hand. "Please think nothing of it, Mr
Filby."

"Well, actually," he contradicted, still apologetic, "must
think of it. Can't have the Earl of Kerslake going about flinging
careless introductions right and left. Not the thing. Been trying
to give him a few hints, but he ain't one to take advice, is he?"

"Indeed, Mr Filby."

Her agreement seemed to cast Filby into deepest gloom.
"Told him so the other night when he kept drinking Blue
Ruin," he said dolefully. "Told him better stick to ale. Told
him he'd regret it." He shook his head. "Seems to be the sort
of thing a fellow has to learn for himself though. M'father
warned me, too, when I was Gerald's age, but did I listen? No.
Sick as a cat for two days."

He continued to look so downcast about this apparently un-
avoidable male rite of passage that Phoebe couldn't help smiling. Her disapproval quite melted away. Clearly, Gerald had
managed to reach a state of disgraceful inebriation without any
assistance.

"Fortunately, Gerald seems to have recovered a great deal
sooner, sir," she said, instinctively dispensing comfort.

He cheered up somewhat at this. "Amazing powers of re-
cuperation," he agreed. "Even woke up long enough to tell

me the way to the garden when we couldn't rouse your butler.''
He lowered his voice and leaned closer. ''Thought you might
prefer him on the back doorstep rather than the front, ma'am.''

''Very considerate of you,'' Phoebe approved, hiding another smile.

''No need to fear Gerald might become addicted to the bottle, though. Told me he wasn't going to touch the stuff again.
Seems to be more interested in ices now.''

This ingenuous observation proved correct. Phoebe looked
around to discover that while she and Mr Filby had been chatting, Gerald and his sisters had descended upon the ice-
vendor's cart and were arguing about how many ices were
needed to quench the apparently hideous thirst engendered by
strolling in the park on a mild September afternoon.

Phoebe sighed. She was about to step forward to do her duty
when a sudden tingling between her shoulder blades made her
turn her head. She found herself gazing straight into Deverell's
glittering aquamarine eyes as he stood watching her across a
stretch of lawn.

Her heart tripped. Her breath caught. Every nerve in her
body pulled taut as if awaiting a signal to stand or flee. He was
still several yards away, but the impact on her senses of his
intense masculinity was enough to suspend every faculty.

It was his size, she told herself, more than a little frantically
as he started towards her. She'd forgotten how big he was. How
powerfully built. Really, there was something not quite civilised about such raw masculine strength, and yet all the politely
behaved medium-sized, *civilised* males within view promptly
faded to insignificance.

''Good God, it's Deverell!'' announced Filby. ''Wonder
what brings him here? Never walks in the Park. Rides sometimes. Very handsome black. Temperamental, though.
Wouldn't like to throw a saddle over him m'self.''

Phoebe experienced a strong desire to order Mr Filby to
cease chattering. It was very distracting when she was trying
to recover her wits. Never had she had such a reaction to a
man's sudden presence. Her senses seemed to have become
almost unnaturally acute. Her heartbeat thundered in her ears;
the scent of newly clipped grass stung her nose. Even the

breeze took on an almost tangible form. She could have reached out and touched it as it brushed her cheek in passing.

It was all most unsettling.

So was the intent gaze Deverell subjected her to when he reached them.

He inclined his head slightly. "Good afternoon, Miss Smith."

Fortunately for her scrambled wits, he didn't wait for an answer. After taking in her new cream muslin gown worn with a frilled spencer of bronze silk shot with green, he shifted his attention to her companion. "Filby, isn't it?" he enquired with a distinct lack of cordiality.

Filby promptly bowed with the flourish of a born Tulip. "Your servant, sir."

Deverell merely looked at him. "I hear you've put my nephew's name up at your club."

"Oh, that. Yes." Mr Filby smiled happily, apparently under the impression he was being thanked. "No trouble at all. Do Gerald good to acquire a little polish. One's always a bit raw when one first comes to Town. Dare say you remember how it was, my lord."

"No, I don't." The words fell into the balmy afternoon like hailstones. "I didn't acquire those particular memories."

"Oh." For a second Mr Filby looked taken aback, then whatever he'd heard in the way of rumours seemed to stir in his brain. "Oh, yes. Yes, indeed, sir. Quite so," he subsided, clearly crushed by the suspicion that he might have committed a social solecism.

"How *very* kind of you, Mr Filby," Phoebe said warmly, finally recovering her voice. She bestowed a beaming smile upon him. "I assure you Lord Deverell is most grateful to be saved the exertion of doing the same thing." She turned a look of heavy meaning on her employer. "Aren't you, my lord?"

He raised a brow.

Phoebe glared at him. This was too much. Not only was Deverell making mincemeat of her wits after ignoring her— *no!* Ignoring his wards—for the better part of a week, he was also being rude to the one gentleman who had taken Gerald under his wing.

"Pay no heed to him, sir," she advised, turning a smile that had more than a suggestion of gritted teeth about it on the unfortunate Mr Filby. "He's a Deverell. They can be exceedingly difficult at times."

"Er…" Filby cast a wary glance from her smile to Deverell's face and began edging backwards. "Yes. Um…that is, dare say you wish to consult with Miss Smith, sir. Be happy to assist by walking with your nieces. Take a toddle around the lake, you know. Your very obedient servant, ma'am."

He retreated at speed, scurrying towards the shelter of the crowd about the ice-vendor's cart.

"Well!" Phoebe turned on Deverell, ready to deliver a pithy lecture on the subject of manners. She encountered a scowl that reminded her of their almost silent parting some days ago. Obviously his mood hadn't improved in the interim.

"'Difficult,' Miss Smith?" he queried before she could start.

"Exceedingly," she repeated with relish. "Not only that, sir, but you will have to cease this habit you've developed of fobbing your wards off on to others. First it was Mr Charlton the other day, and now poor Mr Filby."

"*Poor* Mr Filby?" His scowl darkened. "He didn't look to be in a particularly unfortunate position a moment ago. In fact, you both appeared to be enjoying a most enthralling conversation."

Phoebe blinked. "Enthralling? Mr Filby was good enough to set my mind at rest about G—I mean, about a certain matter sir, and—"

"You mean about Gerald drinking himself under the hatches two nights ago at Limmer's."

"Oh." The wind of righteous indignation whooshed out of her sails. "You know about that."

"Yes. And about Gerald applying to Edward as to how to hire a box at the theatre. Did you expect Edward to pass the matter over to me, Miss Smith? He was only too happy to join your party under the guise of assisting Gerald with the arrangements."

This barrage of information undermined Phoebe's wrath still further. "I was referring to their excursion to the Exeter Exchange the other day," she said in weak accents. Good heavens! First Deverell pulled her nerves in two different directions;

now her mind was being jostled to and fro as well. Had she misjudged him yet again?

"I have been a little concerned about Gerald," she admitted, sending him a fleeting sidelong glance. The rather grim line lingering about his mouth made her feel positively guilty. "But Mr Filby, at least, seems harmless enough."

"Filby's all right," he said impatiently. "Good family, comfortable fortune which he doesn't show any signs of wasting. Gerald won't come to any harm with him—unless he tries emulating Filby's taste in clothes, of course. Then he'll have me to contend with."

Not sure if he was jesting, Phoebe tried a tentative smile. It seemed to have about as much effect as a pin striking steel armour.

"Er...quite so, sir. And if you've been keeping an eye on him—"

"I know what Gerald's been doing, Miss Smith. I haven't been dogging his footsteps."

"Well, I wouldn't expect you to, but—"

Before she could clarify the matter, a young, male voice hailed her from the Row.

"Good afternoon, Miss Smith. Capital day, isn't it?"

Deverell turned.

Phoebe couldn't see his expression, but her youthful acquaintance suddenly changed his mind about stopping to chat. Giving a hasty wave, he rode on, scarcely giving Phoebe enough time to call out, "It certainly is, Lord Bradden," before he departed at a fast trot.

"His mother," she informed Deverell succinctly when he turned back to her, "is your aunt's closest friend. We met them at Lady Grismead's yesterday."

For all the notice he took of this statement, she might as well have saved her breath. His eyes glittered down at her from beneath frowning black brows. "I permitted my wards to remain in London for one reason only, Miss Smith. That reason was not dictated by duty, mawkish sentiment or any of the other dozen reasons you can doubtless come up with. Do you understand me?"

"I understand you're in no mood to be even marginally polite, sir. To me or to anyone. No wonder Gerald displays such a lamentable want of conduct, if this is the sort of example set by other male Deverells. However, if you expect me to believe that you permitted your wards to remain in London because I threatened to leave, you will be sadly disappointed. A mere governess would have no influence on you, my lord.''

''You'd be surprised, Miss Smith,'' he said grimly. ''Come on, let's follow my wards and that idiot, Filby, around the lake. I want to talk to you and if we continue to stand here, every fool in London will feel free to interrupt us.''

''The graciousness of your invitation leaves me breathless, sir. Or was it a summons? Whichever, I decline. I refuse to walk about Hyde Park with a man whose face resembles a thundercloud.''

To her utter astonishment, a reluctant smile started to dawn through the tempest.

''Miss Smith,'' he said, shaking his head, ''you have a talent for confounding me at every turn. Does nothing intimidate you?''

''Is that what you were trying to do?'' she countered, deftly dodging the question.

His smile turned rueful. ''Believe it or not, no.''

''Oh, I see. You only wished to terrify poor Mr Filby and Lord Bradden.''

He narrowed his eyes at her. ''Why do I have the feeling you're enjoying this?'' he asked with a faint hint of menace. ''You know I won't dismiss you and you're making the most of it, aren't you?''

Phoebe smiled sweetly up at him, suddenly realising that, despite his terse speech of a moment ago, she *was* enjoying herself. It was no doubt reprehensible of her, and extremely improper behaviour for a governess, but sparring with Deverell was positively exhilarating.

She was about to continue the exercise when, without any warning, whatsoever, he seized her by the arm and yanked her behind a stout oak.

''What in the world—? Will you kindly explain why I am being manhandled in this fashion, my lord?''

''It's Pendleton, driving his new greys.'' Deverell seemed totally oblivious to her indignant splutterings. ''If we're fortunate, he didn't see us, but if he hails me, for God's sake don't tell him you're a governess."

She stared at him. "Have you run mad, sir? I *am* a governess."

"Not any more. Now you're a companion."

"Well, of all the—— What has that to say to anything?"

When he didn't answer, Phoebe made a concerted effort to gather her scattered wits and tried again. "I thought Lord Pendleton was your friend."

Deverell spared her a quick glance. "He is."

"Well! If you go to these lengths to avoid conversing with your friends, I'm surprised you favoured poor Mr Filby with any discourse at all."

His gaze snapped back to hers before she'd finished, his eyes fierce, glittering, and this time wholly focused on her face. Phoebe felt a jolt in the pit of her stomach; whether it was caused by fear, excitement or both, she wasn't sure.

"It was a near-run thing, if you must know, Miss Smith. Filby may consider himself fortunate that I didn't pound him into the grass."

"Pound him——" Her voice failed her entirely. Then returned with a vengeance when his lips curled in a smile of diabolical satisfaction. "You *have* run mad."

"Very likely. Ah, Pendleton's gone. Let's get the devil away from——"

"Miss Smith! I say, Miss Smith! It *is* you! How happy I am to see you here."

"Good God!" muttered Deverell. He sent an exasperated glance past her shoulder. "How many more of your acquaintances are going to waylay us?"

"Well, if we hadn't been hiding from *your*——"

Phoebe turned on the words and felt her lips freeze in midspeech. Wild notions of dashing around to the other side of the tree darted through her mind. Failing that, she would have been happy to dive into a flower bed and take her chances with the insect population.

The gentleman standing before her was the last person she wished to see. Tall and extremely thin, with a long neck and slightly hunched posture that had always put her forcibly in mind of a depressed crane, the soberly clad individual stood regarding her with a half-hopeful, half-anxious expression on his rather cadaverous face.

"Tobias Toombes," he announced, looking rather more hopeful than anxious when she didn't immediately disclaim any knowledge of him. "The curate at Upper—"

"Oh, yes, Mr Toombes, I remember. How...how very surprising to see you here."

Toombes broke into a pleased smile that revealed a row of very white, tombstone-like teeth. "I came up to Town to see my esteemed patron, Lord Portlake," he confided in a hushed tone such as he might have used at a burial. "I was, if you recall, Miss Smith, in London on a similar errand two years ago when that dreadful scand—"

"Yes, indeed," she interrupted quickly. "I did request the vicar to convey my farewells." Aware of Deverell beside her, listening to every word, she racked her brains for something else to say—preferably in the way of another farewell.

Nothing particularly clever occurred to her. Especially when Toombes took her hand in a bony clasp.

"How very like you, my dear Miss Smith," he intoned, pressing her fingers painfully. He lowered his voice. "That you would think to send a farewell at such a time. I was never more shocked in my life to hear what had befallen you. What you must have suffered! Mr Dorridge told me the entire story, but I *know* you could not have been at fault, whatever ill-natured gossip may say."

"Well..."

"If there is anything I can do for you. Anything at all..."

"You're a little late," Deverell interposed in a voice that sent Phoebe's heart leaping into her throat. Suddenly noticing that Toombes still held her hand, she snatched it back.

"Oh, my goodness, how very rude of me. My lord, may I present Mr Toombes, the curate of...um...that is to say...thank you so much for your kindness, Mr Toombes, but I'm employed by Lord Deverell now as governess to his nieces. No, not governess. I mean companion. Yes, companion. Isn't that right, my lord?"

Deverell raised a brow. "You seem to be somewhat confused about the matter, Miss Smith."

"Yes, well, these things can get very confusing, can't they?"

"So it seems."

"My lord." Toombes was bowing with great ceremony. "Please allow me to apologise for approaching Miss Smith in this unorthodox manner. My surprise at seeing one whom I thought had been cast friendless upon the world—"

"Where did you say you were from?" Deverell interrupted with blunt despatch.

Phoebe groaned silently and raised her eyes heavenward.

"Upper Biddlecombe, my lord. I am the curate there, but thanks to the kindness of my most illustrious patron, Lord Portlake, I am shortly to be presented with the living." He turned to Phoebe and bowed even lower than before. "Miss Smith, may I be so bold as to ask if I may call upon you to discuss such a momentous change in my circumstances? I—"

"Oh, Mr Toombes, I wouldn't wish to delay your return for the world. Think of your parishioners, sir. How they must be missing you. Besides, I feel it would not be proper in me to be entertaining visitors at my place of employment."

"Oh, dear. Yes, yes, you are right, Miss Smith." Toombes looked momentarily discouraged at this setback, but then bared his teeth again in a very determined smile. "But I shall be in Town for a few days and shall hope for another chance meeting. Do you walk in the Park every day?"

"No, she doesn't, Toombes, so don't bother lying in wait." Deverell took Phoebe's arm in a firm grip. "Shall we continue on our way, Miss Smith? We have a great deal to discuss. I'm sure Mr Toombes will excuse us."

"Oh, certainly, my lord, certainly." Toombes started bowing again, then realised he was bowing to empty air. "I shall look for you again, Miss Smith," he called plaintively as she was marched away.

"Don't even think about looking back," Deverell ordered, as she went to do just that. "He's an obnoxious mushroom who doesn't need encouragement."

"I was merely trying not to be rude," Phoebe retorted, trying instead to think of a way to avoid the questions rattling almost audibly in the air around her. After one glance at the implacable determination on Deverell's face, she decided escape was the only solution. She could always come back for the twins when she'd got rid of him.

"And speaking of rudeness, my lord, I have had enough of it for one day." She tried to yank her arm free. "Our discussion will have to wait."

"Oh, no, Miss Smith. You're not slipping through my fingers that easily."

She yanked harder. "I'm not trying to slip," she muttered through clenched teeth. "I'm trying to wrench."

He stopped walking, brows lifting as he glanced down at his long fingers wrapped about her arm as if only now noticing the strength of his grip. She was released immediately.

"My apologies, Miss Smith." He frowned at the way she flexed her arm. "Did I hurt you?"

Deciding she was still in one piece, Phoebe patted herself down in the manner of a small, ruffled bird. "Of course not, my lord. What is a bruise or two?"

He winced. "Yes, I deserved that. I'm sorry, Miss Smith. It was certainly not my intention to hurt you." His mouth twisted. "Strange though it may seem, manhandling women is not something I do on a regular basis."

Phoebe looked up at him, surprised, all notions of escape arrested by the oddly bitter note in his voice.

"That doesn't seem strange to me at all, sir," she said quietly.

His gaze rested rather frowningly on her face. "Thank you. It's no excuse for my lamentable manners, but I've had an extremely busy and...frustrating week."

He'd had a bloody awful week, Sebastian amended silently. And having the cause of it looking up at him with big, searching eyes wasn't improving matters.

So far, he had not discovered one single fact about Phoebe that he didn't already know. And as if that wasn't frustrating enough, images of supple slenderness, a sweetly curved mouth and deep brown eyes that glowed with golden lights one moment and held shadowed secrets the next, were invading his dreams with increasing detailed frequency.

"At least you haven't been busy on your wards' behalf, my lord. Nothing disastrous has happened. Yet."

Her words came to him through the fog of his thoughts. "Depends what you consider disastrous," he muttered. *He* knew what was disastrous. A man in dire need of replacing his last mistress because he had no intention of seducing an innocent girl who was, in a sense, under his protection, only to find himself utterly indifferent to every eligible candidate he'd encountered in a week of intensive hunting.

That was disastrous.

"Well, I suppose we can overlook Gerald becoming intoxicated," Phoebe continued, her mind clearly on more elevated calamities. "Mr Filby seems to think it won't happen again, and since Gerald is now too occupied to indulge in foolish pranks and isn't wealthy enough to be lured to those dreadful gambling houses one hears of, what else is there?"

Sebastian regarded her broodingly. "Women."

She blinked at him. "Women? But Gerald hasn't met any women. Except for the twins' friends, of course, and he's shown no interest in them. It's just as well, really, since he'll be going up to Oxford soon."

Sebastian clenched his jaw and prayed for patience. "Then we have nothing to worry about, do we, Miss Smith?"

Tilting her chin, she glared at him. "There is no need to bite my head off, sir. It was you who wanted this discussion, if you recall."

"That is perfectly correct. There are, however, more subjects of interest than my wards."

Her glare immediately turned mutinous. And defensive. And wary.

Sebastian watched the succession of emotions flicker across her face and clamped his teeth shut on a blistering curse. Wonderful! Now he'd scared her into total silence.

Damn it, he hadn't lost his temper, or even let it slip, in fifteen years, but as soon as he'd called on Phoebe, only to find himself obliged to follow her to the park where she seemed happy to chat with every second male in the place, his vaunted self-control had disintegrated under a cannon blast of sheer primitive possessiveness.

He'd been behaving like something out of a cave ever since. Such behaviour was not likely to win Phoebe's trust. And if he was to discover the source of the shadows in her eyes, her trust was essential.

Leashing the primitive beast inside him that strained to tell her what he intended to do and then set about doing it, he offered her his arm.

"On the other hand, Miss Smith, your devotion to duty is just what one would expect of you. Shall we go on? I believe my wards can't be too far ahead of us."

She eyed him with such a combination of suspicion and scepticism on her expressive little face that Sebastian's sense of humour got the better of him. He smiled.

The peace-offering wasn't returned. She accepted his arm, still in silence, and started walking again, eyes front.

Swallowing this set-down, Sebastian matched her pace while he considered various strategies.

The silence continued.

"Capital day," he remarked at last.

Her lips twitched.

"Obliging of Filby to take the girls off our hands for half an hour."

She pursed her mouth into a prim bow that made him want to kiss her witless. That necessitated a few seconds in which to regain his control.

"Unfortunate name for a curate," he observed after a moment.

She choked.

"Especially with those teeth."

Phoebe broke into giggles.

Sebastian felt himself start to grin like an idiot. "That's better," he said. "I thought I'd terrified you into permanent silence, Miss Smith."

"Very unlikely, I'm afraid, my lord." She sent him a droll look. "After two years with Deverells, I'm beyond terror. Besides, I could never be terrified of you."

The expression that flashed into Deverell's blue-green gaze mirrored her own surprise at the confident statement. But it was true. Phoebe thought, bemused. She had no trouble believing Deverell could be dangerous. He was perfectly capable of making her extremely nervous. But she knew, beyond any doubt, that she would never be truly afraid of him.

"I'm pleased to hear you say that, Miss Smith," he said, almost purring the words. A gleam came into his eyes that caused a sudden, and, she feared, belated resurgence of caution.

"In that case, I'm sure you won't mind clarifying a small point for me. Where the devil is Little Puddleton, or wherever Toombes' unfortunate flock resides?"

"Upper Biddlecombe," Phoebe mumbled. She searched for a distraction and had to concede defeat. "A very obscure village in Dorset, sir. You wouldn't know it. Dear me, how did we ever wander so far from the subject of your wards? What was it you wished to discuss? Gerald's hectic social schedule? The fact that Mr Charlton is calling almost every day? Or—"

"Why don't we start with the dreadful scandal that apparently rocked Upper Biddlecombe two years ago?" he suggested smoothly.

Phoebe promptly stumbled over her own feet. When she glanced up, steadied by the steely support of Deverell's arm, she encountered a smile that could only be described as one of fiendish anticipation.

"What dastardly crime did you commit, Miss Smith, that caused you to be cast friendless upon the world?"

Chapter Five

"That remark, sir, was a gross exaggeration." Phoebe shifted her gaze to a clump of rhododendrons and affected a tone of airy unconcern. "You may have noticed that Mr Toombes tends to speak in flowery periods."

When this defence elicited nothing more than polite but relentless silence, she scowled up at him. "It's true I was dismissed from my last post, but it was due to a most unfortunate misunderstanding."

Deverell's smile took on a faint edge. "It usually is. Who misunderstood whom?"

She sighed. "I'm afraid the squire's son forgot he was expected to offer for my employer's eldest daughter and...er..."

"Offered for you instead?"

"It was not the same sort of offer," she said primly. "But even though I told Mrs Dorridge I had no intention of listening to *any* offer, and had not encouraged the young man in the slightest, she had made up her mind that I was a scheming, ambitious, unscrupulous— Well, I won't repeat the rest."

Despite the warmth of the sun, Phoebe shivered slightly when she remembered the last hideous interview with her enraged and threatening employer. Sensing the sharp glance Deverell gave her, she lifted her chin. "Anyway, it's all in the past now. I can't offer any proof of my innocence, of course, but—"

"You don't need to, Miss Smith," he growled. "You're so

damned innocent you shouldn't be allowed out except on a leash.''

"A *leash!* Well! Of all the—"

"What did you do to discourage the lout? Suddenly start dressing like a dowd and refuse to speak to him?''

She swallowed the rest of her protest. "Er…yes.''

"Exactly as I thought. You little goose, didn't you realise he'd immediately take that as a challenge?''

"Indeed?'' She had realised, of course—too late. "Perhaps you can tell me what else I could have done, my lord.''

He immediately disarmed her with a crooked smile. "Not a thing,'' he admitted. "I'm sorry, Miss Smith, I wasn't being critical, but I suspect it wasn't the first time a disaster of that nature had befallen you. Am I right?''

Phoebe blushed. "I wasn't dismissed from the position prior to that,'' she stated with great dignity. "I resigned.''

He looked down at her. "Because?''

"Because the master of the house decided he wanted an extra mistress,'' she muttered. She winced at the indelicacy of the statement, but then decided if there was anything capable of shocking Deverell, she, for one, would be mightily surprised. A thought occurred that had her rallying.

"In any event, my lord, what is the use of me finally learning a lesson and dressing unbecomingly from the start, only to have you oversetting the scheme?''

"There's a slight difference, Miss Smith.''

"Oh? What, pray?''

"You now have a watchdog.''

A surprisingly thrilling little tremor shivered through her. The sensation was oddly disturbing.

"I would be grateful if we could avoid any more animal metaphors,'' she said faintly. "First I need a leash, now you're a watchdog. I'm perfectly capable of looking after myself, my lord. Or I would be if you'd leave my wardrobe alone.''

"I think we're beginning to argue in circles. But since we're discussing your wardrobe, would you mind telling me what happened to the flounces on that gown?''

"Flounces?'' Phoebe's brain whirled dizzily as she tried to follow this leap in the conversation.

"That dress had flounces on the hem when it left Cecile's.''

"Good heavens, my lord, I had no idea you took such a…a keen interest in ladies' fashions."

He smiled down at her, the glinting light in his eyes causing another of those strange little *frissons* of half-nervous excitement to shimmer through her. She wasn't sure why. His smile wasn't exactly wicked. It wasn't exactly threatening. It wasn't exactly…well, she didn't know what it was…exactly.

"If you must know," she said, hurriedly pushing the question aside, "I removed the flounces for the same reason I had that plume removed the other day. Flounces are frivolous."

"Good God! Flounces are frivolous. Plumes are provocative. I had no idea a companion's life was so hedged about by rules and restrictions. What do you do for fun and excitement, Miss Smith? Sleep?"

Phoebe elevated her nose. "I read novels, my lord. Or I used to," she amended, abandoning dignity for the truth. "Since residing with your wards, I've discovered that drama of some description seems to occur on a daily basis. The experience has taught me that I much prefer a quiet, uneventful life. Constant excitement can be extremely wearing, you know."

"Wearing?" His voice dropped to a deep, husky note that made her feel as if she was suddenly enclosed in darkest velvet. "Yes, possibly. But what about excitement in small doses, Miss Smith?"

"S…small doses?"

He smiled lazily. "Well, to begin with."

"Uh…um…"

"For instance, was I wrong earlier when I guessed you enjoyed turning the governess on me?"

"Ohh." Phoebe blushed and silently berated herself. Goodness, for a minute there she'd thought…

She hurriedly consigned what she'd thought to oblivion. "I see you've found me out, my lord. What can I do but confess?" Stiffening knees that had gone weak with relief, she smiled confidingly up at him. "Perhaps I enjoy talking with you, sir, because I'm secure in the knowledge that you won't make any undesirable advances towards me. You see, I've never had that freedom before."

There was a very odd silence.

"I hope I haven't taken advantage," she queried, suddenly anxious.

"Uh, no, Miss Smith." Sebastian eyed her rather curiously. "Yes, I did promise not to pester you with the undesirable advances that follow sorry details of infelicitous relationships, didn't I?" *He must have been mad.* "I take it you didn't consider the episode in the hackney the other day to be an advance?"

"Oh, no. I know you were only testing me."

"Testing you," he repeated carefully.

"Naturally you wished to be sure that your nieces' companion was a respectable female."

He stared at her, fascinated. "Naturally."

"Well?" She looked up at him with a quizzical smile. "Weren't you? Testing me, that is."

Sebastian gazed down into guileless brown eyes and had to fight a sensation of drowning. God, a man could lose himself in those warm golden depths and not even notice until it was too late. He must be losing his mind. Thanks to that idiotic promise, Miss Phoebe Smith had just managed to completely flummox him. A state of affairs that he couldn't recall ever occurring before. Obviously, unsatisfied desire was a more serious problem than he'd supposed. First he'd lost interest in other women; now he was losing control of the situation.

"You could say it was something along those lines," he murmured at last, completely incapable of disillusioning her.

"I thought so." Phoebe pushed aside a sharp little twinge of disappointment. Really. What foolishness. She had no reason to feel disappointed. Deverell had turned out to be more understanding than she'd supposed. He'd believed her innocent of any wrongdoing—even if his remarks on the subject were less than polite—and he even seemed somewhat protective.

Not that she needed protecting, Phoebe told herself hastily. But just once in a while—only for a few minutes, of course— it was a nice, warm feeling to have.

"Thank you for believing in me," she continued earnestly. "I've always dreaded anyone finding out about...well, what happened. Most people tend to blame the governess in such cases, and there's really nothing one can do. Protests only make it worse."

"You may not be able to do a great deal, Miss Smith; however, should I ever encounter the squire's son from Lower Fiddleton, he will apologise to you immediately or be torn limb from limb."

Phoebe giggled. "Upper Biddlecombe, my lord. Oh, dear, I suppose I should tell you that violent retribution is not the answer, but I must confess I would have found it rather satisfying to have *planted him a facer,* myself. Do I have that right?"

He slanted an amused glance down at her. "You do. I take it Gerald has sullied your ears with boxing cant. How improper."

"I believe you're teasing me, sir. No doubt you consider me *overly* proper, but governesses must be forever mindful of decorum. We have our reputations to think of, you know."

"Indeed you do. So was it after the episode in Little Muddlecombe that you changed your name to Smith?"

Phoebe stopped walking so abruptly her hand fell from Deverell's arm. This time she felt no inclination to correct him. The soft, totally unexpected question sent shock racing through every nerve-ending. Her mind went blank. Her lungs constricted.

"I...I don't know what you mean, sir. My name *is* Smith. I told you..." Her voice dried up.

Deverell took her hand in a warm clasp, but made no move to walk on. "Haven't I shown you that I can be trusted with the truth, Miss Smith?" he asked very gently. "I am no fool, you know. Indeed, it would be plain to the meanest intelligence—"

"My lord," she interrupted, shaken immeasurably by his sudden gentleness. She hadn't expected it. Hadn't known he was capable of it. And yet...

But even as an image of the sculpted Psyche in his library flashed before her mind's eye, even as the bitterness in his tone when he'd apologised for bruising her echoed faintly in her mind, words that would keep him at a distance were tumbling from her lips. "I don't know what has given you the impression that— In short, sir, I can only repeat that Smith is my name. That *is* the truth."

And it was, she comforted herself. More or less.

His intent, searching gaze held her captive for several seconds longer. "Then I can only apologise for upsetting you, Miss Smith." He released her hand and drew back. "Shall we catch up to my wards? I believe they're just ahead of us."

"By all means, sir." It was all the answer Phoebe could manage. The slight coolness in Deverell's tone caused her throat to close up and her eyes to sting. The sudden sense of loss was piercing, a sharp pain in her chest, but what else could she have said? She'd made a promise of her own, and even though the promise had been forced, surely it had still to be honoured.

While her beleaguered brain was struggling with this ticklish question, they overtook the small animated party ahead of them. To her mingled distraction and relief, Phoebe was instantly surrounded by Deverells wanting to indulge in such diverse entertainments as a visit to a bookshop to purchase political treatises on the rights of women, and an excursion to Astley's Amphitheatre to see the equestrienne displays. Cressida was suspiciously quiet, but Phoebe was too beset to worry about this unusual state of affairs.

As they made their way back to the Stanhope Gate, where Mr Filby took his leave of them, she made sure there was always someone between herself and Deverell. It was a depressingly easy task. He seemed to have the same intention.

Phoebe felt so ridiculously low by the time they were standing in the street again that she didn't even raise her voice in protest when she heard Gerald pestering his uncle to take him to Jackson's Boxing Saloon.

"Perhaps some time next week, Gerald," Deverell said brusquely as he turned towards her. "Miss Smith, thank you for a most instructive afternoon." He took the hand she held out before she thought better of it. "No doubt we shall meet again soon."

"No doubt," she agreed, avoiding his direct gaze.

He raised her hand to his lips, dropped a kiss into her palm and released her. "By the way," he said softly, "have your abigail sew those flounces back on your gown before we do."

He turned and was more than halfway down the street before Phoebe managed to get her mouth closed again.

It was Cressida who brought her back to earth. "What abigail?" she asked.

Phoebe made a concerted effort to pull herself together. It wasn't altogether successful. Her mind seemed suspended in the moment when Deverell had dropped that casual kiss into her palm as if...as if...

"Your uncle has a very odd notion of companions, Cressy," she managed at last, abandoning any attempt at rational thought. "I expect he meant the girl Mr Charlton hired to assist the housemaid. Come now. We'd better go home before everyone wonders why we're all standing about in the street."

"You don't need me to escort you home, do you, Phoebe?" Gerald started edging away along the street. "Think I'll take a look-in at the Pigeonhole. Fellow I met at Reggie's club took me there last night. Interesting place. I'll see you tomorrow. Perhaps we can go to Astley's."

"Astley's? Well—"

But Gerald was already out of earshot.

"Oh, dear," Phoebe said again, gazing after him. "The Pigeonhole. Well, that sounds like a nice, harmless place. Perhaps they serve ices."

"Never mind about Gerald." Theo seized Phoebe's sleeve and gave it an urgent tug. "I want to go to Hatchard's on our way home, Phoebe. Edward says they have an excellent selection of political treatises on all sorts of subjects, and—"

"'Edward'? Oh, dear."

"I don't know why you bother with those pamphlets, Theo." Cressida frowned at her sister. "You only annoy people when you quote Mary Wollstonecraft all over the place. The theatre is where people listen. I'll sway thousands. Millions. I'll be famous. I'll—"

"Oh, dear."

"We're going to Hatchard's, Cressy. The theatre can wait."

Taking charge in a manner strongly reminiscent of Lady Grismead, Theodosia took hold of her sister and started off in the direction of Piccadilly.

Feeling quite incapable of protesting, Phoebe followed, only vaguely listening to the argument which continued unabated. The words "persecuted" and "suffering" wafted to her ears, but whether in relation to thwarted theatrical ambitions or oppressed females was not clear. Nor was she inclined to enquire. She wondered if Hatchard's had a nice, quiet room set aside for customers who badly needed peace and solitude.

She devoutly hoped so. It seemed to her that every time she encountered Deverell she needed a period of calm reflection in which to recover.

The following morning, Phoebe found herself in possession of all the peace and solitude she could have desired. The breakfast table, usually a popular and lively place, was entirely devoid of Deverells.

Since the butler had been summoned from Kerslake Park along with a half dozen or so other servants, and had been with the family for years, Phoebe had no hesitation in questioning him about this departure from the normal.

"The young ladies have gone out, miss," he said in answer to her query.

"Already? But it's scarcely nine o'clock. Did Gerald go with them, Thripp?"

"No, miss. I understand his lordship is still asleep." Thripp pursed his lips and allowed himself a small frown of disapproval. "Master Gerald…I mean, his lordship, did not retire until dawn."

"Dawn! Well, I suppose we should let him sleep. Did the twins say where they were going?"

"Not in so many words, miss, but Lady Cressida mentioned something about being thrown out into the snow."

Phoebe gazed towards the window in astonishment. Beyond the open casement, bordering green lawns and gravel paths, gaily coloured autumn blooms nodded in the sunshine. "But it's the middle of September."

"Precisely so, miss." Thripp's tone lowered to a note of heavy foreboding. "Her ladyship may have been rehearsing."

"Rehearsing!" She looked back at the butler in dismay. "Oh, no! The theatres! She wouldn't! Would she?"

Thripp had no trouble following these horrified utterances. "That I couldn't say, miss. But I did happen to notice that Lady Cressida was dressed rather strangely."

"Dressed rather—— In what way?"

"She wore a cloak, miss, and was heavily veiled. Before she lowered the veil, however, I caught a glimpse of her face." Thripp paused for effect before continuing in a voice of doom. "I couldn't be sure, miss, but I think her ladyship's countenance was painted."

"Painted! Oh, my goodness, they *have* gone to the theatres. For heaven's sake, Thripp, why didn't you stop them? No, never mind," she added when the butler turned a look of reproach on her. It was no use chastising Thripp. He was elderly and not overly blessed with quickness of wit. "I know they wouldn't have listened. I'll have to go after them at once. Send the footman out to summon a hackney, if you please, while I fetch my pelisse and bonnet."

"Yes, miss. Shall I send a message to his lordship?"

Phoebe hesitated, trying to push aside her worry so she could think. "No, let him sleep. There aren't that many reputable theatres in London. I'm sure I'll find the girls quite quickly."

"I hope so, miss, but I was referring to Lord Deverell."

"*Lord Deverell!* No! Good heavens, no! He is not to be told about this. Do you hear me, Thripp?"

Inured by long association with Deverells to alarums and starts of a similar nature, Thripp merely nodded obediently and left the dining-room.

Phoebe took a moment to finish her coffee on the principle that she'd need the sustenance, before dashing upstairs to fling on her old pelisse and her bonnet. No doubt Deverell would object to her attire, but this wasn't the time to be fashionable. When she ran downstairs again, a hackney was at the door. She wasted no time climbing into it and directing the driver to take her to Covent Garden.

Thripp stood on the front doorstep as she was driven away, looking mournfully after her. Phoebe wished his expression was a little more encouraging. She also wished she had some company. Even Miss Pomfret's presence would be preferable to sitting alone with her worried thoughts, but although Deverell had summoned Cousin Clara to Town with the servants, Miss Pomfret, in a rare Deverell-like display of defiance, had taken refuge in her bed, citing nervous prostration and thus delaying her arrival.

Still, she wasn't seriously worried, Phoebe assured herself.

After all, Theodosia was with her sister, and they would probably have to wait to see the managers of the various theatres. She would soon catch up with her charges.

But she did not catch up with them.

Three hours later, footsore and weary, Phoebe stood in a tiny malodorous court in the middle of a maze of streets and decided it was time to take stock of her situation.

It was not good. For one thing she was exhausted. She had called first at the Theatre Royal, Covent Garden, where she'd learned that her charges had been turned away by a charming but discouraging Charles Kemble, who had recently taken over as manager from his famous brother.

Undaunted, she had then repaired to the Theatre Royal, Drury Lane where, according to Mr Alfred Bunn, the manager, the twins had received a lecture on the impropriety of young ladies of quality seeking a career on the stage. Disinclined to believe they had taken this to heart, she had proceeded to the Theatre Royal, Haymarket, by then wondering why managers couldn't think of anything more original in the way of names for their playhouses.

Apparently they couldn't think of anything original in the way of lectures either. Her charges, it seemed, had received similar homilies to Mr Bunn's at the Haymarket, the Lyceum and the San Pareil.

"And I'll tell you what else they heard at the other theatres, miss," Mr Scott of the San Pareil had added. "The young lady's acting skills are rather too limited to tragedy and she won't take direction. I'm sure she does very well in amateur theatricals, but even if her station in life didn't prohibit her from the public stage, she wouldn't suit."

"Do you think she might have abandoned the scheme?" Phoebe had asked hopefully.

But to her dismay, Mr Scott had no such good news to impart. Cressida had declared her intention of applying to every theatre in London.

"And some of them, miss, ain't what you'd call genteel," Mr Scott had called after her.

Phoebe had just discovered precisely what he'd meant. After

visiting a succession of lesser playhouses whose productions, while of an inferior nature, were at least respectable, she had finally been confronted by a bevy of scantily clad females rehearsing a very odd-looking tableau.

And the owner of the theatre, a rather oily individual, had seemed to think *she* was looking for employment.

After ascertaining that the man had not encountered any twins that morning, Phoebe had fled. Unfortunately, she had not taken note of where she was fleeing. And now, she realised, looking about her with a shiver, she was quite alone and completely lost somewhere in the labyrinth of courts and alleys surrounding Covent Garden.

No, not quite alone, she thought, glancing quickly over her shoulder. There was no one in sight—indeed, the rickety buildings surrounding the court appeared utterly vacant, their windows, darkened by the grime of years, reminding her unpleasantly of so many empty eye-sockets—but she was being watched. She felt it. The scrutiny of innumerable eyes was palpable, like a chilling brush of air across her skin.

The accompanying silence was even more unnerving.

There had been noise. She remembered a child's wail, quickly hushed; the clatter of a tin somewhere in an adjacent alley; a slow creak that might have been the closing of a door. But now silence hung over the small court like a shroud.

Phoebe frowned and took a firmer hold of her reticule. This would not do. She couldn't stand here dithering all day while hair-raising tales of the crime abounding in large cities chased one another through her head. She would find a shop somewhere and ask for directions.

Two exits led from the court. An archway beyond which she could see another smaller, dingier court, and a narrow alley. She couldn't remember running along the alley on her way here, but it looked the more promising of the two.

She had taken no more than a single step towards it when a door banged open directly behind her.

Phoebe squeaked and whirled about, her heart in her mouth.

A gentleman—yes, unmistakably a gentleman—stepped into the open, a slim ebony cane tucked under one arm while he drew on his gloves, quite as if he was preparing for a stroll in the Park.

She blinked. Once. Twice. And still couldn't believe the evidence of her eyes. In fact, so unexpected was the sight of such gentlemanly elegance in these mean surroundings that several seconds passed before she realised that he, too, was staring as if unable to believe his senses.

When his expression registered, she found herself stepping back a pace, her initial hope that here was someone who might help her receiving a severe jolt. The frozen rigidity of his features was out of all proportion to their encounter. He seemed shocked beyond measure; as if he gazed upon the utterly impossible rather than the startling and unusual.

Had there been anyone else in the court, she would have instantly turned to them, no matter how unsavoury and ruffianly their appearance.

Phoebe took a shaky breath and told herself not to be foolish. There *was* no one else, and at least he was a gentleman.

"I...I wonder if you could help me, sir." Her voice trembled and she stiffened her spine. "I was trying to find the...the Market." Yes, that would do. She could take a hackney from there.

The gentleman frowned at the sound of her voice, his pale, almost colourless blue eyes narrowing on her face as he came closer. "You're lost?" he asked, his voice oddly hoarse. "Who are you?"

Phoebe shifted uneasily. "Yes," she said, ignoring his second question. "That is, I left the Birdcage Theatre by a side door and must have taken a wrong turning somewhere and..."

She let the words trail off. The strange expression of shock had gone but the gentleman was now staring at her in a way that put her forcibly in mind of a collector savouring the imminent possession of a rare specimen. She wanted to shrink into herself, and yet the stranger hadn't threatened her in any way.

But even as this reassuring thought occurred to her, his gaze travelled over her drab costume in a manner that suggested he was coming to some accurate conclusions about her circumstances.

"You must have come from the country," he murmured.

Phoebe took another step back, tales of simple country girls lured to places of ill-repute and never heard of again promptly darting through her mind. "If you wouldn't mind directing me to the Market," she said firmly. "I would be very grateful. This neighbourhood is not exactly comfortable." *And nor are you,* she added silently.

"The Market. Yes." His gaze returned to her face and lingered, seeming to study each individual feature. "How very extraordinary are the machinations of fate," he murmured, and smiled. Quite a pleasant, unthreatening smile. She didn't know why she shivered.

"Sir…"

"Yes. Yes, indeed. The Market." His smile turned faintly chiding. "This is no place for a young lady. Most reckless of you, my dear, to venture away from the main thoroughfare."

Phoebe was too busy straining her ears at a faint noise to object to his familiar mode of address. Had that been a shuffling footstep over to her left?

"But first—though I feel introductions are hardly necessary—perhaps we should observe the niceties. Viscount Crowhurst at your service, Miss…er…"

"Smith," she said briefly, scarcely listening to him. Yes, that had been a shuffle. The feeling of being watched grew stronger, as though the watchers had pressed closer, or perhaps there were more of them.

Her companion seemed to have no awareness of danger at all. "Smith," he repeated slowly, thoughtfully. "Ah. Yes. Yes, of course. It would be. And you were looking for a theatre, my dear?"

"Not precisely. Sir, I'm sorry if I seem impolite, but I'm employed by Lord Deverell and—"

"Deverell?"

The name exploded in the air with such force that Phoebe jerked back instinctively. For a moment she could only stare, her mind reeling beneath the flash of sheer hatred in Crowhurst's pale eyes before he swiftly lowered his lashes.

She shook her head, unable to believe what she'd seen. Surely she was mistaken. Infuriating though Deverell could be, he could hardly arouse such bitter enmity in three short months.

"I'm companion to his nieces," she ventured, beginning to feel rather like someone groping her way through an impenetrable fog.

Crowhurst raised his eyes to hers again, his expression impassive now but watchful. "Is that so, Miss Smith?" He seemed to dismiss the statement with a gesture. "Well, that shouldn't present us with any problems. I don't know how it comes about that Deverell has abandoned you in this sorry neighbourhood, but I hope you'll allow me to escort you—"

He was cut off by the sound of heavy footsteps ringing on the cobblestones of the alley. Already stunned speechless by Crowhurst's assumption that Deverell would abandon a woman in an area patently worse than sorry, Phoebe barely had the wit to turn, heart pounding, as she braced to confront whatever new danger was about to show itself.

A heartbeat later, Deverell strode into the court, a black scowl on his face, his fists clenched, and an expression in his eyes that gave Phoebe a glimpse into the hell awaiting anyone who crossed him.

She had never seen a more welcome sight in her life. Ignoring the waves of lethal menace emanating from him, she flew across the court as if her feet had grown wings. "Oh, my lord!"

He caught her, his hands tightening almost brutally around her shoulders. For an instant she thought he was going to pull her closer, to pull her into his arms and hold her. The impression was so strong she cried out, stunned by the intense longing that swept through her for him to do just that.

And then it was gone. With a stifled oath he swung her to one side, leaving his right hand free. Before she could blink he drew a pistol from his pocket and levelled it with one smooth motion.

Immediately a sense of movement rippled through the court. There was still no sign of life, but it seemed to her that the invisible watchers took a collective step back.

"A wise precaution, my lord."

Crowhurst strolled over to them, his cane swinging gently from one hand. "But the people here know me and have a certain respect for my own weapon." The cane was swung again before being tucked under his arm.

"Sword-stick," said Deverell, nodding. He lowered the pistol to his side but kept it in plain sight.

"Yes. One doesn't venture into these streets unarmed unless

one is a fool. Or ignorant of the dangers,'' he added, glancing at Phoebe. ''Your…er…nieces' companion, I believe.''

Deverell's eyes narrowed.

''Yes, quite so. I was about to offer my assistance, but it now appears unnecessary. I'm Crowhurst, by the bye. I believe we met at the Waterbrooks some weeks ago.''

Phoebe gaped at him, astounded by the unctuous civility. She *must* have been mistaken a moment ago. No man could look like that—so filled with hatred one minute and then able to hide it so completely the next.

And yet, there was something…

''I'm obliged to you,'' Deverell said shortly, reclaiming her attention. ''I'm sure you'll understand that my thanks must necessarily be brief.''

''Of course.'' Crowhurst turned to Phoebe, his pale eyes boring into hers before she could avoid his gaze. ''I shall look forward to meeting you again, Miss Smith. Please be assured that I will not say a word to anyone. About…anything.'' A faint smile curled his lips. He inclined his head, then turned and walked away.

Without so much as a glance at her, Deverell stepped back into the alley, drawing Phoebe with him. Dazed, her mind in a state of suspension, she stumbled after him down the lane-way. Across another court. Along an alley so narrow the upper storeys of the houses almost met overhead.

Whispers hushed through the air behind them. She caught a glimpse of a face, pale, furtive, before a door was slammed shut. A pile of refuse appeared at her feet. She dodged it, then blinked, startled, when they stepped onto a wider street lined with shops and coffee-houses and light struck her eyes.

A hackney was waiting at the curb, its driver leaning down from his perch to peer anxiously into the gloomy tunnel from which they'd emerged.

''Ah, there ye be, gov'nor. I was gettin' a mite worried. The rookeries ain't no place for the likes o'ye, even if ye are a sight larger than most. I see ye found the young lady.''

Deverell's pistol vanished into his pocket as smoothly as it had appeared. He yanked open the door of the cab, stuffed

Phoebe unceremoniously into it and climbed in after her. "Park Street," he said curtly to the driver and slammed the door shut.

She suddenly realised he hadn't addressed one word to her since he'd come upon her in the court. One swift glance at his face told her why. He was furious. Savagely, relentlessly, furious.

Chapter Six

Silent, deadly, his rage lashed through the interior of the hackney, filling the small space until the air felt too heavy to breathe.

A fine tremor vibrated through Phoebe's limbs. The thought of explaining the situation was almost impossible. This was no mere fit of male annoyance. Deverell's brief moment of gentleness yesterday was as distant as the stars, nor was there any hint that humour would come to her rescue. If the rigid line of his jaw was anything to go by, only the most formidable control was keeping his fury leashed.

She did not, however, have a lot of choice. Deverell's nieces were still missing, and she was too anxious to remain silent.

Taking a deep, steadying breath, Phoebe lifted her chin. "Theo and Cressy...?"

"Both at home."

"Oh, thank goodness!" Relief coursed through her, making her sag limply back against the squabs. She straightened immediately. His voice had been as chilling as the frigid depths of the ocean, but in his eyes blue lightning flashed across the raging sea-green surface.

"I know you must be very angry with them, my lord, but—"

"Angry with them?"

"Yes, and it's perfectly understandable, but please don't be too harsh with them. Remember, Theo and Cressy are not used to being disciplined or checked in any way and—"

"You think I'm angry with *them?*"

"Well..." She blinked at him, suddenly wary. "Aren't you?"

A sound that could only be described as a snarl erupted from his throat. "This may come as a surprise to you, Miss Smith, but at the moment the thought uppermost in my mind is not the twins' transgressions. It's you I'm going to strangle. As soon as I get you alone."

"Me! But—"

"What in the name of God did you think you were doing, chasing after my nieces in that reckless fashion? You should have notified me immediately. But no! You'd rather put yourself in danger because you didn't bloody well think first!"

"There is no need to swear at me," Phoebe said, tilting her chin still further. She promptly lowered it again when the lightning in his eyes seemed to leap straight out at her. He looked as if he might strangle her there and then. It was probably not wise to offer any inducement. Such as unrestricted access to her throat.

"And I did think," she muttered. "In fact, I was doing quite well until that dreadful man at the Birdcage kept pestering me to join his tableau."

"You went into the Birdcage?" The words were enunciated with ominous precision.

"I went to all the theatres. And since they were situated on relatively busy streets, I didn't see anything rash in my doing so. Besides, I was in a hackney most of the time."

"God-damn it! The Honeypot isn't on a busy street and you didn't drive there in a hackney!"

The cab slowed down. "Everythin' orl right in there, guv'nor?" the driver enquired, poking his face through the hatch.

"Keep driving!" Deverell roared.

The man vanished.

Phoebe scarcely noticed that the pace picked up considerably. "Honeypot? What Honeypot?"

"That theatre where you met Crowhurst," he snarled. "How did you get there? Fly?"

"Good heavens! That was a *theatre?*"

Deverell eyed the stunned expression on her face and half-raised his clenched fists. "My God, I ought to give myself the pleasure of strangling you now. It would be extraordinarily satisfying."

"Oh, no, I beg you will not," Phoebe said hurriedly. She eyed his fists until he lowered them, then tried an appealing smile. "Only think of the scandal, sir."

This attempt at diverting him didn't have quite the result she'd hoped. He ground his teeth audibly.

"You think the discovery of your stabbed or strangled body in one of the most dangerous parts of the city wouldn't have caused a scandal? You little idiot! Even the girls had enough sense to avoid such places."

"They did?" Phoebe's jaw dropped. "You mean I searched for hours…"

Her defiance collapsed like a deflated balloon, taking her voice with it. She sagged back against the squabs again, torn between outrage and thankfulness that her charges were safe. "Where did you find them, sir? *How* did you find them?"

Deverell sent her a look of grim meaning. "After your visit to Covent Garden, Charles Kemble realised who the girls were and immediately despatched a message to me. I caught them at the Parisian, only to be informed that there was still another female running around loose. Edward took the twins home while I began the search for you. Of course, if I'd known you preferred the company to be found at the Birdcage and its ilk, I would've saved myself the trouble."

Phoebe grimaced. "You must know I wasn't there by choice."

"Then why the devil didn't you send for me the instant you knew what had happened?" he yelled.

Shaken, knowing she was in the wrong but too overset to admit it, she yelled right back. "I didn't want to bother you!"

"*Not bother me?* You came up to London for the express purpose of bothering me, Miss Smith. Why have a change of heart now?"

"Ohh…I…" Phoebe felt tears flood her eyes and turned her face away at once, horrified. Her swift burst of temper disintegrated as abruptly as if Deverell had struck her. And yet his question was entirely logical. She had to answer. She mustn't let him see… She mustn't let him know she'd been nervous about meeting him again, when she didn't know precisely why.

"I thought I would find the girls quite easily," she finally managed, clenching her hands until her nails dug into her palms. She risked a glance at him from beneath her lashes and saw that his savage expression hadn't abated one bit. "I'm very sorry you've been put to so much trouble, my lord."

"God damn it, Phoebe, don't you dare apologise."

"What?" She gaped at him, hastily blinking back another threatening tear. "Why not?"

"Because I'd be obliged to forgive you and you're not getting off so easily." His eyes narrowed abruptly on her face. "Damn it, are you crying?"

She gave a surreptitious sniff. "Of course not, sir. Why would I be crying when everything has turned out all right in the end? I am merely tired."

He continued to eye her rather narrowly for a minute, then said in a milder tone, "I'm not surprised. Perhaps next time you'll think twice before embarking on such an ill-considered action."

"Yes, well, I dare say such a situation will not occur again." She blinked away the last traces of moisture, thankful that both his rage and her tears seemed to have passed. Now if she could only get her insides to stop quaking. "What do you intend doing with your nieces, my lord?"

"I haven't decided, although locking them away somewhere for an indefinite period has a certain appeal."

"They'd only break out," Phoebe warned him. "Besides, Lady Grismead is giving a dance party for them tomorrow afternoon. They can't possibly cry off at such short notice."

"A dance party. To which you're taking them."

"Well, of course." Hoping this information wouldn't start another outburst, she summoned up an expression of earnest appeal. "Dance parties are quite unexceptionable, sir. Only very young girls who are not yet out, such as Lord Braddon's sister and Lady Yarwood's daughters, will be attending. It gives them an opportunity to practise various dances. Naturally, if there's a waltz, Theo and Cressy will be partnered by their brother."

"If you can get him out of bed in time."

She thought it prudent to ignore that remark.

Deverell continued to study her somewhat grimly for a moment. "Lady Yarwood?"

"Yes, do you know her?"

He shrugged. "We've met. I believe Crowhurst is some sort of connection of hers."

"I doubt if Lord Crowhurst will be present at a party got up especially for young girls, sir."

"He'll find a way to be there if he discovers you'll be attending."

"What?" Phoebe's jaw dropped.

"You heard me."

"I heard you, sir, but I don't understand your meaning. I'm sure Lord Crowhurst was merely being polite when he offered his assistance and—"

"Polite be damned. My arrival was the last thing he desired. You'd have seen it yourself if you hadn't been busy fleeing to me as if I was your last hope."

"Oh-h-h!" Heat stung her cheeks, staining them a bright scarlet. "I didn't... He wasn't..."

"You did and he was. He wants you, you little fool. Even in that ridiculous disguise."

"I wondered when we'd get around to my clothes," she muttered. When Deverell gave a derisive snort, she straightened her spine. "I'm not a complete idiot, my lord. I mentioned your name almost at once in case Lord Crowhurst thought I was alone and friendless in London. Although, as it happened, he was a perfect gentleman even before I told him I was employed as your nieces' companion."

"A fact he didn't believe for one minute until I confirmed it."

Phoebe frowned.

"Don't bother trying to recall the words. The situation didn't call for any."

"Oh, I see," she retorted, stung to sarcasm. "It was one of those male rituals that we females consider incomprehensible."

"You don't need to comprehend it, Miss Smith. Just stay away from him."

"I have no intention of encouraging Lord Crowhurst," she declared. "However, if I happen to see him again I can hardly cut the man dead when he offered to help me out of an extremely uncomfortable situation.''

Deverell's eyes narrowed again, but this time he didn't say anything.

Feeling as if she'd at least managed to uphold rational womanhood by having the last word, Phoebe shifted her gaze to the window. They were almost home, she was thankful to see. She would be glad to seek the sanctuary of her bedchamber where she could recover her composure away from rebellious wards and furious guardians.

However, as they swung into Park Street, a glimpse of a nursemaid and her two small charges staring agape at a passing dandy nudged another thought to the forefront of her mind. She remembered Crowhurst's odd familiarity and frowned, glancing across at Deverell.

He, too, was staring at the passing scene. Or, rather, scowling at it. The worst of his rage might have dissipated, but the hard line about his mouth and the deep furrow between his brows didn't invite polite conversation. It was probably unwise to continue with the subject of Crowhurst, but the question in her mind was strangely insistent.

''My lord?''

His gaze snapped to hers. ''What?''

She winced at the bitten-off syllable. ''I was wondering… Is there anyone in London who…looks like me?''

''I shouldn't think so, Miss Smith. I suspect you're unique.''

Phoebe didn't make the mistake of taking that as a compliment. Her own temper stirred. ''I mean,'' she enunciated through set teeth, ''do I resemble anyone closely enough to invite comment?''

Her insistence deepened his frown, the gem-like glitter of his eyes turning sharply interrogative. ''The answer is still no, Miss Smith. Why?''

She shook her head. ''It's probably nothing, but when I encountered Lord Crowhurst, he gaped as if he couldn't believe his eyes and I—''

''It's more likely he couldn't believe your recklessness. Or his good fortune.''

She let that pass. ''No, it was more than that. I think you're wrong about Crowhurst, sir. The way he spoke to me, it was almost as if he knew me. Or…though he did. It was really quite odd.''

"The only odd thing about this entire episode, Miss Smith, is that I've managed to keep my hands from your throat. Don't press your luck. If you wish to remain unscathed, you will give me your word of honour that you'll refrain from dashing off unaided if this sort of situation occurs again.''

"Well, if you lectured the girls the way you've been lecturing me, I shouldn't imagine—''

The trapdoor opened a cautious crack.

"We're in Park Street, guv'nor. Which house is it?''

Deverell's mouth compressed at the interruption, but he glanced out of the window. "You can set us down here," he ordered as a familiar door came into sight.

Thripp was standing on the front doorstep precisely where she'd left him hours ago, holding a bouquet of flowers. As Phoebe stepped down from the cab, she found herself entertaining the wild thought that the butler had been standing there so long someone had planted the flowers on him.

Obviously she was going mad.

"These were just left by a Mr Toombes, Miss," Thripp informed her in mournful tones. "There is also a note." He handed it over.

"Oh, no.'' Phoebe eyed the note with dismay before thrusting it into her pocket. "How on earth did he find out where I live?''

"If his patron is Lord Portlake, it'd be easy enough to make enquiries," Deverell said after paying off the hackney. He glared at the colourful array in Thripp's hands as if the flowers might house particularly noxious bugs. "Thripp, I want a word with you." Grasping Phoebe by the arm, he marched her into the house. "But first I'll speak to my wards. Where are they?''

"Mr Charlton has them under guard in the drawing-room, my lord.''

"Under guard! Good heavens, Thripp." Phoebe bent a reproving frown upon the butler. "The girls are not felons. I'd better see them at once.''

She took a step towards the drawing-room, only to be brought up short by Deverell's long fingers tightening around her arm.

"You're not seeing anyone at present, Miss Smith," he pronounced, using his hold on her to steer her smartly in the other direction. Phoebe found herself confronted by the staircase. "Is Gerald up yet, Thripp?"

"I'm not sure, my lord."

"Go and check. You may inform him that if he isn't down here in five minutes, I will personally see to it that his exit from his bed is immediate and unpleasant."

"For goodness' sake, sir, Gerald is not to blame for this morning's activities."

"The speech I intend to make to my wards," Deverell said as Thripp departed on his errand, "will be made only once. And you don't need to hear it, Miss Smith. You may retire to your room."

"Retire to my room?" Completely forgetting that she wanted to do nothing else, Phoebe stared at him, incredulous. "Well, of all the arrogant decrees. Retire to my room! I'm surprised you're not ordering me to bed without my supper!"

He looked down at her, eyes narrowing until only a glittering aquamarine sliver was visible between the midnight-dark lashes. His voice went very soft. Very soft and very gentle. "An interesting punishment, Miss Smith. I shall keep it in mind. Rest assured, however, that should I resort to such methods, supper will be served."

Phoebe's mouth fell open in shock. At least she thought it was shock. It was difficult to be sure when Deverell's precise meaning seemed to be lost somewhere in the swirling fog invading her brain. His words said one thing, but his eyes—

Before she could recover her thought processes, he brought both hands up to cup her shoulders and draw her around to face him.

"Now," he said in quite a different tone, "do I have your promise that you'll let me know the instant one of my wards goes off on some hare-brained start?"

Promise? She couldn't even think. Surely he hadn't meant that *he* was going to serve—

But that thought, too, shattered when his hands closed more firmly around her much smaller frame and he drew her closer. At least her upper body moved closer; her feet seemed glued to the floor. Phoebe stumbled and almost collided with

Deverell's chest. Instinctively her hands lifted to steady herself and she gasped aloud at the contact. Beneath the fine fabric of his coat he was rock-solid, as hard as the most fiercely tempered steel; but warm, and intensely alive.

"Your promise, Miss Smith," he repeated in a voice so low anyone standing more than three feet away wouldn't have heard it.

"Well, yes...I suppose... That is...not all their starts are hare-brained, sir. At least..."

"No." He moved his hands inwards. Very gently, inch by slow inch, his fingers smoothed up her throat to cup the back of her head. Using the slightest pressure of his thumbs, he tipped her face up until her gaze was caught by his and held, chained by the intent, wholly focused power of those light, glittering eyes.

"No hesitations. No conditions. Your word of honour, Miss Smith."

"My lord, this is most..."

The words vanished on another gasp as his fingers widened, moving gently against the sensitive flesh of her nape. If she'd had the breath, she would have accused him of trying to intimidate her again, except that she wasn't intimidated in the least. Her acute awareness of the formidable strength in those big, powerful hands made her shiver helplessly, but the shivers weren't induced by fear.

Her gaze fell to his mouth. It really was a beautiful mouth, she thought distractedly. Utterly masculine, hard, fierce, and yet passionate. And so close. Another inch or two and his breath would bathe her lips. An inch closer than that and they could almost—

"Promise me, Phoebe."

"Yes," she breathed.

His hold tightened. For a fleeting instant she could have sworn a faint tremor passed through his fingers to the flesh heating beneath his touch. Then he stepped back, releasing her slowly until his hands fell to his sides. Bemused, she followed the movement, watching his fingers curl into fists so tight she saw his knuckles turn white.

"There," he said, his voice intriguingly husky, "that wasn't so difficult, was it?"

"Oh!" Suddenly realising he was no longer holding her, Phoebe grabbed for the stair-rail. What on earth had Deverell done to her? She couldn't remember when she'd last taken a breath. Her head was spinning. Her throat felt tight. She feared she might actually swoon—an action she'd always considered as idiotic as it was useless. Now it seemed not only a real possibility, but rather more useful than she'd suspected.

With an enormous effort, she dragged in a breath and focused her eyes on his cravat. "If you don't mind, my lord, I think I'll...retire to my room. I feel quite...quite..."

"An excellent idea, Miss Smith. You must be exhausted."

"Exhausted. Yes. Yes, that's it. Exhausted. Good day, sir."

"Until tomorrow, Phoebe."

"To—" Her gaze lifted to his. It was a good thing she was still hanging onto the stair-rail, she thought. Because the blue and gold flames blazing in his eyes threatened her senses all over again.

"There's no need to look so alarmed," he said softly. "I intend to see how my wards comport themselves. One taste of me looking over their shoulders and there shouldn't be any trouble for a few weeks."

"Oh. Trouble. Yes. I mean, no. I mean...a very sound notion, my lord."

With a sudden burst of energy, induced by sheer panic, she relinquished her grip on the stair-post, turned and fled up the stairs.

Sebastian watched her go, aware of a fierce elation roaring through his veins. The force of it startled him. He barely managed to stop himself letting out a primitive yell of triumph. He felt as if he'd just taken a giant step forward in the pursuit of something elusive, and yet indefinably precious. Something he wanted...no, *needed* to possess. A need that until yesterday he'd put down to physical desire.

But physical desire did not account for the other emotions he'd recently encountered. The discovery just now that his delectably disapproving Miss Smith was not indifferent to him was, in fact, the only bright spot in a morning that had seen him reel helplessly from violent rage to raw fear and back again. Emotions he hadn't felt since he was nineteen. He had not enjoyed the experience then, and he liked it even less now.

Damn it, that little wretch had played absolute havoc with his control yet again.

But now…ah, now, he understood why. If he hadn't been so distracted by his strange possessiveness yesterday he would have seen it then. He hadn't even known he'd been waiting, but from the moment he'd stood, watching Phoebe across a swathe of lawn, and realised that the softness, the sweetness, the gentle glow haunting his dreams were as real, as enticing, as the strength and humour and intelligence shining in her eyes, he'd known.

This was the one.

Sebastian stared at the now empty staircase and thought back. Had he sensed it from the tone of the letters Edward Charlton had mentioned? he wondered suddenly. The writer's name hadn't stayed with him, but had he known, somewhere deep inside himself, that Phoebe would come up to Town to confront him if no one replied to her missives? Known and waited because he had no intention of returning to the scene of his banishment?

He shrugged inwardly. It didn't matter now. She was his. The one woman with whom he wanted to share his life.

It wouldn't be that easy, of course. Because of his own shadows—and because he suspected her heart would follow where she trusted—he wanted her belief in his honour before he won her heart. And the trust of such a wary little creature would be hard-won. One wrong word or more and she'd probably assume he was going to offer her a *carte blanche*.

She would also be only too ready to throw that promise he'd made her in his face.

A slow, rather anticipatory smile curled Sebastian's lips as he turned away from the stairs and strode across the hall to the room where his wards awaited him. Phoebe hadn't realised it yet, but contained in that promise was a giant loophole. And he was going to make sure she slipped right through it— straight into his arms.

His smile grew as he wondered what his delectably disapproving Miss Smith's reaction would be if she knew he was about to change the terms of her employment yet again.

* * *

Quite some time elapsed before Phoebe found herself recalling the oddly mislaid fact that Deverell was her employer. Her strange forgetfulness was extremely worrying. For the first time in her adult life, emotions and physical sensation had completely taken over her well-ordered mind.

And she didn't know what to do about it.

Restless, she rose from the chair where she'd been sitting, waiting for her senses to return to something resembling normal, and walked over to her dressing-table. She hadn't even removed her bonnet, she saw, gazing at the solemn-eyed image staring back at her through the glass. Thoughtfully, she did so, tossing the drab brown hat aside. Her hair was a mess. Several tendrils had been freed from their severe knot when Deverell had touched her nape, his hands so big and powerful and warm and—

A rush of shimmering heat flowed through her, turning her knees to water. Phoebe sat down rather suddenly, nearly missing the rose brocade stool in the process. She righted herself, glaring at her reflection as she did so.

This was ridiculous. She was going to put a stop to it immediately. The first thing to do was face the truth. She was strongly attracted to Deverell. It was no use denying what was perfectly obvious. Despite all the lectures on the evils of unbridled passion she had received nearly every day of her childhood, she suspected she could have felt very unbridled indeed if Deverell had been intent on passion rather than promises.

Unfortunately, no great illumination resulted from an inordinate number of minutes spent in wondering why she was so powerfully drawn to him. His flashes of humour appealed to her; she was curious about the restraint she sensed in him and the shadows briefly glimpsed beneath the glittering surface of his eyes, but those qualities would hardly turn her brain to mush and the rest of her to trembling blancmange.

No, it must be a case of intense physical attraction. She'd been warned to guard against unseemly urges often enough by her family not to know that ladies were capable of such urges, even if she'd never experienced the phenomenon until now. After all, Deverell was different to every other man she'd ever met. For all she knew, that was all it took.

Or perhaps it was merely a resurgence of her girlish tendencies towards romance, also deplored by her relatives. Or the fact that she'd rather foolishly come to think of her charges as the family she'd always wanted but would probably never have.

"But the Deverells are not my family," she told herself sternly. "In fact—" remembering the note in her pocket and frowning thoughtfully "—unless someone of humble station, such as Mr Toombes, offers for me, marriage is not likely to be my lot in life. And since I wouldn't accept someone like Toombes anyway, the only romance I'm likely to encounter is between the pages of my books."

No argument came to mind to refute that unassailable logic. Phoebe ordered herself to forget romance and concentrate on the real problem: how to cure herself of such an unsuitable attraction.

Her first impulse was to insist that Deverell accept her immediate resignation, but no sooner had the notion occurred to her than she was overwhelmed with dismay. So little did she want to leave, that for a moment she found her traitorous mind entertaining the hope that if Miss Grismead was still unmarried by the start of the next Season, Deverell might need her to stay longer.

"And what good will that do?" she demanded scornfully of her reflection. "You might find your employer interesting— well, all right, fascinating," she amended as her image frowned in disapproval of this mild description. "But nothing can come of it."

"Are you sure?" asked an insidious little voice that seemed to come out of nowhere. "He said you intrigue him and he can be quite charming to you."

Phoebe stared at the glass, wondering if her mirrored self had actually spoken or if she was losing what few wits she had left. Not that it mattered; there wasn't anyone around to hear her talking to herself.

"He said that only once, and I'm not at all sure he meant it," she argued. "As for charm, well, you know what Deverells are like. They're perfectly capable of using charm if they think it'll work. Look at the way he extracted that promise from me."

"But he didn't have to use charm. You'd have promised anyway."

"*He* didn't know that."

This gave her reflection pause. Phoebe took advantage of the lull to point out a few facts. They weren't particularly pleasant, but experience had taught her they were correct.

"Whether or not Deverell could ever be attracted to me doesn't matter. I'm his nieces' companion. And we know what happens when gentlemen develop an interest in governesses and companions. Marriage is not the first thought that pops into their heads."

"Very true. But it might be the second."

Phoebe gaped at the temptress in the mirror. "Have you run mad?" she demanded. "It wouldn't be the third. Or even the fourth, fifth or sixth. I have absolutely nothing to recommend me as wife to a man of Deverell's standing. Not only that, but if *any* gentleman were to offer for me, I'd be obliged to tell him my real name and why I changed it."

Her reflection pursed its lips. "A Deverell wouldn't care about that old scandal."

"How do you know? You're not even sure precisely what happened." She considered that. "Nor am I. Besides, there are other matters to take into account. If I recall correctly, Deverell's barony is not a landed title. If he does marry, he's sure to choose an heiress to a large estate."

Her reflection could do nothing but nod in reluctant agreement to this statement. Phoebe found the response so disheartening she immediately ordered herself to cease such an idiotic conversation.

How on earth had she got onto the subject of marriage anyway? She was supposed to be effecting a cure, not slipping further into fantasy. Instead of wondering what attracted her to Deverell, she might be more profitably employed in compiling a catalogue of his less appealing qualities. There were sure to be plenty. He was a Deverell.

This exercise, once started, proved reasonably successful. By the time she'd reached the end of a list that included arrogance, unjustifiable threats of strangulation and dictatorial tendencies, and had added the suspicion that he deliberately set out to addle her wits—quite unnecessarily—every time they met so he could have his own way, she felt a good deal better.

Quite able to return to her duties, in fact.

When a knock sounded on the door a short time later, she had even changed into one of the gowns Deverell had provided for her. The soft amber-coloured jaconet muslin skirts hushed gently about her ankles as she crossed the room to answer the summons.

She wasn't very much surprised to find the twins standing in the hall outside her room. What did bring a startled exclamation to her lips was the evidence that Theodosia had been crying, not her more dramatic sister.

"May we speak with you, Phoebe?" Theo asked in uncharacteristically subdued accents.

Phoebe blinked at her to make sure she'd got the right twin. Although, since Cressida's made-up face put her forcibly in mind of a badly constructed rainbow, it was difficult to be mistaken.

"Yes, of course, Theo." She stepped back so the girls could enter. "Oh, dear, I did ask your uncle not to be too harsh, but I can see he ignored me as usual."

"It wasn't Uncle Sebastian," said Theo, hovering around Phoebe as though she feared her companion was going to collapse at any moment. "We knew what *he* was going to say. Can we get you anything, Phoebe? A mustard plaster? One of Dr James's Powders, perhaps?"

"Dr James's Powders? A *mustard plaster?* Why on earth…? Cressy, why are you holding on to me? I'm not about to swoon."

"Are you sure?" Cressida queried, peering at her intently. "Perhaps you should lie down. Do you have any smelling-salts? Is there anything we can do for you?"

"We'll even do your mending," Theodosia offered. "Should we dust the ornaments? Would you like me to arrange some flowers?"

"Perhaps we can make you some gruel."

"Yes. You could sip it in bed."

"Do you want us to read an improving sermon or something?"

"An improving sermon!" Phoebe gaped at Cressida as if she'd lost her wits. "Has everyone run mad today? I can't believe your uncle even knows that improving sermons exist. Sit down and tell me precisely what he said."

This command appeared to throw Theodosia into a pit of despair. She plunked herself down cross-legged on Phoebe's bed and propped her chin in her hands. "Nothing we didn't expect," she said dolefully. "We should have thought of the consequences. We should have known you'd come after us. Why did he have to be inflicted with fluff-brained females?"

"Actually, he said pretty much what Edward said," Cressida added. "Except for that last bit."

"Edward?" Phoebe glanced quickly at Theodosia. "I see."

Theo sent her a look of earnest appeal. "We're truly sorry, Phoebe. I mean, we would have apologised anyway, because Uncle Sebastian told us to, but we really mean it." She turned to her sister. "Don't we, Cressy?"

Cressida nodded. "We didn't think our going to the theatres would put you in danger, Phoebe."

"I wasn't in that much danger," Phoebe demurred, deciding to accept this rather ingenuous apology in the spirit in which it was offered. "In any event, nothing untoward happened, so we'll say no more about it."

She fully expected the twins to bounce back to their usual exuberant selves after this speech, but instead Cressy sat down next to her sister and the pair proceeded to stare dismally at nothing in particular.

"Has your uncle forbidden you to go out?" Phoebe queried after a moment, unable to think of anything else that would cast her charges so thoroughly into gloom.

"Oh, no," Cressida said vaguely. "He didn't even threaten to send us back to Kerslake, which we quite expected him to do." She glanced sideways at her sister. "It was Edward."

"Oh. Well, I'm sure he won't remain angry for long, Theo."

Theodosia sniffed. "It isn't that, Phoebe. Edward was quite calm about the whole thing. But he said if women wanted to be given more rights and independence, then we had to be prepared to accept responsibility also, and…and be worthy of those rights. And…he was right.''

"Yes, he was," Phoebe said gently. "But nobody expects you to understand that immediately, Theo. Goodness, at your age most girls think only of gowns and parties, not of rights and responsibilities.''

"She only did it for me," Cressida muttered.

"You see, Phoebe, Cressy needs something to do. I have my interest in the rights of women—Edward and I have the most fascinating discussions, you know—but Cressy isn't like me. She needs something different.''

"But acceptable," Phoebe responded, smiling ruefully.

To her relief, this drew faint smiles in return. Dealing with contrite Deverells was an interesting experience, but it was also somewhat disconcerting. She should have known, however, that the twins would take even contrition to extremes.

"I really did want to be an actress," Cressida said wistfully. "But if there was something else…''

"Why not try writing drama?" Phoebe said, struck by sudden inspiration. "You know you've always enjoyed the Gothic novels I borrow from the circulating libraries. I'm sure you could write one just as interesting.''

Cressida looked doubtful. "Do you think so?''

"Of course I do. What's more, your uncle isn't likely to take exception to the scheme. Especially if you write under a *nom de plume*.''

"I suppose I could try it.''

"You could make Uncle Sebastian the villain," Theo suggested darkly. She scowled. "He certainly has the temper for it. Edward was just as cross, but he didn't threaten to strangle us and throw our bodies into the Thames.''

"Oh, goodness! Is that what your uncle threatened to do?" Phoebe thought of her own encounter with Deverell's temper and was stunned by a sudden return of her earlier gloom. She'd known he wouldn't really carry out his threat to strangle her, but the fact that he'd made the same threat to the twins made her wonder if, in his mind, she belonged in the same category.

Not only another fluff-brained female, but a nuisance. A troublesome duty. A responsibility he didn't want.

The thought was positively depressing.

"That wasn't all," Cressida added. "He said that if anything happened to you, we'd find ourselves on a ship to the Colonies so fast we wouldn't know where we were. Can ladies be shipped to the Colonies, Phoebe?"

"He didn't mean it, silly." Theodosia frowned at her sister, but a moment later her frown took on a rather thoughtful aspect. "But you're right. Uncle Sebastian did seem more worried about Phoebe than about us." She looked at her companion. "Isn't that strange?"

"Quite extraordinary," Phoebe agreed glumly.

Her mood hadn't lifted by the time Thripp announced that dinner awaited them. As far as she was concerned, the only reason for Deverell's concern was that he would have felt in some way responsible if his nieces' antics had led to her being harmed. And since she'd been the one to put him in that position in the first place, it was no wonder he wanted to strangle all of three of them.

Unfortunately for her low spirits, there was no diversion to be found at the dinner table. The girls were still contrite, and Gerald looked as if he hadn't slept for several weeks. Phoebe was quite sure she could detect early signs of dissipation in his heavy-eyed countenance. Something else for her to worry about.

All in all it was a very subdued party who adjourned to the drawing-room and began a lacklustre game of Speculation. The tea-tray was brought in and ignored. Nobody argued when Phoebe decreed an early night was in order.

Chapter Seven

Fortunately for her equilibrium, a reasonably sound sleep did much to restore the balance of Phoebe's mind. She arose betimes, having convinced herself that her usual calm good sense had been overset yesterday by worry about her missing charges.

As for her strange attraction to Deverell: well, she had simply mistaken the novelty of enjoying a man's company—secure in the knowledge that he wasn't going to make any unwanted advances—for a stronger attraction. And she had to admit, annoyingly large and dictatorial though Deverell might be, there was something rather reassuring about those qualities when one found oneself in a potentially dangerous situation.

All she had to do, therefore, was maintain a polite and proper distance and avoid dangerous situations. Especially where gentlemen were concerned.

With this resolute goal in mind, she launched an assault on the gown she intended to wear to the dance party that afternoon. Unfortunately, thanks to the lectures she gave herself all through the exercise, she didn't remember Tobias Toombes's note until after a light luncheon had been consumed.

She was just in time to avert disaster. Mr Toombes had apparently decided that the violence of his feelings outweighed the tricky question of his calling on her at her place of employment. He had, he wrote with a determined hand, a matter of crucial importance to his physical and mental well-being to discuss with her. He would do anything in pursuit of a favourable outcome. He was sure her celestial sweetness would lead her to forgive his disobeying her veto on visits. If not, he would be happy to crawl to her on hands and knees in pursuit of this worthy cause.

Since Phoebe had never given him any reason to suppose that the well-being, physical or mental, of a gentleman who waited for fate to throw her in his path again was of the slightest interest to her, this very pointed note sent her into a frenzy of activity. Her charges were pushed and prodded out of the house a good half-hour before they were due to leave for Lady Grismead's—and a mere ten minutes before the hour appointed by Toombes for his visit—and told that a walk to the Grismead residence would do them good.

The walk was not one of unalloyed pleasure. She didn't know from which direction Toombes would come and at every corner expected to be confronted by the sight of him crawling pathetically towards her, bony hand outstretched. No such hideous vision assaulted her eyes, however, which left her free to lend an ear to Gerald's complaints that he'd wanted to try out his new phaeton, while her mind pondered ways and means of avoiding both Toombes's impending proposal, and Deverell's company.

She needn't have worried about Deverell. When they were ushered into Lady Grismead's drawing-room, there was no sign of him among the crowd of chattering damsels and the male relatives they had coerced or cajoled into accompanying them.

So much for keeping an eye on his wards' behaviour, she thought, irrationally annoyed by this evidence of neglect. She'd spent the last half-hour rehearsing a very cool, proper little greeting and he wasn't even here to receive it.

Then, as her eyes met those of a gentleman standing on the other side of the room, her emotions underwent an abrupt about-face. Elegantly clad in a plum-coloured coat and pale pantaloons, his hand resting lightly on the back of Lady Yarwood's chair, Crowhurst stood watching her with the fixed stare that had made her want to shrink into the background yesterday. The effect hadn't diminished overnight.

"Ah, Miss Smith. At last. Now we can begin." Lady Grismead, resplendent in steel-grey silk, descended upon them, cutting off all retreat. "You will be happy to play the pianoforte," she informed Phoebe. "So much easier to practice the steps of a dance when there is music."

"Yes, ma'am," Phoebe agreed, abandoning at birth any hope of leaving her charges in Lady Grismead's care and making her escape. "And I must apologise for our lateness. We took a wrong turn and walked a little out of our way."

"A little?" muttered Cressida, handing her bonnet into the tender care of a maid. "More like miles."

"You walked?" Her ladyship frowned. "Extraordinary. I am an advocate of genteel forms of exercise, Miss Smith, but one cannot consider wandering, lost, about the streets of London to be anything but unsuitable."

"Worse than that," Gerald grumbled. "I wanted to try my new phaeton."

Phoebe quelled him with a look that would have done credit to a Deverell and bent her mind to the task of placating her hostess. "No doubt we'll soon learn our way about, ma'am. Goodness, I see you have quite a crowd. One would think it the crush of the Season."

She scanned the room, her eyes widening when she recognised several familiar faces, Edward Charlton and Lord Bradden among them. "Gerald has even impressed Mr Filby into service. How did you acquire so many partners for the girls?"

"My parties are always successful," pronounced her ladyship in a tone that would have given pause to any party considering failure. "Even a simple dance party. All it takes is organisation. Organisation, Miss Smith. Next time you walk, consult a map. The pianoforte is behind you by the window. You may begin as soon as you are ready. Theodosia, Cressida, come with me."

Left summarily alone, Phoebe made her way to the pianoforte, wondering if a visit from Toombes wouldn't be preferable to an afternoon spent on tenterhooks, after all. If Deverell ever discovered Crowhurst was here, she'd never hear the end of it. As for Crowhurst, himself, though he showed no signs of approaching her, his pale, unwavering gaze was extremely disconcerting. She could only hope the afternoon would go off without incident.

For a while her hope seemed justified. With a great deal of

laughter from the ladies and instructions from the male contingent, the dancers took to the floor, twirling their way through country dances, the quadrille, and even a waltz, those ladies not fortunate enough to be partnered by brothers or cousins pairing off with each other.

It was when the butler appeared with refreshments that the afternoon disintegrated with positively startling rapidity. Before she could rise from the piano stool, Phoebe found herself besieged by males.

"Miss Smith—" Lord Bradden gazed at her with the earnest expression of a puppy anxious to please "—may I fetch you a cup of tea, or a glass of lemonade?"

"Miss Smith, do try one of these salmon patties." Mr Charlton's smile was a trifle strained. He leaned closer under the guise of offering her a plate. "Do you think Lady Theodosia seems rather quiet today, ma'am? I'm concerned that I may have been too harsh yesterday."

"I say, Miss Smith, you must be fixed to that stool by now." Mr Filby, a blinding vision in bright yellow pantaloons, a white satin waistcoat embroidered with gold hummingbirds, and a gold brocade coat of startling cut and hue, bowed with a flourish. "Care to take a toddle around the room with me? Loosen up a bit, you know."

"If anyone could toddle after being trampled upon by one's partners," drawled a gentleman on Phoebe's other side. "You positively astound me, Filby."

At the sound of the light, mocking tone, Phoebe froze. She didn't know why, but quite suddenly she felt extremely cold.

Crowhurst must have had the same effect on Deverell's secretary. Mr Charlton glanced across at the older man, his fine grey eyes hardening. "Miss Smith, I don't believe you've met Lord Crowhurst," he said, his voice heavy with meaning.

Crowhurst's lips curled. "Oh, Miss Smith and I are old friends," he contradicted easily. "I was, in fact, hoping to see her today. Allow me to congratulate you on your playing, my dear Phoebe. But I know you have many talents."

A strained silence fell on the group. Phoebe suspected that one glance at her face would be enough to inform the others that Crowhurst was lying, or at least exaggerating, but none of them, she realised, was a match for the older man's cool assumption of friendship. Lord Bradden was far too young; Mr Filby, though three or four years older than Gerald, was still no match for a man close to Deverell in age; and Edward Charlton, while looking grim, was clearly aware that a public challenge might place Phoebe in an awkward position.

She was aware of it herself. Rising to her feet, she prepared to do the only thing possible. Abandon the field.

"Allow me to escort you to the refreshment table," Crowhurst said, immediately divining her purpose. His gaze slid over her, lingering on her throat. The square neckline of her gown was quite respectable, but Phoebe had to resist a swift urge to tug it upward. "That is, if you insist on cruelly abandoning your admirers, my dear."

"I do," she stated, feeling a flush of annoyance stain her cheeks. "Furthermore, sir—"

She was pulled up short by the abrupt change of expression that flashed across Edward Charlton's face. Alerted, her gaze flew to the doorway.

Deverell stood in the aperture, broad shoulders filling out a coat of burgundy superfine, long, powerful legs clad in breeches and topboots, one hand stuffed into his pocket, the other clenched by his side, and a scowl on his face that would have quelled the most besieged maiden looking for rescue.

Phoebe's heart did indeed trip and start to race. All in all, Deverell did not look like her idea of a gallant rescuer. In fact, she wouldn't have been surprised to learn that the hand clenched in his pocket was wrapped around a pistol. And yet, despite the ugly expression in his eyes as he stared at Crowhurst, despite the hard, unrelenting line of his mouth, she didn't feel quelled in the least.

Her lips parted as though she would call to him; she even took a step forward, as though pulled towards him by an invisible chain, before she recollected herself.

Oh, goodness! What was she doing? If anyone noticed…if he ever suspected… And he wasn't even dressed for the occasion. It was just like him to arrive in riding clothes when…

Her thoughts scattered like wraiths in a mist. Phoebe's heart almost stopped completely when Deverell's gaze flashed from Crowhurst to her face and the menace in his eyes disappeared. A slow smile curved his hard mouth. A rather pleased smile.

It had the very peculiar effect of making her legs feel as if they were suddenly made of jelly. When he started towards her she had to put a hand on the pianoforte to steady herself.

"Good afternoon, Miss Smith. I trust I find you well?" Deverell took her free hand and bestowed a brief kiss on the inside of her wrist.

Phoebe nearly sank back onto the piano stool in a boneless heap.

"For goodness' sake, my lord," she expostulated in a strangled whisper. "What on earth do you think you are about? Riding clothes! And you should be greeting your aunt and Lady Yarwood, not— Oh, dear, now I have *five* gentlemen…"

She glanced distractedly about her. Filby, Lord Bradden and Mr Charlton weren't paying the least attention to her incoherent stutterings. They were too busy goggling at the hard-edged looks being exchanged by her infuriating employer and Crowhurst.

Images of snarling, sword-wielding warriors instantly presented themselves to her beleaguered mind.

"Oh, my goodness. My lord, don't you think you should greet your aunt before you…before you…?"

"Before I what, Miss Smith?"

With considerable effort she summoned up a glare. "I don't know, sir, but Lady Grismead is your hostess and—"

Deverell laughed softly and glanced down at her. "Who do you think is footing the bill for this little gathering? If I greet my aunt, she's likely to go off in a fit of apoplexy that I dared show my face here to remind her of it."

Fortunately for Phoebe's frazzled wits, she was spared the need to answer this irreverent statement. A lady of about her own age, a cap of feathery black curls and a pair of sapphire eyes proclaiming her Deverell heritage, chose that moment to drift into the room in a cloud of palest blue muslin. Scurrying behind her was a thin, gnome-like little gentleman of sparse hair and harassed mien who, Phoebe deduced, could only be Lord Grismead.

"There! Now your uncle and cousin have arrived. Will you kindly take me to Lady Grismead, sir?"

"Are you sure you wish to be caught in the middle of a confrontation between Deverell and his aunt, Miss Smith? I'm reliably informed that it isn't a comfortable position in which to be.''

Phoebe stiffened as Crowhurst's mocking tones smote her ears again. Really! Didn't anyone have any manners these days? There was Deverell treating his family as if they didn't exist, and now Crowhurst apparently felt quite at liberty to intrude on a private conversation whenever he heard one.

Momentarily forgetting that contact with Deverell had a highly unsettling effect on her senses, she touched his arm lightly. He promptly tucked her hand into the crook of his elbow.

"There will be no confrontation, sir," she informed Crowhurst in her coolest tones. "Gentlemen, if you will excuse me, I have neglected my duties long enough."

The three younger men, who until that moment had been giving an excellent imitation of exhibits in a waxworks, came to life with a collective start.

"Most obliging of you to play the pianoforte for us, Miss Smith," Lord Bradden said earnestly.

Mr Filby bowed. "Your servant, ma'am."

Mr Charlton aimed an absent smile at her, then turned anxious eyes on his employer. "Sir, you did grant me leave of absence this afternoon."

"Yes, Edward, I remember." Deverell bestowed a benign smile on the trio that had them all blinking like astonished owls. "Please continue to enjoy yourselves, gentlemen. I'm sure the other young ladies will be only too pleased to assist in the endeavour." He led Phoebe away, pointedly excluding Crowhurst from the request.

"Well!" After one glance at Deverell's expression, Phoebe valiantly assumed the bright tone of one praising a diligent pupil. "That went off quite civilly."

"Strive for the intelligence I've come to expect from you, Miss Smith."

She abandoned approval with unprecedented speed. "Except for the glares you and Crowhurst were exchanging, of course. Would you mind telling me what that was all about, my lord? Yesterday you were obliged to him."

"Yesterday I had more pressing priorities than feeding Crowhurst his own sword-stick. As for today, you know damned well what it was about. I warned you about Crowhurst. Now are you convinced he wants you?"

"There is nothing more annoying than a person who says I told you so," stated Phoebe, nose in the air. "Lord Crowhurst certainly has a very odd manner, but even though he behaved in that detestably familiar way, it seemed…I don't know… almost natural."

"It is natural, you little goose. The sort of naturalness designed to fluster innocents like you by forcing an intimacy that doesn't exist."

"I don't mean *that*," she said impatiently. "It was just as I told you yesterday. He spoke as if…as if he *really* believes he knows me well. Do you think he might be a little unbalanced?"

"A convenient explanation," Deverell said grimly. Then, quite unexpectedly, he started to smile. "But I must say, my little innocent, you gave him a most delightful set-down."

"Set-down? What—?"

His eyes glinted down at her. "You touched me. Of your own free will. And that, my proper little governess, *was* done perfectly naturally."

Phoebe promptly snatched her hand from his arm. "Obviously, a gentleman's mind exists on quite another plane than that of a lady," she said severely, conscious of the hot colour sweeping into her cheeks. His little governess, indeed! She might be little compared to a Deverell, and no doubt the same applied to being proper, but she wasn't *his!*

It was strange how that realisation made her feel quite alone all of a sudden.

"A lower plane," she clarified, shaking off these useless maunderings. "I merely requested your escort, my lord. And, I might add, I would not have needed to do so if you hadn't been glaring at Crowhurst as if you were about to call him out."

"If what Edward discovered for me this morning is more than rumour, Crowhurst needs whipping rather than a chance on the field of honour."

"Good heavens!" Phoebe's eyes widened. "You've been asking about Crowhurst? Whatever for?"

"I prefer to know my enemies, Miss Smith."

"But Crowhurst hasn't done anything to you." She tilted

her head, considering that statement. "For that matter, he hasn't done anything to me."

"He shows every sign of pursuing a lady who is under my protection," Deverell said with soft menace. "He is a man whose reputation with women is not that of a gentleman. Have you forgotten precisely where you met him, Miss Smith? The Honeypot isn't a theatre that caters to the usual crowd of play-goers."

"Oh, goodness!" Phoebe came to an abrupt halt near a bay window where several young people were engaged in animated conversation. "No, I suppose not. Well, if the manager stages plays like that very peculiar tableau—"

She stopped, glaring, as Deverell started to grin. "Yes, you may well laugh, my lord, but I found nothing amusing in having to talk my way out of a career as a sea-nymph!" She thought back and shuddered. "As far as I could tell, their costumes consisted of fish scales painted on muslin and wrapped around their legs and very little else."

"Nothing else, I expect," Deverell said, a wicked light in his eyes. "But although that creature at the Birdcage deserves a good thrashing for insulting you, Miss Smith, I can't fault his taste. You would make a delightful sea-nymph. Not for public edification, of course."

"Not for—" Under Deverell's amused gaze, Phoebe struggled valiantly to recover her powers of speech. "No, of course not. As if I would... Oh, goodness me, what am I saying? Really, my lord, this is a most improper conversation. I can't think how... Kindly remember where we are, sir."

Good advice, she thought distractedly. *She* hadn't even remembered to keep a polite and proper distance. Or to avoid perilous situations. Actually, now she came to think of it, perilous situations and Deverell seemed to go hand in hand. Immediate rescue was imperative.

"Dear me, where is Lady Grismead? Ah, over there on that sofa. If you'll excuse me, sir, I'll—"

"In a moment." Deverell prevented her escape by the simple expedient of taking her hand in a gentle and totally unbreakable clasp. He contemplated their joined hands for a moment, then lifted his gaze to her face. All traces of wicked amusement had gone, leaving his eyes intent and wholly serious.

"I don't know what Crowhurst said that annoyed you," he began. "But next time you encounter him, Miss Smith, cut him dead. Letting yourself bandy angry words with him will only whet his appetite."

This instruction—from one who took a fiendish delight in bandying words with her at every turn—incensed Phoebe so much she said the first thing that came into her head.

"Indeed, sir. In that case, I shall expect you to follow your own advice."

"What the deuce does that mean?"

"It means that I expect you to support my statement to Crowhurst that you will not pick a fight with your aunt."

His eyes took on an unholy gleam. "What if she picks one with me?"

"Then I will expect you to conduct yourself in a manner worthy of your position, my lord."

The gleam disappeared. "In that case, Miss Smith, I wish to claim another concession. An answer." He glanced quickly around the room then bent until he could speak directly in her ear. His voice lowered to a soft growl. "Where the devil is the chemisette that belongs to that dress?"

"Oh... Well—I—" Phoebe stuttered to a halt, her mind going unnervingly blank. Oh, heavens! What was he doing to her *now?* Just because Deverell's mouth was two inches from her cheek was no reason to shiver. If anything she felt extremely warm—another reason why tiny shivers had no business chasing themselves around in her stomach.

"Yes?" he purred, straightening.

"You know very well where it is," she retorted, recovering her wits with the safety of a respectable distance. "The chemisette was very frilly so I took it off. However, before you say anything else, my lord, I intend to sew the wretched thing back on as soon as I return home."

His mouth curved in a slow smile. "Oh, I don't know. We wouldn't want to make a hasty decision, Miss Smith. That peach colour is really quite delectable against your skin. And it would be a crime to hide so graceful a throat."

"Graceful! Yesterday you wanted to strangle it!" she squeaked, torn between indignation and the shivery sense of excitement still rippling through her.

"Yes," he said, laughter, and something more intense, glittering in his eyes. "But, you see, I would have strangled you very, very gently, Miss Smith. You wouldn't have been hurt at all."

Phoebe nearly choked without the assistance of any hands around her throat. Before she could recover her breath to annihilate her tormentor—always supposing she could think of a lethal enough response in a matter of seconds—he fired another question at her with a speed that left her brain reeling.

"And while we're on the subject of yesterday, what did Toombes want?"

This was too much. Phoebe drew herself up to her full height and, ignoring the risk of a cricked neck, stared Deverell straight in the eye. "Nothing that concerns you, my lord. You may be right about Crowhurst, although he hasn't— But that is neither here nor there. If Mr Toombes has any intentions towards me, you may be sure they're honourable. And that is the last concession you are going to wring from me. I am going to sit with your aunt and you, sir, will behave yourself."

Snatching her hand free, Phoebe turned on her heel only to be brought up short by Deverell's voice, still soft, still amused, but with something beneath the gentleness that set her spine tingling.

"Remind me to tell you, Miss Smith, that you are not my governess. That is to say, you are not the arbiter of my behaviour."

She would not answer. She would treat all such remarks with dignified disdain. She would take refuge in the small alcove behind Lady Grismead and, what was more, she would take great pleasure in composing a letter of application for the post of companion to an elderly lady who possessed no male relatives, no male friends and no male acquaintances. And as soon as she found this mythical person she would—

"Ah, Miss Smith!"

Lady Grismead, one imperious finger crooked in Phoebe's direction, promptly put a spoke in this particular wheel.

"You may sit with us," she commanded as one bestowing a great favour. "Lady Yarwood wishes to compliment you on your playing. And I don't believe you have met dear Pamela."

Meeting dear Pamela was not high on Phoebe's list of de-

sirable treats, but after exchanging polite greetings with Lady
Yarwood, an attractive, fair-haired matron in pale chartreuse
silk, she found herself turning to Deverell's cousin with an
alacrity she told herself had nothing to do with the fact that
he'd followed her and was greeting his aunt.

Fortunately, Miss Grismead showed every promise of living
up to her reputation. Draped limply over a small sofa, she managed a wan smile in response to her parent's introduction that
would have led the uninitiated to suppose she was in the last
stages of a fatal decline. Phoebe was not of their number. There
was a determined set to Miss Grismead's lips that looked all
too familiar.

"You play delightfully, Miss Smith," Lady Yarwood said,
smiling kindly. "But you must be quite exhausted. Do come
and sit down. Ottilia tells me you're an excellent governess,
but your charges are safely occupied with the other young people at present, so you may relax for a moment."

"Miss Smith is most conscientious," Lady Grismead stated,
shifting her steely-eyed gaze from where Deverell was now
conversing with Lord Grismead to her friend. "And very properly behaved, I was pleased to see, Miss Smith, that you did
not linger among the gentlemen. No doubt they were only being polite, but a lady in your position must always guard
against attracting a certain type of attention."

"Er—yes, ma'am."

"Isn't that correct, Almira?"

"It certainly is." Lady Yarwood looked anxiously at
Phoebe. "Please don't take this amiss, my dear, but I thought
you seemed a little *distraite.* I hope Lord Crowhurst didn't say
anything improper."

"Oh. No, ma'am. That is…"

"Forgive me if I seem inquisitive," Lady Yarwood murmured, apparently taking Phoebe's hesitation for embarrassment. "But you must know that before my marriage I, too, was
a governess. I know how very uncomfortable one can be made
to feel on occasion. Really—" she turned to her hostess "—I
can't imagine why Adrian would put himself out for us today.
He doesn't call above two or three times a year, but there he
was just as we were climbing into the carriage; when I told
him where we going, he at once offered his services. Of course,

Amabel and Caroline were positively in alt, but I think it very odd.''

"What does he want?" asked Lady Grismead in accents of grim foreboding. "That is the question you must ask yourself, Almira. When a man offers to assist his family, you may be sure he wants something in return.''

Only the greatest exercise of self-control stopped Phoebe from glancing at Deverell to see if he'd heard this cynical pronouncement.

"Well, he did say he'd come to seek information," Lady Yarwood continued, "but that since he was going to attend your party, it might turn out to be unnecessary. It seems very odd to me. How did he know it might be unnecessary before he'd made his inquiries?''

Both ladies turned to contemplate the subject of this question as if an answer was to be found writ large on his countenance. Phoebe followed the direction of their gazes. A faint ripple of unease drew her brows together when she saw Crowhurst talking to Gerald. Not that there was anything wrong in that, of course, but judging by the expression of eagerness on Gerald's face, Crowhurst was putting himself out to be pleasant to the younger man.

Phoebe frowned again, annoyed at the instant suspicions wafting about in her mind. This was what came of listening to Deverell. Even if Crowhurst had nefarious intentions towards her, Gerald would hardly help in the endeavour. He might be young, but no one had ever accused a Deverell of being a fool.

Reflecting darkly on the influence one particular Deverell seemed to be wielding on her calm, well-ordered mind lately, she brought her attention back to the conversation that had resumed next to her.

"Not that I know anything against him, Ottilia, because you may be sure if I did I wouldn't have accepted his escort, Yarwood's cousin or not. But it can't be denied that since that unfortunate affair fifteen years ago, Adrian has suffered from very strange moods.''

"So I've heard." Lady Grismead frowned portentously. "I am not one to encourage maudlin behaviour in anyone, Almira, and in a gentleman it is particularly displeasing. One cannot deny, however, that the effect upon a young man of an unsuitable liaison is to be deplored by all persons of character. Especially," she added with a darkling glance behind her, "by their unfortunate families."

This time Phoebe turned her head before she could stop herself. It couldn't have been clearer that Deverell, also, had been involved in an unsuitable liaison in his youth. He was utterly still, the expression in his eyes as he stared down at his aunt as cold and deadly as the unfathomable depths of the ocean.

Phoebe found herself clasping her hands together, almost in supplication. Oh, dear. He was going to take Lady Grismead's comment as condemnation. She wondered if he'd heard even a hint of the concern and regret in her ladyship's voice.

Her mind whirling with conjecture, conscious of an odd little ache in the region of her heart, she gazed up at him, silently pleading with him not to retaliate with a scathing response.

As if he sensed her gaze, Deverell turned his head. The cold expression vanished. And in its place dawned a light she recognised—and yet still couldn't name. The same light, she realised with a tiny jolt, that had puzzled her in the Park.

Her brows knit as she gazed up into the aquamarine eyes gleaming down at her from between midnight-dark lashes. The touch of wickedness she recognised. And amusement—as if his aunt's strictures, though annoying, hadn't truly enraged him. But the disturbing gleam held something else. Something warm, and…

She didn't know. And wasn't sure why her ignorance bothered her. In another man, that warmth alone would have rendered her wary, but Deverell had promised not to pester her with attentions.

And she trusted his word.

Why did that thought make her feel so low? Why, in fact, was she feeling inexplicably confused about so many questions at once that her thoughts seemed to be scurrying back and forth like extremely busy mice? Whatever had happened to Deverell in the past—whether the unfortunate liaison had led to his banishment or not—was none of her business. But…

Not only Deverell but Crowhurst, too, it seemed, had been involved in an unsuitable liaison years ago. Was that the real source of the enmity between the two men? Had they been entangled with the same woman? But they'd only been introduced a few weeks ago; Crowhurst had said as much in that horrid little court.

Phoebe blinked, suddenly realising she was still staring over her shoulder at Deverell, and that the smile in his eyes was beginning to reach his mouth. That same pleased little smile that had curved his lips earlier.

Dismayed, she whipped her gaze to the front and addressed the first person she saw.

"I believe you take a keen interest in poetry, Miss Grismead. Have you—?"

The rest of Phoebe's question lodged in her throat as the conversation between the two older ladies ceased as abruptly as if a door had slammed shut. From the corner of her eye, she saw Deverell's shoulders begin to shake with silent laughter.

Oh, how like him! She had just sunk herself beneath reproach and he had the temerity to laugh.

"Pamela has more practical interests than poetry," stated Lady Grismead in quelling accents. Passing over Phoebe's flushed countenance, she cast a gimlet-eyed glance behind her. "Isn't that so, Grismead?"

Lord Grismead jumped like a startled rabbit and looked more harassed than ever. "Oh. Yes. Yes, indeed, my dear. Mathematics, for instance. Really, she is quite—"

"A lady does not profess to understand complex mathematical equations." Her ladyship's tone dared anyone to contradict her. "It is not a talent valued by gentlemen."

"Oh, I don't know, Aunt." Deverell bestowed a brief glance of approval on his cousin. "When the bills start rolling in, Norvel might be grateful for Pamela's talent with figures."

"Well, as to that, Sebastian, nothing has been arranged, you know." Lord Grismead blinked several times, his resemblance to a hunted rabbit becoming more pronounced than ever. "That is, there has been no formal announcement or—"

"You will oblige me by changing the subject, Grismead. There will be no announcement until Mr Hartlepoole comes to his senses. And even then, the outcome is by no means certain."

This provoked a response from an unexpected quarter. Miss Grismead, who until then had been watching the other occupants of the room as if their very animation was too much for the depleted state of her health, abandoned her air of exhaustion.

"Dearest Norvel is coming to see you tomorrow, Papa, and if you don't immediately send an announcement to the *Gazette,* it will be the meanest thing!"

"Now, my dear, you know Mama and I must think of your future, which is not likely to be felicitous if you're forced to live in penury. Nor is this precisely the time or place—"

"I don't care." Miss Grismead pouted prettily, but there was a steely light in her blue eyes. "If you don't send an announcement to the *Gazette,* then *I* will."

"But, dearest, females don't send notices to the *Gazette.*"

"Well, I'll send it somewhere else then."

Lord Grismead goggled at his daughter. "Somewhere else? But—"

"Silence, Grismead. I will deal with this."

His lordship subsided, his demeanour that of one long accustomed to being crushed between two determined Deverells.

Phoebe could only sympathise. On the other hand, she mused, his lordship must have known the fate in store for him. After all, he'd married a Deverell. Perhaps he'd expected his wife to give birth to a Grismead. But no. True to form, she'd produced a Deverell. Really, he'd been foolish to think otherwise. If *she* married into the family, she'd expect to produce a Deverell, too, and—

Oh, good heavens! Had her mind run completely mad? How could she possibly marry into the family? The only Deverell of suitable age was—

Her mind seized before she could finish the thought. Phoebe stared straight ahead of her, very much afraid that her countenance was taking on a distinct resemblance to Lord Grismead's. With an additional element of stunned stupefaction.

Mercifully, before anyone could notice her sudden paralysis, several ladies arrived to collect their various offspring. Suddenly the drawing-room was all bustle and confusion. She could only be grateful for the small reprieve. At the moment, she seemed to have no conscious control over herself at all.

To think of marriage and…

To think of marriage *at all!* Really, she'd reminded herself only yesterday to put aside girlish dreams for the reality of her life, but here was her well-ordered mind dashing down forbidden paths two days in a row.

What she needed was distraction. Immediately. The Grismeads were no help. Father and daughter were still arguing about impecunious poets; while Lady Grismead was farewelling her guests. Nothing would induce her to speak to Deverell again until she had her wits about her. That left Lady Yarwood.

And, suddenly, inspiration struck.

"Excuse me, ma'am." Thanking Providence for the timely notion, Phoebe turned to Lady Grismead's friend. "I can't help but wonder what sort of woman would trifle with a young man's affections. From the point of view of a governess of boys Gerald's age, of course," she added mendaciously. "The lady who caused Lord Crowhurst such pain, for instance. What did she look like?"

Fortunately, Lady Yarwood didn't appear to find anything odd in this request. She smiled and answered readily enough. "I never saw her, my dear. The affair took place in the country. A fortuitous circumstance, I've always considered, for I believe she was already married and several years older than Adrian. Only imagine the scandal if such a liaison had been carried out under the eyes of the *ton*. As it is, her identity remains a mystery to this day."

"I see." Phoebe pursed her lips thoughtfully.

"In any event, it's long forgotten now." Lady Yarwood smiled again and patted Phoebe's hand in her friendly fashion as she prepared to depart. "I do hope you'll bring the girls to visit Amabel and Caroline one day, Miss Smith. Please don't think they must wait until Ottilia is available. You are very welcome."

"I'm sure Miss Smith appreciates your concern, cousin." Crowhurst approached, a faint smile on his thin lips. "It must be a great comfort to her to encounter one who was once in her…er…position. Are you ready to leave? Not that I wish to hurry you, of course, it is just that one has so many engagements."

"Then you should have said so, Adrian," Lady Yarwood returned, with what Phoebe could only consider to be great self-restraint. "I will fetch the girls immediately."

Phoebe watched her ladyship cross the room, then turned a look of displeasure on Crowhurst. "Were you trying to embarrass your cousin, sir, or me?" she demanded, too annoyed to remember Deverell's instructions regarding the Viscount.

His smile held a touch of spite. "You must pardon me, my dear Phoebe. A petty remark, wasn't it. But, you know, it was very naughty of you to go off with Deverell. And quite unnecessary."

"I don't know what you're talking about, sir."

"Oh, I think you do. You escaped me once before, my dear Phoebe, but not a second time."

Seeing her eyes widen, Crowhurst seemed to realise he might have gone too far with that remark, because he wiped the unpleasant sneer from his face and replaced it with a smile. As far as Phoebe was concerned, the change wasn't an improvement.

"I don't believe I've given you leave to use my name, sir," she retorted. "I was grateful yesterday for your offer of assistance, but I would prefer you to address me correctly."

His voice lowered to a sibilant whisper. "Are you saying you want me to use your surname, Phoebe? Oh, no." He shook his head. "I don't think so. Not here. No, I don't think you'd like that at all."

And with his mouth still curled in that sly smile, he bowed and walked away, leaving Phoebe with a mind once more whirling with surmise and conjecture.

None of the possible explanations for Crowhurst's enigmatic remarks were reassuring, but she wasn't, she saw, to be allowed the luxury of brooding over them now.

Lady Grismead, having despatched the last of her guests, returned to the drawing-room and the attack. Apparently considering Deverell and his charges capable of seeing themselves out, she commanded her now weeping daughter to adjourn to the morning-room.

Adding heartrending wails to her repertoire, Pamela obeyed.

Under the awed gazes of her younger relatives, her ladyship, undaunted by the rapidly increasing volume of the performance, prepared to follow. She paused with her hand on the doorknob and swept the room with a basilisk glare.

"It is all very well for Pamela to say she has a talent for

managing finances," she stated sternly. "So has Deverell. But have we seen any advantage from it? Pray tell me that."

No one was foolhardy enough to volunteer an answer. Indeed, since her ladyship swept out of the room on the words, Lord Grismead hard on her heels, Phoebe was not certain if she'd expected a reply. The question did, however, set up a new train of thought in her mind. She was seizing on it with an eagerness that bordered on the desperate when Deverell planted himself in her line of vision. He appeared to be torn between annoyance and amusement.

"I have to say, Miss Smith, that infuriating though our charges may be at times, they at least refrain from performances guaranteed to shatter the ears of anyone in the immediate vicinity. Are you ready to depart? Since my esteemed uncle has chosen to add his mite to the melodrama being enacted across the hall, there's nothing to stop us. Let's escape while we can."

Phoebe was in no mood for flippancy. The past few hours seemed to have been filled with one disaster after another. And they could all be laid at the doors of the gentlemen involved.

She turned to their interested audience and took a leaf from Lady Grismead's book. "Gerald, you will oblige me by escorting your sisters to your uncle's carriage and waiting for us there. I presume your carriage *is* downstairs, my lord?"

He raised a brow. "Since I gave my coachman instructions to meet us here at four o'clock, it had better be." He nodded to Gerald, who reluctantly withdrew with his sisters, then winced as several despairing shrieks reverberated across the hall before the door was closed again. "Do you have any further orders, Miss Smith?"

Phoebe regarded the sardonic lift of his brows and glared at him. "If your aunt is correct in saying you're a financial genius, my lord, it would better become you to assist your family than to make fun of them. It seems to me that Miss Grismead is sincerely attached to her poet and—"

"If Nermal, or whatever his name is, really wishes to marry Pamela," he shot back, "he'll cease this idiotic notion he has of cutting himself off from his family for no good reason."

"But that is precisely what I mean!" she exclaimed. Pleased at his ready understanding, she momentarily forgot her other tribulations. "I knew you would comprehend the matter perfectly, my lord. First of all, you could give Lord Grismead a nudge in the right direction. Financially, I mean, and then you could speak to—"

"Have you lost your mind, Miss Smith?"

"No, of course not. Only think. It's much more likely that Mr Hartlepoole will listen to someone who really was estranged from his family for years. You could tell him how very uncomfortable it is."

"You *have* lost your mind."

Grappling with details, Phoebe waved this away as one absently brushing aside a bothersome insect. "Really, I'm surprised I didn't think of it before. Just think how relieved and happy the Grismeads will be. It will heal the rift beautifully and—"

"I wonder if my aunt has a blue powder in the house."

"Very likely. Now, would it best if you—"

"Yes, I believe you're right. Blue powders must work on Pamela, otherwise the neighbours would be forever complaining. Now, if I can only prevail upon my aunt to spare one, I'm sure you'll soon feel more the thing."

That got through. Phoebe ceased contemplating the brilliance of her scheme and bent a severe frown upon him. "You seem to forget, sir, that your aim is to have your aunt take charge of Theo and Cressy as soon as possible. She won't oblige you in that until Miss Grismead is suitably married. And if the only impediment is Mr Hartlepoole's intransigence, then the sooner he is convinced of the foolishness of his actions, the better."

She didn't expect this admonition to be greeted with exclamations, of delight, but the abrupt narrowing of Deverell's eyes sent a tingle of alarm down her spine. He went very still. The stillness of a predator about to spring.

"Do you know, Miss Smith, I'd forgotten how anxious you are to leave us. How very remiss of me. However, in case you're considering ways of escape, you may disabuse your mind of the notion that Toombes is a likely prospect. He'd drive you mad within a week."

Phoebe's mouth fell open. "Well! Really, my lord. This time you go too far! What I do about Mr Toombes is none of your business, although escape certainly has a definite—"

"Damn it, Phoebe, as your employer I have a right to know if you're considering accepting an offer from Toombes!"

His outburst momentarily stunned her into silence. Phoebe took a deep breath, contemplated the grim line about Deverell's mouth and decided she'd better answer.

"No, I am not!" she exclaimed, goaded. "Not that I expect him to take any notice of me," she added disagreeably. "Like all men, he doesn't listen to anything he doesn't want to hear."

Without a word, Deverell grasped her by the elbow and marched her over to the door, snatching up her pelisse from a chair near the piano where she'd placed it earlier.

"You won't be required to say anything, whether or not Toombes wishes to hear it," he grated through set teeth as he propelled her down the stairs. "From now on, Miss Smith, you will refer any offers, of any kind, from any gentlemen, to me. Is that perfectly clear?"

Phoebe clenched her own teeth. "Perfectly," she muttered. And refused to say another word all the way out to the carriage.

The Grismeads' butler looked enviously after them as they exited through the front door while the sounds of battle continued unabated from the floor above. Phoebe found herself in entire sympathy with Miss Grismead's piercingly uttered desire to send a notice to the *Gazette* at once. She would very much like to place an advertisement therein herself.

For the mythical male-free, elderly lady she'd imagined earlier.

Chapter Eight

Several days later, Phoebe had not changed her mind about the advantages of a household free of gentlemen. In fact, she told herself, rubbing salt into the wound, if she'd remained at Kerslake, she could have looked forward to such a household once Gerald was settled at Oxford.

But no. She'd insisted on bringing Deverell's wards to London and look what had happened. Instead of alleviating all her problems, she now had a whole new set to worry about. All of which had to do with males.

She never seemed to be rid of the creatures.

Coming down the stairs, she bumped into Mr Filby on his way up to haul Gerald from his slumbers. She tripped over Lord Bradden in the drawing-room. Mr Charlton appeared to have taken up residence in the library. Only the sounds of Mr Toombes's measured tones wafting into the morning-room prevented a disastrous encounter in the hall.

She couldn't even take comfort from the fact that Crowhurst hadn't called. Instead, he was bombarding her with flowers that came attached with invitations to dinner at a discreet coffee-house at a time of her choosing. As if he had only to ask!

Her bedchamber was the only place where she could be guaranteed any peace and privacy. And even that seemed to have been invaded by memories of her last encounter with Deverell. For some strange reason, she was constantly beset by a desire to tell him that she wasn't at all anxious to leave his employment. It was very odd. Why should she care if he'd taken her helpful suggestions the wrong way? It was just like him, she'd fumed, pacing up and down in front of her mirror, to be the only gentleman to make himself scarce precisely when he was needed to oust the others. Typical Deverell behaviour.

Rallying her spirits with that stricture. Phoebe tried valiantly to oust him from her mind.

Her efforts had not been crowned by any great success when she ventured cautiously into the dining-room in anticipation of breakfast two days later.

She immediately perceived another problem. The room was mercifully free of gentlemen, but it was *too* empty. Phoebe eyed the vacant places at the breakfast table with foreboding. They did not augur well.

When Thripp tiptoed into the room after her and carefully placed the coffee-pot on the table, her uneasiness increased twofold. One glance at the butler's face aroused the unpleasant suspicion that another breakfast was about to be rendered hideous by disclosures she would rather not hear.

Phoebe fortified herself with a mouthful of coffee and braced for the worst. "Don't try to break the news gently, Thripp. Tell me at once. Where are they?"

Thripp shook his head. "That I couldn't say, miss, but I doubt the young ladies have gone to the theatres."

"Well, that's a relief. I think. What makes you say so?"

"They prevailed upon his lordship to lend them his new phaeton, miss, which they would hardly do if they intended to pay frequent visits to theatres."

"Gerald lent them his phaeton?" Phoebe contemplated her empty plate while she mulled over that bit of news. It wasn't reassuring. Theo was an excellent driver, but this was London.

"So I understand, miss. And very smart they looked, too, in their greatcoats."

"*Greatcoats!*" Her head jerked up. "Greatcoats? Thripp, ladies don't wear greatcoats."

"Well, as to that, I couldn't say, miss, but greatcoats they were. With capes," he added helpfully. "Several capes. And large brass buttons."

A variety of nerve-racking pictures chased one another through Phoebe's head. She didn't like any one of them.

"I don't suppose you managed to see what they were wearing under the greatcoats, Thripp?" she asked, hoping against hope that her sudden suspicions were too wild to be true.

"Nothing you could take exception to miss," responded Thripp, quite as one who was an expert on suitable fashions for young ladies. "Very pretty gowns, I thought. Blue and yellow stripes."

Phoebe's suspicions took a giant stride towards certainty. Several remarks passed by Theodosia on the subject of female drivers echoed ominously in her head. Oh, why hadn't she taken more notice of the twins' activities over the past few days? It was no use only now recalling hurried forays to the shops, and several meetings with other young ladies, conducted in hushed voices and accompanied by excited gigglings.

Distracted by the possible reasons why Deverell had formed no part of the male invasion, not to mention Gerald's increasingly haggard countenance, she'd been only too relieved that the girls were happily occupied. And now...

"Thripp, go upstairs and tell Gerald if he isn't down here in five minutes his exit from his bed will be even more unpleasant than what Lord Deverell had in mind for him."

Thripp's countenance immediately fell into its usual mournful lines. "His lordship has not as yet returned home, miss."

"Good heavens! Where is he?"

"I couldn't say with any accuracy, miss, but his lordship has been very flush with the ready—" Thripp coughed discreetly behind his hand "—I beg your pardon, miss, I'm sure. That is to say, very well-heeled lately. If you take my meaning, Miss."

"Oh, my goodness! Do you mean Gerald has been *gambling?*"

Thripp looked cautious. "I believe his lordship has taken quite a liking to a place called the Pigeonhole."

"The—*Pigeonhole!* Of course! Pigeons! For the plucking. Oh, how could I have been so foolish, so neglectful?" Abandoning all thought of breakfast, Phoebe leapt to her feet. "I'll have to see Deverell immediately. Thripp, go and summon a hackney, and then send the footman out to search for Gerald.

I don't care where you find him or what he's doing. Tell him he's needed at Lord Deverell's house at once!''

Wasting no more time, Phoebe dashed out of the room. She was still chastising herself several minutes later as she leapt into a hackney, pelisse half-buttoned and bonnet askew. What a dreadful mess she'd made of everything. She'd known what she was dealing with but, too busy brooding over Deverell, she'd forgotten the schemes his wards were capable of concocting.

On the other hand, Deverell was supposed to be applying a firm hand. He'd told her he was keeping an eye on Gerald. What was he about, to let an inexperienced boy throw money around in every gambling hell in town? And who had given Gerald the money in the first place?

She hadn't reached any satisfactory conclusions when the hackney arrived at Deverell's townhouse. Paying off the driver, Phoebe ran up the steps and wielded the knocker with violent force. The door was opened by a startled butler. Phoebe raced past him into the house as if pursued by demons and demanded its master.

''His lordship is Upstairs, Miss Smith,'' intoned the guardian of the door in frigid accents. ''I will see if he can Be Disturbed.''

''Good heavens, does everyone in London spend half the day abed?'' she cried. ''Tell his lordship he'll be extremely disturbed if he doesn't come down here immediately. His entire family will be disturbed. The whole of Society will be disturbed. In fact—''

''What seems to be the problem, Miss Smith?''

The calmly voiced query did not come from the butler. Phoebe looked up—and felt her throat seize in mid-sentence. Not that she didn't have plenty to say, she tried to remind herself, but it was, she suddenly discovered, impossible to deliver a tirade when its recipient stood two floors above her, dressed only in breeches, topboots and a shirt that, with sleeves rolled up and half-unfastened, exposed a good deal of tanned throat and powerful forearms dusted with a covering of dark hair.

Phoebe swallowed and wondered why the sight of Deverell

interrupted in the process of dressing for the day should have the very peculiar effect of suspending every faculty.

He stepped forward to the head of the stairs, a faint smile curving his lips. "Won't you come up, Miss Smith?"

"Come up?" She repeated the words. That is, her lips moved. She still seemed incapable of uttering a sound.

"You obviously have news of great moment to impart. Dawby, would you be good enough to bring some tea up to the studio for Miss Smith?"

Her gaze still fixed on Deverell, Phoebe moved towards the stairs as one in a trance. "Oh, no. Nothing, thank you. I—"

She started to climb, her breath growing shorter with each step. It was no use telling herself the stairs were particularly steep. It was the way Deverell watched her that was rendering her both breathless and witless. She was too far away, at first, to see the expression in his eyes, which were shadowed anyway by the downward sweep of his lashes, but when she reached the landing there was no mistaking the intensity of his gaze.

Unable to meet it, she looked at his throat instead and found herself instantly transfixed by the pulse beating there. And lower still, just where his shirt was fastened was the veriest hint of the same dark hair that covered his forearms.

Phoebe felt a shiver ripple every nerve in her body. She tried to tell herself that Deverell wasn't the first male she'd seen in a state of *déshabillé*. She'd once come upon Gerald *completely* bare-chested when he'd been swimming in the stream at Kerslake. But somehow it wasn't the same. Gerald was a stripling, a boy. Her only reaction had been to order him to don his shirt before he encountered Miss Pomfret and sent her into a fit of the vapours.

Deverell, on the other hand, was all adult male. At least a foot taller than her, broad and solid across the shoulders, all powerful muscle and sheer primitive masculinity. And she felt a shockingly primitive urge to draw closer, to lift her hand to his chest, to feel the strength and power she'd felt once before and could now see.

Oh, dear, such urges were definitely unseemly. Extremely unseemly. And it didn't help that she could feel Deverell's intent gaze on her as if he was about to *do* something unseemly.

Completely unnerved, Phoebe whirled about and scurried

through the nearest open doorway. She immediately froze, squeezing her eyes shut. Oh, heavens! This was worse. She was probably in Deverell's bedchamber! What was she to do *now?*

She didn't stop to contemplate her options. Spinning about, eyes still tightly shut, she dashed back towards the hallway and cannoned straight into Deverell.

Heat enveloped her instantly. If he hadn't grasped her arms, she would have collapsed in a heap right there at his feet. The thought was so shocking, she didn't realise he continued to hold her a mere inch away until his breath stirred the curls at her temple.

"Did the sight of this room startle you so much, Miss Smith?"

Phoebe took a deep breath and opened her eyes. The triangle of his open shirt met her gaze; feathery black hair almost tickled her nose. She swallowed, wrenched her gaze upward and met a wry, heart-shaking smile that was totally unlike the fiendish grin she'd half-expected.

"I...that is..."

Her voice was a mouse-like squeak. She dragged in another breath and tried again. "I shouldn't be here, my lord."

Something glittered in his eyes behind the smile. She felt his hands tighten very carefully. "This is precisely where you should be," he murmured. And turned her around. "Look."

Phoebe obeyed, and then blinked as light and space bombarded her senses. They weren't standing in Deverell's bedchamber after all, but in a room that appeared to her astonished gaze to be filled with items of statuary in various stages of construction. Several finished pieces stood on pedestals against one wall, and in front of her stretched a long bench covered with a liberal coating of whitish dust and holding an array of tools whose purpose she could only guess at.

"Oh, my goodness." Blinking again, she glanced down at the long fingers still wrapped about her upper arms. They, too, wore a coating of dust. She transferred her gaze to his face. "You're a sculptor, my lord."

He continued to hold her for a moment longer, looking down into her face. He didn't appear to be put out by her discovery, she thought. Or annoyed that she'd invaded his privacy. Rather, his eyes held a watchfulness, an almost wary stillness; every emotion carefully hidden.

Then as her awareness of him, warm and solid against her back, set her pulse tripping, he released her and moved away to a table holding a porcelain basin and ewer. Pouring some water into the basin, he began washing the dust from his hands.

"It's merely a hobby. I started years ago, whittling pieces from wood to pass the time."

"Pass the time?"

He threw her a sidelong glance from beneath half-lowered lashes. "It can be rather tedious waiting in the mountain regions of India for bandits to show themselves."

"Oh." So her initial assessment of him as a warrior had been accurate.

Unable, for the moment, to do anything except ponder that point, Phoebe watched him withdraw his hands from the basin, shake them and reach for a cloth that lay folded nearby.

Big hands. Powerful hands. The hands of a warrior.

And, she mused wonderingly, remembering the candelabra in his library, hands capable of creating delicate beauty.

"The Psyche," she murmured, then blushed, recalling the statue's paucity of civilised clothing.

"Guilty, I'm afraid." The corners of his mouth curled upward. "I hope she didn't shock you, Miss Smith."

Phoebe valiantly fought back a hotter blush. "Of course not, my lord. Your Psyche is formed quite in the classical mode. A most accurate…er…rendering of the ancient Greek, um… That is to say…"

She subsided when Deverell tossed the cloth aside and strode towards her, a distinctly amused light in his eyes.

"Are you feeling overly warm in here, Miss Smith? There are a lot of windows, and it is a particularly sunny day. Perhaps if you were to move out of the direct light—"

"I am not overly warm," Phoebe retorted, recovering somewhat under this goad. She assumed her primmest posture and levelled a disapproving frown at him. "It is just—I'm not in the habit of conversing with a gentleman who hasn't taken the trouble to don his coat before receiving visitors."

"But I didn't know you intended to visit," he returned inarguably. He stopped in front of her and subjected her to a swift examination. "And I hardly think your strictures are fair, Miss Smith, when you appear to have flung your clothes on in some haste yourself." The words were followed by a slow smile. "In fact, your bonnet is listing quite dangerously to the left. If you'll allow me…"

Phoebe just managed to prevent a startled gasp escaping her lips when Deverell's fingers brushed her throat. She stood still, every muscle rigid, as he placed her bonnet at the proper angle and began retying the ribbons.

He was obviously going to take his time about the task. She wondered why her heart seemed determined to leap out of her chest; why she couldn't breathe; why the feel of Deverell's fingers, warm and hard against her bare flesh made her nerves quiver like harp strings recently struck. He was only touching her neck, for heaven's sake.

But then he rested the backs of his fingers against the pulse beating wildly in her throat and she ceased thinking at all. A strange melting lassitude made her legs go weak and her insides dissolve. She wanted to lean on him, to feel his arms go around her, supporting her, holding her.

Oh, dear, this was beyond unseemly urges. She was crossing the line into unbridled passion. And it *was* dangerous. Her family had been right to warn her. Instead of raising her voice in protest, she could only gaze, mesmerised, into those half-narrowed, intensely glittering eyes, and picture his hands, fashioning, moulding, smoothing over the feminine contours of the statue he'd created.

No, not just picture them. *Feel* them. On *her*. Even though he hadn't moved an inch.

She trembled once, violently. Then, with an incoherent whisper, wrenched herself away and fled to the other side of the room.

She found herself confronted by an array of statuary and at once began babbling. "Good heavens, my lord, you *have* been busy! Marble, wood, clay. You're certainly versatile. What a very interesting statue of a child. It looks just like…"

The spate stopped abruptly as her mouth formed a silent "oh" of surprise. "It looks just like Gerald," she finished slowly, turning to face him.

But Deverell was no longer watching her. He stood before

the bench, fists thrust into the pockets of his breeches, apparently deep in contemplation of the block of ebony wood in front of him.

"It is Gerald," he said curtly. "As I remember him. Always pestering me for a ride."

Eyes wide, Phoebe stared at the unyielding line of his shoulders and wondered uneasily what had brought about the demise of all traces of devilishness. He'd spoken so tersely, so dismissively. It could be in response to the possibility of her remarking on his work. She hoped so. It was bad enough that her nerve-endings still felt as if they were simmering under some invisible source of heat. If Deverell knew how shockingly she'd reacted to his touch, she would be forced to leave him. And...

She didn't want to.

"I see," she managed, and turned to the statue again. Blindly, at first, her thoughts in a turmoil. But then her vision, strangely blurred, cleared, and she did see. More, perhaps, than Deverell realised, she thought, distress and embarrassment forgotten in the wonder of discovery.

She studied the upturned marble face, the chubby outstretched arms, and felt something move deep within her. A little child wanting to be lifted, and yet there was something in the way the arms reached upward, something about the face...

Then she shifted slightly—or perhaps the angle of the light changed—and the child's features seemed to alter, to harden, to show hints of the man he would one day become. And in that moment, Phoebe knew, with absolute certainty, that it was Deverell reaching out; that he was innocent of whatever scandal had seen him banished from his home; that he'd been hurt, terribly; was still hurt, by that banishment.

"You're very talented, my lord," she murmured, hearing the huskiness of repressed tears in her voice. She cleared her throat, hoping he hadn't noticed, trying desperately to think of something else to say. What was the matter with her? Why did this particular man cause these strange emotions that tempted her to draw perilously close to the invisible line beyond which lay scandal and disgrace?

But even as the faintest whisper of an answer threatened to

creep into her consciousness, she fought it back. She didn't want to face the reasons for her odd behaviour. She didn't even want to think about it. Now wasn't the time. Later she could put it down to overwrought nerves. Surprise that a warrior could also be an artist. Something she'd eaten.

Anything.

Right now the only line she was prepared to cross was that of employee telling her employer precisely what she thought of people who abandoned their responsibilities—

"Oh, my goodness! What on earth are we about? My lord, we can't stand here chatting about statues. We must go at once! At once, I say!"

Deverell turned to face her, his hands still thrust into his pockets. His gaze was rather searching, causing uneasiness to flutter again like tiny moths in her stomach, but his voice held a familiar sardonic note.

"I am, of course, only too happy to oblige you, Miss Smith. Not, however, until I now where we're going and why."

"I'll explain on the way." Phoebe glanced hurriedly around the room. "Where's your coat? Why is nothing ever where it should be? You'll have to send a message to your stables, my lord, and then—"

"No."

She gaped at him. "No?"

"No."

"But...there isn't a moment to lose. Disaster will overtake us at any moment. Think of the scandal, sir! Think of your nieces' reputations! Think—"

"Aha. So that's the cause of this precipitous visit. I did wonder if I was to be called upon to rescue you from the estimable Mr Toombes, or even Crowhurst. How very disappointing."

"What?" Phoebe shook her head as if trying to clear her brain. "What on earth have they got to do with anything? I'm here because I think Theodosia may have started a club for female whips based upon the Four-in-Hand and—" She glared at him as he started to smile. "There is nothing amusing about it, I can assure you."

His smile widened. "I dare say, Miss Smith. If I'm amused, it's because you're a constant source of delight to me. But surely your reaction is unnecessarily exaggerated. Theodosia

may have spoken about a whip club, but she won't get far
without a carriage.''

"She has a carriage, sir. Gerald's phaeton. And while we're
wasting time arguing, the twins are driving to Salt Hill with
heaven's knows how many other young ladies. Also in carriages.''

He shrugged and turned back to the bench to start putting
tools away. "Then, I dare say, if they adhere to the rules of
the genuine Four-in-Hand Club, they'll eventually return.''

"Is that all you have to say?'' she cried. "Didn't you hear
me? I said they're driving to *Salt Hill!* They intend to dine at
a public inn. Imagine the spectacle they'll present! Good heavens, most of them aren't even out yet. Their parents will never
forgive you.''

He sent her a look over his shoulder that clearly stated his
indifference to parental disapproval.

"Well, if that doesn't move you, my lord, consider the fact
that I'll give you no peace until you agree to accompany me.''

"A telling threat, Miss Smith.'' His mouth curved wryly as
he abandoned his task to lean casually against the bench. "You
know,'' he mused aloud, "I returned to London for some
peace. Strange. I wonder what made me think such a com-
modity could be found here?''

"I have no idea,'' Phoebe snapped with some asperity.
"Peace is not something one readily associates with Deverell's.
Now, will you send a message to your stables, sir, or shall I?''

"You realise, of course, that we may be setting off on a
futile enterprise. Theodosia may be doing nothing more innoc-
uous than tooling Gerald's phaeton around the Park.''

Phoebe considered the suggestion with a quick uprush of
hope, only to dismiss it. "I'm afraid not, sir. You see, I over-
heard the girls talking.'' She wrung her hands in self-reproach.
"I know I should have taken more notice at the time, but it all
sounded so far-fetched I didn't think anything could come of
it. Theo was setting out some sort of rules and regulations. That
they would drive to Salt Hill, just like the gentlemen's Four-
in-Hand Club, in single file at a strict trot, with no overtaking.
And they'd even wear the same sort of costume.''

"Good God!''

She nodded gloomily. "I am very much blame, my lord. I'm

fully aware of it. I can only hope that no one has met with an accident. If I recall correctly, only men with a great deal of experience in driving a team are admitted to the Four-in-Hand Club. Some even take lessons from professional coachmen. Heaven knows what we'll find. But,'' she added hopefully, ''I've sent a message to Gerald to meet us here, so we'll have some help.''

''You can't imagine how that reassures me, Miss Smith.''

Phoebe hung her head. ''I'm very sensible of the patience you're exercising, my lord.''

''Hmm. First threats, now remorse.'' Straightening, he strolled over to her and tipped her face up to his with one long finger under her chin. Amusement, and something that made her breath quiver, glittered in his eyes.

''Forgive me for saying so, Miss Smith, but you're more than a match for any Deverell. I'll accompany you—if only for the pleasure of seeing you cope with what is sure to be a shambles if the young ladies are indeed emulating the Four-in-Hand Club.''

Phoebe shuddered, but straightened her shoulders. ''We must save them from scandal, my lord.''

And while she was about it, she'd better do the same for herself, she reflected, taking a careful step away from his touch.

She was still expounding silently on this theme when Deverell, having left a message for Gerald with his butler, handed her up into his phaeton. The vehicle appeared to be fashioned more for speed than safety, a sight that heartened Phoebe somewhat. Deverell might appear to be less than concerned about the situation, but clearly he didn't intend to waste any time.

He had just walked around to climb up next to her, when the clatter of several wheels on cobblestones had them both turning their heads. Bowling up the street towards them came a bright yellow curricle drawn by two chestnut horses. Mr Filby, resplendent in a greatcoat with wide lapels of the same hue as his carriage, held the reins, and seated beside him, looking slightly rumpled, was Gerald.

Two or three more curricles, all crowded with young gentlemen, followed hard on their wheels.

Deverell watched the approaching cavalcade for a moment,

then turned a narrow-eyed look on Phoebe. "How many females did you say were in this club?"

Phoebe decided it would be prudent to keep her eyes lowered. "Um…I didn't say precisely, my lord, but…several."

"Several." He muttered something indecipherable, climbed into the carriage and gathered up the reins. "And several of Gerald's cronies have obviously entertained second thoughts on the wisdom of lending their various equipages to their sisters."

"Er…it would seem so, sir."

He continued to eye her for a moment longer, his lips set in a grim line. Then, without waiting for Mr Filby to come up with them, gave his horses the office to start.

Followed by the astonished stares of a number of passersby, two youthful crossing-sweepers and assorted loungers and tradespersons, the procession headed out of Town.

"Don't worry your head about an outbreak of scandal, Miss Smith."

The sound of Deverell's voice, abrupt in a silence broken only by the rapid rhythm of horses' hooves, shook Phoebe out of the gloomy contemplation of her probable future that had occupied her for the first few miles.

They were driving through some rather pretty country, the autumn hues of the trees and hedgerows painting everything in sight in warm russets and golds. The road wound through a small wood enclosing them in a dim, sun-dappled tunnel. Birds flew, twittering, between the branches, seeming to dart from sunbeam to sunbeam.

She hadn't noticed a thing.

"I cannot help but worry, my lord."

"Unnecessary, I assure you. Thanks to your quick action in coming to me immediately, we'll overtake the little beasts before they reach Salt Hill."

When she failed to take exception to this unloving description of the miscreants, he cast a quick glance at her face. "And if they're decked out in identical costumes, as you say, they'll probably pass for pupils from a young ladies' academy. Taking driving lessons," he added helpfully when she turned a look of scepticism on him.

"Without any teachers?"

"We were delayed."

"How?"

"One of the horses threw a shoe."

"And they went on without us?"

He grinned. "They're pupils. The couldn't get their horses to stop."

Adjuring herself not to respond to that wicked grin, Phoebe returned her gaze to the road. "I don't think that will work, sir."

"Why not? You're already wearing your governess costume. Again."

When she once more refused the challenge, his voice changed. "All right, Miss Smith, let's have it. What else it causing that line between your brows?"

Phoebe contemplated ignoring the demand, then decided that delivering herself of another lecture might keep her mind on her proper sphere in life. Despite all her strictures to herself, it still seemed possessed of a regrettable tendency to dwell on such inappropriate matters as the way Deverell's mouth kicked up at one corner when he smiled in that wry fashion, the brilliant intensity of his eyes, the strength of his hands as he handled the reins with easy competence.

"If you must know, sir, I am extremely worried about Gerald. If you didn't notice it before, the merest glance over your shoulder should tell you how haggard he's looking."

"If you don't mind, Miss Smith, at this speed I'd rather keep my eyes on the road."

"You told me you were keeping an eye on Gerald," Phoebe pointed out. "But this morning I learned from Thripp that Gerald is spending night after night at some dreadful place called the Pigeonhole."

"Hmm. Gambling hell. St James's Square. Precisely what one would expect of a young fool."

"I can see you're beside yourself with worry," she observed with heavy sarcasm. "It is not good enough, my lord. Poor Gerald could fall into the clutches of evil moneylenders at any moment. Be cast into the Fleet. Throw himself into the river! What will you do then?''

"You've been reading novels again, Miss Smith."

"If you don't do something," she threatened, sweeping over this accusation with magnificent disdain, "then *I* will. I cannot stand by and watch Gerald ruin himself, even if I have to drag him out of that dreadful place myself."

"If you go anywhere near the Pigeonhole, Miss Smith, or any other hell for that matter, I'll put you over my knee."

Phoebe's mouth fell open. The action didn't seem to restore the air to her lungs. While she was still struggling with outrage, Deverell apparently forgot the dangers of driving at speed along a winding road and looked down at her.

"Phoebe."

He waited until she glared back at him.

"You are worrying to no purpose," he said very softly, and looked straight into her eyes.

Phoebe could only gaze back, her mind whirling. She could have sworn a full minute passed before Deverell released her from the spell of his gaze. Even then she could hardly think. She stared at the ribbon of road unfurling ahead of them and wondered how one direct look could deflate her wrath so thoroughly.

No answer seemed forthcoming, but that and every other consideration was abruptly forgotten when they swept around a bend.

The road ahead, empty of traffic only seconds ago, was crowded and congested beyond belief. Horses, carriages and people milled about in a seething kaleidoscope of confusion and noise.

Trapped in the middle of the turbulent sea of humanity and horses was a large stage-coach, its driver standing upright on the box, his mouth opening and closing, arms waving frantically. Passengers hung out of windows or shook their fists from the roof. Since no one could be heard over the shrieks, shouts and equine squeals that filled the air, their efforts were useless.

"Oh, my goodness!" Hands pressed to her mouth, Phoebe stared in horror at the scene before her. Even as she watched, one young lady, who had apparently considered herself competent to drive tandem, managed to free her carriage from the fray only to have her lead horse turn in its traces and try to rejoin its fellows. She promptly succumbed to hysterics while her pair exchanged nips and uncomplimentary pleasantries.

"Oh, my goodness! This is impossible!"

"I'm surprised you know the word, Miss Smith." There was a suspicious tremor in Deverell's voice as he pulled his horses to the side of the road. "Here—" thrusting the reins into her hands "—try to keep my greys from adding to the disaster."

"But what—?"

She didn't get any further. Before the enquiry was fully formed in her mind, Deverell put his head in his hands and laughed so hard he almost fell out of the carriage. If she hadn't been fully occupied in preventing the greys from backing into Mr Filby's curricle, Phoebe was certain she would have given him a helping push.

"For goodness' sake, my lord, have you run mad? Don't just sit there laughing! *Do something!*"

He straightened, still grinning. "Have *you* run mad, Miss Smith? Anyone fool enough to wander into that pandemonium will be trampled underfoot."

"I say, sir." Gerald appeared at the side of the phaeton, looking as frantic as Phoebe felt. "What is to be done?"

"It's your phaeton, I believe." Deverell turned a look of sardonic mockery on his nephew. "You rescue it. And while you're about it," he added, his gaze sweeping over the crowd of young gentlemen gathering about Gerald, "every one of you had better be prepared to pay compensation to the coach driver and his passengers. Unless you want news of this episode to reach the ears of higher authorities."

As one his audience blanched.

A silence fraught with dismay followed.

"My lord, I don't think Gerald is quite up to this task." Her hands still full of reins, Phoebe tried to put as much of a plea into the words as possible. She didn't *think* Deverell would abandon his wards to their fate, but she wasn't above a little pleading if it got results.

Apparently reaching the same conclusion, Gerald and his cohorts did their best to look pathetically guiltless.

Deverell's eyes narrowed slightly. He glanced from his nephew to Phoebe then, rising to his feet leaned over and spoke very softly in her ear. "You, my love, are going to be knee-deep in debt to me. Don't move from this spot."

He sprang down from the phaeton, waded into the fray and started giving orders.

He tended to do that a lot, Phoebe reflected, struggling with a pair of edgy horses and even more turbulent nerves. On the other hand, she didn't know of anyone else who could cope with a disaster of this magnitude. Softly spoken threats and inappropriate, heart-stopping appellations were a small price to pay, she decided.

Besides, he hadn't meant it. He'd been infected by the madness of the moment. Who could wonder at it?

Chapter Nine

It was well past noon by the time the procession returned to Town, at a slightly more decorous pace than when it had started out.

Theodosia was the only female still driving. The other young ladies sat beside their grim-faced brothers and tried, earnestly or tearfully according to their wont, to explain that if the guard on the stage-coach hadn't decided to blow his yard of tin just when Miss Forsythe was trying to prevent her pair from committing the heinous crime of overtaking the carriage in front of her, the entire débâcle would never have occurred.

Their explanations fell on deaf ears. So, too, did Gerald's dissertation on the matter. From her seat in Mr Filby's curricle, Phoebe had seen Gerald gesturing and talking all the way home. Deverell had appeared deaf and blind to his nephew's efforts.

She could only be thankful she'd retained enough wit to shove the greys' reins into Gerald's hands when he'd emerged, more rumpled than ever, from the mêlée, so she could take refuge with Mr Filby.

Listening to that Tulip's ambitious plans to start a new fashion of greatcoats with lapels to match one's carriage was a lot less nerve-racking than listening to an account of the debt she owed Deverell.

Unfortunately, her reprieve was not indefinite. Mr Filby, after one glance at Deverell's countenance as he alighted from his phaeton, very basely drove off the instant her feet touched the ground. Phoebe gazed after the rapidly disappearing curricle and reflected on the general cowardice of males.

Then she caught sight of Deverell herself, and Mr Filby's cowardice was instantly elevated to the status of strategic retreat. In fact, it would, she decided, be wise to follow his example while Deverell was occupied in directing Gerald to take the reins from his sister, and in making arrangements for the disposition of his own phaeton and horses.

Before the thought was fully formed, Phoebe was scurrying up the front steps and into the house. If fortune smiled upon her, she might even reach the safety of her bedchamber while Deverell was further occupied in lecturing his wards.

Fortune did not feel inclined to smile upon her that day.

"Miss Smith! I *knew* you would return. I knew I would be wise to wait. Your butler has been trying to tell me—"

"Oh! Mr Toombes." Phoebe skidded to a stop in the middle of the hall, and stared at her visitor in dismay. "Oh, dear, what else is going to—? That is, I didn't expect to see you still in Town, sir."

"The gentleman insisted on waiting," Thripp muttered, eyeing Toombes with disfavour. "But what's one more gentleman cluttering up the house?" He sniffed and prepared to depart to the nether regions. "London. I knew how it would be."

The front door opened again.

Phoebe refrained from demanding why, if Thripp had known how it would be, he hadn't warned her, and braced herself for the addition of yet another gentleman into the house. If Deverell could be described as such.

As she turned, Theodosia and Cressida slipped past her like wraiths. It was quite a feat, considering they were still clad incongruously in greatcoats.

Deverell didn't try to slip anywhere. He took in the situation with a lightning-swift glance and stopped less than an arm's length from Phoebe.

"Theodosia, Cressida, the morning-room. Now."

The twins halted in mid-step. Clasping each other's hands, they changed direction.

"And take off those ridiculous coats."

"But, Uncle Sebastian, they're part of the costume of the Two-in-Hand Club for Lady Whips."

"The Two-in-Hand Club for Lady Whips is now defunct. *Off!*"

"My lord!" Toombes started bowing as though to royalty. "No doubt you are wondering why I am here. My presence, when you are aware of Miss Smith's very proper notions on such conduct, has startled you. One can readily understand your surprise. I'm sure you did not mean to speak so harshly to these poor, innocent—"

This highly inaccurate description of Deverell's nieces came to an abrupt halt as the coats were removed. A stunned silence filled the hall as everyone blinked at the barrage of brilliant blue and yellow stripes thus revealed. The paralytic effect was not lessened by the addition of white cravats decorated with large black spots.

Deverell closed his eyes as if in acute pain. "I know why you're here, Toombes." Opening his eyes again, he waved his nieces towards the stairs. "Go! I'll deal with you later. Miss Smith—"

"A wise decision, my lord." Toombes beamed ferociously. "I'm sure after a rational discussion with another gentleman of sensibility you will be able to perform the sacred duty of directing your wards' footsteps on to the proper path with patience rather than brutality and—"

"A rational discussion, Toombes?" Deverell's lips curled back, baring as many teeth as Toombes. "If you're here to discuss Miss Smith's future, no discussion will be necessary. Rational or otherwise."

"If, by that, sir, you mean you have no objection to my intentions, I am happy to hear you say so. However—" Toombes glanced at Phoebe, who was standing, frozen, as one waiting for the sword to fall "—although one does not like to keep a lady in suspense, I would prefer to make myself perfectly clear to you."

Deverell narrowed his eyes. "Clarification is certainly needed on several points around here. Very well, you can have five minutes."

"Five minutes!" Toombes's smile disappeared. He struck

an attitude. "Sir, it would take me forever to describe the exquisitely elevated nature of my feelings for Miss Smith."

"Then I trust you will refrain, because when five minutes have elapsed—"

"My lord." Bowing to the pressure of the moment, Phoebe tugged frantically at Deverell's sleeve. This was no time for such extravagant luxuries as panic. She had to take action before Toombes was laid out insensible at her feet.

"Ah, yes, Miss Smith." Deverell glanced down at her, a particularly fiendish light in his eyes. "I hesitate to behave in such a brutal fashion, of course, but you may consider yourself banished to the drawing-room."

"But, sir, I—"

"You heard Mr Toombes. He doesn't want to keep you in suspense."

Toombes beamed again.

"But—"

"The drawing-room is right over here, Miss Smith." He grasped her elbow.

"I know where it is," Phoebe muttered through gritted teeth as she was marched inexorably forward.

When Deverell opened the door for her and showed every sign of thrusting her unceremoniously into the room, a change of tactics seemed called for. She lowered her voice to an urgent whisper. "My lord, what are you going to say to Mr Toombes? No doubt you mean well, but pray remember that, even as my employer, it isn't your place to be receiving offers on my behalf."

"It's either that or leave you to handle Toombes on your own. I'm choosing the lesser of two evils, Miss Smith. Comfort yourself with the reflection that you'll now be hip-deep in debt to me."

Smiling grimly, he propelled her over the threshold and shut the door in her face.

Phoebe resisted the urge to thump the door panels with her fist and, muttering, began to pace back and forth across the carpet. After several passes, she finally caught sight of herself in the mirror over the mantelpiece and realised she was still wearing her bonnet and pelisse.

Removing the garments restored a measure of composure.

Pacing wasn't going to help. She needed to decide how she was going to deal with Deverell when he'd finished with Mr Toombes.

She wasn't quite sure how she was going to go about the task, but she was *not* going to behave as if she really was hip-deep in debt to him. She would, of course, be grateful if Deverell managed to rid her of her unwanted suitor. She was extremely grateful that she hadn't been left to cope alone with the abrupt demise of Theodosia's Two-in-Hand Club for Lady Whips. But anything else was out of the question.

She absolutely refused, for instance, to allow herself even a *hint* of a tender feeling for a gentleman who was so ungallant as to render an account whenever he was asked to come to her rescue. Or even when he wasn't.

Not that the odd little sensations hovering around her heart lately could be described as "tender feelings." No, no, not at all. Naturally she'd been deeply touched by the poignancy of the statue she'd seen that morning. She admired Deverell for using his talent as an outlet for his feelings rather than allowing bitterness to ruin his life. He also had an appreciation of the ridiculous that appealed to her, and there was that fleeting sense of protection she'd experienced once or twice in his company, but—

Phoebe frowned uneasily at the mirrored reflection in front of her. Protection, she reminded herself, wasn't all she was capable of feeling in Deverell's company. He seemed to have the knack of arousing some extremely disturbing, not to say positively scandalous, sensations whenever he came too close.

She couldn't understand it.

Or didn't want to understand it.

The insidious thought flitted across her mind and was instantly quelched. There was nothing *to* understand. However unseemly her urges, she'd observed enough to know that without tender feelings such urges didn't last long. And she'd just finished telling herself that she didn't have any tender feelings for Deverell so—

The sound of the door opening had her mind going blank in a singularly unnerving fashion. Every thought, every stricture, every resolve vanished as if it had never been as Deverell strode into the room and shut the door behind him.

Phoebe turned slowly to face him—and was instantly beset by an intense longing to run to him, to fly straight to the warmth of his arms. He looked so big standing there, watching her. Big and powerful and, somehow, protective.

Which was really quite ridiculous, she thought distractedly, because he was the cause of her dilemma.

"My...my lord." Somehow, from somewhere, she conjured up a bright smile. He mustn't know. That was the one clear thought in her head. He must not know.

What, precisely, he wasn't to know she wasn't prepared to admit.

"I've been waiting here on tenterhooks forever. You haven't strangled Mr Toombes, I trust."

"No," he purred, his lips curving in an anticipatory smile, "that is a fate I'm reserving for you, Miss Smith."

For some reason, this response restored a semblance of normalcy to the situation. Threats of strangulation were as nothing. She was becoming quite accustomed to them.

"Now, my lord, I know the morning has been...er...fraught with strain, but there is no need to lose your temper."

He began to stalk slowly towards her. "I never lose my temper."

Phoebe's jaw dropped. "But you just threatened to strangle me. Not for the first time, I might add."

"That's right. And I'm going to enjoy every minute of it."

She skipped nimbly behind a chair. "Quite out of the question, sir. Besides, I know you don't mean it. Your family might be fooled by such threats because they're inclined to dramatic utterances themselves, but you're a great deal more controlled than they are and—"

"If you think that, Miss Smith, you're even more innocent than I supposed."

The chair began to look rather flimsy. Phoebe retreated to the far side of the sofa. "Nonsense, my lord. Apart from your outburst in Covent Garden last week, which was quite understandable, you've always behaved with perfect control."

"I'm all too aware of that, Miss Smith. That's another item you can add to the account." He moved closer.

"I'm afraid I don't understand you, sir." Phoebe sidestepped along behind the sofa and measured the distance to a small writing desk. "Perhaps we should sit down and discuss the matter."

"You seem to be more interested in dancing around the furniture."

"I'm trying to avoid being strangled," she retorted with some asperity. "It is not a practice I approve of, sir."

He halted his advance and eyed her consideringly. Phoebe took the opportunity to dart across to the writing table. It wasn't as solid as the sofa, but it was wider.

"You deserve to be strangled," he growled. "Just what would you have done if you'd returned here, alone, to find Toombes waiting for you?"

"I'd have sent him about his business precisely as you did." She paused and thought for a moment. "Er…how did you send Mr Toombes about his business, sir?"

The fiendish gleam came back. "I told him the truth about your position here."

"What!" Phoebe's eyes widened. "What truth? My position here is perfectly respectable."

"You and I know that, Miss Smith, but Mr Toombes, I'm sorry to say, seemed not to approve of the fact that you've visited me, unescorted, on two occasions before most people have left their beds. And when I pointed out that Lord Portlake, not to mention the worthy parishioners of Little Muddleford, wouldn't understand how it came about that you allowed me to purchase your clothes, he—"

"Good heavens! You didn't have to tell him *that!*" Phoebe's voice soared. "What did you think you were about? Are you trying to ruin every shred of reputation I have left?" Forgetting her present danger, she took an agitated turn in the small space behind the table. "Not that I care what Toombes thinks of me, but—"

"I am, of course, relieved to hear you say so, Miss Smith."

"Yes, that's all very well," she retorted, coming to a halt so she could glare at him. "But what if he goes to Lord Portlake with the information that you're providing your nieces' companion with her clothes?"

"Perhaps I should also explain that Toombes left here with the additional impression that if he so much as lets your name pass his lips in future, it will be the last thing he'll every say."

"Oh, my goodness." Phoebe put a hand to the desk and wondered why, when she was absolutely certain Deverell would never strangle *her*, she didn't have the same assurance about Mr Toombes's continued good health. "Really, my lord, you can't go about threatening people like that."

He quirked a brow. "You did want to see the last of Toombes, didn't you?"

"Well, yes, but—" After a futile effort to gather her thoughts, she abandoned the attempt to bring her tormentor to a sense of his inappropriate behaviour. Such attempts were seldom crowned by success when dealing with Deverells anyway. "I don't think I wish to know what you said to the twins," she muttered.

"A wise decision, Miss Smith. However—" he took a deliberate step towards her and fixed her with a narrow-eyed stare "—what *I* wish to know is why you didn't see fit to inform me that this house is being overrun by males and that Crowhurst has been sending you notes capable of making you appear extremely worried, not to say frightened."

"Thripp!" she exclaimed, flushing. "Really! How dare he tell such tales? He's as bad as the rest of you Deverells. I am *not* frightened of Crowhurst. Merely, I thought if I ignored his notes he would eventually desist."

"Indeed." He took another step forward. "And has he?"

"Well…" Suddenly realising she was being stalked again, Phoebe scuttled to the end of the table. She discovered, too late, that an overzealous housemaid had placed a chair at an inviting angle to the desk—right behind her.

In front of her, Deverell loomed.

Phoebe stiffened her spine. "These things take time, my lord. Patience. Resolve." She raised an admonishing finger. "One must stand by one's guns. Hold the line. Um…"

"Never mind the rest," he ordered, coming right up to her. "Miss Smith, you and I are going to come to an understanding."

"We are? I mean…" She raised her finger higher. "*You* must understand, my lord, that—"

"Miss Smith," he interrupted again, very gently, "if I hear one day that one of Toombes's parishioners has strangled him in the middle of a sermon, I will be most understanding. My understanding, however, does not extend to you placing yourself in awkward or dangerous situations with the male half of the population."

Phoebe pursed her lips. "Well, actually, my lord, I believe the proportion of population is not quite half and half. In fact—"

"Obviously words aren't going to do the trick," he muttered. He caught her still-raised hand and tugged.

Phoebe squeaked, stumbled, and found herself landing in a disordered heap against Deverell's chest. Stunned, she gazed mutely from their clasped hands to his face.

"Allow me to remind you once again, Miss Smith, that you are not my governess. As a matter of fact, at present, you are not anybody's governess."

"Yes, I know that, my lord, but—"

"And I'm beginning to believe that your talents as a companion are rather limited. So far this morning I've been compelled to spring my horses out of Town, engage on a battleground that would cause Wellington to blanch, deal with my wards and set an idiot vicar straight on one or two crucial points. All without giving vent to the famous Deverell emotions, Miss Smith."

"Yes, I know that, too, sir, but…"

"Even a controlled Deverell, Miss Smith, has his limits."

"But—"

He circled her waist with his free arm and drew her even closer. Phoebe tried frantically to remember what she'd been about to say. She couldn't seem to think at all. A shivery sense of excitement was racing along every nerve-ending. Her heart fluttered somewhere in her throat. Her breathing halted.

She watched, mesmerised, as he lowered his head until their lips were less than an inch apart.

"And before you remind me of it, Miss Smith, I know this is not part of our agreement, but keep in mind that no sorry details of infelicitous relationships have recently crossed my lips."

His mouth closed over hers with devastatingly gentle mastery.

A thrilling, utterly shocking torrent of excitement poured through her. Sweet, melting weakness followed. Every muscle went limp. She felt his arm tighten across her back, supporting her, holding her locked against him. Heat and strength enveloped her, wrapping her in a mindless haze of increasingly dizzying pleasure as his mouth moved slowly on hers.

Her lips parted on a tiny yearning sigh and suddenly the pressure was no longer gentle. His mouth was hot and hard and fiercely demanding; the arm across her back like iron.

He stroked his tongue across the tingling curve of her lower lip, but even as pleasure burst inside her in streamers of heat, Deverell broke the kiss, jerking his head back so abruptly she felt as if she'd been picked up and tossed about by a wildly eddying whirlwind, only to be as swiftly dumped back to earth. She had to cling to him, her face pressed to his coat, until the room and her senses stopped spinning.

He held her like that, his arm around her waist, his free hand still wrapped about her smaller one. Almost as if they'd been dancing, she thought dazedly, raising her head at last.

Except that her breasts throbbed where they'd been crushed to the hard planes of his chest. She felt unutterably soft and vulnerable and yielding inside. And she doubted the fierce expression glittering in his eyes was to be found in any ballroom.

She drew in a shaky breath, suddenly, overwhelmingly conscious of his much greater strength, of her own softer femininity, and he loosened his hold enough to put an inch or two of space between them. His hand remained at her waist. Big and powerful, it burned like a brand through her gown.

She didn't know why he kept it there. Fleeing from the room wasn't an option. Her legs wouldn't have carried her.

"Well, Miss Smith—" his voice was low, and strangely husky "—at least I didn't strangle you."

"No." Phoebe struggled desperately to think, to follow his lead. If he could shrug off a kiss, then so would she. She could collapse later. "You showed great…self-restraint, my lord."

He smiled at that. A slow smile that made her tremble inside. "You have no idea, Miss Smith."

"No. I…I mean…am I now out of debt, sir?"

For the first time since she'd known him, Deverell seemed to hesitate. His gaze shifted to her mouth. Very slowly he bent his head and brushed his lips lightly across hers. "No," he murmured.

And, releasing her, he turned and strode out of the room.

Phoebe was left staring after him, her mind a complete blank. She didn't move for several minutes. Then, quite abruptly, she put out a hand and lowered herself to the chair behind her. Her other hand lifted to touch her mouth.

What had she done?

The answer was all too evident in the tingling heat and softness of the lips beneath her fingers. She had allowed Deverell to kiss her. She hadn't raised her voice in protest for as much as one second. She had *wanted* him to kiss her.

That was scandalous enough. What was infinitely more devastating was why.

Phoebe groaned and leaned forward to rest her elbows on the desk. She lowered her brow to her clasped hands. Hiding her face, however, did nothing to disguise the truth. The answer could no longer be ignored. The moment of revelation could no longer be pushed aside to wait until later. She had done a very foolish thing. She'd done the most foolish thing a governess could do.

She had fallen in love with her employer.

When had it happened? she wondered, raising her head to stare blankly into space. When Deverell had rescued her in Covent Garden? At Lady Grismead's dancing party? When she'd discovered the statue of Gerald in his studio that morning?

Or earlier, in the Park, when he'd almost tempted her with gentle persuasion to tell him all the secrets of her past?

"Oh, what does it matter?" she exclaimed, leaping to her feet and pacing restlessly to the window and back. She'd had this conversation with herself before. Nothing but disaster could come of such a situation. If she had any sense of self-preservation, she would go upstairs and pack as fast as she was able.

Phoebe stopped pacing and dropped onto the chair again. It was a lowering thought to discover she hadn't any sense at all. Obviously she was more like her mother than she'd been told, because she was actually contemplating throwing away everything, including her reputation, for a love that was unlikely to be reciprocated and could only lead to scandal and disgrace.

That was if Deverell really wanted her. *Truly* wanted her. He might have kissed her, but then he'd all but informed her she should be grateful he hadn't strangled her instead.

This reminder caused a kindling light to dawn in her eyes. If Deverell had sworn undying devotion after that kiss it would be one thing. But no—typical infuriating male—he'd talked of debts. She *should* go upstairs and pack. It would serve him right to be left to cope with his nieces, and Gerald's gambling, and the Grismeads, *and* Miss Pomfret, because that lady would have to be summoned immediately from Kerslake.

But even as she rose and stalked over to the door, Phoebe knew she wasn't going to carry out any revenge. In fact, she admitted gloomily, while one part of her mind was busy ordering herself to dash off a letter to Mrs Arbuthnot's Employment Registry, the other half was issuing reminders that she still had a lecture to deliver to the twins.

And she really should look closely into Gerald's activities.

Then there was the fact that Miss Pomfret's last letter had contained ominous mention of the restorative tonic that had failed in its purpose.

A responsible companion simply couldn't abandon her charges at this point.

But she would not go to Deverell again. Oh, no. If she mentioned Gerald's troubles to him, there was no saying where the debt would end up. Over her head, no doubt. And until she managed to discover some sort of cure, she would be all too willing to drown.

Phoebe sighed and opened the door. For the first time she wished she knew more about the scandal that had sent thunderous reverberations echoing through her own family. She'd known her mother had been cast off; that her father had become a recluse. She'd listened for most of her life to warnings and reproaches every time her behaviour was less than exemplary. But she didn't know the hideous details.

Perhaps she should write to her aunt and ask. Hideous details might help her avoid a path that could only lead to more scandal and recriminations.

She was just wondering why that thought should put

Crowhurst into her head, when the front door bell rang with a particularly urgent-sounding summons.

Still deep in thought, Phoebe absent-mindedly waved Thripp away and crossed the hall to answer it herself. She was speedily snapped back to full attention when Lady Yarwood hurried through the aperture.

"Miss Smith, you're home. Thank goodness! I came as soon as Caroline told me what was afoot. If only she'd mentioned it earlier. But perhaps it is not too late."

"My dear ma'am, please don't fret yourself." Gathering her wits to cope with this relatively minor calamity, Phoebe ushered her breathless visitor into the drawing-room. "You've come about Theodosia's club, I expect. Really, it is too bad. Those dreadful girls! I'll summon them downstairs immediately to apologise for putting you out like this."

"You mean they're here? Safe?" Lady Yarwood sank onto the sofa and fanned herself with one hand. "Thank heavens."

"Yes, indeed." She turned to the butler who had followed them and was watching her with mournful disapproval. "You may take that look off your face, Thripp. Nobody cares if I answer the door on the odd occasion."

"What if it'd been Mr Toombes again?" Thripp demanded in sepulchral accents. "Or that fellow sending notes?"

"Yes, I'd like a word with you about that," Phoebe retorted. "Later, if you please. In the meantime, you may ask Lady Theodosia and—"

"No, no, don't bother them, Miss Smith." Lady Yarwood sat up and straightened her bonnet. "If Caroline's news was precipitate, I'm only too happy to hear it."

"Well, as to that, ma'am, if Miss Yarwood was referring to the first meeting of a certain club for young ladies, she was quite correct. Thanks to Lord Deverell, however, the first meeting was also the last."

"His lordship told me to keep an eye on all the gentlemen running in and out of this house," Thripp declared, Deverell's name apparently stirring him to animation. "Just as well, if you ask me. Someone should know what's going on around here."

"Yes, well, Lord Deverell already has quite enough to do." Phoebe waved Thripp away and sat down beside her visitor.

"It was very good of you to come, ma'am, but I can assure you that the girls are indeed safe. All of them."

"All?" Lady Yarwood blinked at her in dismay. "How many were there?"

"Six or seven," Phoebe admitted, shuddering as she remembered her first sight of the disaster. "If it hadn't been for Deverell— But never mind that. You may be thankful, ma'am, that Miss Yarwood had the good sense not to take part in such an ill-considered romp."

"Believe me, Miss Smith, Caroline is as silly as any young miss with more hair than wit. It was only her brother's refusal to lend his phaeton, and his representations on the matter, that convinced her to come to me in the first place. I dashed around here at once."

"Oh. Well..." Phoebe hesitated and looked down at her hands. "You...er...didn't think to go directly to Deverell, ma'am?"

"Perhaps I should have done so, Miss Smith, but I do know something of the strained relations between Deverell and his family. It occurred to me that if his intervention was necessary, you would have more influence when it came to persuading him to set things right."

Phoebe felt herself turning pink. "I...beg your pardon, ma'am?" she asked weakly.

"Perhaps I'm wrong, my dear, but from the way Deverell's attention scarcely left you the other day—except when he was glaring at any other gentleman who looked as if he might venture too close—I received the distinct impression that his interest in you was more than that of an employer."

"Oh, no. Surely you're mistaken, ma'am."

Lady Yarwood gave her a thoughtful look. "I don't think so, my dear."

"But—"

She stopped, anything as useful as rational thought beyond her. Tremulous hope, niggling doubt and an awareness of harsh reality jostled about in her head until she scarce knew what to think.

"Nothing but disaster could come of such an interest," she finally managed.

"I see you believe you have reason to say so, Miss Smith.

And I must admit that when Yarwood first showed a hint of interest in *me,* I was considerably incensed, having already suffered one nasty experience. But remember, not all men prey on vulnerable females.''

"I dare say not, ma'am, but Deverell has never shown a hint... That is..." She blushed fierily as the memory of his kiss returned in full force. "Well, *that* wasn't what I would call a *hint,*" she blurted aloud before she could stop herself.

Lady Yarwood laughed delightedly.

"Oh, dear, I shouldn't have said that." Phoebe wrung her hands. "What I mean was, that Deverell has never *said*... Indeed, he promised at the outset..."

Again her words tangled in her throat. He'd promised, yes, but suddenly a giant omission from that promise loomed large in her mind.

"Yes, I made it very clear to Yarwood that there would be no undesirable advances if he wished me to join his employ," her ladyship said drily. "It didn't take him long, however, to discover that *his* advances would be far from undesirable to me."

"Oh, dear." Phoebe wrung her hands again.

Lady Yarwood leaned over and stilled her writhing fingers. "There, my dear, I didn't mean to distress you. I may be quite mistaken in Deverell's interest. Although," she added shrewdly, "perhaps you should ask yourself if he would have chased after his nieces at Ottilia Grismead's request."

"He refused to do so at my request, ma'am. I had to threaten him."

Her ladyship looked amused again. "I doubt there are many people in this world who have threatened Deverell and managed to escape unscathed, Miss Smith."

This remark, though clearly intended to reassure, had the opposite effect. Phoebe sank immediately into gloom.

"Yes, ma'am," she agreed sombrely. "I doubt it, too."

Lady Yarwood bestowed a last pat on her hand and rose to her feet. "In any event, whether Deverell is interested in you or not, Miss Smith, I hope you know I would like to stand your friend. If you need assistance or advice at any time, please don't hesitate to come to me."

"Thank you, ma'am." Phoebe rose, also, and tried to paste a polite smile on to her face. "You're very kind."

"Not at all." Lady Yarwood gathered up her reticule and moved towards the door. "I know precisely how difficult your situation can be. And Deverell, unlike everyone else in his family, is a great deal harder to read than Yarwood ever was."

For the second time that day, Phoebe was left staring at the drawing-room door while she contemplated her visitor's parting remark.

It was not, she discovered after a moment of intense examination, altogether discouraging. She, herself, knew that Deverell was harder to read than the rest of his family—and in his dealings with others, it was perfectly true. But, she realised with a quick little uplift of her heart, he had shown her several different sides to his nature. Annoyance, anger, laughter, understanding.

And although she'd always been aware that he possessed the arrogance of a warrior completely sure of himself, this morning she'd seen the vulnerability of a boy unjustly banished from his birthright.

This morning she'd looked into his soul.

Had he meant that to happen?

Phoebe pondered the question for quite some time before she rose and walked over to the door. A new decisiveness was in her step. She might be more foolish than ever. She might be putting a rather desperate sort of faith in Lady Yarwood's opinion. She was definitely risking the destruction of her reputation, and the possible devastation of her heart.

But she knew she couldn't leave Deverell without knowing why he'd allowed her that glimpse of his soul.

Chapter Ten

Despite the improvement in her spirits, Phoebe did not spend the night in restful slumber.

For once, Deverell wasn't wholly to blame for this state of affairs. After Lady Yarwood had left, she had thought to distract herself by concentrating on her charges, her first task being the delivery of a stern lecture to the twins on the differences between the freedom enjoyed by gentlemen of the *ton,* and that allowed young ladies.

Theo and Cressy had watched her with close attention throughout the homily, but Phoebe was left with the impression that they had not listened to a single word. When she ran into Gerald outside the girls' bedchamber, however, her vague suspicions were forgotten. Gerald had been marched down to the drawing-room and ordered to render an account of his recent activities.

He had been all reassurance. There was nothing to worry about. No, no, not a thing. Yes, he had been keeping rather odd hours lately, but everything was all right and tight. Anyone would look pale after spending so much time indoors, but a run of luck had to be pursued. There was absolutely no need for her to concern herself—and could she possible inform him if a minor could draw up a Will?

Phoebe had been so stunned by this mind-numbing question that Gerald had made good his escape while she was wondering if she'd heard him right.

* * *

By three o'clock the following afternoon she was still fretting over the question, and was further thrown into anxiety when Mr Charlton was shown into the drawing-room and immediately demanded to know what was this nonsense about Gerald needing to draw up a Will before he'd reached his majority.

"For I don't mind telling you, Miss Smith, that I'm seriously concerned," he went on, accepting Phoebe's offer of a chair. "I'm all too aware that Gerald has been gambling every night for the past couple of weeks. God knows what sort of company he's fallen into."

"Oh, dear." An anxious frown creased Phoebe's brow. "You don't think he's been so rash as to accuse someone of cheating, do you, sir? What if there should be a duel? Gerald has never engaged in such a thing in his life."

"We can only hope not," Mr Charlton said heavily. His tone held out no hope at all. "But you know what Deverells are like. Try as I might, I can think of no other reason why Gerald would express this sudden desire to draw up his Will. It's not the sort of thing he'd normally consider."

"No." Phoebe thought for a moment, then cast a fleeting glance at her visitor. "I take it, you haven't told Lord Deverell of your suspicions, sir?"

Mr Charlton looked a little self-conscious. "Er…no, ma'am. In light of yesterday's events, I hesitated to bring Deverell's wrath down upon Gerald before I have all the facts. Gerald is very close to his sisters, however. Perhaps, if we were to ask them…"

His suggestion was cut off as the drawing-room door opened to admit the sisters in question. They greeted Mr Charlton with every sign of pleasure, and had scarcely sat down when Lady Grismead, a wilting Pamela in tow, sailed into the room. She did not waste time.

"Never have I been so mortified!" she declared, sweeping Mr Charlton from her path with a puce silk-clad arm as he rose politely. She appropriated his abandoned chair and fixed her nieces with a fulminating eye.

"Perhaps you could tell me," she began ominously, "why it comes about that every young lady in London is this minute explaining chipped paintwork and dented carriage doors to their fathers.''

''Well, Aunt Ottilia, you see—''

''And stripes! How could you, Theodosia? If the gentlemen wish to make fools of themselves by dressing in blue and yellow striped waistcoats, that is one thing. Deverells do not emulate such fashions.''

''But, Aunt Ottilia, we wore dresses.''

Her ladyship shuddered, then proceeded to chastise her nieces in no uncertain terms. Her main grievance seemed not to be the fact that Theodosia had started the Two-in-Hand Club for Lady Whips, but that she'd allowed incompetent drivers to join the ranks.

Shaking her head at the predictable unpredictability of Deverells, Phoebe was about to retire to the window-seat to wait out the storm when the door opened yet again. Gerald and Mr Filby strolled into the room, took one look at its occupants and promptly began to retreat.

''Gerald!'' Phoebe darted forward, raising her voice to be heard above the din created by arguing Deverells.

''Can't stop now, Phoebe,'' Gerald said hastily. ''Reggie and I are on our way to Manton's Shooting Gallery. Just stopped in to collect my pistols.''

This statement, delivered in a tone of airy unconcern, was enough to cause Phoebe to grasp Gerald's coat with both hands and haul him bodily back into the room. The thought crossed her mind that had it been Deverell she'd been trying to haul, the tactic would never have worked.

She instantly dismissed such useless meanderings.

''Just for once,'' she told Gerald in minatory accents, ''you can stay here and help entertain your aunt and cousin. And I believe Mr Charlton has something to say to you.'' She turned to Filby with a determined smile. ''Mr Filby, I have been wishing since yesterday to hear more about your brilliant idea of coat lapels to match one's carriage. Shall we sit over there by the window?''

No fool, Filby began to look hunted. Unfortunately for him, his manners precluded any other action but compliance. He followed her to the window-seat, his demeanour that of one approaching a designated place of execution.

"See you have quite a crowd," he began with rather desperate chattiness as Phoebe seated herself. "Bit hard on the ears, so many Deverells at once. Not that Miss Grismead ever says much. Seems to prefer draping herself over the furniture. Always wondered, y'know, if she actually has any bones."

Phoebe smiled despite herself. "An interesting theory, Mr Filby."

"Once had a bet on it at White's," he confided, looking more at ease. "But no one could think of a way to prove anything one way or the other."

"Indeed, sir." Phoebe firmly suppressed the urge to laugh and turned an uncompromising look on him. "I believe the Betting Book at White's is not the only form of gambling enjoyed by some gentlemen."

"Well, if you mean Gerald," said Filby, apparently deciding to take the bull by the horns, "no need to worry he'll end in the River Tick. Inherited Deverell's talent for mathematics. Never loses."

"Never?" Phoebe's brain reeled. She'd been so beset by visions of Gerald signing away Kerslake Park to some monster who preyed on green boys from the country, and in despair challenging said monster to a duel, that she'd never even considered the alternative.

Perhaps Deverell was right. She *had* been reading too many novels.

"Soon be rich," Filby added, not without a touch of pride. "Well, richer than he is now. Never seen anything like it. Figures the odds before you can say knife. Wants to repair the family fortunes, you know."

"Well, I'm sure that's very commendable," Phoebe began, still coping with this reversal of every plot she'd ever read. "But, in that case, why would Gerald wish to draw up his Will? And why is he going to Manton's?"

"Oh, nothing in that. Everyone goes there. Well, not ladies, of course, but…"

"Mr Filby, has Gerald accused someone of cheating and demanded satisfaction?"

He began to look hunted again. "No, no, nothing of the sort. Other way about. I mean—" he gasped as one going down for the last time "—all an unfortunate misunderstanding."

"Oh, good heavens! Then there *is* going to be a duel!"

"Shouldn't mention such things to ladies," Filby yelped frantically. "Only send you into a fit of the vapours."

"Mr Filby, it seems to be you who is having a fit of the vapours, but let me assure that I will immediately join you in the exercise if you don't tell me everything you know. Right now!"

Filby blinked several times in an agitated fashion, then capitulated. "Told Gerald he shouldn't play at the Pigeonhole," he whispered, as if anyone could have heard him over the voices of Deverells *en masse*. "Full of Sharps and Flats." Heartened by an encouraging nod, he continued. "Trouble was, once everyone at the proper clubs realised how good Gerald was, they'd only play a few games at a time with him. One thing about Sharps, they always think tonight will be the night they'll fleece someone, so they continue to play. But Gerald didn't get fleeced."

"The Sharp turned into a Flat?"

"Very neatly put, ma'am. Rather well-heeled Sharp, though. Didn't seem too concerned about losing, at first. Usually when that happens they cast about for another victim, but two nights ago he suddenly accused Gerald of cheating."

"Oh, my goodness!"

Filby nodded soberly. "Very nasty business. Ain't likely a Deverell's going to take that in the face and walk away. Took three of us to keep Gerald from beating the fellow to a pulp. Creech—that's the Sharp—challenged him at once, and Gerald accepted. I'm one of his seconds," he added, sinking into gloom. "Offered immediately. Nothing else to be done."

"Oh, yes, there is something else to be done," Phoebe announced trenchantly. "I understand the first duty of a second, Mr Filby, is to effect a reconciliation."

"Already tried it," Filby answered. "Very obstinate fellow, Creech. Seems determined to put a bullet in Gerald. Wouldn't apologise, even when I pointed out that Gerald couldn't have cheated because they were playing with the House cards. Surprised he didn't challenge *me* when I said that. Not the thing at all."

"But did you also point out that Gerald is a minor? I'm not

perfectly certain about such things, but surely any gentleman would hesitate to shoot a boy Gerald's age.''

Filby shook his head. "Tried that, too. Creech told me he'd never withdrawn from an affair of honour and he wasn't going to start now.''

"You mean this dreadful creature has fought duels before?'' Phoebe gazed at Filby in dismay while hideous visions of Gerald's lifeless body being carted into the house flashed through her mind. "Then there's nothing else for it. Gerald will have to go to Deverell.''

Filby so far forgot himself as to sink his chin into his cravat. "Won't do it, ma'am. Suggested it m'self, but he refused point-blank. Seems Deverell likes to go about strangling people. Doesn't sound too likely to me. Haven't heard of any corpses lying about, for one thing, but Gerald seemed very certain.''

"Oh, for goodness' sake, of course Deverell doesn't strangle people,'' Phoebe exclaimed, quite exasperated. "Although, after this, he'll probably make an exception in Gerald's case.''

After this unanswerable conclusion, a rather melancholy silence descended upon them. Phoebe tried vainly to think of a way to extract Gerald from his obligations without involving Deverell in yet another disaster. Mr Filby appeared to have sunk into a mindless torpor.

"You said you're *one* of Gerald's seconds,'' she finally recalled. "Who's the other?''

"Crowhurst,'' Filby answered glumly. "He was playing at the next table that night. Good of him to offer, I suppose, but he hasn't been particularly helpful.''

"Perhaps not to you, Mr Filby, but surely he wouldn't refuse a lady's request.''

Filby frowned. "I don't know, ma'am. I know you and Crowhurst are friends, but to tell you the truth, he's not quite…''

"Lord Crowhurst exaggerated when he called us friends,'' she interrupted hastily. "I hardly know the man, but—''

Before she could explain the situation further, they were interrupted from an unexpected quarter. Miss Grismead floated up to them, obliging Mr Filby to rise to his feet. Under his fascinated gaze, she crumpled slowly and gracefully onto the window-seat, transforming herself into a limp heap of pale blue muslin.

"Miss Smith," she breathed in accents that would have led anyone to believe her next words would be her last, "I wonder if I might have a word with you?"

Only too happy to take a hint, Filby swept a magnificent bow. "Must pay my respects to your mother, Miss Grismead. Your very obedient servant, Miss Smith."

"We shall continue our conversation later, Mr Filby," Phoebe said with heavy meaning. But Filby was already making good his escape.

Not that he was going far, Phoebe consoled herself, as she watched him fall into the clutches of Lady Grismead. She heard her ladyship demand his expert opinion on the proper costume for a Ladies' Driving Club and decided Filby would still be within easy reach when she'd finished with Pamela.

When she turned to her visitor, Miss Grismead fixed her with a soulful gaze and managed the enormous effort of clasping her hands together. "Miss Smith, I must and will speak with you. You're my Last Hope."

"I am?" Phoebe blinked at her, momentarily distracted from Gerald's problems.

"Yes, indeed. I know you are aware of my situation. How could you not be, when Papa so brutally refused to countenance my betrothal to dearest Norvel the other day? In front of *everyone!*"

"Well, I don't think he refused precisely, Miss Grismead. He seemed to think—"

"It is all of a piece," stated Miss Grismead, waving away anyone else's thoughts on the matter. "But I was struck, Miss Smith, by your sympathy. By your courage in mentioning the Fatal Word in front of Mama. By your—"

Phoebe gazed at her, mesmerised. "Fatal Word?"

Miss Grismead glanced about the room, assured herself that no one was listening, and leaned closer. "Poetry," she whispered.

"Oh. That Fatal Word."

"I knew in that moment you'd been Sent."

"Sent?"

"To aid me in my affliction."

"Well, actually, I came up to London to demand help on my own account, but—"

"Yes, I know. From Deverell. You see. It is all Meant."

"Meant?"

Pamela nodded. "Deverell will never listen to me, Miss Smith, but if *you* ask him to help us, he won't refuse."

Phoebe started to wonder if she'd missed something, somewhere along the line. "Naturally, I'd be happy to help you in any way I can, Miss Grismead, but—"

"*Thank you,* Miss Smith, thank you. I knew I could depend on you." Pamela rose to her feet. She managed the task so gradually that Phoebe held her breath, expecting her visitor to collapse back onto the seat at any moment. So fascinated was she by the procedure, she completely failed to comprehend that Pamela considered her task done.

"I knew you wouldn't refuse to exercise your influence to ensure the Happiness of one who will be Forever Grateful."

"Influence!" Phoebe's pent-up breath rushed out in a startled whoosh. By the time she'd recovered, Miss Grismead had drifted back to the sofa where she appeared to fall asleep. Phoebe was not fooled. She had just been struck by the unpleasant realisation that Miss Grismead's languishing pose gave her plenty of opportunity for observation.

Heat stung her cheeks as she wondered what, exactly, Pamela had observed to cause her to say practically the same things that Lady Yarwood had said yesterday? Had she betrayed herself in some way before she'd even been aware of her own feelings for Deverell? But even if she had, surely Deverell hadn't done anything to cause two such diverse personalities to assume she had any influence over him?

Phoebe gripped her hands together, fighting a whirling torrent of emotions while her mind see-sawed dizzily between alarm that she'd made a public spectacle of herself, and a quite improper hope that Deverell wasn't indifferent to her.

Hope, she discovered to her shock, even a tiny, tremulous hope, was stronger than any amount of alarm. It took several minutes of severe self-chastisement before she managed to drag her mind back to more important matters. She had to prevent Gerald's untimely demise on the field of honour. And she would also try to persuade Deverell to help Pamela.

She wanted to see him reconciled with his family, she realised, with a little pang of her heart. She didn't want him to be alone anymore. He had stopped being a warrior. Now it was time he…

Before she could finish the thought, the door was flung open with a flourish, and Thripp ushered Deverell into the room.

Phoebe's entire body went rigid. She went hot all over. She was positive she was one big blush. Every thought in her mind vanished, leaving only the memory of his kiss. The warmth and gentleness; the strength of his arms; the fierce demand of his mouth on hers in the instant before he'd wrenched away.

Dismayed, trembling, suddenly realising that all conversation had been momentarily suspended, she whipped her head around to face the window, fighting the sensations aroused by his arrival. Given the choice, she would have fled from the room, but what would everyone think?

On the other hand, she couldn't stay here, gazing rudely out of the window when the drawing-room was full of visitors. What if Deverell ignored everyone else and approached her as he'd done at Lady Grismead's dancing party? Every eye would be upon them. Everyone would think what Pamela and Lady Yarwood were already thinking.

Completely unnerved by the possibility, Phoebe leapt up and scurried over to take cover in the crowd. Collapsing onto the chair next to Mr Filby, she pressed a hand to her middle. A futile gesture, she thought despairingly. It was going to take more than a shaking hand to still the butterflies dancing a reel in her stomach.

"Cressy, perhaps you might ring for some tea," she managed distractedly, breaking into that damsel's conversation with Mr Filby.

"Yes, of course, Phoebe." Cressida glanced at her uncle, then gave her a sweet smile that had alarm bells jangling once more in Phoebe's head. She felt more like an insect on a pin than ever.

"Glad you came over," Filby muttered out of the corner of his mouth. His furtive manner had her mind struggling back to Gerald's plight. "Got something to say. Better say it quick. Deverell's chatting to his secretary, but no telling when that might change. After all, he can talk to Charlton any time, can't he?"

She resisted the urge to scream. "Do you have an idea, Mr Filby?"

He nodded. "Brilliant notion. Can't think why it didn't occur before. Deverell won't give me the time of day. Will only strangle Gerald." He paused and beamed at her. "*You'll* have to tell him."

"*Me!*" She stared at him. "Oh, no, not you, too, Mr Filby."

He blinked. "Beg your pardon, ma'am?"

"Oh, dear. What am I saying? Really, I hardly know... Please take no notice, sir."

"All a bit much," he said with perfect understanding. "Shouldn't have suggested it. Bit alarming, isn't he? Rather large. Can quite understand why you wouldn't want to be strangled either, ma'am. Better try Crowhurst first."

"Yes," she agreed weakly, quite unequal to the task of explaining her incoherence. "Perhaps you're right, Mr Filby."

"No hurry," he assured her, rising. "Meeting's not for another two days. Insisted that Gerald have time to practise. Only fair."

"Oh, my goodness."

"Must go. See Deverell wishes to speak with you. Very obedient..."

He was gone before the last words were out.

"What a very strange effect I seem to have on Filby," Deverell observed blandly as he approached. He turned Filby's vacated chair slightly towards her and sat down, one arm resting along the low curved back. "Why do you suppose that is, Miss Smith?"

She shook her head, not risking even the most fleeting of glances at him. She didn't need to look at him to know that his hand was resting only inches from her shoulder, that his gaze was fixed unwaveringly on her face. She could feel the heat and intensity in him as if they were actually touching.

"Hmm. I see I've put myself beyond the pale." His voice lowered, sending a shiver down her spine. "Aren't you even going to greet me, Phoebe?"

"Good afternoon, sir." Her own voice showed a distressing tendency to squeak. Phoebe cleared her throat and sat up straighter. "Did you wish to consult with me about something?"

"Nobody would remark upon it, if I did, you know."

Her gaze flashed to his.

He smiled, but those aquamarine eyes were watchful. "That's better. Would you mind telling me why you're behaving as if I kissed you in front of my entire family yesterday, instead of privately?"

"For goodness' sake, my lord! You must have run mad!"

His smile turned wry. "An unnerving possibility."

"No, not because of *that!*" She gestured wildly in her agitation. "What if someone had heard you just now?"

Deverell obligingly followed the direction of her hand. "Gerald and Filby have escaped, Theodosia and Edward aren't paying the slightest attention to anyone else, and my aunt is arguing with Cressida about which theatre to attend tomorrow night. Pamela appears to be the only one interested in our conversation, and that's probably because she's hoping you'll persuade me to cast a vote in Nermal's favour."

"Norvel," she corrected faintly. "And how did you know that, sir?"

His lips twisted. "I know my family, Miss Smith. However, before you embark on a futile course of action, I wish to apologise to you."

Phoebe's mouth fell open. She instantly clamped it shut again.

"Deverells do apologise on occasion," he murmured, a wicked smile lighting his eyes.

"Yes," she agreed by now quite distracted. "Bowls of gruel."

A quizzical brow shot up. "I beg your pardon?"

"Nothing, my lord. I mean…" She made a heroic effort to pull herself together. "Every time Theo and Cressy apologise, they offer me bowls of gruel or mustard plasters. Heaven knows why."

"Probably fell into the habit with Cousin Clara," he suggested drily. He hesitated, then seemed to choose his next words carefully. "I'm afraid I can only offer my regrets that I've made you uneasy in my company, Miss Smith. It was inexcusable of me to take my frustrations with my wards out on you."

"Frus— Oh. Yes. Yes, I see."

"I doubt it," he muttered, then, raising his voice, "it would have given me great pleasure to have despatched them back to Kerslake yesterday. Unfortunately, I'm unable to do that."

"No, my lord. Er...why not?"

He met her gaze. "And abandon you to your fate, Miss Smith? Or have you leave?"

"Oh," she said again. "Yes, I suppose I did threaten you, sir."

He laughed softly. "You did. But don't let your conscience bother you. There have been...compensations."

Oh, dear, how was she to take *that?* Now her heart didn't know where it was supposed to be. It was probably safer to leave it in the vicinity of her feet, whence it had plummeted as soon as Deverell had implied he'd kissed her out of frustration with his nieces. But then, what compensations was he referring to? So far, all she'd done was involve him in one imbroglio after another. Something he didn't seem to appreciate.

Especially as no one in his family seemed to appreciate him.

But he was wrong, she thought, intercepting a fleeting, keen-eyed glance from Lady Grismead. She was sure her ladyship would soften towards him, given the chance.

And she was going to see that he received that chance, Phoebe vowed again. She knew what it was like to be isolated through no fault of one's own. He shouldn't have to endure his aunt's disapproval, when a simple favour might put things right. He shouldn't have to spend his life fashioning statues, whose pleading arms wrenched at her heart.

If she did nothing else for him, she would heal the rift with his family.

"Compensations," she repeated brightly, as though suddenly struck by the notion. She avoided the amused gleam in his eyes and gathered her thoughts in the manner of a general mustering troops. "Well, I'm pleased to hear you say so, my lord. That is one thing about Deverells. They're seldom boring. I'm sure as you come to know your family better, you—"

"I wasn't talking about my family, Miss Smith."

"Well, I was!" she retorted, cross at this lack of cooperation. "Whether you like it or not, my lord, you do have a family. I..." She hesitated and her voice softened. "I know you were treated harshly in the past, but surely your father's actions can't

be laid at the Grismeads' door. If you would only offer to
help—''

The faint smile in his eyes vanished abruptly beneath a layer
of ice. ''I have no intention of assisting any member of my
family in the follies they choose to commit, Miss Smith.''

Phoebe heaved an exasperated sigh. ''My lord, it is no use
trying to make me believe you are heartless. You aren't.''

''Indeed?''

''No. You'll always assist your family, even if you don't
particularly like some of them.''

His eyes narrowed. ''Why would I do that?''

''Because you are a man of honour, sir. Don't bother trying
to convince me otherwise. I know better.''

''Do you? What makes you so damn certain of that?'' His
voice was even more frigid than his eyes.

Phoebe took a deep breath, as though she was about to
plunge into those icy depths. ''Because you think your family
believes otherwise, and that hurts you,'' she all but whispered.

The silence hanging between them almost vibrated with the
echo of her words. Sebastian stared at Phoebe, buffeted by so
many conflicting emotions he could only hold himself savagely
in check while the storm howled within him. The sensation
was stunningly similar to the one he'd felt when he'd been
confronted by his father all those years ago. The sudden sense
of vulnerability, the frustration, the helpless rage at having the
hurt place deep inside him stripped bare.

But...this time...there was something else. Something that
held him here, waiting. Something that warred viciously with
his desire to draw Phoebe closer. Something that goaded him
to see how far he could push her blithe certainty, even while
the fear that he could push her too far sank icy claws into his
gut.

The conflict was so intense, so agonising, he had to glance
away from her before he could speak.

''You're mistaken, Miss Smith.''

She shook her head. ''Actually, you know, they don't consider you dishonourable in the least.''

''Oh?'' He looked back at her, one brow raised. ''You have
an intimate acquaintance with their innermost thoughts as well
as my own?''

"No," she said softly, ignoring his sarcasm. "But I do know Deverells, and I shouldn't think Gerald and the girls have given the matter a moment's thought. They would have been far too young when you left England to have had an opinion on the subject. As for the Grismeads, you intimidate them. You see, instead of chastising you, your years away have made you very much stronger than they are. They know it, and they know you know it. That's why they're so wary of you."

She smiled with sudden mischief. "You also take a delight in giving your aunt apoplexy, but she is still ready to approve of you if you'd only give her the chance."

That smile went straight to his heart. She hadn't even taken his bad-tempered denials into account. Sebastian realised. She was far too busy trying to convince him that his family no longer considered him a disgrace. *She* believed in him, and that was that.

He went utterly still as the knowledge sank into the dark place in his soul.

Phoebe believed in him. Without any evidence to the contrary.

The raging conflict within him abruptly coalesced into a surge of desire so violent he almost shook with it. His hand clenched hard around the back of the chair. He didn't dare move a muscle. It took every ounce of self-control he'd learned over the years not to reach out, drag her into his arms and make her his here and now.

He'd known she was necessary to him, but this sudden savage desire…this *need*. This yearning to sink into her warmth and belief in him so he'd never be alone again—he'd never felt anything like it. His body ached with wanting her, but it was more than that. His heart…his very soul…hungered.

God damn it, he was starving for her.

Shaken, Sebastian managed to unlock his clenched jaw so he could speak. "My aunt doesn't approve of anything, Miss Smith."

She tilted her head slightly, the mischievous gleam taking on a touch of provocation. "Why don't you try it and see?"

The challenge dragged a reluctant laugh from him. "I did say, didn't I, that you're more than a match for any Deverell? Little did I know how true that was."

She clasped her hands. "Then you'll do it?"

"What, precisely, is 'it,' Miss Smith?"

"Merely what you do so well, sir." Her mouth curved in a way that deepened the tiny dimples at its corners. "Intimidate Mr Hartlepoole into behaving sensibly and assist the Grismeads out of their financial quagmire."

Sebastian took a deep breath. "Is that all?"

She nodded.

"And what do I receive in exchange?"

For the first time, since he'd startled her out of her nervousness, she began to look wary. "Er…your family's gratitude?"

He started to smile. Damned if he was going to be the only one suffering here. Leaning closer, he deliberately lowered his voice. "Not enough, Miss Smith."

She looked more wary than ever. "Um…the knowledge that you've done the right thing?"

"Still not enough."

"Well, I don't know what more you expect, but—"

"Keep in mind that, despite your little speech on the subject, I'm not doing this for my family but for quite a different reason, and I'm sure the answer will come to you."

Phoebe swallowed, immediately rendered speechless. A shivery sense of excitement raced through her body as though tiny bubbles of heat were sizzling in her veins. Everything tingled, even her fingers and toes. The tremulous hope that Deverell wasn't indifferent to her was both thrilling and terrifying.

Thank goodness she hadn't mentioned Gerald's predicament to him, she thought inconsequentially. She was already drowning in those intense, glittering eyes. When they lowered to her mouth and lingered there for a heart-stopping moment, it was almost as if he was kissing her again.

"Yes," he growled very softly when his gaze returned to hers, "you know the answer, Miss Smith."

She swallowed again. "I don't think…"

He smiled slowly. "There's no need to think. The details will have to wait until a more convenient time anyway." He rose, still watching her from beneath half-lowered lashes. "I shall report back to you, Miss Smith, when my tasks are done."

Phoebe couldn't summon the breath for even the briefest of

farewells. She watched Deverell bow to his aunt—while sending a glinting sidelong look at her that plainly told her he was adding the courtesy to her debt—and leave.

Before the door was fully shut, her thoughts were whirling around and around like ribbons on a maypole. She couldn't seem to catch hold of any one of them. The arrival of Thripp with refreshments went almost unnoticed. She was aware of Theodosia dispensing tea and cakes, but it was like watching everything from another place.

What was she to do? What was she to make of Deverell's remarks?

She felt torn, unbearably torn, between her belief in his honour and the painful awareness that the most honourable man in the world might not offer anything but a *carte blanche* to a governess whose past was still largely shrouded in mystery. She had no dowry, no land, no prospects, and a family who refused to publicly acknowledge the connection. What else was she to think?

And yet he'd said she was innocent.

Phoebe felt her heart constrict so sharply her lips parted on a silent cry of pain.

There *was* one other alternative. One she hadn't considered until now. One that filled her with so much desolation she couldn't bear it.

If an honourable man had no intention of marrying her, he wouldn't offer anything at all.

He might tease her because she'd persuaded him to go against his personal inclinations in assisting his family. He might even kiss her because he'd been driven to the edge of his control.

But he wouldn't ruin her.

The realisation that she wouldn't care about being ruined occurred and was dismissed. It no longer had the power to stir so much as a ripple. She loved him. She would accept an offer of any kind, for as long as Deverell wanted her. Because when love was placed on the balance, the consequences weighed nothing.

Unfortunately, despite several hours spent in contemplation of the subject after the guests had departed, she couldn't think of a way around the situation. Knowing that Deverell had been unjustly punished for suspect conduct in the past, precluded her from trying to tempt him into definitely scandalous conduct now.

Even if she'd known how to deliberately tempt a man against his more honourable inclinations.

All she could do was treasure every moment she spent with him in the months she had left. To gather memories and store them. To hold them in her heart against the time when she'd have to leave. There was really no other option.

The prospect was so depressing, it was almost a relief to turn her mind to the problem of how she was to approach Crowhurst.

Chapter Eleven

In the end it was all quite simple. She sent a message to Crowhurst, asking him to call on her the next day on a matter of business, and when he arrived she stationed Thripp, already forewarned, in the hall.

At least, it was meant to be quite simple. Her plan should have worked. Unfortunately, she had forgotten that she wasn't dealing with a gentleman.

"You'll have to pardon me if I seem a little surprised by your invitation, Phoebe," Crowhurst began to say as he sat down on the chair she indicated. His pale brows rose slightly when Thripp departed, leaving the drawing-room door wide open and remaining in plain sight in the hall, diligently polishing the stair-rail.

"And in view of the fact that Deverell has informed me that the next note I send you will be my last, isn't it a little indiscreet for us to be meeting under the roof he's providing for you, and under the eye of a butler who's engaged in a task more suited to the under-housemaid?"

"No doubt you're accustomed to noticing such nuances, my lord," Phoebe retorted before she could stop herself. "You may also have noticed that it is Lord Deverell's wards who live under this roof. They, or rather one of them, is the reason I asked you here today."

Crowhurst smiled mockingly. "Yes, I can appreciate that you'd prefer some privacy."

She took a deep breath, determined to ignore the implied insults. "I wish to speak with you about Gerald, sir. About his forthcoming engagement with a certain Mr Creech, to be exact."

Crowhurst's eyes narrowed. He watched her for a few unnerving seconds, then sat back and crossed one leg over the other. "I take it Filby has been busy. You'd better get rid of the butler, Phoebe. Or close the door."

"Thripp is completely devoted to Gerald," she informed him. "If he does hear anything, it will go no further. Besides," she added, descending from these lofty heights, "I've already informed him of the situation. He knows I'm trying to save Gerald."

She didn't add that Thripp had threatened to go to Deverell with the tale if she didn't succeed.

"How very heroic of you, my dear," Crowhurst drawled. "I wish you every success."

Phoebe straightened her spine. The interview was not going as she'd planned, but she refused to give up. "Success, sir, may depend upon you. Mr Filby has already failed in his attempt to bring about a reconciliation, but there's still hope. This Creech person may listen to an older man."

"You expect me to visit him?"

"Will you not do so, sir?" She leaned forward, clasping her hands. "The fact that Gerald has never fought a duel in his life, and is still a minor, must weigh heavily on a gentleman acting as a second. Surely you'd wish to do everything in your power to bring about a happy resolution."

Another silence fell as Crowhurst seemed to consider both her and her words. His expression never changed, but Phoebe felt her skin start to crawl under his appraising stare.

"A happy resolution," he repeated. "That, my dear Phoebe, might take considerable effort on my part. I believe…" He paused and smiled faintly. "Yes, I really do believe that if I help you, some recompense will be in order."

Phoebe rose at once. "Then this interview is at an end, sir. Good day."

"You think so?" he snarled suddenly, coming to his feet. His hands clenched and unclenched by his sides. His lips drew back in a grimace of rage as he glared at her.

The transformation from mockery to menace was so swift, so unexpected, that Phoebe's entire body jolted. She backed away, putting her chair between them, the similarity of the situation to the one two days ago when she'd retreated from Deverell's wrath striking her with stunning force.

The same circumstances; two such different men. How could anyone think Deverell dishonourable, she thought, angry and hurting for him, when men like Crowhurst existed?

"Do I have to call Thripp to show you out?" The ice in her voice, born of anger and contempt, seemed to throw Crowhurst off stride for a moment. He shook his head, as if he hadn't expected her to respond like that, and made a visible effort to control his fury.

"We haven't finished, Phoebe."

"We never started, sir. I was labouring under the misapprehension that, as Gerald's second, you would wish to assist him. I see I was mistaken. There's only one thing to be done, and I should have done it in the first place. Go to Lord Deverell."

The expression that flashed into his pale eyes had her hands gripping the chair tightly, but his voice was still controlled. Sibilantly soft, it slid over her nerves like ice-water over bare flesh. So might a snake speak, she thought, before striking.

"Why do you think I'm reluctant to serve you in this regard, Phoebe? Go to Deverell, by all means. Pour out the tale of Gerald's woes. I'm sure you'll find he's already aware of the situation and intends to do nothing about it."

Her hands gripped the chair tighter. "What do you mean?"

"It's all quite simple, my dear. Ask yourself who would have reason to desire Kerslake's death. Who will benefit from the likely outcome of this duel? Who, indeed, is in a position to arrange for such a challenge to be issued in the first place?"

Phoebe stared at him, shocked speechless. "You're mad," she whispered at last. "Deverell has no reason to want Gerald dead. Why should he?"

"Why? There's the title for a start. Then—"

"But Deverell has his own title." Still reeling from Crowhurst's insinuations, she shook her head. "He's wealthy, he…"

"Ah, yes. Wealthy. Riches he acquired as a result of exile. Do you think even wealth such as Deverell's would influence a man bent on revenge against the family who banished him in the first place? As for his title: what's a new barony against an earldom several centuries old? I think you'll find, Phoebe, that when the evidence mounts up—"

"That evidence may weigh with you, sir," she retorted, abruptly restored to her wits. "But as has already been made perfectly clear to me, you and Deverell are entirely different. Kindly take your leave. I will strive to forget that this conversation ever took place."

"Strive to forget it?" he hissed back, taking a step forward and speaking so quickly the words almost slurred together. "Do you think to fob me off so easily? Do you think I'll forget you asked me here to assist a Deverell? Do you think you can crook your finger and I'll come running, even while you're living under another man's protection? Go to him, then. See who's right and who's wrong. See—"

"My lord, for goodness' sake..." From the corner of her eye, she saw Thripp move towards them.

"You come to London to haunt me. You set up house with Deverell. The one man you knew it would kill me to see you with. You—"

"My lord, *please*..."

Crowhurst stopped. He glared at her, his eyes unfocused, staring blankly at something—or someone—only he could see.

Phoebe swallowed and tried to think of something to say. She'd been rendered totally off-balance by Crowhurst's attack. Not only the unexpectedness of it, but the extent of his rage was beyond what was reasonable. Clearly he wasn't entirely sane. Especially on the subject of Deverell.

And it was all too obvious that, in his frenzy, he'd mistaken her for the lady with whom he'd had that long-ago affair. She didn't know what to do. All she could think about was the fastest method of getting him out of the house, and yet she couldn't help feeling a sense of pity.

Glancing past Crowhurst, she motioned Thripp to remain in the hall. "Look about you, sir," she said, gesturing to their surroundings. "Do you see any sign of Deverell living here? I'm companion to his nieces, nothing more. Nor do you do yourself—or, indeed the lady you once cared for—any credit by insulting me like this."

"Do you think I care about that?" he muttered. The fixed glare was fading, but he continued to stare at her with a kind of brooding purpose that was even more disturbing. "I haven't cared about anything since you left."

"My lord…" Phoebe took a deep breath and tried to instil as much gentle firmness into her voice as possible. "I'm very sorry for your pain, but…I'm not who you think I am."

He seemed not even to hear her. "I know who you are," he grated and, turning on his heel, walked out of the house.

Several hours later, Phoebe had forgotten all about Crowhurst and his problems. Indeed, she was so worried about Gerald, who hadn't put in an appearance all day, she even managed to prevent her heart from somersaulting more than once or twice when Deverell at last strolled into the drawing-room.

She stopped pacing to scowl at him. "My lord! At last! Where have you been? Didn't you receive my notes?"

"All three of them," he replied, crossing the room to her. A wry smile curved his mouth. "I'm willing to do a lot for you, Phoebe, but being in three places at once is impossible. Even for me."

"But I haven't asked you to be in three places at once! Really, my lord—" She stopped, her indignation vanishing under the impact of his wicked smile. That same smile that at once puzzled and disturbed and excited.

Wrapping her arms across her waist, she took a firm grip on her elbows. It was better than flinging herself at him and taking a firm grip on him, which was what she really wanted to do.

"*Where* have you been?" she demanded, forcing her mind back to the matter at hand.

"I," he said virtuously, "have been obeying the first of your orders, Miss Smith. I've been engaged with Nermal."

"Oh, my goodness," she uttered weakly. "You didn't call him 'Nermal' to his face, did you?"

Deverell tilted his head while he considered the matter. "Actually, now I come to think about it, I don't remember calling him anything at all. I merely pointed out a few facts." He regarded the way she was holding on to herself and raised his eyes to her face. ''I take it you don't wish to hear about the interview?''

''No. Yes! I mean...not now, my lord. Something much worse than Nermal's stubborn— Oh, heavens, now you've got me doing it. I mean, something much worse than Mr Hartle-poole's—''

''Phoebe...'' His voice lowered and went dark. A large hand was laid across her lips. ''Hush.''

Phoebe went utterly still. Even her breathing stopped.

''Unless,'' he continued very softly, ''the girls have taken up scientific experiments that threaten to blow up the house while we're in it, I really don't care what has happened.''

She tried to take a breath and felt her lips brush against his fingers. Tiny shivers of sensation coursed through her body, tightening her throat and turning her knees to water. She made an inarticulate sound and he lifted his hand. But only to trace the line of her jaw with one long finger, to stroke the curve of her ear, to retrace the path to her chin. He tilted her face up to his.

''If...if only that was all,'' she managed to say, amazed she could speak at all. She'd never known that a light caressing touch to her ear could cause such a quivering in the pit of her stomach. She focused desperately on Deverell's cravat and tried to recall why she'd summoned him. ''It's Gerald.''

''Gerald?''

''He's engaged himself to fight a duel with a dreadful man called Creech.''

Deverell smiled faintly and lowered his hand. ''Yes, I know.''

''You know?'' Phoebe's gaze flashed up to his. The faint echoes of sensation quivering inside her abruptly stilled. ''*You know!* Then what do you intend to do about it, my lord?''

''I've already done it,'' he said calmly. ''Creech has been...ah...persuaded to acknowledge the rashness of his challenge by apologising on the field.''

''Oh, thank goodness!'' Phoebe's stunned expression changed with lightning speed to a brilliant smile. ''Now Gerald will be able to cease pretending that he hasn't been worried out of his mind for the past few days.''

Deverell didn't seem unduly moved by the prospect. ''Not

quite. You, Miss Smith, will behave towards Gerald as if nothing has happened. It won't hurt him to lose a few nights' sleep over the matter. He's as much at fault for being cozened into playing in an out-and-out Hell in the first place."

"Oh." Her smile lost some of its brilliance. "You want to teach Gerald a lesson."

"Precisely."

"Well, I suppose your intention is admirable, my lord, but—"

This time he captured her chin on the edge of his hand. "I thought I asked you to trust me, Phoebe."

"I do trust you," she retorted, valiantly striving to ignore the resumption of dancing butterflies in her stomach. "But how was I to know you were even aware of the situation?"

"There were any number of people at the Pigeonhole that night who were only too ready to apprise me of it," he said drily. "If anyone should have remained ignorant of the situation, it was you." His brows met. "Don't tell me Gerald ran to you for help."

"No, of course not."

"Then it must have been Filby. No wonder he fled yesterday. Damn it, I ought to seek him out and throw a real scare into him for upsetting you like this."

"It wasn't Mr Filby's fault. He tried to persuade Gerald to confide in you, but because you're forever threatening to strangle your wards, Gerald refused to do so."

"So now it's my fault?" A faint smile edged his mouth. The fist beneath her chin stroked briefly, gently.

"Well…" She swallowed, intensely aware of the size and warmth of his hand. She didn't know whether she was supposed to ignore his touch or object to it. When his knuckles stroked down her throat and back again, she shivered and rushed into speech.

"Threats of strangulation are not conducive to happy relationships, my lord. It is one thing to strangle bandits in India. I dare say they were trying to rob you at the time. It must have been vastly inconvenient, but—"

"There's nothing for it," he murmured. "I see I shall have to kiss you again."

"Oh. Oh. Well…"

"If you have no objection, of course."

"Objection?" she squeaked. She felt herself blushing wildly as his other arm went around her, drawing her closer until she was nestled against him...melting against him, she realised in wonder, her softer curves accommodating themselves to his bigger, harder frame as though they'd been lovers forever.

The thought made her tremble. Somewhere in the back of her mind she couldn't quite believe her own recklessness, but she knew she was going to grasp the moment and hold on tight. Her voice was barely a whisper. "Well...as you pointed out yesterday, my lord, no sorry details of infelicitous relationships have recently crossed your lips."

The smile in his eyes was suddenly heart-shakingly tender. The hand beneath her chin uncurled to cup her face. "My sweet, trusting, innocent little Phoebe. How did I ever live without you?"

Fortunately for her scattered wits, he didn't seem to expect an answer. He lowered his head and with the same irresistible, utterly overwhelming mastery that had rendered her helpless yesterday, covered her mouth with his.

Phoebe found herself drowning in sensation instantly. Heat and excitement, deliciously thrilling, poured through her from her head to her toes. Her lips parted, her arms lifted to cling to him, and this time...this time when his arms tightened in response, when his mouth hardened on hers in fierce demand, he didn't draw back, leaving her dizzy and bereft.

His tongue caressed her lower lip, gently, insistently, as though preparing her for his deeper claiming, and then he was tasting, touching, possessing every soft, hidden part of her mouth, coaxing her into a hesitant response until she was kissing him back as deeply, as passionately, until she lost all awareness of anything but their embrace.

When he lifted his head aeons later, she was limp and trembling in his arms, her heartbeat wild, her breasts deliciously crushed against his chest, a strange insistent ache throbbing through her lower body. She sorted the sensations out one by one and then was suddenly flooded with the knowledge of Deverell's violently leashed desire. Every muscle in his body was rock-hard with tension.

Her eyes flew open. She gazed into the golden flames blazing in his aquamarine eyes and felt herself melting all over again. Not even the crushing strength of his arms, or the frankly intimidating male arousal pressed against her had the power to restore a semblance of caution.

"Phoebe." He kissed her again, briefly, her name a whisper against her lips, and then pressed his mouth to her temple. His heart thudded, powerfully, against her breast. "Don't be afraid. I want you, but—" His breath shuddered out and his arms tightened. "Just give me a minute."

"I'm not afraid," she breathed in the same hushed tone.

"You're trembling." He drew back to look down into her face.

She blushed at the raw hunger in his eyes. He made no effort to disguise his need, continuing to hold her so closely she could feel the faint vibration of muscles held rigidly in check. And yet she'd spoken the truth. She wasn't afraid. Her awareness of the fierce restraint in him was as thrilling as all the rest.

Only one thought had the power to disturb her.

"It's just…when you kissed me yesterday…" She faltered, then met his gaze openly. "You're not angry, or frustrated, today, are you, my lord?"

His mouth curved. "I think under the circumstances, Phoebe, you might call me Sebastian."

"Oh." She felt herself turning pink again. "You're not annoyed with anyone, are you…Sebastian?"

He bent and brushed her mouth with his, a half-groan, half-laugh escaping him. "I didn't know until now that the sound of my name had the potential to drive me mad. Phoebe—" He held her impossibly closer. "No, I'm not angry, or annoyed. And as for frustration, I think I can survive another day or two of it." The rueful laughter that sprang into his eyes was as swiftly banished. "Phoebe, you do know, don't you, that there's no debt between us? That I was only teasing you the other day?"

She smiled on a dizzy rush of happiness. *He cared.* He cared about her feelings.

"Of course I do," she assured him. And added confidingly, "Crowhurst said much the same thing, you know, about favours and recompense, but he meant it. The difference was glaring."

And so, without any warning, was Deverell. The hands that had been lightly stroking her back abruptly ceased their movements. He seized her by the arms and stepped back a pace.

"Crowhurst was here?"

"Yes, but—"

"What gave Crowhurst the idea he would be welcome in this house?"

"Well...I sent for him."

"What?"

She winced. "Please, my lord. I have had quite enough of gentlemen yelling at me today."

His voice immediately went ominously soft. "Crowhurst yelled at you?"

Phoebe began to perceive that whatever Deverell might have felt before, he was now *very* seriously annoyed. She set herself to rectifying the situation. "He wasn't himself, my lord. Or, perhaps he was," she amended, recalling Crowhurst's erratic behaviour.

"Make up your mind. Whether Crowhurst was himself or not may be the deciding factor in whether he continues to exist at all."

She ignored this growled threat. "Do you know, sir, I believe Lord Crowhurst must be quite unbalanced. Not only has he constantly mistaken me for someone else, but he actually had the temerity to imply that you were somehow involved in Gerald's duel." She gazed up at him anxiously. "Perhaps you'd better have a word with him, my lord. If he were to spread it about that—"

"I'll have a word with Crowhurst, all right." He released her, but only to clench his fists. "Several words. Unlike you, Miss Smith, who will never speak to him again if you wish to avoid the inconvenience of being unable to sit down for a week."

Phoebe's eyes widened. "Now you're threatening to beat me? Well! Of all the— I was only trying to help Gerald."

His teeth met. "I'm aware of that."

"All I did was send Crowhurst a note—" She stopped, abruptly recalling something else her earlier visitor had said. "And that's another thing, my lord. Did you threaten

Crowhurst with retribution if he sent me any more notes, because if you did—"

"Yes?" Deverell didn't appear to move, but suddenly he was looming over her, eyes glittering. "If I did, Miss Smith?"

"Nothing," she said, metaphorically retreating with as much dignity as possible. "I have no wish to receive notes from Crowhurst, but since I needed to see him I had to send *him* a note. You must know he's one of Gerald's seconds. How else was I to speak to him about the situation?"

Deverell continued to loom. "You weren't supposed to speak to him about anything," he grated. "But just so I have all the pertinent facts, where did this interesting conversation take place?"

"In here, of course."

"Crowhurst was in here? Alone? With you?"

"Thripp was in the hall the entire time and the door was open."

There was a moment of menacing silence. Deverell continued to study her with ominously narrowed eyes. Then he scowled.

Phoebe rewarded this evidence of self-restraint with a brilliant smile. She was far too hasty.

Deverell reached for her. His hands, big and immensely strong, closed around her shoulders.

"I don't know how you manage to drive me straight to the edge," he muttered, dragging her not entirely gently into his arms. "But right now I don't particularly care." His mouth came down on hers.

A tidal wave of male passion and outrage washed over her. Phoebe trembled under the impact. Deverell wasn't so much kissing her as staking a claim. From a deep well of feminine awareness, she recognised the difference instantly and responded to it, clinging closer, yielding the moist secrets of her mouth, letting him know she was his.

And as if her response was all he'd been seeking, he gentled at once. His arms tightened, but they cradled her. He broke the kiss, but only so he could trace the curve of her throat with warm lips. She trembled again as his mouth nudged aside the lace-trimmed neckline of her gown to caress the soft skin beneath, and he murmured something she couldn't understand, nor barely heard over the pounding of her heart.

"You're mine," he whispered. "Only mine, Phoebe."

"Yes."

The word was lost in his kiss as his mouth returned to hers. He began to stroke her, his hands caressing the curves of her waist and hips, until she felt his fingers come to rest just beneath her breast.

She shivered in almost unbearable anticipation. Then he moved his hand upward and enclosed one soft mound with the sureness of absolute possession.

Phoebe cried out softly and clung to him. Liquid warmth unfurled inside her, the muscles in her thighs went soft. She was helplessly adrift on a sea of the sweetest pleasure she'd ever known, and yet caught, held safe, in the arms of the man she loved.

Even when he raised his head and looked down at his hand cupping her so intimately, she made no protest. She blushed. She trembled inside and knew he felt it. But she had never felt such a sense of rightness as the warmth of his touch.

"You trust me." He sounded awed, as if he'd just discovered the most priceless treasure in the world.

"Absolutely," she whispered.

He raised his eyes to hers. Something fierce blazed in the blue-green depths for an instant. Desire was blatant; she thought she recognised glittering triumph; but behind it was something so dark, so vulnerable, that she made a tiny sound of protest.

"It's all right," he said swiftly. And releasing her, cupped her face in his hands. The breath he drew in was audible. "Phoebe, I—"

The drawing-room door opened with a crash.

"Phoebe! You must read this at—whoops!" Theodosia started to retreat.

Flushing with confusion, Phoebe tried to back away from Deverell. He promptly prevented her escape by seizing her hand.

"It's all right, Theo," she managed to say when he whipped his head around and fixed the intruders with slitted eyes. "Come in."

"No, it's not all right." Deverell all but snarled. "Go away."

Theo giggled. "Sorry, Uncle Sebastian, but from the look of Phoebe's face, I suspect the moment is lost."

"I'll be the judge of that. Vanish."

"Really, my lord." Phoebe tried to summon up a reproving frown. She suspected the effect was sadly ruined by the bright colour staining her cheeks. "Is that any way to speak to your wards?"

"Yes."

She frowned even more severely.

"You're not still angry with us for starting a driving club, are you, Uncle Sebastian?" Cressy gazed at her uncle with an air of innocence that didn't fool Phoebe for a minute.

She stared at the twins more closely. They didn't appear to notice anything odd in the fact that their uncle was holding their companion's hand in a particularly possessive grasp, and showed no inclination to release it. Their eyes were certainly sparkling with excitement, but it didn't seem to stem from any anticipation of scandal.

Phoebe's wits reeled. What lost moment had Theo been talking about? Surely her charges didn't suspect she was willing to become Deverell's mistress?

"Be assured," Deverell responded in a tone that wouldn't have reassured anyone in possession of their senses, that this latest crime puts the Two-in-Hand Club for Lady Whips in the shade. Leave."

"But we haven't told you our news." Theo waved a thick wad of paper under his noise. "Cressy has written a melodrama."

"I'll be the first lady playwright."

"We're going to show it to Mr Kemble at once."

"I'm sure he'll wish to produce it."

"But if he doesn't, well take a copy—"

"In the first instance," Deverell interrupted in crushing accents, "Cressida is not the first lady to write plays. And in the second instance, as much as I'd like to be rid of you, you will not pester Kemble, or anyone else, with anything."

"But, Uncle Sebastian, you don't understand. I'm going to write plays instead of acting in them. I'll be famous."

"Unlikely."

"I'll sway millions."

"The theatres only seat thousands."

"That is quite enough, my lord." Phoebe tugged at her hand. This time she succeeded in freeing herself. The fact that she did so only because Deverell chose to release her wasn't lost on her. "Cressy, I would be delighted to read your play. Perhaps I should do so before you take it to Mr Kemble. I consider myself something of an expert on melodrama, you know."

Out of the corner of her eye she saw Deverell start to grin. While the twins conferred in excited voices, she turned and fixed him with a minatory stare. "And I believe you have several other people to visit today, my lord. Now that our discussion is finished, you mustn't let me keep you."

"Our discussion is far from finished," he growled in a low voice. "But you're correct. I still have Grismead to see and a long-overdue account to settle with Crowhurst before I can be sure of your undivided attention." He recaptured her hand and raised it to his lips. "But I'll be back, Miss Smith, be certain of that, at which time I intend to see we have some privacy. I have a very important question to put to you."

The sudden cessation of chatter had Phoebe glancing at the twins. They were watching the proceedings with bright-eyed interest.

"Well...I cannot imagine...that is..."

"Don't let your melodramatic imagination run away with you while I'm gone," he murmured against her fingers. "It's a very straightforward question, requiring a very straightforward answer."

His brilliant aquamarine eyes smiled straight into hers for a heart-stopping second, then he pressed a lingering kiss into her palm, released her and left.

Phoebe gazed after him, suddenly floating so high on a bubble of happiness that she scarcely noticed the twins' scurrying out of the room after him.

Deverell wasn't going to offer her a carte blanche. His intentions were honourable. There could be no other explanation for his words or his actions. If he'd intended to make her his mistress, he would never have spoken or behaved with such frank purpose in front of his nieces.

And with that thought whirling through her mind, she finally realised what had continually puzzled her about that very wicked, very inviting smile. She'd seen the warmth and amusement, she'd seen the devilish invitation to share his humour, but she hadn't recognised the intimacy or the promise in his eyes.

The promise of a man of honour, she thought wonderingly. The impossible seemed to have happened. She didn't know how it had happened. She didn't know what Deverell saw in her that placed her above ladies of wealth and beauty and position, but he wanted her. He cared about her feelings; about her reputation. He might even—

Oh, did she dare to hope for so much? He might even grow to love her as she loved him.

Phoebe hugged herself and executed a small skip of uncontained excitement. For the first time in her life, the future was full of hope and promise. For the first time, she dared to believe that the fantasy she'd dismissed several days ago might come true. The impossible really had happened.

Deverell was going to ask her to become his wife.

Her euphoria lasted until she sat down to a solitary meal in the dining-room. Gerald still hadn't returned, and the girls were attending a concert with Lady Yarwood and her daughters, thereby allowing their companion a free evening.

It was a pity she didn't want a free evening.

Phoebe studied the silent, empty room and wished she'd thought to pay a visit to Hatchards. The latest calf-bound novel from the Minerva Press would be preferable company to the doubts that were beginning to crowd into her head.

Not she doubted Deverell's intentions. Not for a minute. But he'd practically expressed those intentions before she'd put him in full possession of the facts. And three pertinent facts were now staring her most unpleasantly in the face.

Her circumstances were perfectly suited to becoming a mistress.

A wife was another matter.

Before Deverell said another word, she would have to tell him the truth.

She would have to do more, Phoebe told herself, a sharp ache already piercing her heart at the thought. She would have to point out every disadvantage, every possible repercussion, every drawback to a marriage between herself and Deverell. She would have to do it even if he loved her—and he hadn't said a word about love.

He *wanted* her. She had no doubt about that. The memory of the fierceness of his embrace and the heated demand of his mouth on hers caused tingling little shivers of sensation to dart about inside her every time she thought about it.

But he was a Deverell. When Deverells wanted something, they tended to go after the object of their desire and worry about the consequences later. If he married her and later regretted it, she knew the heartbreak would be unbearable.

Because she loved him, she would have to bring about the possible destruction of her dreams.

Phoebe sighed and pushed her unfinished meal away. She propped her chin on her hands and stared unhappily at the window. Dusk had fallen, shadowing the garden in shades of grey. She could vaguely make out her own reflection in the glass. Doom and gloom emanated from her like a shroud that threatened to engulf her entire surroundings. The destruction of her dreams seemed all too imminent.

When Thripp opened the door, she turned with a sense of foreboding.

He carried a small white envelope. The logical explanation seemed to leap out at her from the shadows.

She wasn't going to have to explain things to Deverell after all. She'd forgotten he was more controlled than the rest of his family. He'd already had second thoughts.

"This was just delivered for you, miss." Thripp glanced down at the note he held, but made no move to give it to her.

Phoebe braced herself and straightened. She held out her hand. "Thank you, Thripp."

He didn't move. "It's from that Crowhurst fellow."

She frowned. "How do you know?"

"After all them notes, miss?" Thripp indulged himself with a most unbutler-like snort. "I'd know his hand anywhere."

"Oh. Well…" She tried not to let her spirits revive too much with the small reprieve. "No doubt he wishes to apologise for his very peculiar behaviour today. I'm sure Lord Deverell won't object to me reading it."

Assuming his most mournful expression, Thripp handed over the note.

Phoebe ripped open the envelope and drew out the single sheet of notepaper. Its message was brief. She had to read it twice, however, before the meaning sank in. When it did, she leapt to her feet, sending her chair crashing to the floor behind her.

"Oh, dear God! Oh, my goodness! Thripp, what—? Where—? Oh, heavens, what are we going to do? Crowhurst has kidnapped Gerald!"

"Knew that note boded no good." Thripp nodded several times. He seemed more satisfied at his own acuteness than appalled at this latest calamity.

Phoebe was too busy scanning the note again to pay attention. "He says if we wish Gerald to remain alive, I'm to come to the Black Mole Inn on Hounslow Heath before eight o'clock tonight. Alone. He gives directions on how to find the place."

"His lordship isn't going to like that, miss."

"*I* don't like it, but what choice do I have? Gerald's life could be snuffed out at any moment. Good heavens! This must be why we haven't seen Gerald all day. Crowhurst must have kidnapped him this morning in case I refused to…er…repay him if he prevented Gerald's duel."

"Why would he do that, miss? He didn't know you were going to ask for help. Any road, even if you'd gone off with Crowhurst all meek and cosy, Master Gerald would still have a tale to tell."

Phoebe stared at him in dismay. "Perhaps Crowhurst doesn't intend to keep Gerald alive. He seemed to be quite irrational earlier, but now—he must be insane, and there's no saying how such a mind works." Her own was racing. "He even accused Deverell… But what if it was Crowhurst who arranged for that awful man to challenge Gerald?"

"So the innocent young lady'd be forced to ask for the villain's help," Thripp concluded knowledgeably.

When Phoebe blinked at him, he gave a discreet cough.

"Mrs Thripp likes to read them news pamphlets, miss. You've no idea what some folks get up to. A right disgrace it is and no mistake!"

"Good heavens!" Her mind remained suspended for a moment on the image of the Thripps poring over scandalous half-penny pamphlets before she managed to wrench it back to the present.

"I'll have to obey Crowhurst's instructions, there's no question about that. But if he thinks I'll tamely succumb to his threats, he's very much mistaken."

She thought for a moment longer. "Thripp, while you instruct Gerald's groom to bring the phaeton around, I'll write a note to Deverell. Tell the footman he's not to rest until he's delivered it into his lordship's own hands. Oh, dear..." She wrung her hands and glanced at the clock on the mantelpiece. "Crowhurst might be insane, but he's not entirely stupid. It's past seven now and I have to be at this place by eight."

"Aye." Thripp nodded gloomily. "Just the time when his lordship has likely gone out for the evening. Henry'll have to search for him all over, and by that time who's to say where you'll be?"

His words were an all-too-accurate reflection of her own fears. Phoebe scowled at him. "Let's not sink to the level of your pamphlets, Thripp. If Deverell has already seen Crowhurst, which seems likely since Crowhurst has resorted to threats, he may still be at the Grismeads'. If not, try his clubs."

"Aye, miss."

"And I'd better leave another note for the girls. There's no saying when I'll return."

She wouldn't say "if," Phoebe told herself, as Thripp hurried away to summon Gerald's groom. Of course she would return. When Crowhurst saw that she'd followed his instructions to come alone, she might even find an opportunity to help Gerald escape. Even if she didn't, Deverell would come after her, she was sure of it.

If only she could be as certain that Gerald was still alive. Her fear for his safety was all too real. Crowhurst would soon realise—if he hadn't already—that he could hardly release his bait without serious repercussions to himself.

Pushing the chilling thought aside, Phoebe raced into the

drawing-room. Her hands were shaking, but she managed to pen the note to Deverell and stuff it into an envelope.

The clatter of carriage wheels outside the window told her the phaeton was ready. She scribbled a hasty note to the twins, thrust the missives into Thripp's hands and threw on the bonnet and pelisse a maid had fetched for her.

As she dashed out into the night she could only hope and pray that Deverell wouldn't be too far behind her.

Chapter Twelve

Hounslow Heath was not a comforting place to be in broad daylight. By night, for a lone traveller, it was eerie in the extreme. One tended to see footpads and highwaymen lurking behind every bush. When Phoebe finally drew up outside a small inn crouched by the side of the track in the meagre shelter afforded by a few stunted trees, she released a huge sigh of relief.

A curricle and pair drawn up to one side of the building was the only indication that she was in the right place. The lantern over the door was unlit, and the sign creaking in the wind was so grimy, only the most keen-eyed observer would have discerned the figure of a small, sly-eyed creature. In the faint glow from the downstairs windows, Phoebe decided the creature was a black mole.

The inn named for the animal did not appear to be the most well-run hostelry. No ostler came running to hold the horses. No host was bustling through the doorway with offers of refreshment.

She began to regret having left Gerald's groom a mile or so back where the rutted lane, leading to the track she herself had followed, left the main road. Mindful of Crowhurst's instructions, she had thought it safer to come on alone. The groom had argued vociferously, but Phoebe had been adamant. They had already taken several wrong turns, having passed the ill-defined lane in the darkness before the moon had fully risen.

Jem had been ordered to hold the lantern and keep a look-out for Deverell.

She wondered what time it was. Sending up a prayer that she wasn't too late and that Deverell was hard on her heels, she tied the reins and climbed down from the phaeton.

The door of the inn opened as her feet touched the ground. Hazy golden light spilled into the yard. The illumination didn't improve the scene. Turning, she saw that an attempt had once been made to pave the yard, but now tufts of grass poked up between the stones and weeds grew in wild profusion. Leaves and refuse blew and eddied across the small space every time the wind gusted.

Phoebe shivered in the cool breeze and started to chafe her arms. She froze in mid-gesture as Crowhurst strolled through the open doorway, a smile of triumph twisting his features.

The memory of her first encounter with him flashed through her mind. She shivered again and glanced around her. At least, then, she'd been in the middle of a city. The Black Mole seemed to be situated in the middle of nowhere.

"Ah, Phoebe, my dear. I was beginning to wonder if you'd been so foolish as to ignore my instructions."

"Where is Gerald?" she demanded without preamble.

Crowhurst smiled again and gestured to the doorway behind him. "Won't you come in? We may as well discuss the situation in comfort, don't you think?"

Ignoring the question, Phoebe swept past him into the inn. She halted at once, transfixed by dismay and a spine-tingling silence.

Comfort was not the word she would have used to describe the interior of the Black Mole. The door opened directly into an evil-smelling taproom that hadn't seen a broom or mop for years. Several seedy-looking individuals were seated around the solitary table. Their eyes bored into her with avid interest. A tankard clunked as it was put down on the table. One of the men made a remark beneath his breath and was answered with coarse snickers.

Crowhurst ignored the crowd. "In here," he said, opening another door off the taproom.

Thanking providence that she didn't have to walk past those men, Phoebe followed Crowhurst into what was clearly a private parlour. It was no less gloomy than the taproom, lit only by a branch of candles on the centre table, but at least it was cleaner and a fire burned in the stone fireplace opposite the window.

She crossed to it, holding her hands to the warmth. The flames seemed to have little effect on the chill sweeping through her body.

"I must apologise for these crude surroundings, Phoebe." Crowhurst closed the door and crossed the room towards her. "But the Black Mole has been rather convenient for my purposes over the past few years. Out of the way. No one asks questions. And we won't be staying long."

Phoebe raked him with a scornful gaze. "You would seem to have a taste for low company, my lord. First that grimy little theatre, and now this."

He laughed. "Always the haughty madam. But I'm no longer a boy to be kept dangling at the end of one of your strings."

"Gerald," she prompted coldly.

He raised a brow at her lack of response to his comment, then indicating the wooden settle by the fire, seated himself at one end and picked up a glass of wine from the table beside him. Phoebe remained standing.

"Still playing cards at White's, I expect," he murmured casually, raising his drink to contemplate the reflection of flames through the dark liquid.

She stared at him.

He smiled and lifted his glass to her before taking a sip. "You didn't think I'd really kidnap Gerald, did you, Phoebe? That would have been a very foolish thing to do. And far too much trouble."

"You lied?" She almost whispered the words. Her brain struggled to take them in.

"Indeed. You see, I'd been watching Gerald today in pursuit of my original scheme. An exhausting process, I must say. First I trailed him to Filby's, then Tattersall's, then Manton's. Then he and Filby must needs lunch at a coffee-shop, and visit Filby's tailor. I knew he hadn't been home all day, and the idea of setting a trap for you by claiming he'd been kidnapped occurred to me. Once I saw him settle at White's, I doubted he'd ruin my plans by making an inconvenient appearance before you left London, so—'' he spread his hands ''—here we are.''

She could only continue to stare at him, incredulous. ''And you think you'll get away with this?''

He lifted a shoulder. ''Why not? By the time anyone realises the truth, we'll be long gone.''

The comment had a rather nasty ring of truth. Phoebe took a steadying breath and tried to think past the quick jolt of fear spreading ice through her veins. Somehow she had to prevent Crowhurst from taking her further afield. The Black Mole was unprepossessing, but she was safer here where Deverell had a chance of finding her. If she could just manoeuvre for some time.

''What was your original scheme?'' she asked, her mind scurrying to think of ways to keep him talking.

He hesitated, then shrugged again. ''I don't mind telling you, since you won't be going back to Deverell anyway. As soon as I realised the duel I'd arranged wasn't going ahead, I formed the notion of making a more overt attempt on Gerald's life.''

''You wanted to kill *Gerald? Why?*''

''No, no,'' he said irritably. ''Of course I don't want to kill Gerald. Don't you see? If an attempt had been made on his life, everyone would've thought Deverell was behind it. He would have been imprisoned. At the very least disgraced. He'd have left England again.''

''No,'' she murmured, shaking her head. ''No one would believe Deverell capable of harming Gerald.''

Crowhurst sent her an impatient glare. ''They would after I'd reminded everyone of the old scandal. It's common knowledge that Deverell has no love for his family, nor they for him. And then, you see, you would have been mine, and *he*'d have been punished for trying to take you from me.''

The gloating satisfaction in his voice momentarily deprived Phoebe of speech.

''Why did you change your plan?'' she finally asked, hoping he couldn't hear the faintness in her voice.

His air of triumph dropped from him like a cloak. He turned to her with an almost boyish eagerness that made her want to cringe. A combination of fear and pity roiled inside her, making her feel sick to her stomach.

"I thought you wouldn't like it if Gerald got hurt, Phoebe. Even though I wouldn't have killed him, I'd still have had to make it look like a real attempt on his life. That was when I thought of the kidnapping scheme. I knew you'd come."

"My lord, surely…" Dear God, how did one reason with a disordered mind? "Do you honestly think you'll get away with this? Deverell will come after me, but it's not too late if you'll only—"

"Let him come after you!" Crowhurst shot to his feet and flung his glass into the fire with a violence that made her flinch. The glass exploded, sending sparks hissing up the chimney and illuminating the sudden viciousness of his expression.

Phoebe remembered Lady Yarwood's comment about Crowhurst's moods and tried to force herself to stillness. Her ladyship hadn't known the half of it. Nor was the memory going to help her now, she thought, glancing at the door. Had he locked it? But if she tried to escape, Crowhurst was close enough to catch her. And she doubted those men outside would lift a finger to assist her, even if she screamed.

"I don't mind killing *him*," Crowhurst snarled. "You'd like us to fight over you, wouldn't you, Phoebe? You always played one of us off against the other. How many were there? Two? Three?"

Trembling inside, she put a hand to the back of the settle to steady herself. "Sir…" She swallowed and tried again. "I am *not*—"

"No!" He cut her off with a jerk of his hand and, frowning, took a few agitated steps towards the window. Again she saw him try to master his rage. "I know! I know. Not her. Keep forgetting."

"I'm sure…I'm sure that's quite understandable," she faltered. "It's clear I very closely resemble the lady you once loved, and…I'm sorry for that, but—"

He wasn't listening. "Not her," he muttered, peering through the glass.

Phoebe's heart leapt as she heard a faint noise outside. Had Crowhurst heard? Could he see anything but their own dim reflections?

"Not her," he continued to mumble. He turned and started back towards her. "Look the same. Yes, that's it. Exactly the same. She's you."

Ice water flowed down Phoebe's spine. She stopped straining her ears for sounds beyond the window. "Who?" she whispered.

Crowhurst halted and peered at her in the hazy light. "Your mother," he said as if surprised she should ask. "Just like her."

"My *mother?*" Phoebe dropped to the settle as if her legs had turned to water. Scenes from her childhood whipped through her mind with a speed that left her reeling. Suddenly several things began to make sense. "You were in love with my mother?"

"Her name was Phoebe, too."

"No." She shook her head, still dazed. "Charlotte. It was Charlotte."

"That's what her family called her." Crowhurst dismissed the name with a gesture. "We used her middle name. She said it made her feel like another person. Not hedged in by that puritan family of her husband's. Phoebe. Like you."

"And Deverell?" she whispered, staring at Crowhurst. "Was he...? Did he...? But you met him only weeks ago. Was that a lie, too?"

"We never met. She kept us apart. But he took her from me!" he shouted suddenly. "She ran off with him. She was supposed to leave your father for *me*. But she chose him. She chose Deverell."

"Not quite, Crowhurst."

"Oh, thank God! *Sebastian!*"

Her cry was lost beneath the crashing of the casement against the outside wall. Before the echoes had died away Phoebe leaped from the settle, darted around Crowhurst and flung herself at Deverell as he came in through the open window.

He caught her as he straightened, holding her close for a moment before drawing back to look down at her face. His gaze, dark and concerned, swept over her. "Are you all right, little love?"

She nodded. It was all she could manage. A rush of relieved tears sprang to her eyes. She blinked them away, and was open-

ing her mouth to speak when she found herself abruptly thrust
to one side.

Crowhurst launched himself at Deverell, his lips drawn back
in a snarl of rage.

Before Phoebe could so much as gasp, Deverell took one
step forward and lashed out with his clenched fist. The full
strength of his body was behind the blow. Crowhurst's jaw
cracked under the impact. He went down in a sprawl of arms
and legs and lay there, groaning.

"Oh, good heavens." Phoebe unglued her hands from her
mouth. "He's just lying there. Do you think you've broken his
jaw, my lord?"

"Very likely." Deverell didn't appear to be unduly dismayed by the prospect. He stepped over his victim and stalked
towards the door. He opened it and subjected the occupants
beyond to a flint-eyed stare.

Phoebe felt the sudden stark silence from where she stood.

Deverell shut the door without a word and waited until the
faint murmur of conversation started up again.

Obviously, Crowhurst had been right when he'd said no one
asked questions at the Black Mole. Phoebe glanced at him and
immediately went rigid. "Sebastian!"

Deverell drew a pistol from his pocket with a deceptively
casual movement. "Don't bother looking around for your
sword-stick, Crowhurst. It's over by the fire and I'll bring you
down before you can take one step towards it."

"Bastard!" Crowhurst's voice cracked but apparently his
jaw was still in one piece. He could speak. Crawling to a chair,
he pulled himself painfully to his knees, then to his feet. "I'll
see you ruined for this. I'll see you both ruined. She came to
me. She came to *me!* I didn't force her."

"Depends on how you look at the situation." Deverell
nudged the settle closer to the fire with one booted foot. "I
seem to recall being told quite recently by a certain governess
that blackmail is a form of threat." He beckoned to Phoebe.
"Come here, love. You're shivering."

Phoebe obeyed, reflecting on the very peculiar effects of
shock. The gentler note in Deverell's voice and the careful way
he seated her—while holding a gun in his other hand—was

having a strange effect on her nerves. She began to wonder if she was growing slightly hysterical.

"I didn't blackmail her," Crowhurst repeated. He eyed Deverell for a moment, then his features twisted into a look of cunning. "She came to me to avenge her mother!"

"What?" Phoebe's eyes went wide. She snapped back to life. "What *are* you talking about, sir? You wrote me that dreadful note. I can produce it right now!"

"Sweetheart—"

"Don't you know?" Crowhurst burst out. "Your mother killed herself when Deverell abandoned her. Her family cast her off. She couldn't stand the loneliness and disgrace and—"

"God damn it!" Deverell roared. "Will you shut up, Crowhurst!"

"It's all right," Phoebe said quickly. She glanced up at him and felt her heart turn over at the glittering rage in his eyes. "I knew my mother had been cast off. I was going to tell you, but…"

Oh, dear God, what a way for him to learn the truth. Would he ever believe that she was going to tell him everything at their next meeting?

"I was going to tell you," she repeated. "Everything. That my name is really Phoebe Everton-Smythe and—"

"I know, love." She saw his eyes narrow as he controlled his anger. "I heard Crowhurst ranting while I was prising the window open, and put most of it together. Until tonight, I don't think any of us knew all the facts. We'll talk about it later."

"Will you tell her the truth, Deverell? That you only want her because you were forced to give up her mother and your family shipped you off to India to avoid the scandal."

"In the first place, Crowhurst, I neither abandoned Phoebe's mother nor was forced to give her up. She was having an affair with my brother, not with me. Unfortunately," he added into the stunned silence that greeted his announcement, "on the evidence at the time, my family thought as you did."

Both his listeners continued to stare at him, speechless. Crowhurst looked as if Deverell had struck him again. Phoebe had already received so many blows to her senses that she could scarcely think. The sweeping sense of relief washing over her was immediately followed by another stronger wave of foreboding.

She'd been wondering how Deverell could ever love the daughter of the woman who had caused so much pain in his life. She was still wondering, Charlotte Everton-Smythe hadn't broken his heart, but she'd been the unwitting cause of his banishment.

"Your brother?" whispered Crowhurst. His face had turned a sickly pale colour.

"Yes. Your revenge has been for nothing, Crowhurst."

Deverell nodded, glanced down at the pistol in his hand and returned it to his pocket. "That threw me for a while. Crowhurst's obsession with you made it obvious that you closely resembled a past lover, and taking into account my brother's series of affairs and Crowhurst's enmity towards me—despite the fact that we'd never met—it seemed all too probable that he and Selwyn had been rivals. When he inveigled Gerald into playing at the Pigeonhole, I thought he was trying to revenge himself on Selwyn's son by ruining him."

He turned to Crowhurst who was now slumped in brooding silence. "But it was me you were after, wasn't it, Crowhurst? The only trouble was, you didn't have the guts to tackle me personally, so you decided to strike at me through Gerald. Quite a neat scheme, but you should choose your tools more wisely. Creech crumpled as soon as I told him you'd been seen together."

"You can't prove anything from that," Crowhurst said sulkily. "I dare say I've been seen with everyone who's played at the Pigeonhole."

Deverell appeared unperturbed by the claim. "Quite true. But men who make a living by fleecing young sprigs from the country aren't noted for their superior intelligence. Creech not only admitted that you paid him to accuse Gerald of cheating, but added the interesting fact that you promised him swift passage out of the country and enough money to live on for several years if Gerald was fatally wounded. Then you would've sat back and waited for Society to remember the old scandal."

Crowhurst's already pale face turned a ghastlier hue. He plucked at his sleeve with shaking fingers. "What are you going to do?"

"Strange though it may seem, I have no wish to ruin you. I can even sympathise with your desire to wreak vengeance on my family." His expression hardened. "I spent several years harbouring similar fantasies. But you made a fatal mistake when you involved Phoebe in your schemes."

"I wouldn't have hurt her. I just wanted her back."

Deverell's eyes flashed with such savagery even Phoebe gasped. He strode forward, yanked Crowhurst up by the collar of his coat and slammed him against the wall. His voice lowered, each word emerging with deadly clarity.

"Phoebe is not her mother. Do you understand me, Crowhurst? She is not yours. She never will be."

Crowhurst stared at Deverell as if mesmerised. "Not mine," he whispered obediently, and then his face crumpled. "I loved her," he choked. "And now she's dead."

"Oh, Sebastian."

He silenced her with a look. "She died a long time ago, Crowhurst." He released the other man and stepped back. "Unfortunately for both of us, she died before she could right a few misconceptions."

Phoebe couldn't tell if Crowhurst had heard that last remark or not. He crumpled to the floor and stayed there, utterly beaten. She looked up at Deverell, her eyes widening at the grim set of his mouth, and wondered what was going to happen next.

The answer came from the vicinity of the window.

"I say, Uncle Sebastian, what on earth is going on here? Is Phoebe safe?"

She blinked in astonishment. "Gerald? Is that you?"

Deverell turned in time to see his nephew swing one leg over the windowsill and clamber into the room.

"Of course it's me," he said. "You feeling all right, Phoebe? You look a little pale. No need to. Thought I'd better come and tell you I haven't been kidnapped."

"How...very considerate of you," Phoebe uttered in faint accents.

"We had, however, already deduced that useful fact," Deverell added. "May I ask how you found us?"

Gerald grinned. "Got home to find the girls in an uproar over Phoebe's note. Bad decision to leave one," he tacked on, sending her a reproving frown. "Took me ten minutes to calm everyone down."

"But I wrote that note so they *wouldn't* worry."

Deverell raised his eyes heavenward.

"Anyway," continued Gerald, correctly interpreting this expression, "I followed Phoebe's directions. She was driving my phaeton, of course, so I had to dash off a note to Reggie."

"Good God! Don't tell me you brought Filby with you."

"Very obedient servant, sir." As if at a signal, Filby's head and shoulders popped up at the window with the suddenness of a plump, particularly fashionable jack-in-the-box. He beamed at Phoebe. "Very happy to see you, ma'am. No trouble at all to bring Gerald. Curricle took only a minute to harness. Sorry to be a little delayed just now. Had to tether the horses. Gerald's, too. Looked as if they might wander off. See you left your phaeton down the lane with Gerald's groom," he added chattily, turning to Deverell. "Don't blame you. Yard's getting a bit crowded."

Phoebe couldn't help it. She had to succumb to the madness of the situation or go mad herself. Her peal of laughter earned her a glare from Deverell that threatened to set her off again.

"It was very gallant of you and Gerald to come to my rescue, Mr Filby," she finally managed. "Won't you come in?"

Filby eyed the windowsill with a dubious expression, then looked down at the pale blue pantaloons he wore beneath his greatcoat. "Might use the door, if no one minds," he chirped, and vanished as suddenly as he'd appeared.

His place was promptly taken by the twins. Phoebe blinked at them and wondered if she was losing her mind. She heard Deverell swear comprehensively.

"What the devil are they doing here?" he demanded of his nephew.

Gerald scowled fiercely at his sisters. "I thought you promised to stay in the curricle until Reggie and I discovered what was afoot."

"You have discovered it," Theo pointed out inarguably. "And we're tired of sitting there, doing nothing." She hopped nimbly over the windowsill, followed by her sister, and glanced about with interest. "Besides, we heard Phoebe laugh so we know she was all right. You are, aren't you, Phoebe?"

"Gerald," began Deverell before she could answer, "if you wish to survive until tomorrow, you will take Filby and your sisters and—"

He was interrupted by the sound of horses' hooves entering the yard at a smart trot. At the same time Filby pushed open the parlour door.

"Strange set of company Crowhurst keeps," he remarked, strolling into the room. "Think someone else has arrived, by the bye."

"Surely not," Deverell said sarcastically. "I could have sworn we're all here."

Filby turned a look of polite enquiry on the figure still crouched on the floor. "You expecting anyone, Crowhurst?"

As though emerging from a deep trance, Crowhurst started and managed to push himself upright again. His voice was not the one to answer Filby, however.

"This cannot be the place. Look at it. You, my good man. Are you the innkeeper? You should be ashamed of yourself. And who are all these slovenly persons? Get rid of them at once! Disgusting! Sitting there drinking while villainous crimes are going on under their very noses. I've a good mind to summon the nearest magistrate."

"Good God!" muttered Deverell.

Before he could enlarge on the theme the door was flung open, narrowly missing Mr Filby. Lady Grismead sailed into the room, followed by Mr Charlton.

"Bloody hell," growled Deverell. "I thought I left you explaining finances to Grismead, Edward?"

"Kindly moderate your language, Deverell." Lady Grismead came to a halt in the middle of the parlour and swept the occupants with a single gimlet-eyed glance. "I," she announced with awful meaning, "have come to find out what is Going On." She let her gaze rest on Deverell. "If you think, sir, that you can receive an urgent summons while in my house and dash off without an explanation, you may think again."

Deverell sighed. "Nothing is going on, as you so succinctly put in, Aunt. Miss Smith found herself obliged to leave town and requested my escort."

"Indeed? I suppose that is why Mr Charlton and I encountered a groom skulking in the lane, and why there are carriages everywhere one looks." She paused to let this sink in, then softened her tone.

"I am not quite a fool, Sebastian. Mr Charlton and I hastened to Park Street and found Miss Smith's note. It was clear she was in a great deal of danger. And although I dare say you are capable of managing any number of unpleasant situations, there are some that require the Presence of a Woman. You," she added, with the air of one throwing in a clincher, "have been extraordinarily helpful to us today; now I wish to return the favour. That is what families are for."

While her nephew was swallowing this piece of worldly wisdom, she turned to Phoebe. "Perhaps you will enlighten me, Miss Smith."

Predictably, everyone except Phoebe started to talk at once.

"All an unfortunate misunderstanding," Filby stated positively.

"Crowhurst told Phoebe he'd kidnapped me," Gerald informed his great-aunt. "Of course, he was lying, but—"

"Phoebe didn't know that," Theo put in, glancing anxiously at Deverell. "It wasn't as if she ran off with him."

Cressy nodded emphatically. "She was duped." She glanced around, spotted Crowhurst and turned on him with such ferocity that he shrank. "Villain! Blackguard! You knew if you put a limit on Phoebe's time, she wouldn't be able to check the truth of your story. I hope Uncle Sebastian spits you on the end of his sword."

Gerald rolled his eyes. "Cressy, Uncle Sebastian isn't wearing a sword."

"Well, I hope he shoots you full of holes."

"Please, Cressy." Phoebe's voice wobbled as laughter threatened to overtake her again.

"Leave this to me, Miss Smith." Lady Grismead took charge. "No one will be riddled with holes, Cressida. I do not approve of violence. However—"

As the full force of the argument about what to do with Crowhurst began to rage about her, Phoebe subsided. She was only too happy to let her ladyship have her way. She was starting to feel rather shaky. The result of too much excitement, no doubt. She slumped a little on the settle and felt Deverell glance down at her.

Mr Charlton claimed his attention before he could do more than touch a gentle hand to her cheek.

"Sir, do you want me to get rid of Crowhurst for you? It's the least I can do since I'm here."

"No, what I want you to do is get rid of everyone else."

His secretary winced. "I claim ignorance of your wards' intentions," he pleaded hurriedly. "And I'm sorry about bringing your aunt along, but when you walked out leaving me with Lord Grismead, I doubt a juggernaut would have stopped her."

Deverell grinned unexpectedly. "You're forgiven. But only because you had enough sense to leave Grismead, Pamela and Nermal in London."

"Pamela and Mr Hartlepoole," pronounced her ladyship, overhearing this and abandoning the argument, "are engaged in composing a notice to be placed in the *Gazette*. Thanks to Deverell," she added graciously. "However, poor Grismead is probably worrying himself into one of his dyspeptic fits, so—"

"Aunt," interrupted Deverell firmly, "if you really wish to repay me for knocking some sense into that idiot poet and advising Grismead on financial matters, would you please take the girls back to London? Gerald and Edward will accompany you. And Gerald's groom, of course. You'll be perfectly safe."

Her ladyship frowned. "What about Miss Smith?"

"She'll be perfectly safe, too."

"Hmm. You do realise, I suppose, that Miss Smith has been through a most harrowing experience."

"No, really, I'm—"

"I realise it," Deverell said with unaccustomed patience. "Don't worry, Aunt. We won't be far behind you. I have one more matter to make clear to Crowhurst, after which I'll take Phoebe home."

Lady Grismead considered this statement for a few moments, glanced at Phoebe, then gave a brisk nod. "I see Miss Smith trusts you implicitly, Sebastian. No doubt we have been wrong about you all these years. You shall tell me the truth tomorrow.

"As for you, sir—" her ladyship swept a basilisk glance over Crowhurst, who seemed to be trying to make himself as small as possible "—if I see your face in town in the near future, I shall make it clear that your predilection for unsavoury theatrical productions renders you unfit to be received by all respectable persons. I trust you understand me.''

"Good heavens!" exclaimed Phoebe, startled. She looked up at Deverell. "How did she discover that, sir?"

"I'm afraid I made the mistake of warning Grismead after Crowhurst attended my aunt's party," Deverell answered in the same low tone. "Obviously, she prised the story out of him." He bent and covered her tightly clenched hands with one of his. "Just a few more minutes, sweetheart, then—"

"Uncle Sebastian, do we really have to go with Aunt Ottilia?" Cressida bounced up to them with so much energy, Phoebe felt like a wilted leaf in comparison. "I know Theo is happy to go off with Edward, but I want to hear precisely what happened. Think what a tale this could make. I could write—"

"Wouldn't do," stated Filby, coming up to them with the air of one anxious to quit his surroundings. He peered worriedly at his sleeve and flicked off a cobweb. "Heroine rescued before she's been ruined. Nephew full of gig. Wicked uncle turns out to be the hero. No good at all. Are you ready to depart, Lady Cressida?"

"No good, sir?" Cressida drew herself up. "What, pray do you know about melodrama?"

Filby appeared completely unaware of her outrage. "Well, m'mother likes to put on amateur theatricals at our Christmas house-parties and—"

"She does?" Cressy clasped her hands. Her scowl vanished.

Still inspecting his coat, Filby nodded. "Thought you might be interested. Lot of fun. Often acted in them m'self."

"You have?"

"Tell you all about it on the way home. You ready, Gerald?"

"A moment, Gerald." Deverell bent, picked up Crowhurst's sword-stick and handed it to his nephew. "Send this around to Crowhurst's lodgings tomorrow, will you? And see if you can stay out of gambling hells until you go up to Oxford. If you're serious about repairing your fortunes, I'll help you, but—"

"Oh, will you, Uncle Sebastian? That would be—"

He was propelled through the doorway by Mr Charlton. As everyone departed, arguing about which carriage to occupy, Deverell's gaze rested for a moment on Filby and Cressida.

"A match made in heaven. Why didn't I see it before? Do you know, Phoebe, I believe I may have underestimated Filby." He turned and smiled down at her. "I must have been preoccupied at the time."

"No doubt, my lord," she responded demurely. She glanced at the open window. "Have they really all gone? I don't wish to sound ungrateful, but being rescued by an entire phalanx of Deverells is rather overwhelming."

"I trust you'll that find one Deverell can do the job quite as well," he replied solemnly, and walked over to the window. "Hmm, we're not safe yet. Gerald and the girls seem rather anxious about one of the wheels on Gerald's phaeton. You didn't collide with anything on your way here, did you, Phoebe?"

"Of course not, sir." She smiled faintly. "Fortunately, the road was free of stage-coaches."

"Fortunate, indeed. Ah, at last. They're going."

He closed the window and latched it before turning to Crowhurst. The smile edging his mouth vanished. "And as far as I'm concerned, we've had enough of your company, too, Crowhurst. Before you leave, however, let me make it clear that, like my aunt, I don't wish to encounter you for some considerable time. I suggest you take an extended tour abroad for reasons of health."

Crowhurst merely nodded dejectedly and shuffled to the door. He didn't even glance at Phoebe.

Deverell watched his progress through slitted eyes. He waited until Crowhurst reached the door, then spoke. His voice was quiet, ice-cold, and utterly convincing.

"One more thing, Crowhurst." The other man paused. "Come near Phoebe again and I'll break your neck."

Phoebe's eyes widened. If Deverell had threatened to strangle Crowhurst, she wouldn't have taken much notice. She had no trouble at all picturing him snapping Crowhurst's neck in two without even thinking about it if he so much as looked sideways at her.

Crowhurst knew it, also. He shuddered, glanced back fearfully into eyes that glittered with all the deadly chill of a naked blade, and hurried away.

For a moment silence filled the small room. Then Deverell

took two long strides towards her, snatched her up and, yanking her bonnet off with jerky, impatient fingers, wrapped her in a crushing embrace. He pressed his face to her hair; his heart thundered wildly against her breast.

"God! I never want to go through anything like that again as long as I live," he muttered. "I kept telling myself that Crowhurst wouldn't hurt you. At least not immediately. But I couldn't be sure."

"I knew you'd come." Phoebe clung to him as desperately absorbing the reassuring warmth and strength of his body. "But I was so scared, Sebastian. He was going to take me somewhere else."

"It's over now." He relaxed his hold a little and drew back to trace the line of her cheek with gentle fingers. "However—" his hand stilled "—it may not have happened in the first place if you'd confided in me. Perhaps you can explain, Miss Everton-Smythe, how it comes about that a daughter of one of Yorkshire's most starched-up families is masquerading under the name of Smith and earning her living as a governess."

"Precisely because they are so starched-up," she said drily. "When I decided I'd had enough of reprimands and reproaches and being treated like an unpaid drudge, my family decided they wanted nothing to do with such an ungrateful person. In fact, they said I'd probably end up like my mother, and made me promise to drop the Everton name so no one would connect me with them, or be reminded of the scandal she caused."

Deverell's eyes narrowed. He released her, shoved his hands into his pockets and took a few steps away to stand staring into the fire.

Phoebe sank back to the settle, feeling abruptly bereft. She had the distinct suspicion that the next few minutes were not going to be pleasant.

"It suited me, too," she ventured. "I had my living to earn, and a governess with a scandal attached to her name doesn't find employment easily."

He turned his head to frown at her. "Damn it, the scandal wasn't of your making. Perhaps you didn't mind changing your name, but what the hell was your father about to cast you off like that?"

"My father died several years ago. Although he probably

would've done the same thing," she added after a moment's thought. "The Everton-Smythes are so puritanical they refuse to attend the Assemblies at Harrogate or York. Dancing can lead to improper behaviour, you know. Even to smile is a crime. As for coming to London— Well, you can imagine what they think of the Season."

"I don't give a damn what they think of the Season. If they didn't isolate themselves, someone else besides Crowhurst might have recognised you and we might've put everything together a lot sooner."

"Perhaps," she said doubtfully. "I suppose my father was only too thankful to keep the scandal contained. Even I didn't know the details until tonight. When my mother left, he banned all mention of her name, and sent me to live with his parents." A wry smile touched her mouth. "For a short time I believed it was so his mother could take the place of mine, but I soon learned it was because I resembled Charlotte so closely."

"He couldn't bear to be reminded of her?"

Phoebe shook her head. "Only because she'd brought shame on the family. First by her affairs, obviously, and then...her suicide."

His expression gentled. "Did you know she'd killed herself, Phoebe?"

"I...wasn't sure," she said painfully. "I was only nine when it all happened, and although I knew my mother had done something terrible—sense it, as children do—it was soon made very clear that I wasn't to ask any questions."

He studied her rather thoughtfully.

"It didn't change my life to any great extent," she went on, shifting under that steady gaze. "She was always rather distant. I didn't know her very well."

"We both seem to have been somewhat unfortunate in our parents," he observed, looking back at the fire.

"So it seems, sir, if you were punished for your brother's actions."

One corner of his mouth kicked up. "You're showing great self-restraint, Phoebe. I'm sure you wish to know how that came about."

She ducked her head to hide a quick smile. "Every sorry detail, I'm afraid."

"That won't protect you, you know."

Her head snapped up again. Before she could decide if he was referring to the promise he'd made her, he continued speaking.

"My brother was several years older than I and my father's favourite. Only the most iron-clad evidence would have convinced him that Selwyn could do anything wrong. And all the evidence pointed at me."

"But…you couldn't have been more than nineteen or twenty."

He shrugged. "I was wild. Even by Deverell standards. You think Gerald's prank with the unmentionables was shocking. Well—" he sent her a glinting, sidelong glance "—I wouldn't have wasted time with the unmentionables, but spent it with their owners."

"Oh." She levelled her brows at him. "Indeed, sir."

He grinned unrepentantly. "To put it bluntly, Phoebe, I, too, was involved in…er…liaisons, the only difference being that the women concerned were unmarried. Unfortunately, Selwyn's mistress began to want more than an illicit affair. Probably because her husband had cast her out, as we now know.

"Selwyn, of course, had no intention of disillusioning my father, and risking his own position, by leaving his wife and becoming embroiled in what promised to be a scandal of epic proportions. The result was a series of increasingly impassioned letters, addressed, to avert suspicion, to the Hon. S. Deverell instead of Viscount Kerford, as Selwyn was then styled."

"What happened?" Phoebe prompted when he fell silent.

He shrugged. "The inevitable. One can only assume that your mother was suffering from extreme distress to have behaved so rashly. Since Selwyn and I shared the same initial, far from averting suspicion, a barrage of letters addressed so simply in a feminine hand could mean only one thing as far as my father was concerned. That I was causing trouble again. He opened them and, since endearments rather than names were mentioned, all hell broke loose."

"But you must have protested your innocence. And surely

your brother didn't allow you to be punished so terribly for his wrongs.''

"Protests didn't do much good when I couldn't prove anything. As for Selwyn—" his mouth twisted "—there was no love lost between us. Imagine a Deverell determined to hide his true nature behind a façade of pious respectability, and you have Selwyn. Whenever the two of us were alone, I scorned him for his hypocrisy. I might've been wild, but it was out in the open and Society be damned."

"Also just like a Deverell," she murmured.

He smiled reluctantly. "Yes. I'm afraid I also had more than my fair share of Deverell pride. If Selwyn wasn't going to confess, then I wasn't about to accuse him. And when my father refused to believe me without proof, I ceased trying to convince him."

Phoebe shook her head. "That was very foolish of you, my lord."

"I didn't think so at the time." He hesitated, then added, "I did try to trace the lady who'd written the letters, but by the time I'd beaten her whereabouts out of Selwyn, she was dead. He didn't tell me her real name anyway, only the one she was using by then, which is why I didn't make the link between you until tonight."

"Your brother provided for her?"

"No, he'd abandoned her along with everyone else, but he knew where she was living. One wonders why desperation didn't send her to Crowhurst."

"No wonder his mind became disturbed," Phoebe mused aloud. "She preferred death to running off with him."

"Perhaps he wasn't offering marriage in the event that your father divorced her," Deverell suggested drily. "Apart from the fact that she'd had other lovers, she must have been several years older than him and would always be associated with scandal. Not insurmountable drawbacks in a mistress. A wife is another matter."

Phoebe glanced fleetingly up at him. "Precisely my own words, sir."

There was a rather charged silence. Phoebe could feel Deverell's gaze on her, but she kept her own eyes lowered, even when he reached out a hand to her.

"Phoebe..." He drew in a breath and let his hand fall back to his side. "You must be tired, little one. We'll talk further tomorrow. I'll ask the landlord to fetch you a glass of brandy while I bring my phaeton to the door. It'll warm you before we start out."

Phoebe felt her throat tighten for some inexplicable reason. She nodded and managed a small, rather wobbly smile.

It seemed to do the trick. Deverell strode to the door. He paused for a second to study the empty taproom.

"It's a lowering thought," he observed, "that I had to come in through the window in case that crew in here were in Crowhurst's pay, while my aunt swept the place clean with a few well-chosen words."

He sent her a swift grin over his shoulder and walked into the other room. Phoebe could hear him summoning the landlord. She bent to pick up her discarded bonnet, crushing the ribbons between tense fingers.

She had absolutely no idea, she realised, of Deverell's thoughts on the situation now that the past had been laid bare. Apart from that brief, fierce embrace, his present manner was that of a concerned friend. And although he'd used that most precious endearment, he had never, even earlier that day, mentioned anything about being in love with her.

Of course, there had hardly been time for a discussion on the subject, but they were alone now. What had happened to the very important, very straightforward question he'd wanted to ask her as soon as they had some privacy?

Phoebe gazed unseeingly into the fire and remembered her earlier doubts. It was no use repining, she told herself. Nothing had changed—except that Deverell was now aware of her unsuitability as a wife, which saved her the trouble of pointing out that fact. She should be grateful to be spared the duty.

And she was, after all, still willing to become his mistress. No doubt her heart would be shattered some time in the future, but she wouldn't think about that right now. She might not even have to worry that he wouldn't make any sort of offer at all. He *knew* she was willing to become his mistress. Of course he knew it. She'd responded to him without reservation only that afternoon, before he'd so much as hinted at marriage.

Well, she simply wouldn't act like a woman who expected

a marriage proposal. The task shouldn't be difficult. Up until several hours ago, she hadn't had any such expectations.

Nodding at the logic of her reasoning, Phoebe sat up straighter and arranged her features into an expression of calm composure. She wondered when Deverell would be back so she could get her performance over and done with.

Chapter Thirteen

Deverell was back in two minutes, a very thoughtful look on his face.

"Phoebe, little one, are you certain you didn't collide with anything on your way here? Or run over something on the road?"

Phoebe blinked up at him, distracted from the bracing speech she was delivering to herself. In her fragile state of mind, she was inclined to take umbrage at his question.

"Well, I know I was extremely worried about Gerald, my lord, but I think I would have noticed a collision. Why do you ask?"

He didn't immediately enlighten her. Instead, a slow smile started to spread across his face. "Those devious, diabolical little Deverells."

Phoebe eyed the smile with foreboding. "What have they done now?"

"I should have made sure they climbed into the right carriages. Gerald has very kindly taken my phaeton and left his for us."

"Good heavens. Why would he do that?"

"Probably because he knew his days would be numbered if he damaged mine."

When she only continued to stare at him in bewilderment, he elaborated.

"You may recall, my love, that I thought Gerald seemed anxious about his phaeton."

"I don't think I want to hear this."

"Gerald, no doubt with the connivance of his sisters, has splintered the cotter pin on each wheel. As soon as we hit the first pothole in the road, we'll find ourselves sitting in it."

"He *what?* Why—? Oh, this is too much! Just wait until I see him again. I'll—" She stopped, her eyes widening as the full force of their predicament struck her. "What on earth are we going to do, my lord?"

"Not a great deal, I'm afraid. It's some distance to the nearest town where I'd be likely to find a wheelwright, and even if I was willing to leave you here while I made the trip on the landlord's cob—which I'm not—I doubt the gentleman would be willing to return with me at this hour."

"But—"

The landlord appeared in the doorway before she could voice even one of the protests whirling about in her head.

"Yer horses're stabled, me lord, and the wife's lighting a nice fire upstairs."

"Fire? Upstairs?" Phoebe stared from one man to the other in horror. "But...you're not suggesting we stay *here!*"

"Why not?" The landlord appeared to take offence at her tone. "The room up yonder's as good as this 'ere. The last owner had 'em built on for himself," he confided to Deverell. "Thought him and his rib was a cut above, if ye take me meaning, sir. But *I* says a bedchamber's there to make money." He grinned ingratiatingly, displaying several gaps between his teeth. "There's even a bolt on the door, so ye'll be reel private, like."

"Not to mention solvent in the morning," Deverell remarked, treating the landlord to a hard stare. "Which is when you'll be paid."

"Oh, aye, sir. Wotever yer honour wishes. And I hope yer both has a very good night." Chuckling, he withdrew.

"Oh, my goodness." Phoebe sagged limply against the back of the settle. "Whatever are we going to do now?"

Deverell raised a brow. "Take over the landlord's best bedchamber. What else?"

"How can you be so calm about this, my lord?" Her voice

soared to a note the great Catalani would have envied. "Don't you understand? If we stay here all night, you'll be placed in a compromising position!"

He stared at her as if she'd suddenly expressed a desire to fetch the wheelwright herself. "You're worried about *me* being in a compromising position?"

"Of course I am. What else would I be worried about?"

"Your own position?" he suggested.

She dismissed her own position with an agitated wave. "This is terrible! Just when everything was going so well; when everyone will know you were unjustly accused and... We must *do* something, my lord."

"Before you manage to whip yourself into a real fit of the vapours, Phoebe, let me remind you that no one knows we're here."

"Your aunt does," she wailed, not in the least mollified by this unhelpful remark. "And your wards. And Mr Filby. And—"

"Please." He held up a hand. "Spare me the list. If we leave early in the morning, everyone concerned will think we got home tonight."

"But—" She paused, frowning. There was a flaw in there somewhere, but she couldn't put her finger on it.

A second later the thought fled from her mind. Deverell strode forward, a look of determination on his face, and scooped her up off the settle before she realised his intention.

"However, if I'm going to be in a compromising position, I might as well take advantage of it," he muttered, and carried her out of the room.

Phoebe could have sworn her heart stopped. She flung one arm around his neck in an instinctive reaction to suddenly finding herself in motion while several feet off the ground. Her other hand still clutched her bonnet. "My lord, wait! Are you sure you know what you're doing?"

He grinned. "Positive."

"But..." After several futile attempts, she found her voice again. It sounded very small. "Well, then...what *are* you doing?"

"Carrying you up to bed so I can make love to you."

"Oh." Her heart did stop. "Oh, my goodness."

"Don't worry, love," he murmured, and smiled straight into her hugely rounded eyes. "This only puts things forward a little."

"Things? Oh, yes. Things."

She searched vainly for something else to say. Nothing came to mind. It didn't matter because her breath had stopped, as well. All of a sudden Deverell seemed bigger and more overwhelming than ever. The easy way he carried her up the stairs was daunting enough; she could also feel every powerful shift and surge of muscle against her softer form.

The rhythmic movements began to render her unaccountably weak inside, but at the same time she was gripped by a wholly unexpected feeling of apprehension. Deciding to become a man's mistress was one thing. The actual physical act was something she hadn't exactly thought about until this very moment.

Now it seemed to be all she could think about, as she was carried into a bedchamber at the top of the stairs and set down before a small fire. A branch of candles, their flames reflected in the brandy bottle beside them on the mantelpiece, was the only other source of light in the room. A large, comfortable-looking four-poster seemed to take up most of the space.

Phoebe glanced at it and started to shiver inside.

Deverell strode back to the door, closed and bolted it, then turned to face her across the bedchamber. "Ah, I see the landlord had the happy idea of bringing the brandy up here," he observed, glancing past her. He came forward and picked up the bottle. Glasses clinked.

Struggling for the same casual aplomb, Phoebe burst into speech. "I can't tell you how pleased I am that you're finally reconciled with Lady Grismead, my lord, and… Oh!" She took the glass of brandy he handed her. "Thank you, sir."

"I've recently discovered that life holds a lot more promise if you're not continually looking back," he murmured. He replaced the bottle and turned so that she stood side-on to him, her shoulder brushing his chest. She knew he was watching her. He lifted a hand to briefly touch a curl that had come loose from its tight knot. "You taught me that, Phoebe."

For some strange reason the low, husky note in his voice made her shiver even more. "Oh?"

"Yes." He reached down, gently prised her tense fingers open and removed her bonnet from her grasp. "You won't need this, little one."

She watched as the bonnet went sailing onto a nearby chair.

"And I think you'll be more comfortable without your pelisse," he went on, still in that low, almost soothing tone. He began undoing buttons with one hand.

Phoebe held her breath, torn between an impulse to stop him and a trembling awareness of his fingers moving downward between her breasts. She didn't *dare* breathe. The thought of him touching her there again made her legs shake. She began to wonder if she could stay upright.

The last button slipped free. Deverell pushed the folds of material aside and pressed his hand, just for an instant, to the softness of her stomach. Even through her gown and petticoat, the heat of his touch burned her. There was something primitive about the gesture; something intensely possessive.

Phoebe's hand shook. Brandy sloshed dangerously close to the edge of the glass. She brought her other hand up to steady it, suddenly realising that he'd been talking softly the whole time he'd been unfastening buttons and she hadn't heard a word.

"I...I beg your pardon, my lord?"

His smile sent more shivers chasing one another down her spine. "I said, when I first returned to London I thought it would be amusing to sit back and watch my family tumble into the pit of financial ruin yawning at their feet. I didn't even have to lift a finger to bring it about. They were doing such a good job of it, themselves."

"But you ch—"

Her throat seized when he shrugged out of his coat. He flung it across the chair and loosened his cravat. The strip of snowy muslin went the way of the coat. Phoebe followed its progress, then looked back in time to see him hook a finger in the neck of his shirt and yank it open.

A touch of indignation seeped into the maelstrom of emotions whirling about her head. If he wanted to converse, that was perfectly all right with her. In fact, it might help her regain her balance. But how were mistresses supposed to carry on an intelligent conversation while clothes were casually being removed right and left?

"You changed your mind?" she managed to say, racking her brain to recall the thread of the discussion.

"No," he murmured. "You changed my mind."

"I...I might have given you a new slant on the situation, sir."

"Let's just say, then, that your view of the situation put a new slant on it for me." He began pulling his shirt out of his breeches.

Phoebe decided that if she wasn't to faint right then and there, drastic measures would have to be taken. She glanced down at the brandy in her hand, raised the glass to her lips and took an indecently large sip.

Heat spread through her veins almost instantly. She stopped shivering. At least outwardly. Her shivers were replaced by tiny internal flutters that were surprisingly pleasurable. She eyed the brandy with approval and took a larger mouthful.

The glass was gently removed from her hand and replaced on the mantel.

"Sweetheart." Deverell tipped her chin up on the edge of his hand. She was piercingly aware of the heat radiating from him; of the fact that his shirt hung open, revealing the powerful planes of his chest and the rigid muscles of his stomach.

"I want you more than my next breath," he said softly, "but not if it makes you so nervous you have to toss brandy down your throat. Nothing has to happen here and now. Would you rather I spent the night downstairs?"

"Downstairs?"

His smile was crooked. "If I climb into that bed with you, little one, I don't think I can trust myself not to make you mine every way there is before morning."

For a moment the words stunned her. Then, just as abruptly, Phoebe was flooded with their meaning. He wanted her. His desire was tightly leashed, but it was there, straining against the barriers of his formidable control, apparent only in the narrowed intensity of his eyes and the taut, waiting stillness of his body.

Despite his gentle tone, despite the wry amusement in his smile, he really *did* want her that badly.

And suddenly she thought of the way everyone was always wanting something from *him*. Protection, money, rescue. It didn't matter what. She thought of the way his family had ignored him for years. She thought of the statue of a child with its arms outstretched.

And she thought of the way she loved him, with all her heart and mind and soul.

What good was that love if uncertainty made her hesitate to give freely the one thing he wanted from her? What good was it if she hesitated to take whatever he was offering of himself? Love, she discovered in that moment, transcended everything. Her upbringing, her own innate caution, a woman's vulnerability—all were powerless against the overwhelming need to give.

She smiled up at him, filled with the same sense of rightness she'd felt that afternoon, and lifted her hand to touch his wrist with gentle, questing fingers. "Sebastian. Please stay with me."

His hard warrior's face lit with a smile that almost took her breath away. For a fleeting second she saw the boy he'd been. Passionate, reckless, wild, but with a rock-solid sense of honour that had been forged in fire, making him the man he was today. The only man she would ever love.

"Phoebe," he whispered, and bent to brush a gentle kiss across her lips. "Don't be afraid. We're going to be perfect together."

She lifted her mouth, wanting more, and with a half-stifled groan he thrust his fingers into her hair and kissed her with a fierce ardour that sent arrows of pleasure darting down her thighs. She felt her hair tumble down as pins went flying, and a delicious sense of freedom raced through her.

"I've been wanting to do that forever," he muttered, breaking the kiss to run his fingers through the honey-brown tresses. His hands were shaking, she realised in bemusement. "It's like silk. The finest, softest silk."

With another muffled exclamation, he untangled his hands from her hair and started undoing the ribbon beneath her bodice. Phoebe scarcely noticed. She was no longer worrying about clothes being removed. She gazed with fascination at his bare chest, its covering of thick, dark hair drawing her fingers like moths to a flame.

He shuddered heavily as she flattened her hands on him. "Yes, sweetheart. Touch me. I've been wanting you to touch me for weeks."

Her eyes widened and he smiled in rueful acknowledgement of her effect on him. "Didn't you know?" he asked. "I've wanted you since that first day. That first second."

"Even when I was wearing those old clothes?" she asked, smiling with a hint of mischief.

"All I have to do, little one, is look into your eyes and I want you."

"Ohh."

His mouth curved, she thought with tenderness, but his eyes were glittering, intense. He bent to kiss her again, long and hard and deep. Until her arms went up around his neck and she was pressing so close she could feel the quiver of muscles under relentless control. A heady sense of feminine power went through her. He made her tremble with longing; she'd never dreamed she could have the same effect on him.

Then, with a muttered imprecation, he drew back, whipped his shirt off and turned her around to unfasten the tiny buttons that ran down the back of her gown. She heard fabric tear.

"Bloody hell, do there have to be so many of the damn things?"

Phoebe giggled. Her laughter faded, however, when Deverell turned her again and pushed her gown down to her waist. It obligingly fell the rest of the way to the floor. But it wasn't the fact that she was standing there wearing only her petticoat and chemise that caused amusement to change to awed wonder.

He was the most beautiful male she'd ever seen. Tall and perfectly proportioned, his shoulders and arms hard with muscle, his chest deep and wide, and covered with the dark pelt of hair that made her fingers itch to explore the fascinating new territory spread before her.

"You're beautiful," she whispered, utterly enthralled.

He shook his head, slowly, as though barely hearing her. The heat of his gaze almost seared her skin. With one finger he traced the ribboned edge of her chemise before slowly freeing the laces.

Phoebe trembled as he lowered the straps. In another second she would be as bare to the waist as Deverell. She felt herself blushing and squeezed her eyes shut. The thought was shocking. It was positively scandalous. But the thrilling excitement pouring through her veins prevented even the smallest protest.

Cool air brushed over her, she heard him say something, his voice so hoarse she couldn't make sense of the words, then she cried out in stunned pleasure as his big, powerful hands closed around her soft flesh, cupping her, shaping her, stroking her. The sensation was indescribable, sending tingling streamers of heat from her breasts to a place deep inside her that throbbed with a longing she'd never felt before.

"Sebastian..." Her legs quivered with the effort to stay upright. "I can't...stand..."

She was swept off her feet before the next word was out. Phoebe's eyes flew open as Deverell carried her to the bed and lowered her gently to the mattress. He stood looking down at her, his aquamarine eyes brilliant, glittering, reflecting the moonlight filtering through the window beside the bed.

When he bent to remove her petticoat, leaving her in her stockings and bunched-up chemise, Phoebe wondered how it was possible to feel utterly abandoned and wicked, and blush all over at the same time. Despite the excitement and longing pouring through her, she flexed her knee in an instinctive attempt to shield herself from that intense gaze.

"It's all right, sweetheart. My lovely Phoebe." His voice was shaking almost as badly as his hands, Sebastian realised. God! If he didn't stop looking at her, he'd fall on her like a ravaging warlord intent on taking the spoils of battle.

But she wasn't the spoils of battle. This was his innocent, trusting Phoebe. He'd barely reassured her about their future, hadn't said a word about anything other than wanting her—a totally inadequate description for the grinding, wrenching need tearing at his gut—and still, she lay there, gazing up at him with a fascinated wonder that threatened to rip his precarious control to shreds.

He wrenched his gaze away from the sight of her lying there waiting for him, and sat down on the edge of the bed to yank off his boots. It was no use worrying about the things he hadn't said. He could hardly speak, let alone string the right words together. He felt as if he was going to explode if he didn't sink into her warmth and softness. He could give her all the right words and reassurances later.

He hauled off his second boot and tossed it after the first, then froze when Phoebe reached out a hand and touched his arm.

When she ran questing fingers up to his shoulder and flexed them to test the strength there, Sebastian knew he was going to go mad. The knowledge didn't prevent him from shifting to face her so she had access to his chest. He watched her lips part in a delighted smile as she touched him, saw the innocent feminine appreciation in her beautiful eyes and nearly groaned aloud as the ache in his body intensified to the edge of agony.

"You're so hard," she said wonderingly.

He drew in his breath sharply as one little finger stroked across a male nipple.

"I'm aware of that fact," he muttered through clenched teeth. "Painfully aware of it."

"Sebastian?"

"Don't worry about it." Surging to his feet, he wrenched open his breeches. "If you don't wish to receive the shock of your life, my innocent little governess, I suggest you shut your eyes."

Phoebe smiled happily up at him. "I'm not completely ignorant, Sebastian. I have seen statues of males, you know, and—" Her eyes blinked wide. "Oh, my goodness!"

His ragged laugh sounded as if it had been torn from him. He lowered himself to the bed beside her and gathered her into his arms. She came willingly, but he could feel her trembling.

He brushed his knuckles gently over her cheek. "There have been several times when I've wanted to silence you, Phoebe, but not, believe me, by terrifying you."

"I am not terrified," she informed him, blushing so rosily he could feel the heat beneath his fingers. "It's just that… well…you're very large, aren't you? All over, I mean."

Despite the need clawing at him, Sebastian couldn't help himself. He grinned. "You're worried about the discrepancy in our sizes?"

Phoebe blushed again. "Well, it is rather pronounced."

"Phoebe, sweetheart…" He bent to kiss her. "My innocent darling, do you really think I'd do anything to hurt you?"

"Of course not, Sebastian, but—"

"You've given me so much of your trust. Can't you trust me in this, too?"

She sounded indignant. "It isn't that I don't trust you, Sebastian. But…well…one can hardly ignore the evidence of one's eyes."

"Oh, God." He rested his forehead against hers, unable to decide whether to laugh or swear. What other woman would stop proceedings at this point and expect an explanation that was utterly beyond him? "Just trust me, darling. *Please.*"

He felt her hesitate, then she relaxed and curled against him, snuggling closer. Sebastian groaned softly and bent to kiss her throat, at the same time pushing her chemise lower. "Lift up, sweetheart. Let me get this off you."

The softly growled command sent a tremor of mingled excitement and apprehension through her. Phoebe obeyed, then went very still as he stripped her chemise and stockings off and let his gaze travel over her naked body.

His chest expanded on a ragged indrawn breath. He touched one finger, just the tip of one finger, to her throat. As if he didn't quite trust himself with a firmer caress, she thought wonderingly. Then he laid the flat of his hand against the pulse beating wildly in its small hollow and she trembled in uncontrollable response.

Such big, powerful hands. Such gentleness. The contrast made her melt and then shiver with excitement. When he moved his hand to trace the small bones below her throat, her flesh pulsed with heat where his touch had been.

He bent his head to retrace the same path with his mouth. Phoebe gasped as his kisses went lower. Her breasts felt flushed and heavy, the tips aching. Then he closed his mouth over one rosy crest and she cried out sharply at the sudden, piercing pleasure.

"Yes," he growled against her throbbing flesh, and she shuddered at the raw sound of his voice.

"Sebastian…" Her own voice was barely audible. "I feel so…"

"Yes," he said again. "Tell me, sweetheart."

Tell him? she thought dimly. *Tell him?* She could hardly speak. She felt his hand stroke down her body until his fingers tangled in the soft triangle between her legs and all the muscles in her lower body seemed to dissolve.

"*Sebastian!* Ohh, I thought…I felt unbridled passion when you kissed me, but this…is beyond anything."

"Not yet," he grated. "But it soon will be."

Her eyes flew open at the stark promise in his voice, then widened even further at the savage look of arousal on his face as he watched his hand caress her so intimately. His touch was still achingly tender, but the expression in his eyes held all the fierceness of a warrior; the muscles beneath her hands were coiled springs waiting to unleash the full force of his passion.

He was holding himself in check by the merest thread, she realised. Every tendon was rigid with self-imposed restraint. And, in that fleeting moment of awareness, she knew his restraint was costing him.

The last remnants of nervousness vanished. All that power. All that power, leashed, held in check. For her. She shivered in helpless response to the thrill of anticipation coursing through her.

"I want you," she whispered, stunned by the truth of her words. Not even her own boldness shocked her. The sensations he was arousing with the gentle, insistent touch of his hand and mouth swept her beyond anything but the strange throbbing emptiness only he could satisfy. "Oh, Sebastian, I love you."

"*Phoebe.* Oh, God, sweetheart, I can't wait any longer for you. I have to have you. I won't hurt you, darling. I swear. I'll be so careful…"

Not even aware of what he was saying, knowing only that he couldn't bear to frighten her, Sebastian pressed her legs further apart and lowered himself over her.

She made a soft whimpering sound of pleasure and longing when his weight came down on her that threatened to send him straight over the edge. He paused, teeth clenched, feeling sweat break out across his back as he fought for control.

She lifted her hips beneath him in an instinctive seeking movement that was so utterly female, so unbearably arousing a harsh groan tore from his throat.

"Phoebe, don't! Be still, little one. Let me…" He raised

himself on his forearms to look down at her and felt as if the breath had been kicked out of him.

Her lashes fluttered upward. She gazed up at him, her lovely eyes cloudy with desire, her lips soft from his kisses, her hair a silken fan against the pillow. He remembered that he'd wanted to know how she would look in his arms. Now he did know. Small and soft and heart-wrenchingly vulnerable.

Dear God, how did the sight of such fragile delicacy arouse him to almost crazed desire? The violence of his own need shook him to his soul. And yet something—was it the utter trust in her eyes?—managed to leash the wild hunger straining to break free so he could enter her slowly, lead her gently into an intimacy that had to be new and frightening in its very intensity.

"It's all right," he whispered when she made a small frantic sound and clung to him. He gazed deeply into her eyes, willing her to relax, to accept the intrusion of his body. "I won't hurt you, love. Just be still."

"Sebastian? I don't think…"

"Shh. Relax, darling. Yes, that's it. *That's it*. Oh, God, *Phoebe*—"

Phoebe gasped as he thrust forward, possessing her completely. Her nails bit into his shoulders. He hadn't hurt her, but the thrilling anticipation and excitement was abruptly swamped by the shock of his invasion. She vaguely realised that Sebastian had gone rigidly still, holding her in a grip of iron while her body struggled to adjust to his. His heart pounded against her breast with a violence that would have terrified her if she hadn't been so caught up in the incredible sensations of joining with him.

"Are you all right?" he asked, sounding as if his teeth were ground together.

Phoebe managed a small nod and relaxed her grip on his shoulders. In truth, she was beginning to feel more than all right. The feeling of being invaded was passing and a delicate quivering sensation was taking its place. She tried a tentative movement and almost fainted as a piercingly sweet ripple of pleasure coursed through her.

His arms tightened so convulsively she squeaked. Then he lowered his head, buried his face in her hair, and began to move with a restrained power that brought all the thrilling excitement rushing back.

Phoebe clung with all her strength, eager now to follow wherever he led. Her entire world narrowed to this moment; this man who held her with such fierce tenderness; this act of total surrender of all that she was. The intimacy was shattering, tearing apart any preconceptions she might have had and over-whelming her with the reality of feeling him all around her, inside her, enveloping, sheltering, possessing.

Sweet, hot tendrils of pleasure began coiling inside her, tighter and tighter, until the tension was almost unbearable, until she cried out in intolerable need. And, as if her cry snapped some invisible leash, Deverell's control exploded in a passionate assault that sent her hurtling into ecstasy. If she hadn't been held so fast in his arms, she would have flown into a thousand pieces.

Amazement, helpless delight, love so intense she could hardly bear it, streaked through her in the instant before she was swept into a torrent of exquisite sensation, pleasure throb-bing through her with every pulsing beat of her heart, filling every part of her, taking her to the edge of consciousness. Dimly, she heard the harsh sound that erupted from his throat. He held her as if he would never let her go, shuddering against her, whispering her name over and over in a litany of passion, until he sank heavily onto her, crushing her into the bedding.

Phoebe came back to herself very slowly. She felt as if she was sinking into a soft, endless sea. All her bones seemed to have melted. An incredible feeling of lassitude flowed over her. Vaguely she was aware of questions floating somewhere in the back of her mind, but it was too much trouble to think about them. Too much trouble to speak. The moment was too precious.

Lying with Deverell like this, still holding him within her body, feeling his weight over her, sheltering and warm, was almost sweeter than what had gone before. She had never known such a complete and utter sense of belonging. Whatever happened in the future, whatever life held for them, she would always be a part of him. As he would be part of her. Forever.

"Sebastian," she murmured, and let the sweet lassitude take her into sleep.

His name roused Sebastian from the torpor of satiation. He withdrew as gently as possible, knowing he had to be tender, and gazed down at her.

She was already deep in slumber, her lashes delicate silken fans against her cheeks, her lips still rosy from his kisses and softly parted.

A wave of protective tenderness swept over him, making his body clench and shudder violently in reaction. The intensity of emotion stunned him. Phoebe had taken the pain and emptiness from his heart and filled it with something he'd never known before.

Tenderness.

Until she'd burst into his life, he hadn't known he was capable of so much feeling.

He thought about waking her and telling her how much she meant to him, but she looked so fragile. She was probably exhausted. And he was, after all, the one who had exhausted her. He could wait until morning.

Gathering Phoebe close to his side, he pulled the covers over them and lay back against the pillows. She felt sweet and warm in his arms. Sebastian smiled as another thought occurred to him.

Tonight he had turned his delightfully disapproving Miss Smith into a creature of fire and passion. She had responded to him with an innocent sensuality that had set his senses reeling.

But more importantly—she had given him her heart.

Making a silent vow to cherish her gift for the rest of his life, he fell asleep, feeling at peace for the first time in years.

An early morning mist still hovered in the air when Phoebe settled herself on the seat of Gerald's phaeton and watched Deverell climb up next to her. Around them the trees hovered, insubstantial shapes in the seamless grey of mist and sky. The Black Mole crouched, an unlikely harbour in the stillness.

"It's certainly a relief to be on our way," she remarked chattily as he gave the horses the office to start.

She winced at the inanity of the remark, but decided that if Deverell required anything more in the way of witty conversation at this hour he shouldn't have woken her before dawn in a fashion guaranteed to addle her wits for the rest of the day.

And then, she remembered, having reduced her to a deliciously limp state, he'd dressed, bounded downstairs, *whistling*, and appropriated the entire inn.

Phoebe had been inclining towards a hazy sort of indignation until the landlord's wife had appeared with breakfast, the makings for a hot bath, and the news that her spouse had fetched the wheelwright and repairs were underway.

They had both been fully occupied ever since.

"Oh, I don't know," he said now, sending her a wicked, sidelong glance. "I'm going to have some rather fond memories of the place, myself."

Phoebe tried to look severe and failed dismally. The task was impossible when she was blushing. And she seemed to have run out of chatty responses. In fact, now that she and Deverell were alone, she found it difficult to think about anything except her uncertainty about the immediate future.

The trouble was, she reflected, she didn't have any experience at being a mistress. She'd been touched by Deverell's thoughtfulness in ensuring her privacy this morning, but that was at an isolated inn. What was going to happen when they returned to town?

She cast a quick glance at his profile and decided that since she didn't know the rules of mistressly behaviour, he would have to explain them to her.

"My lord?"

He grinned. "Yes, Miss Smith?"

Despite herself, Phoebe giggled. "Oh, dear, I suppose that did sound absurdly formal after...after..."

"After you spent the night lying naked in my arms?"

"*Sebastian!*" She felt herself turning an even brighter shade of pink. "I did not... Well, I *did*, but..."

He laughed and covered her hands briefly with one of his. "I'm sorry, darling, but when I'm confronted by the prim and proper Miss Smith, I can't resist teasing her. What is it you wished to ask me?"

She took a deep breath. "Well, I was wondering what we

are to do now. I mean, you might wish to spend another night...um...that is to say..."

"You're perfectly correct, my love. I will wish to spend another night making love to you. Every night, in fact."

"Ohh." She was momentarily distracted as a tingling echo of pleasure rippled through her. When his mouth curved, she hurried into speech again.

"Yes, well, that is precisely what I mean. But you can't very well visit me at Park Street. What would Theo and Cressy think? Especially if you were to stroll around without your shirt on as you were doing this morning. Not that I wish to live in another big house," she added hastily, in case he might think she had mercenary tendencies. "No doubt you are thinking of a little cottage somewhere. I'm sure it will be quite delightful."

There was a rather ominous silence from the figure beside her. Too anxious to notice anything amiss, Phoebe broached her greatest concern. "And perhaps—only if the occasion were to arise, of course—you might give me a...a suitable recommendation?"

Deverell hauled on the reins so abruptly, Phoebe almost found herself hurtling from her seat. She looked down, fully expecting to see sparks fly as the horses skidded to a jarring halt. Wood shrieked hideously against wood as he yanked on the brake.

"What?" he roared.

The pair in the traces promptly took exception to his tone.

"God damn it to bloody hell!"

The next few minutes were spent in a lively tussle with Gerald's horses.

When Deverell finally got them calmed down, secured the reins and turned an enraged countenance on her, Phoebe was put forcibly in mind of black thunderclouds hurling bolts of aquamarine lightning. It finally dawned on her that she was in a great deal of trouble. The only good thing about the situation was that they were still sitting in the carriage. At least he had to keep his voice down.

"A recommendation?" he repeated with deadly inflexion. "As *What?*"

"A...a governess, of course," she ventured. "I mean...I couldn't very well ask for a recommendation as a mistress, because I'm not terribly experienced at it yet, and besides, Sebastian, even if you tired of me, I would never want to belong to another man anyway, so a recommendation wouldn't be..."

He made a strangled sound of frustration and clutched at his head.

Phoebe eyed him anxiously. "Oh, dear. Are you all right, sir?"

"No, I am not all right, Miss Smith. I am rapidly going mad. And you are the cause of it." He straightened, took hold of her shoulders and gave her a none-too-gentle shake.

"Phoebe, you little idiot. After last night, what insanity makes you think there'd ever come a time when I wouldn't want you? Not only as a mistress, damn it, but as a *wife!*"

Her jaw dropped. "A wife?"

Her action seemed to enrage him all over again. "What the devil did you think I meant yesterday when I said what I did in front of the twins?"

"Well—" Her brain reeled dizzily. "I did think...*then*. But after last night, you must know how ineligible I am, and..." She looked up earnestly into his furious countenance. "Indeed, Sebastian, you said it yourself. Someone associated with scandal is not suitable as a wife."

"I didn't mean you, damn it!" He closed his eyes, then opened them again to fix her with a glare that made her feel as if she'd been transfixed by one of the lightning bolts.

"Phoebe, I will put up with my aunt's managing ways and my wards' peccadilloes. I will tolerate Pamela and that dimwitted poet. I will even refrain from strangling Filby. But I will not accept idiocy from you! Is that clear?"

"But..." She faltered, eyes wide with anxiety and tremulous hope. "Sebastian, are you sure you're not just doing the honourable thing because we were placed in a compromising position last night and everyone will—?"

"I don't give a damn for Society's opinion," he interrupted roughly. "You know that."

"Yes, but you care about your family's opinion." She gave him a gentle smile. "And, although I doubt Lady Grismead would wish to welcome a daughter of Charlotte Everton-Smythe into the family—especially as I have absolutely no expectations—she'd still expect you to do the correct thing."

"Sooner or later, Phoebe, you'll learn that the day I do what my aunt considers proper will be the day they discover the earth is flat, after all. Why the hell do you think I made love to you after discovering we were stranded? Because I knew if I asked you to marry me last night, you'd start babbling about obligations and compromising positions, even if I'd convinced you that I couldn't care a snap for a scandal that had nothing to do with you."

There was a short silence while she digested this speech. Then Deverell smiled dangerously and leaned closer. "As it is, my love, thanks to my forethought, you do not have a choice. Fortunately for me, you do care about Society's opinion, therefore you have to marry me."

Phoebe eyed the pleased triumph on his face with a disapproving frown. "Are you threatening me with possible consequences again, my lord?"

"Yes."

She took a deep breath and grasped her courage with both hands. "Why?"

"Why?" He scowled at her. "*Why?* Because I love you, God damn it. Why the hell else would I want to marry you?"

As a declaration, this thundered avowal of devotion left much to be desired. Its effect, however, was potent. Phoebe flung herself into his arms, so deliriously happy she couldn't speak. She rained fervent little kisses over his face instead.

Deverell's response was instant. His entire body went hard. He pulled her into a crushing embrace, but instead of kissing her as she'd expected, he wrenched off her bonnet and buried his face in her hair, holding her so closely she could feel every heartbeat, every breath. Her own breath caught in wonder when she realised he was shaking.

"Phoebe, I love you," he said hoarsely. "I love you so much. You must believe me. Until you stormed into my life, believing in me, trusting me despite all you'd been told, I didn't know what need was. I didn't know trust like that was possible. Now I'd fight the entire world to keep you."

"Oh, Sebastian." She clung closer, instinctively giving, instinctively reassuring. "You'll always have my trust. Just as you'll always have my love."

"Sweetheart!"

He drew back for a moment, gazing down into her face as though making very sure. And then his mouth came down on hers with an urgency that made her senses swim. But even as she trembled and melted against him, he gentled, kissing her so deeply, so slowly, with such intensely possessive ardour, she felt as if he was filling her with all the love in his heart, as if, with just that kiss, they would be joined for all time.

The moment was so sweet, so tender, Phoebe felt tears of happiness fill her eyes.

She blinked them away as Deverell drew back to smile down at her. "God, you give yourself so completely. If you knew some of things—darling, you're so innocent sometimes, you scare me."

She shook her head. "If I was that innocent," she said, gently reproving, "I would have believed Crowhurst last night."

Without warning, the hard edge of power returned to his face. "That's when I knew I'd do anything to keep you, Phoebe. Your trust awed me. Humbled me. What Crowhurst said was pretty damning, if you didn't know the truth. Especially as *he* believed what he was saying. And I know it shook you to hear about your mother like that."

"The only thing I feared was that you'd once loved her," she whispered. "But I knew if you had, you would never have abandoned her."

"You're the only woman I've ever loved," he said, gazing deeply into her eyes. The truth reverberated in his words, irrevocable, unchangeable. "You're the only woman I ever will love."

Phoebe's face lit with a smile that was radiant with love and so much happiness she could have soared into the cloudy sky and flown on the wind. "In that case, sir, I can face any amount of Aunt Grismeads and doubtful Deverells. Let us be off."

Sebastian laughed out loud, catching her mood. He released her and bent to untie the reins. "My love, you're forgetting two things. One, my wards were obviously aware of my intentions and last night decided to hasten the inevitable conclusion in their own ruthless fashion. And two, my aunt is a Deverell. Not only that, at present she's a grateful Deverell. What does that tell you?"

"That you think you'll be able to do precisely as you like while her gratitude lasts," she answered, exchanging her smile for a severe frown.

The frown didn't seem to have much effect. He grinned down at her, his eyes glittering with an expression that reminded her vividly of the passion of the night. "Precisely. We'll get married today. You see, I also had the forethought to procure a special licence."

"*Today?* But—"

He leaned over and silenced her with a kiss as they started off.

Several minutes later, Phoebe emerged from the embrace, flushed and flustered. "My lord! Kindly keep your attention on the road when you're driving. I do not wish to end up in the ditch."

"Ah. I wondered where she'd gone. Now you see why we mustn't delay our nuptials a moment longer than necessary, my love. I need my delectably disapproving Miss Smith to keep me in line."

Phoebe pondered that for a moment, then pursed her lips. "Clearly a difficult task lies ahead of me," she concluded. She nodded, her prim expression belied by the laughter dancing in her eyes. "However, you will be happy to know, my lord, that I have considerable experience in dealing with Deverells."

"And last night you added to your talents in that direction," he murmured.

"*Sir!*"

"I beg your pardon, Miss Smith. What I *meant* to say is that you're perfectly placed for the task."

When she sent him a mischievous sidelong look, his mouth curved in a smile of heart-wrenching tenderness. "Right where you are now," he said softly. "In my heart."

The sun broke through the mists as they turned onto the main road to London, lighting their world with golden promise.

* * * * *

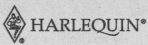

HARLEQUIN®

makes any time special—online...

eHARLEQUIN.com

your romantic escapes

●—Indulgences————————

♥ **Monthly guides to indulging yourself, such as:**
- ★ **Tub Time: A guide for bathing beauties**
- ★ **Magic Massages: A treat for tired feet**

●—Horoscopes——————————

♥ **Find your daily Passionscope, weekly Lovescopes and Erotiscopes**

♥ **Try our compatibility game**

●—Reel Love————————————

♥ **Read all the latest romantic movie reviews**

●—Royal Romance——————————

♥ **Get the latest scoop on your favorite royal romances**

●—Romantic Travel————————

♥ **For the most romantic destinations, hotels and travel activities**

HINTE1

You're not going to believe this offer!

**In October and November 2000, buy any two Harlequin
or Silhouette books and save $10.00 off future purchases,
or buy any three and save $20.00 off future purchases!**

Just fill out this form and attach 2 proofs of purchase (cash register
receipts) from October and November 2000 books and Harlequin will
send you a coupon booklet worth a total savings of $10.00 off future
purchases of Harlequin and Silhouette books in 2001. Send us 3 proofs
of purchase and we will send you a coupon booklet worth a total
savings of $20.00 off future purchases.

Saving money has never been this easy.

I accept your offer! Please send me a coupon booklet:

Name: _____

Address: _____ City: _____

State/Prov.: _____ Zip/Postal Code: _____

Optional Survey!

In a typical month, how many Harlequin or Silhouette books would you buy <u>new</u> at retail stores?

☐ Less than 1   ☐ 1   ☐ 2   ☐ 3 to 4   ☐ 5+

Which of the following statements best describes how you <u>buy</u> Harlequin or Silhouette books?
Choose one answer only that <u>best</u> describes you.

☐ I am a regular buyer and reader
☐ I am a regular reader but buy only occasionally
☐ I only buy and read for specific times of the year, e.g. vacations
☐ I subscribe through Reader Service but also buy at retail stores
☐ I mainly borrow and buy only occasionally
☐ I am an occasional buyer and reader

Which of the following statements best describes how you <u>choose</u> the Harlequin and Silhouette
series books you buy <u>new</u> at retail stores? By "series," we mean books within a particular line,
such as *Harlequin PRESENTS* or *Silhouette SPECIAL EDITION*. Choose one answer only that
<u>best</u> describes you.

☐ I only buy books from my favorite series
☐ I generally buy books from my favorite series but also buy
books from other series on occasion
☐ I buy some books from my favorite series but also buy from
many other series regularly
☐ I buy all types of books depending on my mood and what
I find interesting and have no favorite series

Please send this form, along with your cash register receipts as proofs of purchase, to:
In the U.S.: Harlequin Books, P.O. Box 9057, Buffalo, NY 14269
In Canada: Harlequin Books, P.O. Box 622, Fort Erie, Ontario L2A 5X3
(Allow 4-6 weeks for delivery) Offer expires December 31, 2000.

PHQ4002

If you enjoyed what you just read,
then we've got an offer you can't resist!

Take 2
bestselling novels FREE!
Plus get a FREE surprise gift!

Clip this page and mail it to The Best of the Best™

IN U.S.A.	IN CANADA
3010 Walden Ave.	P.O. Box 609
P.O. Box 1867	Fort Erie, Ontario
Buffalo, N.Y. 14240-1867	L2A 5X3

YES! Please send me 2 free Best of the Best™ novels and my free surprise gift. Then send me 4 brand-new novels every month, which I will receive before they're available in stores. In the U.S.A., bill me at the bargain price of $4.24 plus 25¢ delivery per book and applicable sales tax, if any*. In Canada, bill me at the bargain price of $4.74 plus 25¢ delivery per book and applicable taxes**. That's the complete price and a savings of over 15% off the cover prices—what a great deal! I understand that accepting the 2 free books and gift places me under no obligation ever to buy any books. I can always return a shipment and cancel at any time. Even if I never buy another book from The Best of the Best™, the 2 free books and gift are mine to keep forever. So why not take us up on our invitation. You'll be glad you did!

185 MEN C229
385 MEN C23A

Name	(PLEASE PRINT)	
Address	Apt.#	
City	State/Prov.	Zip/Postal Code

* Terms and prices subject to change without notice. Sales tax applicable in N.Y.
** Canadian residents will be charged applicable provincial taxes and GST.
   All orders subject to approval. Offer limited to one per household.
   ® are registered trademarks of Harlequin Enterprises Limited.

BOB00   ©1998 Harlequin Enterprises Limited

Presenting...  HARLEQUIN®

REGENCY ROMANCE

Experience the opulence of the era captured vividly in these novels. Visit elegant country manors, town houses and the English countryside and explore the whirlwind of social engagements that London "Society" revolved around. Embark on captivating adventures with the feisty heroines who unintentionally tame the roguish heroes with their wit, zest and feminine charm!

Available in October at your favorite retail outlet:

A MOST EXCEPTIONAL QUEST by Sarah Westleigh
DEAR LADY DISDAIN by Paula Marshall
SERENA by Sylvia Andrew
SCANDAL AND MISS SMITH by Julia Byrne

Look for more marriage & mayhem coming in March 2001.

$1.00 OFF!

The purchase of any 2 of the following HARLEQUIN or SILHOUETTE books:
Harlequin Regency Romance, Harlequin Intimacies, Harlequin Prescription Romance,
Silhouette Dreamscapes & Harlequin The Best of Betty Neels Collector's Edition.

RETAILER: Harlequin Enterprises Ltd. will pay the face value of this coupon plus 10.25¢ if submitted by customer for these specified products only. Any other use constitutes fraud. Coupon is nonassignable, void if taxed, prohibited or restricted by law. Consumer must pay any government taxes. Valid in Canada only. Nielson Clearing House customers—mail to: Harlequin Enterprises Ltd., 661 Millidge Avenue, P.O. Box 639, Saint John, N.B. E2L 4A5. Non NCH retailer—for reimbursement submit coupons and proof of sales directly to: Harlequin Enterprises Ltd., Retail Sales Dept., 225 Duncan Mill Rd., Don Mills (Toronto), Ontario, M3B 3K9 Canada.

Coupon expires June 30, 2001.
Valid at retail outlets in Canada only.

 HARLEQUIN®

Limit one coupon per purchase.

52602854

Visit us at www.eHarlequin.com

PHREG1CCAN

Presenting... ◆ HARLEQUIN®

REGENCY ROMANCE

Experience the opulence of the era captured
vividly in these novels. Visit elegant country manors,
town houses and the English countryside and explore
the whirlwind of social engagements that London
"Society" revolved around. Embark on captivating
adventures with the feisty heroines who
unintentionally tame the roguish
heroes with their wit, zest
and feminine charm!

Available in October at your favorite retail outlet:

A MOST EXCEPTIONAL QUEST by Sarah Westleigh
DEAR LADY DISDAIN by Paula Marshall
SERENA by Sylvia Andrew
SCANDAL AND MISS SMITH by Julia Byrne

Look for more marriage & mayhem coming in March 2001.

$1.00 OFF!

the purchase of any 2 of the following HARLEQUIN or SILHOUETTE books:
Harlequin Regency Romance, Harlequin Intimacies, Harlequin Prescription Romance,
Silhouette Dreamscapes & Harlequin The Best of Betty Neels Collector's Edition.

Retailer: Harlequin Enterprises Ltd., will pay the face value of this coupon plus 8¢ if submitted by the customer for this specified
product only. Any other use constitutes fraud. Coupon is nonassignable, void if taxed, prohibited or restricted by law. Consumer
must pay any government taxes. Valid in U.S. only. Nielson Clearing House Customers—mail to: Harlequin Enterprises Limited,
P.O. Box 880478, El Paso, TX 88588-0478, U.S.A. Non NCH retailer—for reimbursement, submit coupons and proof of sales
directly to: Harlequin Enterprises Ltd., Retail Sales Dept., Duncan Mill Road, Don Mills (Toronto), Ontario M3B 3K9, Canada.

Coupon expires June 30, 2001.
Valid at retail outlets in the U.S. only.

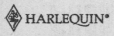

◆ HARLEQUIN®

Limit one coupon per purchase.

5 65373 00033 5   (8100) 1 06734

Visit us at www.eHarlequin.com   PHREG1CUS